GIRL ON THE EDGE

GIRL ON THE EDGE

by

Rachel V. Knox

HONNO MODERN FICTION

Published by Honno
'Ailsa Craig', Heol y Cawl, Dinas Powys
South Glamorgan, Wales, CF6 4AH

The author would like to stress that
this is a work of fiction and no resemblance
to any actual individual or institution
is intended or implied.

A catalogue record for this book is available from The British Library.

ISBN 1 870206 754

Cover design: Vivid
Cover image: Stone

Printed in Wales by Gomer

For my parents, Carol and Kevin,
who let me live in an inspiring place,
and my daughter, Holly,
who wants to be a writer.

ONE

By the time they left Hiraethog it was too late. The strange but mostly silent alliance between Tom, Geraint and the Crow Woman had never been made to last. The secret that had created their reluctant union would eventually make it out into the open, leaving the very person Tom had wanted to protect, exposed.

Can a place be your doom? Tom had thought this over and had decided that it could. Everything was implicated, even the bland, whitewashed face of Hafod; it had lured them with its crude beauty like a siren on the rocks. And then there was the changing face of Hiraethog, the moor, a place that might have been designed to attract a wandering romantic like Lio. It was poetry and art to her, a place rich with inspiration for a creative soul.

On that Wednesday when they first looked upon Hafod, beaming down from its apex at the top of the climbing road, they gained an excited sense of its height in a dark place and its beacon-like luminosity. Hafod's isolation was complete; the only other dwelling in sight was the uninhabited Gwylfa Hiraethog, a melancholy ruin that loomed blackly against the skyline with an air of neglected grandeur. Gwylfa Hiraethog had been abandoned many years before and left at the mercy of the winds that crossed Hiraethog in the colder months. And it played its music for them like an *agent provocateur*: unearthly songs with deep, sonorous notes sounding whenever a gust of wind raced through its hollow shell. The ruined lodge boomed like a giant wind instrument, vibrating with each formidable note as if it might be uprooted from the hill at any moment. It had been captivating at the time, but Tom had one day come to hate its music.

And then there were the cliffs over the river, Afon Ddu. A place really could be your doom, but what would the statistics prove if this were investigated empirically? What would have happened if they had lived somewhere else? Tom had come to the conclusion that events had relied to a large extent on their setting. But not completely. This thinking was perhaps more constructive than much of that which had occupied him over the years. Sometimes he despaired at the dark circles that his mind turned around, dark circles that were linked in a chain. He would jump with a gasp from sleep or reverie, like a drowning man re-surfacing, only to find himself drowning again. When he became conscious it pained him to see where he had been, his subconscious retching up that which he tried to repress. It was only by working constantly that he could keep the darkness at bay and this he tried to do.

He still had Lio's copy of Kandinsky's 'Concentric Circles' on the sitting room wall and though he hated the circles it was the only splash of colour in a very neutral room. Lio had been a splash of colour. She had loved Hafod at first sight and insisted that she would die if they did not move there. Tom had felt much less enthusiasm though he had been barely conscious of the small tug of grief in his heart as he smiled back and said it was as good as theirs. Only a year later it was and Lio had given birth to a baby girl whom they named Leila. She was born at home in a small sitting room they called the snug, during a late spring snowfall, and as she grew up, she liked to force the story of her unconventional birth from her father whenever she could, because she enjoyed it and because she somehow knew he did not like telling it.

For a short time they were content, though they were never compatible. Tom was an academic and Lio an artist and they made a brilliant but mismatched couple, who were already moving apart even before Leila's birth. It was perhaps this opposition in genes and in the environment around her that brought about the mark of oddness in their daughter. But while they were together, the three reeled and spun unruly orbits about each other, like separate planets on separate paths, whirling in all their glorious colour and contrast and always in danger of colliding. Lio was a woman of opposites, sometimes warm and accommodating like her homely pottery, at other times as extravagant and volatile as her gaudy art. When they could stand to be together all at once, they sat in the snug together listening to the winds over Hiraethog, but most of the time they clashed violently, Lio's garish paintings and trinket pottery fighting its way across the kitchen table against Tom's college papers and cooking. This bedlam was enjoyed by Leila, who shook with excitement as her parents sparred. She would pull up a chair and stand on it, tapping her toys out between them, her hands controlling small theatres of real life as she staked her claim to a part of the universe. Her memory of those short early years seemed coloured by her mother's paintings, the red she liked to use and the red she liked to wear. The slash of red lipstick on her mother's mouth and the slash of red paint on the canvas… Leila had no name for the peculiar atmosphere that excited her earliest days, that raised her blood and made her shake and laugh, but later she called it passion. Her mother's passion had ignited everything around her, and would burn them all.

It was when Lio moved into the barn, creating her own studio that Leila had to choose one parent over the other. She usually followed Lio because she liked to watch her mother throw her brushes at large sheets of paper. Sometimes Leila helped and Lio laughed with irony as she let the child do her work. It was only with hindsight that Leila was able to observe that her mother and father were rarely together in the same room during this time.

'Where is my mum?' Leila had demanded one day after it

seemed that the pitched battles were a long distant memory and an awful quiet had descended. Leila hadn't been able to find her mother in the studio or the kitchen, nor indeed anywhere else. She'd searched madly, beseeching her father who would not speak and was blinded by his own tears and then, afterwards, she had been mute for almost a year. She'd become used to seeing her father with his head on the table, sleeping in his own grief. Tom had taken a year off work and during that time they saw few people. When he did return to work and made friends with a female colleague called Ann, Leila was already a loner. She was closest to her father when he was oblivious to it, when she played on the warm stones, her fingers black and her face smeared with coal dust like a camouflage kid of the fireplace. Only her eyes were bright; vivid green like emeralds and full of a life and intelligence that was beyond her age. With cheeks flushed by the fire, she listened and heard.

She liked to make herself invisible.

Being invisible allowed her to listen to grown up conversations, usually in the kitchen, which was comfortable and always warm. There were two easy chairs in front of the fire, draped with blankets and bolstered with cushions. Tom and Ann would sit on these after dinner with their wine. Leila would follow them and perch quietly on the logs and the coal sack in the small alcove next to the fire. This had been her retreat during her father's intense grieving, a place where she was close enough to him to know that at least physically she was not alone, and at the same time she was far enough away to feel safe from the relentless grief, the smell of Scotch and the aura of sadness and desperation that somehow pervaded her own emotions like a contagion. For years afterwards she continued to use this retreat, reluctant as she was to give up the anonymity she gained from it, and when she bathed there was always a film of coal dust floating amongst the bubbles in the bathwater.

By the time she was six, she was cunning and the alcove had become a useful hiding place for a child interested in going unnoticed while eavesdropping. Here, while playing around the warm stones, she was able to assess the threat posed by Ann and her daughter, Imogen.

Imogen was also six and far more sociable. Her reading and writing skills were superior to Leila's, whose school attendance had at best been patchy. Leila was mystified by Imogen's obsession with writing on scraps of paper and her insistence on reading out these rather repetitive and boring inscriptions. It was easier for adults to interact with Imogen and Leila did not try to compete with the attention afforded to her stepsister, acting instead as if she did not need it by turning to look in the opposite direction, at her dusty alcove retreat, as if it was an ally, or at the comforting view out of the window if she was nearer to it.

'When is my mum coming back?'

'She isn't coming back.'

'I want her, not you.'

Tom wondered at her rejection of him. Was she testing him? Or was she only dealing out rejection in response to his apparent rejection of her? It bothered him, but never quite enough because he too was preoccupied and behind the carefully placed reading glasses his grey eyes were haunted.

He found comfort in his friendship with Ann. Lio had been a brief fire and he had been burnt, now he wanted to feel safe with someone.

It was on an early train to a conference in Cardiff that Tom decided to ask Ann to marry him. The pain of his loss had somehow subsided when Ann had become his friend. It wasn't just the pain of loss, it was the pain of feeling that he had loved more than he had been loved. And the pain of the shocking way in which Lio had died. It all became endurable with Ann. It became background. Ann was not like Lio but that was a good thing. He knew he could trust her. She could be a bit of a stickler with the children and with cleanliness, she often took two showers a day, but these were things he could live with. And Imogen would be the sister and friend that Leila desperately needed, should have had.

It was not like him to sleep on the train but he slipped away in the darkness before dawn and woke sometime after sunrise to the first cold, blue light of day with the train stopping in Crewe station. He sought out shelter and a hot drink at one of the station's breakfast bars and as he sat awaiting his connection with a coffee cradled in his hands, he looked out at the pillars and the sharply azure station lights, on a morning when everything was pristine and pure, cobalt and lapis lazuli; created afresh for him. That first cerulean light possessed for Tom new birth and a leaf turned, a freshness and hope. He would go and buy a ring that very day and it would be a sapphire; for the blue of Ann's eyes and the blue splendour of an early morning new beginning.

And so, a year after Ann and Imogen first moved in, there had been a wedding, a low-key affair at a registry office.

'Why did my mum go away?'

Over the years Leila learnt much by listening. It was in the midst of the ebb and flow of Tom's kitchen conversations with Ann that she gradually learnt about her mother. She could attune her hearing to the frequency required – with patience, because it was elusive. In adulthood she would have the sharpest hearing of anyone she knew, as if her childhood had sharpened this one sense to the point of brilliance. She learnt to focus in with her hearing, like a hawk on a rabbit, zooming in on the lowered voice, the whisper, the mention of her mother. Leila listened so intently to spoken words that sometimes she could hear nothing else and other sounds became no more significant to her than the constant ululation of her own blood.

She came to understand that her mother was the source of a rift between her father and Ann, though not enough to prevent their marriage of comfort and convenience and she waited in vain to hear when Mum was coming back or at least for information on where she had gone. They had told her that Lio was dead and had gone to heaven, but Leila still looked out of the window when someone knocked, just in case. The photos given to her by her father were all she had and she kept them under her pillow. She knew from these that her mother was dark-haired and green-eyed and always smiling with the smug look of someone who had lived in a past golden age. She seemed to embody perfect happiness, allowing Leila to believe that this was at least a possibility.

'Where is heaven? Can I go there?'

As she grew older Leila became aware that most of the community avoided her, like they avoided walking under ladders. She had a habit of staring right through people, as if they consisted of nothing more than vapour. Her resemblance to Lio did not include the radiance or beauty that her mother had possessed; she was rather a morose child and her only real friendship at this time was with her stepsister, Imogen, who was happy to follow her flawed leadership. Imogen was the only person who really listened to Leila, while Leila's father only tolerated her by ignoring her and though he stayed near her geographically until his dying day, he was a continent away in reality. She would grow to love Hiraethog as he hated it, feeling that she was attached to it by her soul, which pulled within her like a silvery fish. Pushing, pulling, and flipping against her, held only by the thinnest, glittering cord.

The truth was that Leila was Lio all over again. She had the same intense attachment to Hiraethog, and it pained Tom to see it. He knew that Lio and Leila would have been good together, if only Lio had survived. Hiraethog was like a remnant of the mythical Wales Lio had loved. She had tried to encourage Tom to love it as she did.

'You don't have to be born in Wales to be Welsh, you know,' she had said, 'nor do you have to be able to speak Welsh fluently. It is rather a sense of belonging.'

Tom never belonged, though he accepted that she was right in thinking that birth and language might sometimes be pre-requisites but they were not always. He simply did not want to belong, though he never again lived in any other country.

Lio belonged as if it had been created for her. The lonely Afon Ddu cliffs became one of her favourite places and it was here that she had died on a hot, dry August day with a strong southerly breeze and heat hazes warping the distance.

TWO

By the time Leila was almost thirteen, her sombre looks set her apart. If it hadn't been for Imogen she would have been without friend or ally.

Sometimes, in the early hours of the morning when skeins of fog veiled the moors in a peculiar nebulous light, Leila experienced false awakenings. She would feel her mother's presence near her and even saw her as if she were alive again; unclear in the dimness before dawn, but real enough, her spilled blood returned to her body by the alchemy of dreams. Leila often initiated these experiences through desire and awareness before falling asleep. Until the day came when it all went bizarrely wrong.

It began with Leila waking to the feeling of a kindly, mothering hand pushing aside her clammy fringe. Leila opened her eyes and sat up, and thought she saw her mother's face retreating into the shadows by the door with a quiet smile. With some difficulty Leila lifted her hand to touch her forehead where a trace of her mother's touch still lingered. But before she could even feel the usual sadness that the touch was gone and that she could not imitate it, she was hit by something else. Suddenly she could not hear anything but an awful rushing that filled her ears. She felt as if she was awake but could not see. Something from a deep darkness within seemed to be trying to speak to her. But she could not understand the language of that part of her. It was attacking her, she knew that and it was not coming from outside herself, but from inside: a devastating assault that was causing something like strong waves or currents to wrack and wrench at her from a place beyond the physical. Leila was frozen in terror, yet a wiser part of her was able to oversee and understand in part what was happening. But her dimmed consciousness in terror thought a building had fallen onto her and she was somehow being blended into the rubble that was crushing her. In the midst of the rushing noise and the waves that seemed to brutalise her very soul, she thought that she must be dying. She did not know whether her eyes were open or not, nor whether her limbs were flailing or still, she was just a vessel feeling this foreign sensation without any control over it. Then, as abruptly as they had begun, the inner convulsions stopped and she fell still again even though her outer body had not actually moved. The terrible rushing in her ears ceased and she found herself sitting up in her bed with her eyes open. She could dimly see her bedroom again and her vision was returning gradually. After about half a minute the room brightened suddenly, as if a light had been clicked on and she was once again able to hear the wind outside on Hiraethog and see the figures on her alarm clock glowing. It was 5:14 am.

They had finally told her what had happened and it was a scratchy, ill-fitting story, incomprehensible like smudged ink on warped, brittle paper. She had heard it as many times as she could make anyone tell their version and it remained somehow unsatisfactory. She was too frightened to go back to sleep so she lay there, thinking of it.

She had been told that her mother was walking along the Afon Ddu cliffs when she had somehow lost her footing on the highest, rockiest section and fallen about a hundred feet. She was later found lying near the river, her neck broken. She was dead, of course.

Leila turned the pillow over for the cool, dry side and then threw herself onto it. She had the strangest feeling that there was more to the story she had been told. She had seen it: flashes of something terrible in her father's eyes.

It was eight o'clock when she next awoke, though she had not meant to sleep. At least the terror had ridden away on her sleep and she sat up, happy to be back on blissful, misty Hiraethog. She always woke before her stepsister Imogen, whose slight figure was wrapped foetus-like around a double duvet and several strategically placed pillows. Imogen felt the cold up on Hiraethog. She had lived in a cosy terrace in Denbigh before and even that had never been warm enough.

Leila occupied the favoured southern window and on the mornings when she was warmed by a bright patch of sunlight, she would wake earlier. On this occasion, she leapt up and crawled down her bed to open the curtains and look out. It was a low window, just level with her bed. Her window onto the world outside.

The air was pleasantly balmy and she could hear the affectionate twittering of skylarks ascending over the moor. She moved onto her window seat and tucked her knees up under her nightdress for a chin rest, feeling almost as if she were outside herself, suspended in the air like a bird on a thermal. Then she opened the window and leaned out, extending her head and upper body outside in order to peer downwards at a dizzying angle. She liked to dare herself to lean out further and further over the walls that fell away with a dazzling whiteness beneath her, the ground was a death-fall away and out in the airy space beyond, the moor watched her suicide games.

From the front of the house she could espy the narrow lane, which led towards the moors on upwardly sloping ground. After Hafod's three acres of land, there was a rough area of grazing owned by the farmer Mr Parry, which gradually turned into marshland, characterised by pale, yellowish rushes. Beyond this a small band of pines had been planted and formed a dark green boundary line, almost like a moat, in-between the hill on which

Hafod stood and the higher hill with its ruin, which rose to a spinning height on the other side.

This was the beginning of the moor, bathed in pallid light by a morning sun struggling through swathes of mist. She knew a perfect May morning was on its way, even now the moor shone with a supernatural, variegated brilliance and she was still and silent with a peculiar but powerful feeling of joy. This was her home.

The moor was quiet today, nothing but the occasional salt-thick cries of curlews returning from the sea. Ahead of her, the closest hill rose in a perfect arc and though her eyes were drawn to the dark contrast of the ruin, the moor was beautiful; adorned by clouds of greenish brown heather crowned with tiny buds that would become flowers later. Green lipped paths wound their way in their steep climb to the summit, skirting the silvery glint of exposed rocks polished to smoothness by the elements. The great abundance of colour and contour caught the eye and was at first overwhelming. Time was needed to absorb the brilliance of a landscape unrolling a riot of mottling and depth, of sunlight and cloud shadows chasing fast breezes. She would never tire of looking, but it was Saturday and the aromas of a cooked breakfast lured her away.

Down in the kitchen, the stepmother, Ann was sitting on her stool repairing a broken vase. She would often take up repair jobs after weekend breakfasts in this way. The back door was open and Leila's father was already in his lounger on the short alpine grass outside the back door, reading his paper. These rituals were comforting and Leila climbed onto her stool for the usual weekend breakfast fare: eggs, fried mushrooms and bread.

Imogen appeared half an hour later, yawning noisily and stretching two long, pale arms. Ann was making the girls their first picnic of the year.

'Don't go further than the standing stone,' said Tom. The warning was principally for his daughter, who he suspected was a bit of a wanderer.

Like her mother.

Leila was watching the stepmother's smooth hands spreading butter onto bread with a faint feeling of disgust. They were mean little hands and she had a real dread of small, smooth adult hands.

'And don't forget,' Tom continued, 'if the weather changes, head home.'

He was still looking at Leila and when she realised this she looked out of the window. She had never given up looking out of the window when her father spoke to her, though by now she had reluctantly outgrown the alcove by the fire. She had seen many things through the window over the years, seeing more as she grew taller and no longer had to crane her neck to find something to focus on. She saw the season's subtle change on the moor and the paint slowly cracking, peeling and curling from the window frame as if it no longer fitted... The buzzards circling and waiting for prey, the old farmer's mad dance with his stick and his dog like a jackal, waiting to be unfaithful. Then she turned back to her father, finding always that he had given up on her, his reading glasses were back on and he was muttering to his papers. It was as if he too had hit the rocks of Afon Ddu, accidentally breaking their father-daughter relationship because it was just an egg that needed a mother to keep it warm.

That day they followed the pale lane up onto the moor. There was grass growing in the middle and rivulets of water trickling down the edges from the recent rains. The banks on either side were steep and high so that little beyond the lane could be seen until they reached the end where the rusty gate appeared and the banks fell away to reveal the rolling, brown moor, spreading out on all sides. It was always surprising, this sudden appearance of the moor and Leila never quite got used to it, never quite stopped being excited as she scrambled over the gate and dropped down onto the other side where Mynydd Hiraethog really began. There was an airy feeling of being released and of shaking off the dry scales of civilisation.

They often visited the stream. It was an ecstatically fast, narrow torrent of cold, clear water that forever seemed to buoyantly race up and down the contours with a hearty, jaunty babbling and cheeriness. Leila could sit for ages and watch the swirling currents and the glittering sparks of light reflected from the sky, which she found hypnotic and reassuring. Sometimes she lay back and rested by the stream, hearing its light-hearted babble as if it were a host of voices, chattering hurriedly as they were carried away from her down the hill. The stream was a great source of interest; it ran through the bottom of a narrow chasm whose sides had been intricately moulded and sculpted into graceful curves by the strong currents. Lying on their stomachs on the mossy banks they were able to peer into the deepest sections of this miniature valley and observe the details of a world of moss, stones and eddies. In some areas the stream babbled deep under its banks and elsewhere it rose up and re-appeared from the chasm, bubbling up towards them, before plunging downhill and away from them. It was good for dam building since its shallowness meant it was easy to block up with a mixture of sticks, stones, moss and mud, and its velocity meant that the placid pool which built up soon reached the top of the dam and began cascading over it in the form of a miniature waterfall. Eventually the torrential little stream would always run their dams into the ground.

It was through following the stream on that first occasion, that they had unintentionally left the path and made their way downwards towards the forbidden marshes. They meandered on until Leila suddenly grabbed Imogen's arm and pointed to a spot somewhere above them.

There was a man watching them. An outlandish looking man. He was approaching them rapidly, leaning over a stick. Leila recognised him to be the old farmer she had often caught staring at her from a distance. He owned a small hill farm, a mile west of Hafod, situated on another pale lane that ran parallel to theirs. They had only come across his dilapidated farm once, when Leila's father had taken the opportunity to lecture them on the evils of drink. The farmer had grazing rights on Hiraethog and could often be seen rambling over the moors with his sheepdog, Euros. He was an overweight and hulking figure of a man, who usually overdressed for the weather, though they had once seen him in an old Jimi Hendrix T-shirt with a pair of tight fitting Bermuda shorts that were trying to take refuge beneath his hanging gut. Leila, who sensed his nihilism, found herself drawn to him as much as she was repelled.

He approached them along the path, leaning on his stick, breathless as an old buffalo, swaying and baulking, his eyes fixed on them in a stare.

'Where are you girls from, then?'

His voice crawled from beneath the bedclothes of alcoholic torpor and every cell in his body seemed to whisper ill health.

Leila was quick to dislike the man. She might have one day identified with him, but that day she only noticed how his bottom lip drooped and curled to one side as he spoke. She gave him a level look of defiance and refused to reply. He chuckled at that and turned to Imogen.

'Are you the girls from Hafod?'

Imogen nodded and pointed towards the white shape of their cottage in the distance. She was hoping his gaze might leave her and follow her pointing finger, but it did not.

He went to hold his side and shake a little and they were unsure as to whether the sound he made was from chuckling or choking. However he made a quick recovery with a swig of the amber liquid from the bottle that poked its snout from his jacket pocket.

'Well watch out for the bogs. Be good and go home now.'

'Why?' Leila asked.

He smiled and fixed her with his small eyes once again, his mouth dropping to reveal a graveyard of leaning and broken teeth.

'Why should we go home *now*?' she repeated, not liking his stare. 'We haven't had our picnic yet!'

He was motionless except for the quick squinting of his eyes, his smile suspended in animation. Imogen pulled her gloves off and then put them on again for no apparent reason.

'Well *cariad*,' he said at last, 'you're off the public path and that makes you trespassers. And it's going to rain. Look at the sky if you don't believe me.'

He watched her as she looked.

'See how the sheep are walking downslope? They know. Just like my cat, who was sat with her back to the fire this morning. You listen to me, *del*, and you'll learn something.'

Leila was not impressed, she folded her arms and frowned uncooperatively.

He waved his whisky bottle in mid-gulp and appeared to shake with irritation as some of the precious liquid was wasted. Then he held out his hand, a hard glint in his eye.

'As I said, you are trespassing.'

He jabbed his finger into a point at the sour child's face, though the words to match the gesture died on his lips as he recognised the green eyes. He seemed to quake a little then and quickly turned away, offering Imogen a handshake because he felt he had been rather harsh. His big red hand was warm and so chapped that there were red fissures in the palm. Then he turned and went on without another word.

THREE

With the passage of each month of that year it became more apparent that Leila and Imogen were testing boundaries. They were no longer satisfied with playing within the grounds of Hafod and found themselves wandering further afield, drawn towards some of the intriguing characters that inhabited their community. They often followed the raucous farm boys, who played rough inbetween harvesting hay on the lower slopes, and sometimes, from a safe distance, they spied on the abominable Crow Woman... Until, one day in August when they weren't expecting it, she swooped on them.

Leila had seen her close up once before, from the safety of Ann's car. The Crow Woman had stared after them as they passed, with a sad look, the rifle that often accompanied her tucked under her arm. Ann seemed to hate her and always found something unpleasant to say, while Tom maintained a deathly silence.

She was a stout woman, wild eyed and probably in her early fifties. Leila could not decide if she was attractive and concluded that she had the look of someone who had been slim and pretty once. However she now looked like a person who was becoming overwhelmed by a widening girth and skin that was sagging around her jaw line, creating sad-looking jowls. There was something in her aloneness, the rifle and the heavy, tasselled skirts that suggested eccentricity or possible derangement. Her wayward hair unwound itself from a bun, its tendrils reaching out like Gorgon's serpents. Her Roman nose was in opposition to the elongated dark eyes that pierced through Leila, even from a distance. More than once she had seen her lift a rifle to shoot at the noisy rooks and crows that cawed from the tall trees next to her house and had heard her cursing them in a voice that was itself a corvid croak. This was how Leila had come to call her the Crow Woman. She was intriguing and frightening, like someone who might be endowed with supernatural powers.

It was a windy autumn day when Leila found herself crossing the small hump-backed bridge that led towards the Crow Woman's dilapidated old house. Imogen was following her, lured by a sighting of a hoary old fox. When they spied Mr Parry, the farmer, approaching, Leila grabbed Imogen's arm and pulled her at a run towards the Crow Woman's house. They knew they should have been heading home but instead they jumped into a patch of sedges in a deep ditch at the bottom of the Crow Woman's driveway. From there they watched Mr Parry pass by, muttering to himself in customary fashion. He had become a joke to them. A ridiculous drunken figure of a man with his belly emerging as if bidding for freedom from beneath his clothes, leaping over his trousers like a pig over a gate. The cold lips of a whisky bottle were never far from being lifted to his drooling lips and he was constantly muttering to himself in the manner of one who has been alone, and against his wishes, for too long. Holding conversations with make-believe companions and imagining voices in the winds because no one real would talk to him. Though Leila felt some pity, she laughed at him wickedly as children do.

She was so pleased to have outwitted him that she sat sniggering and whispering with Imogen in the ditch for a few minutes until she was ready to leave. But before they could stand up, a shadow fell over them. They looked up to find the Crow Woman towering over them.

'I see I have trespassers,' she cawed.

No matter how marginally, they had dared to encroach onto the Crow Woman's land, and now looked up at the dark, glinting eyes, still crouching, to see how they would be dealt with. She was even more crow-like than they had expected.

'All right,' she said, appearing to find their cowering vaguely amusing, a slight, suppressed smile lifting her jowls.

'I know who *you* are, but you have nothing to fear from me. As for him,' she motioned towards the retreating figure of Mr Parry, 'he's the sort of man your parents should have warned you about.'

Then she softened a little, seemingly not wanting to frighten them but rather wanting them to stay for a while.

'If you want,' she said, 'I could give you a quick tour of my place. You always seem interested enough when you pass me in your car. Would you like that?'

Leila nodded. 'We'd like to see your ducks and hens,' she said. 'Dad mentioned you, he said you were friends.'

'Oh did he, that's nice,' said the Crow Woman, the corners of her mouth twitching into a smile. 'We were once.'

She appeared wistful for a moment and then she waved them up the twisting driveway. 'Follow me. I'll show you how to live off the land.'

She led them to a yard full of suspicious hens. Leila and Imogen were uneasy with the idea of her killing her meals with her own hands and she seemed to sense their distaste because she pointed out that some of the fowls would never be eaten.

'I don't eat the old ones. They'd be as tough as leather.'

The Crow Woman's closest companion was her sheepdog Boadicea, though she also kept a small friendly herd of goats and sheep. She was a crack shot with a rifle too, and could bag herself a rabbit or pheasant for dinner when she fancied.

On the south side of her house, there was a large vegetable patch and an old greenhouse, this was where most of her food came from.

'I caught a big old fox sleeping here under my rhubarb leaves, one afternoon. It had quite a shock when it saw me coming up with my spade.'

'What did you do?' Imogen asked anxiously.

The Crow Woman laughed. 'Foxes have never troubled me, they eat rabbits so I don't interfere with them. Mr Parry claims he loses lambs but I think most of his losses are through cold weather and neglect. He's a drinker.'

Imogen was eyeing the Crow Woman curiously. 'What do you mean by "a drinker"?' she asked.

The Crow Woman led them inbetween the rows of vegetables, watching vigilantly for any garden pests that she could pick out with her birdlike fingers. She did not answer for some time, so Imogen began to think she had not been heard or even worse, was being ignored. But the Crow Woman was merely musing on something she had not thought about for quite some time.

'He's a drinker, just like my husband was. I'm talking about a serious drinker, not just one of them that enjoys a tipple like I do.'

'Oh I see,' said Imogen.

'What happened to your husband?' asked Leila.

The Crow Woman cleared her throat. 'Oh not a lot. I left him because of the drinking, he was a changed person with it and not a very nice one. He died about ten years ago with a bottle at his side.'

She walked ahead of them purposefully and then stopped as she bent to pull out weed seedlings.

'I've got everything here, almost every fruit and vegetable you can buy in the shops and even a few of the exotic ones in my greenhouse. I think August is a wonderful month, especially when it burns hot like it is this year. It almost turns this place into a paradise.'

She paused as she began picking up her gardening tools. 'Perhaps you would like a drink? I'm forgetting my hospitality. I don't see many people these days.'

They agreed to a glass of juice. So she gave them apple juice with ice and they sat on the wooden bench she had made herself, in a patch of warm sunlight against a wall covered in roses.

'I'm harvesting now and I have a great deal of surplus. I sell a lot of it, but you can take some fruit and vegetables back with you when you go. The tomatoes are good this year and so are the cauliflowers. This is my favourite month because it is so abundant.'

'My mother died in August,' said Leila suddenly.

'I know,' said the Crow Woman, quickly, almost as if she had expected it. 'It was a day like today.'

Leila noticed the immediacy of her reply but remained silent.

Far away a golden plover was calling from the moor, the sun was moving into the west and Leila thought they should be going home, but could not bring herself to move or say anything. Then Imogen asked the question that was on both their minds.

'What do you know about Leila's mother?'

The Crow Woman's lips tightened. 'Oh not much,' she said, though there was a curious glint in her eyes as she spoke. 'Do you still visit Afon Ddu with your father to leave flowers there?' she asked shiftily.

Leila nodded, 'Yes, we're going next week.'

Tom expressly forbade Leila from going anywhere near the spot where her mother had fallen. Just once a year he relented, on the anniversary of the tragedy, when they would lay flowers there and say a prayer. He believed this ritual was necessary to give Leila a kind of contact with her mother and to remove some of the mystique and attraction of the tragic place, but he worried too and she noticed this, even when she was very small. She saw her father fidgeting near the edge of the cliff where her mother had fallen. Did he think that being there might prompt something? Was that why he never let her stay long?

The three were silent together for a while, staring away beyond the Crow Woman's vegetable garden to where a patch of rough ground had become overgrown with weeds and the brick wall was falling down under the stranglehold of clutching ivy. The girls had finished their apple juice and the shadows were beginning to grow long, but while Imogen waited for a cue from Leila, Leila sat unmoving, held by things that were remaining unsaid. Things about her mother. Finally she spoke.

'Was my mother's death really an accident?'

The Crow Woman appeared a little taken aback by this question, she stared at Leila for a moment before attempting to answer her.

'Of course,' she said kindly. 'There can be no doubt that it was a terrible accident.'

Leila nodded and closed her eyes so that it was all dark. Dark and red.

They had told her that her mother's death would have been instantaneous; her world blacked out so suddenly that she would have known nothing.

She had died on August 17th and because of that, August could be a dark month. Dark and sticky. When her father took her to lay their flowers on the cliffs every year, something would be triggered afterwards and for days she would find reasons to feel sick and often would not go out at all. The sun could be burning outside and the moor a purple paradise, but Leila would be indoors in the shadows. And if she did go out, things seemed to happen, like the day she trod on a rotten dead sheep, hidden in the heather, a horrible paradox of hard bone and soft skin and wool. The crunchy feeling through her shoe seemed to remain for ages afterwards though she furiously wiped and pounded it in the heather. And there were things she didn't like to see, like Mr Parry walking downhill with two shot rabbits dangling from his hand, their funnel ears glowing pink and sensitive in the late sun. The moor was like a sunken ship on such days, too dark to walk on, and she would turn her back to it and try to pretend it wasn't there.

'Perhaps you girls will come again. I've enjoyed your company,' said the Crow Woman kindly. 'It's getting late now but I will show you my house next time.'

'Yes please Mrs...' said Imogen.

'You can call me Arabella.'

Leila wanted to ask more about her mother, but the questions had not yet formed themselves, there would be time yet, another visit would yield more.

'Have you met anyone since your husband?' asked Imogen as they got up to go.

The Crow Woman's answer was pensive: 'Yes, I've been hurt again since, quite badly…though he's a good man, really.'

They asked her who he was, but she shook her head and stood up, so they asked her if she had any children instead.

'There were never any children, maybe there should have been,' she said with a wan smile.

Before they left, she gave them a basket of strawberries, tomatoes and lettuce to take to their parents and waved to them, making them promise to call on her again. They were excited as they walked back over the bridge and along the winding road that eventually brought them home to Hafod. Leila felt a sense of change in the air. It was as if the summer had gorged on its own heat and would soon expire.

Arabella watched them for a while, though they did not look back. She observed their brisk walk and heard their excited chatter as indistinctly as the skylark that was climbing invisible ladders in the air with its musical twittering. The long crisp white socks and the lemon skirt on the blonde girl made her yearn for her own girlhood. Days of freedom, days when the grown ups had taken care of things, days of picking daisies and throwing sticks into streams. They were freer now than they would ever be again and the envy she felt was of the sweeter kind. Not like the bitter envy she had felt for the dark haired girl's mother. She had never had much time for the artistic mother; that one was always too full of herself. She remembered her disappointment when she discovered that another artist had moved into the area. As she had come to know Lio and Tom that initial disappointment had branched out like a growing tree. A twisted, poison tree of jealousy, hatred, anger and desire.

She was alone in her view that she was the better artist. However she was not alone in thinking that Lio's looks and vitality were instrumental in marketing and selling her art as much, if not more, than any modicum of talent. It still rankled, even though the woman was dead. The value of Lio's work had inflated even before she was buried and her last works were quickly cleared from galleries around the county and beyond.

Arabella shut the door with a gentle snap and leaned against it for a moment. The child was different to the mother. She had seen how the girl's eyes were rather strained for her young age. This she was sorry for. There was something about this girl that she liked. Even as she saw a quick, livid curiosity in her eyes, it changed and became something else. A cool air of depression. A vague happiness moved Arabella as she stood there, leaning on the door and staring into space. It was a little like the excitement that sometimes lifts a person and turns their body into a body of light, a feeling of fascination, a bit like falling in love.

FOUR

After the heat of August, autumn blustered in with a bountiful ration of rain and gales, and even a sprinkling of snow. It was safer to stay inside and listen to the winds racing around Hafod's thick stone walls. While Tom and Ann sat in the kitchen with their wine and work-related conversations, Leila read about famous murders by lamplight and Imogen moved between homework, ballet and the TV, impatient and fluttering.

It was well into November before the weather calmed down and it was no longer a feat to walk unbattered from door to car, car to door. Though whatever had bashed and clouted them had worn itself out, it was still; deathly still and bitter cold. The girls were itching to get out of the house and Leila slyly took this opportunity to lead Imogen into the shadow of Clocaenog. By the time Ann realised they were gone, they were already on the edge of the great plantation forest on the other side of the moor, far beyond the mossy standing stone that was meant to mark out their boundary. Leila had always hankered after Clocaenog, even while she was revulsed by something she felt was hiding there. Whenever she entered the shadow of its trees, her senses were overtaken with vivid memories. The scent of evergreens, the damp fingers of mist, the coolness and the stark, dark stillness… She knew she had been there many times before, when she was very small and with her mother, not her father. But her memories were mostly atmospheric and she recalled no real detail of what she and her mother had actually done in Clocaenog.

It was a damp day, full of the whiteout of low cloud becoming fog and the hostility of cold, frost-tinged pines. Even in warm weather the old part of the forest, into which they had ventured, was a dead place. The trees were too tall and too closely planted to allow any light to penetrate and had strangled out all other life. This was a silent place where the air did not circulate well, but lay inert in a heavy, cold wedge that penetrated to the bone. They found themselves shivering and it was not just from the chill.

'I don't like it here,' complained Imogen as she tried to pull her anorak tighter around her. 'Why on earth did we come here?'

The pine trees were showering her with frost whenever she brushed against them, frost that slid down her spine and inside her wellies and turned back into cold water almost instantly. She shuddered violently whenever this happened, which was often. On top of that she hated the feel of the rust coloured pine needles underfoot. They put her in mind of dead hedgehogs.

'Leila! Where are we going? Tell me!'

'I don't really know,' said Leila stopping and turning to Imogen. 'I just wanted to come here because my mother used to.'

'I don't know why,' snapped Imogen. 'Where exactly are we heading? Everything looks the same here. There isn't anything here but trees and it's cold. Which way is the way back? I'm going back.'

'You can't just go, Imogen.'

'Why not? Just point the way.'

'I don't know the way,' said Leila. 'I'm trying to work it out.'

'You mean we're lost!' Imogen was aghast. 'I knew I shouldn't have come with you. You're nuts!'

'Shut-up Imi, I can't think with you nagging. We only left the road because you moaned it was boring, if we had stayed on the road we would be all right. Now we just need to find it again, so come on.'

'I've never known such a cold, horrible place,' Imogen whinged, as she pulled her anorak tightly around her in hope of extracting every ounce of comfort from it.

'I bet it's minus something centrigade. About three, or four, or even five. Maybe it's dropping while we speak and soon it'll be minus ten and we'll be frozen ice blocks.'

'Stop whinging will you,' growled Leila.

'And it's all your fault!'

Imogen was too busy with her usual muttering and complaining to notice the twig snap some way behind them, but to Leila it was like a gunshot. She looked anxiously over her shoulder. Imogen was following like a grumpy shadow, her head was down and she was fiddling with her gloves, and behind her there was nothing except for the frosty silhouettes of Norwegian pines, their edges touched by the thickening fog. Leila was becoming frightened, she suspected they were not alone with the trees but she wasn't going to let Imogen know, so she pressed on with her ears pricked.

'Why did I come out here?' she thought. 'On such a horrible day too and why *did* mother ever like to walk here? It's so gloomy.'

She had not been in the forest as often as she had told Imogen. She knew there were three reservoirs and a recreation centre somewhere in the thick of it, but they were walking in the part near the moor where the trees were older, taller and more closely planted and where everything looked the same. She was beginning to feel desperate, the stock-still, frozen pines seemed to be gathering in and the still air was strikingly cold. Like a tomb.

There it was again, unmistakeable…. a twig snapping from somewhere behind them. Leila looked round but there was nothing there.

'Come on Imogen, if we jog, it'll keep us warm and we'll get there quicker,' Leila's voice was shaky, she felt they needed to lose whatever it was that was tailing them.

'But my feet are so numb it hurts to run!'

'No, come on, you will get your circulation going better.'

As soon as they began to jog, Leila felt herself gripped by fear and an instinct that told her to fly, and she found herself running and choking at the same time as if someone had caught her by the throat so she couldn't breathe.

The dead forest floor had once been moorland open to the sky, and it was not easy to run on since the mat of needles concealed dead wood and potholes designed to twist ankles. Even as Leila thought of this, her foot wedged into a small hole and she was catapulted, hands out, into the awful mixture of wet and frozen mud and matted vegetation. A cry was knocked from her lungs, from shock rather than pain.

'That'll teach you!' cried Imogen from behind, she was a feeble runner and had fallen back. 'I thought you said, "jog". Well I'm not following you anymore because you're going the wrong way.'

'What do you mean?' said Leila, picking herself up and looking anxiously behind.

There was only the forest.

'I mean, look over there,' cried Imogen pointing back to Leila's right. 'There's light shining through, it looks like a road.'

'Yes, you're right. Let's go.'

They tracked across, down a slippery slope where Leila noticed large boot prints in the wet mud and splintered ice close to; and onwards towards the light, but it was not a road, it was a clearing.

'Well, it's something at least,' she said, looking back into the forest.

'It's not home,' grunted Imogen.

'I know. But don't you think the pines look pretty with frost on them?' asked Leila, though it was a rhetorical question and Imogen merely pulled a face for a reply.

The clearing was surrounded by tall Sitka Spruce, Norwegian Spruce and Scots Pine. A hoar frost had danced all over their forms, picking out and highlighting every intricacy and inventing many more. The long meadow fescue that grew plentifully in the clearing had been dead and yellow until the hoar frost fairy had danced her wand over it, clothing it in a fragile white dress that seemed to have a fluorescence all of its own. The fluffy heads looked like the lively heads of old people with lots of white hair. A slight breeze ruffled them even as Leila looked and they merrily danced a little jig while some of the frost shivered down from the nearest trees and was gathered by them. The trees here were larger and majestic with spreading branches, thanks to the space, and quite unlike their tall, thin-branched neighbours. The closest one was so covered in frost that its long branches hung down and the spaces between its needled twigs were joined by frost like webs strung by a prolific ice spider.

Leila looked over her shoulder again. Perhaps they were not safe after all.

'Why do you keep looking behind you?' asked Imogen.

'Just checking for bears. Come on, the trees are thinner here, the road could be nearby.'

'I hope so because I'm getting tired,' said Imogen. 'And there aren't any bears in Wales, you dimwit.'

The light, albeit an eerie kind of foggy light, was a huge relief. Leila continued to glance over her shoulder, but she felt less uneasy now they were out of the dark forest and on firmer ground. At the other side of the clearing they found a vehicle track, which they followed hopefully.

'This will lead to a road if nothing else does,' said Leila. 'I just hope it's the road we want.'

Imogen had stopped to pick up a frosty pinecone; she was too annoyed to speak.

'Come on, Imogen, we need to hurry.'

'What's the point, we've been ages, a bit longer won't hurt,' snapped Imogen. 'I want to stop a minute and see if I can wring my socks out. I think my welly has a hole in it.'

'We need to keep moving.'

'Why? Anyway I have to do this.'

She already had one of her wellies off, just as they were reaching a bend, which Leila suspected led them out onto a road.

'Imogen, I heard noises behind us earlier, that was all.'

'What kind of noises?' asked Imogen anxiously, her pale, naked foot dangling without sock or welly.

'Just like someone walking and snapping twigs with their feet.'

Imogen stuffed her foot back into her welly without the sock and began to limp quickly after Leila.

'You should have *told* me,' she muttered.

'I didn't want to worry you.'

They rounded the corner and found a road before them. Imogen waved her wet sock in relief, while Leila looked quickly behind.

'Anyone there?' asked Imogen.

'Nothing. Look, we might still be lost. I'm not sure if this is the road we wanted, we'll just have to see where it takes us.' Leila was frightened now. The forest ahead seemed darker as if they were further in – or was it just the mist that had become thicker?

They began to jog together, when Leila heard another sound, a thundering of feet, as if someone was running towards them, fast. This time it did not come from behind them, but alongside them, in the dark trees. She smothered a cry of fear that rose birdlike in her throat and looked at Imogen, but it appeared that with her heavy, laboured breathing, Imogen had once again not heard.

A man stepped from the trees, stopped in front of them and stared. He materialized so quickly and quietly that it was almost as if he was not real at all, but a manifestation of the gloom; his pale hair full of condensed fog and his eyes large and dead like rabbit burrows. A branch above him was waving and showering him with its frosty coating, like tiny snowflakes. Landing in his hair.

They stopped less than ten feet from him and stared back. Mesmerized, they felt they could not take their eyes off him, because that was when something unpleasant might happen. Leila felt that funny gripping, constricting feeling in her throat as if someone had taken hold of it and was squeezing. Why was he staring at her with that strange look, as if the ghost had seen a ghost?

She put her hand to her throat to try and stop the squeezing. He smiled then, and like a cold breeze through the still pines, a sense of vague familiarity surprised Leila, but she could not remember who he was or where she had seen him.

'Who are you?' asked a small voice somewhere to Leila's left.

It was Imogen. The sound of her voice seemed to bring Leila to her senses and the strange man stopped staring as if he too were recovering from a surprise, though he looked ill at ease. Leila noticed Imogen put her hand into her pocket where she kept her usual weapon (a rock, self-defence) concealed and wished she had one. The man put his hand through his fine hair, perhaps self-consciously and laughed lightly.

'Did I scare you?' he asked, 'I didn't mean to, but what are you doing here alone?'

'Just walking,' said Imogen. 'We're going home now.'

'It will be dusk soon, do you want a lift?'

The words seemed to hang in the air for a moment with both girls recoiling inwardly.

Imogen answered again. 'No thanks,' she said.

'You're probably right to refuse,' he said with a slight nervous laugh again. 'I don't know what I was thinking ... you don't *know* me of course,' there was a pause, he seemed reluctant to leave them. 'Let me walk you, at least some of the way, then I'll feel better if I see you on the road home. You live at Hafod, don't you?'

He had addressed the latter question to Leila.

'We *are* from Hafod,' she replied. 'Who are you?'

The pale-haired man was slow to answer this question.

'Geraint,' he said finally, 'I'm local, I live here in Cloc, over towards the southern side where it is a bit brighter. You know, if you really want to walk in Clocaenog that is where you should go. This part is so dark, and it is too easy to get lost here.'

'So why are you walking here?' asked Leila, knowing fully how insolent she sounded.

'Good question,' he said appearing vaguely amused. 'I came looking for gloom today. It's away from the tourists, and there are memories here for me.'

It occurred to Leila that it was extremely unlikely that there would be any tourists in any part of Clocaenog on a chilly day in November. He started to walk along the road ahead of them but then stopped as if having second thoughts. He stood still for a moment and they waited behind him with a sense of unease. Just as Leila was going to ask him what was wrong (they could not see his face), he suddenly turned on his heel and said, 'This way,' without looking at them. They were now walking in the opposite direction and he was silent. They followed after hesitating and exchanging nervous glances that failed to reassure. Leila had noticed how the man's accent was very well spoken and English, like her father's, and how it seemed odd somehow in this setting. It was difficult to tell his age in the gloom, but he looked to be in his thirties, particularly since the initial fear in his face had transformed into hardness, with a slight twitch on the left side of his jaw. Leila felt he was watching her, as if he knew her. She wanted to ask why he had been following them, but thought better of it.

'How did you know we are from Hafod?' she asked instead.

He seemed to clench his jaw, 'You get to know everyone in these parts.' The tone of his voice had altered as if he was annoyed by the question. 'People round here talk a lot and you get to hear all their business whether you want to or not.'

He paused and was quiet for a while. Then he looked at them, smiling warmly once again, his mood apparently swinging like a pendulum.

'You're stepsisters aren't you?'

'Yes,' replied Imogen.

'Did you know my mother?' Leila asked suddenly.

'Your mother?' he paused and looked away. Leila noticed his hands were shaking as he put them into his pockets.

'Yes, I must have spoken to her a few times... she had an unusual name. It was Lio wasn't it?'

'Yes, it was.'

His face was inscrutable and his voice had become a monotone.

'She used to walk here sometimes, just like you are today. I remember seeing her with a baby in a carrier, which I expect was you,' he looked at Leila and she noticed the strange way in which his dark eyes glittered. 'That is why I stared when I first saw you,' he said softly. 'You look like her, younger perhaps … but like her.'

There was a short pause when only their footfalls echoed amongst the silent evergreens.

'Do you remember me?' he asked looking again at Leila.

'Well, I don't think so,' she said. 'But…I do have some memories from that time, and you look sort of familiar like I have seen you before, but can't remember when.'

If there was an answer that could please the man, this was not the one. It was as if a shutter had gone down on his face and he looked away again. A feeling of panic was rising within Leila and she wanted him to go away. She walked onwards as fast as she could without appearing too afraid. Imogen on the other hand seemed much more at ease with him and had taken her hand off her rock.

'Perhaps you will come again for a walk in the nice part of the forest,' he said suddenly after it seemed he would not speak again. 'There are rabbits, foxes, birds and even a badger's sett near me. I could show you a nice walk, there is a nature trail you can follow.' He was smiling and seemed friendly once more, except for his unnatural eyes.

But Imogen was beguiled. 'Have you seen the badgers?' she asked, because badgers were her favourite animals.

'Yes, I have,' he replied and then suddenly gave Imogen his full attention. 'Perhaps I could show you one day. I like to guard the sett from unwelcome intruders. I'm always on the lookout for suspicious characters or people I don't know in the area.'

'Is that why you were following us?' asked Imogen, innocently.

There was the vague embarrassment of one caught out and he seemed to try and lift his head and his facial expression out of their reach and with a laugh said: 'Yes, but I wasn't a very good detective if you saw me.'

'I didn't,' said Imogen. 'It was Leila who knew you were there.'

Geraint looked at Leila then. A dark look that made her shrink back. His striking looks both drew and repelled her. A ghost from the past. Her throat felt tight and a feeling of nausea was fighting its way upward and making her weak. Why did he keep looking at her? She was like her mother, but what was the significance for him? She was relieved when the roar of a car urgently approaching the upcoming junction interrupted them. She saw Geraint stiffen and the glare in his eyes. Her relief grew when she saw it was the stepmother's car, even with the inevitable scolding.

'It's Mum,' said Imogen, half disappointed. She turned to say goodbye to the mysterious Geraint, but he had already withdrawn and was walking, without a word of farewell, back into the trees and the gloom from which he had appeared.

Ann was furious when she discovered they had been talking to a stranger. She said she did not know Geraint and then put her foot hard on the accelerator as if she couldn't get away fast enough.

As they drove away, Leila turned in the back seat of the car to look back towards the forest, but Geraint was already out of sight. They fell into a pensive silence, busy thinking over their encounter. Leila was flattered when someone commented on her likeness to her mother, was pleased that she resembled the face that was always smiling from those old photographs. She wanted to be like her mother when she grew up, though it was difficult to know what that would mean...

'And where exactly were you going, anyway?' said Ann suddenly.

'We were coming home to you, Mum,' said Imogen.

'Tom will go crazy if he finds out you were... there,' said Ann. 'Especially you Leila. If I don't tell him then you must never do that again while you are under my care.'

'We *were* coming home,' said Leila.

Ann said nothing. They had been walking in the wrong direction, towards Geraint's bungalow, but she would not say anything. It could do no good.

FIVE

Ann and Imogen had their own family, who lived mostly in Camarthen, and it was customary for this family to receive an annual visit shortly before Christmas. It left Leila alone with her father for several days, something that was not always a pleasant experience. When Ann was away the house was not heated as well and Leila's father had a habit of leaving food on the counter in the kitchen instead of cooking a proper meal to sit down to or eat in the lounge off a tray. It had happened this time, with things like cold, wrinkled chicken drumsticks bought pre-cooked from the supermarket and a wrap of gorgonzola cheese, some tomatoes that probably needed washing, a bowl of pears and grapes that probably did too and some pasta salad. Anyone would have thought he didn't like cooking. Perhaps it was more that he couldn't be bothered. There was only *her* after all. Well she wasn't going to eat any of it – in protest – see if he'd notice. Of course, she was aware that this could be a dangerous game to play.

It was excruciatingly cold this time. A cold snap before Christmas and the house felt like a morgue. Leila found herself in the little study room, where her father's books were stacked along one wall opposite the organised clutter that concealed his desk. It was strangely quiet in the house without Imogen's wittering and Leila had found herself tiptoeing and whispering as if she were in some hushed place where quiet was obligatory.

As her fingers traced lines in some of the dustier tomes, she remembered her father's big book on the earth. With a sudden passion she began looking for it. The book had been unique, something they had shared, something that had brought them together; no matter how briefly. Leila had been five then, still young enough to believe that she was the planet around which the bright sun revolved. At the same time she had known that she was odd in some way, and had come to identify through the book with the lonely blue planet as it was first seen from the moon. Her father had shown her.

'When we landed on the moon we could see at last how alone and how insignificant we really are on our lonely, little blue planet earth,' he had said in a kind voice that she had never forgotten, the big book open on his knee and his glasses halfway down his nose.

'At last we could see how small we were swimming in the big black sea of space. And so alone.'

Leila recited this after him, to herself in a whisper.

She requested the book over and over and though it was heavy, she took it to him, dragging it along the carpet and lifting it with a mock groan onto his knee. Until, one day when she was seven, she saw a tear fall onto the book and looked up to see her father crying. After that the book was not there anymore.

Her search was futile as she had expected, the book had not returned. Leila found her father doing his marking in the kitchen and sat herself down at the other end of the table.

'I'll be finished in a minute,' he said, acknowledging her presence without looking up. 'Perhaps you could help me make some Christmas cards.'

This was a surprise. She nodded suspiciously though he did not see.

'Where was I when mother died?' she asked suddenly.

Tom looked up quickly and then out of the window, as if mimicking his daughter's habit. And perhaps in an attempt to dull the sharp shock of her question he muttered to himself that there was something Siberian about the weather after all the gloom and fog of November. There were two days left until Christmas, too. The room suddenly felt rather cold and he realised he hadn't lit the fire. Leila's question rattled in his head and he closed his eyes as if to suppress it.

'You were with me,' he said finally. 'You were with me.'

Perhaps if he repeated himself now, she wouldn't ask again later and he wouldn't have to feel his own heart sink again. She needed to keep hearing the story, but he was fed up of having to say it all yet again; burdened by an odd mixture of nausea and boredom.

Weariness dragged at his features, he could almost feel himself ageing. It was as if Leila was draining him. How she had drained his life away! She was unaware of how such small gestures and efforts on her part had slain him. Now she was watching him with her mother's eyes, waiting for more answers. Like a ninety year old he mustered his reply: 'You were with me while your mother went out for a walk alone. She sometimes liked to walk alone. You were doing a jigsaw.'

It occurred to him that there is an edgy boredom to repeated lies. Did he tell it exactly the same each time? Or did the utter boredom of repeating the lie make him clumsy with details?

'Why did she like going out alone?'

'She was an independent woman,' said Tom, speaking as if his voice had become detached from himself. 'She made friends easily enough but she also loved her own company. Until you were born, she spent the vast majority of her time alone, sketching, painting... creating.'

At least that bit was true, though it was still an effort.

'Did anyone see mother fall?' Leila asked.

He slumped in his seat as if something ailed him, 'No, Leila, only the birds in the sky I expect.'

'Well I wish they could speak so that I would know *exactly* how it happened.'

He did not answer but closed his eyes.

It was difficult for him to be the man he once was. Leila seemed to grow more like her mother every day and sometimes the reminder was not pleasant. There were things he felt compelled to tell her, but he procrastinated and so lived with the fear that she would find out from someone else. These secrets were a burden, requiring continuous work to suppress. The death of Lio had gained a life all of its own and a kind of mythology had grown up around it. He often thought it might be time to enlighten Leila. She was thirteen now, if he left it much longer she might react badly; puberty could be a difficult time for a girl. But the truth was that he did not want to tell her. He was considering putting Hafod on the market and leaving the area altogether. That was how far he would go not to have to tell her.

It was their last day alone together, so he consciously chose to spend some quality time with her. He told Leila how Lio used to create her own Christmas cards and brought out some he had kept. They were crinkly and haphazard with a rich assortment of dried leaves and flowers, holly berries, glitter, tinsel, crepe paper and tin foil. He didn't like them much but he was right in predicting that Leila would love them. The gesture was an effort, tired him to his core, but he thought it was worth it.

'Do you miss her at Christmas especially?' Leila asked.

He nodded as he watched her kneeling by the Christmas tree looking at the cards. It was his own fault of course; if he had not wanted to talk about Lio, then he should not have chosen the cards for this father-daughter bonding session. It would be a while before he would try anything like it again.

He sent her to bed at nine o'clock, a little earlier than usual, because he could no longer bear it. She seemed to want something special from their time together, but his preoccupation with past and future meant he could not be there in the present. Afterwards he sat at the kitchen table, his elbows on its reassuring wooden thickness. Holding him up as it had many times before. He could still see the cup rings on its weathered surface from when he had not cared about using mats. Then with a horrible sense of *déjà vu* he went to the cupboard and took out the Scotch.

Leila was crestfallen. She had made three cards copying her mother's style and having finished, had sought her father's approval. However he appeared distant and unimpressed. When she tried to force his attention, he seemed annoyed by her. His aloofness hurt her most when they were alone and there was no Imogen to turn to. She climbed into bed and wrapped herself up like a mummy, disappearing.

She lay still for a while but could not sleep. The room was cold. Too cold. She felt she was ebbing away like a chilled inland water. She was cold and a part of her wanted to stay cold, to lie there and feel the ice edging in like a small, gleaming black millipede, edging closer towards her shiny, silvery soul. If she closed her eyes tight she could see it was losing its brilliance. It was becoming tarnished. A darker hue with no sheen was spreading like a void and it was almost easier to lie still and let the cold seep in, slowly. Her father had forgotten to turn on the heating in her bedroom because he didn't care.

Then suddenly, angry and wanting to fight, she jumped out of bed, pulled the duvet from Imogen's bed and threw it over her own.

On Christmas Eve morning Ann returned with Imogen and they were allowed to visit the Crow Woman to give her one of the handmade cards. It was a cold day, too cold for snow, so the girls went out heavily clothed like igloo people. The lane was ghosted with frost and like a rink beneath their thick boots. About halfway between Hafod and the Crow Woman, when they were passing the house that was half-built, they heard heavy footsteps clumping behind them and a suspicious growl. They turned to see Mr Parry and his dog gaining on them.

'Quick, walk faster,' said Imogen, but even as she said it Leila had encountered an ice patch and had fallen back with a yelp. Mr Parry chortled. There was no stopping him from catching them up now. His heavy boots crunched up behind them and he slapped his knee as he laughed.

'You be careful,' he said, 'or you'll be all bruised.'

He squinted at Leila then, with a bemused look. Leila sighed heavily in the fashion of her father and rose to her feet.

'You look like her…' said Mr Parry quietly.

Leila did not need to ask whom he was talking about. She frowned in reply, pulling her hood over her head in attempt to conceal herself from further scrutiny.

Mr Parry's dog had run off and his attention was diverted. He grunted as he looked around and then shouted. 'Tyrd!'

While he was calling his dog back, the girls tried to escape but the dog was ahead of them and with a whistling from Mr Parry it stopped in front of them and growled. They halted and looked behind, Mr Parry was catching up again.

'Move your dog please,' said Leila, daring to show anger in her voice.

He smiled, revealing his tombstones. 'I will help you, if I see any ice patches I'll shout.' He chuckled and then muttered to himself. There was a conversation to be had with some of the people inside.

Then in another voice he said: 'She always looked nice,' and he lifted his chin like a struggling actor in an empty theatre. 'She used to walk over the moor like she was going somewhere, always with some purpose, making sketches, painting scenes…'

'Who are you talking about?' asked Leila in annoyance.

'Her of course, *del*,' he said, turning his head slowly towards Leila as if he deemed his only audience unworthy. 'She was lost and full of longing… but happy too. All that the Welsh are; all that *hiraeth* means. No English word can convey the meaning of *hiraeth*. You see there is no English equivalent.'

They watched him sweeping his arm over the moor, as if he was playing a part and for a moment he was someone far nobler. He was almost handsome, but only for a moment. Then he became

Mr Parry again and he leered at them.

'You'd better watch out for that mad English man!'

Leila recoiled, wondering whom he meant. Her father perhaps? She was too afraid to ask.

'Come on Imogen,' she cried suddenly. 'Let's hurry or we'll never get to Arabella's.' She tried to pull Imogen along, but Mr Parry suddenly caught hold of her arm.

'I don't think you should be going there and I will tell your father when I see him,' Mr Parry was wagging his finger at them now, the colour rising in his cheeks.

'He knows!' cried Leila shaking off the chapped hand that was clutching at her coat.

'Bobol bach!' exclaimed Mr Parry. 'Is *it* back on or something?'

'What do you mean?' said Leila, still trying to escape.

He laughed incredulously and shook his head, muttering unheard sentences of English and Welsh that curled around one another like crooked corkscrews. And then he turned back angrily and let them go.

'It just shows, he wasn't going this way, he just wanted to follow us,' said Imogen.

Leila nodded but didn't speak. She wondered at what Mr Parry had meant about 'it' being back on and then her thoughts drifted back to what he had said about her mother and she saw that perhaps he was right. *Hiraethog: welcome, isolation, longing without direction, bliss and fear. A word with music, a word whispered, belonging to its place in the world, hugging like a cloak and so stark standing out from an old, crooked white signpost, pointing to everything and pointing to nothing. She could feel within how her mother was there.* Her grasp of Welsh, learned at school as a second language, allowed her partly to understand.

When they arrived at the Crow Woman's house they saw smoke rising from the chimney and the rooks gathered as usual in the tall broomstick trees. They were cawing as if mocking the Crow Woman who was without her rifle.

'Blasted birds!' she said, and then her arms extended for a hug as she went to meet the girls, with a black shawl hanging from them like a large pair of wings.

'How lovely to see you!' she cried. 'And on Christmas Eve too. Come on in, I've got the kettle on.'

Her house had a warm atmosphere. They had been several times since that first meeting back in August. Leila loved the lounge with its great wrought iron fireplace and the way in which the sofa and armchairs huddled around it. All around the room were bookcases bursting to their brims with books thick and thin. The humble and homely atmosphere was partly countered by an air of eccentricity in the arrangement of the house and its possessions. Now that it was Christmas the lounge was further adorned with seasonal wreaths of holly, firethorn, cotoneaster, laurel and ivy and a handmade garland of red ribbons, pinecones, berries and baubles hung over the roaring fire. There were dried flowers packed into tin cans tied with ribbons, a Giant's Causeway of church candles and on the coffee table a glass bowl of water full of floating candles and reflected firelight. Arabella had been in the process of twisting raffia for another garland when they arrived. Now she cleared the table so they could sit down together with hot drinks and biscuits. It was all for them. There was no one else to see it.

Leila and Imogen found a pleasant spot on the worn old sofa with the Crow Woman, basking in the firelight and listening to the crackle and hiss of burning wood. The sheepdog Boadicea lay snoring at their feet while they sat clutching hot mugs with cold outdoor hands and Imogen began whining about her frozen feet, now being toasted over the fire despite a thriving collection of chilblains. Leila told the Crow Woman of their meeting with Mr Parry.

'He's always pestering women and children...any who are unlucky enough to cross his path anyway,' said the Crow Woman. 'It's best if you avoid him, he needs professional help.' She stopped then and thought of how he was not the only one who did.

After a short silence, she looked at Leila, 'I expect you know how that old buffoon of a farmer used to follow your mother as she walked on the moors. I saw him myself and when I told her, she said she knew.'

'What exactly do you mean?' asked Leila.

'Did your father not mention it?' asked the Crow Woman, though her eyes were appraising as if the question was rhetorical and she knew very well that he had not.

'Well,' she continued, 'at first your mother seemed to pity him, she was perhaps too kind to strangers for her own good. She made the effort to speak to him and so he became fixated with her. The last time I ever spoke with her, she mentioned that she had managed to avoid him by changing her walk to the path into Clocaenog...'

'Clocaenog forest?' asked Leila eagerly.

'Yes.'

'We met a man there who knew her,' said Leila. 'Do you know him? His name is Geraint.'

The Crow Woman appeared puzzled.

'He had blonde hair and very dark eyes,' said Imogen.

'No, I don't believe I do. You really shouldn't have been out there alone. Do your parents know?'

They nodded together.

'We won't be doing it again,' said Leila. 'What were you saying about my mother?'

The Crow Woman looked momentarily exasperated and it took her a moment to recall what she had been saying.

'Well, as I said, your mother had begun walking in Clocaenog and also along Afon Ddu in order to avoid Mr Parry. I suppose she just wanted to be alone. She told him to leave her alone, but I don't believe he did. He was just more careful.'

Leila was silent. The unwanted attentions of Mr Parry had forced her mother into taking the Afon Ddu walk, the cliff walk along which she had met her death. Had he even followed her mother there one day and pushed her? It was possible. She looked at the Crow Woman and thought there was something else, something glinting in the birdlike eyes.

'Are you all right Leila? Would you rather we changed the

subject?'

'No, please, I want to know more,' said Leila quickly. 'Was my mother alone when she died?'

There was a hesitation and the Crow Woman's face seemed to change, almost to withdraw and while she said, 'Yes', Leila thought her eyes shone strangely. She grabbed the Crow Woman's arm in a sudden fit of panic and pleaded with her, 'Tell me, was my mother pushed? You have to tell me!'

'Oh no,' said the Crow Woman, appearing shocked. 'It was all a terrible accident, that was the verdict.'

They watched her swallow hard, gulping like an ostrich.

'But how do we know if there was no one there?' cried Leila. 'What if he pushed her because he was obsessed with her? What if he killed her and has got away with it?'

'Oh dear, no,' said the Crow Woman, her voice rattling in her throat. 'I'm sorry, I only intended to warn you about Mr Parry. To ask you to be careful because you are *like* your mother. This idea that he killed your mother, it's wrong. Here let's have another drink, you've both finished already.'

Leila watched the Crow Woman's rapid exit to the kitchen. There was something about it that reminded her of her father.

Arabella returned with another teapot and after she had poured, she put her arms around each child, though she felt a darkness descending on them as if the sky outside was being blacked out. After a while she tried to explain.

'It really was no more than a tragic accident and there was no evidence to the contrary. I only felt I must warn you about that man because I don't think your father realises how far you wander on the moors.'

Leila was calmer now, with the glazed look of a child putting her faith in adult explanations.

'Is that it then?' she asked after a long hesitation. 'My mother just accidentally fell?'

Arabella nodded. 'Yes dear, but ask your father to tell you. You are old enough and should hear it from him. Of course, there are some things that we will never know and probably just aren't meant to know.'

Eventually Arabella was able to turn the conversation around. She stoked up the fire and they ate pâté and cucumber sandwiches together. She beamed over the card Leila had made for her and then left them alone for a few minutes while she went upstairs to get their presents. Two small art kits, good quality and expensive, but not too obviously extravagant. She had wrapped them carefully because they were the only presents she would have to wrap this year. She admired them for a minute, she had made the packaging herself, the brown cinnamon scented paper decorated with holly berries and matching square cinnamon scented gift tags. The dark red velvet ribbon finished in a bow had been bought from the exclusive gift shop in Chester that had been buying her hand crafted greetings cards for the past three years. The day she had bought the paper the old man had commented that he had done business with someone who had a similar address. It was some years back and she had died in a terrible accident. Did she know her? Glamorous looking, but he couldn't quite remember the name. She had replied angrily that she did not know of any such person, all the time with an uncomfortable sense of irony as she purchased ribbon for the dead woman's daughter.

She did not want to talk of Lio, except to Leila and Imogen. This was how she could keep them coming to her, with titbits and morsels thrown haphazardly. She would not tell too much, just a little at a time. She would be mysterious, she would weave a smoke screen, and in return for love she would give information because she could. But then she stopped and looked down at the beautifully wrapped presents. She knew what had happened, but could she really ever tell all? The sudden emotion that rose in her brought her close to weeping. No, she wasn't going to cry. Not now, too many years of weeping alone. She would drive them away. Deep breaths. She had been too long upstairs, looking at the presents but not really seeing them. She walked to the mirror and wiped carefully under her eyes, it was a good job she had checked because the eyeliner was beginning to migrate downwards. She didn't want to look over made up, but she remembered how Lio had done her eyes smoky-looking and thought Leila might like that. Leila was particularly vulnerable with no mother figure in her life. It was clear that Leila had not accepted Ann, indeed she made no secret of her open dislike of the step parent, even in front of Imogen. This was something else Arabella knew she could play on, for she too did not like that thin, mean looking woman. But she had to do it carefully, without alienating Imogen. There was a leaden weight in her heart as she straightened her skirt and picked up the presents, she would be alone on Christmas morning as usual, with the TV turned up to mask the silence that went on and on.

'Thanks, it's really nice,' said Leila when she was given her present.

'You've wrapped it so beautifully,' gasped Imogen, in her fey, excitable way. 'It's too nice to open!'

'Thank you for keeping me company,' said Arabella, and then realising that she did not want their pity, she rose up in her seat and said cheerfully, 'but it's time for you to go home now.'

'Oh, do we have to?' complained Leila. 'It's so nice and warm here. Dad's been half freezing me to death the last few days.'

Arabella could not suppress a pleased smile, but did not give in. If they were to come regularly of their own volition, they must never stay long enough to be bored. It was as she locked the door behind her and trudged to her Land Rover that she thought of speaking to Tom and how it was likely that Leila would try to eavesdrop.

At Hafod they found Ann in the process of updating the Christmas decorations in accordance with the latest fashion. Everything was perfect as always but there was something about her decorating that left Leila cold. Always at Christmas she wished for her mother and particularly when it snowed; she had a photograph of Lio building a snowman.

The entrance of the Crow Woman had elicited a sigh and an annoyed toss of the head from Ann and she began complaining to Imogen about how long they had taken. Leila held onto the Crow Woman's hand for a while, this made her immune. The Crow Woman was precisely the kind of person Ann disliked. She was about the same height, but there the similarity ended. In contrast to Ann's manicured, stick-like figure, the Crow Woman was a heavily boned and large featured woman who walked as if permanently astride a small, thin horse. Over her large frame she wore dark, loose clothing; large embroidered Indian tops and tasselled skirts. Skirts for small children to hide behind. Leila found herself admiring the power of the Crow Woman who defied fashion and walked with her own grace and what seemed to be formidable self-assurance.

'I would like to speak to Tom if he's here.'

Leila heard the booming quality in the Crow Woman's voice, but she did not see how her hands were clasped together and trembling slightly.

Ann frowned but sent Imogen to find him.

The room was silent, except for the rustle of the decorations being hung by Ann. The Crow Woman was standing watching her and there was an atmosphere of ill feeling between them, which probably stood for more than differences in clothing and looks. Leila wondered why the Crow Woman wanted to speak to her father, but was unable to discover anything from the forbidding silence that ensued. When Tom finally arrived, looking awkward and a little afraid, the Crow Woman asked him if they could have privacy. Ann looked irate. Tom led his visitor into the kitchen and the door shut.

'Why don't you two go out for a walk?' snapped Ann.

'But we've only just come in!' whined Imogen, who always seemed to whine when speaking to her mother.

'Well go upstairs then.'

'But what are they talking about?'

'I don't know,' Ann was exasperated. 'Grown up business. Not for your ears. Just leave me in peace!'

'She wants to listen in herself,' said Leila disappointed.

'What about trying from upstairs?' whispered Imogen.

They both knew they could pick up conversations from below if the windows were open. They had discovered it by accident in the summer and Leila was particularly good at it.

'Of course, the kitchen window might not be open,' said Imogen.

'Come on there's only one way to find out,' Leila was already running up the stairs.

Kneeling on Leila's bed they were able to open the window and hang out over the white walls looking down on the kitchen. They were in luck, the kitchen window was open. However the air was so cold that Imogen withdrew almost immediately, teeth chattering.

'They're too far from the window,' she said. 'We won't have a chance of hearing them.'

'Don't give up straight away,' said Leila.

She leaned out, forcing herself against the cold air and pushed until she was in the precarious position of balancing on her hips, with the majority of her body hanging out of the window and her hands braced against the wall.

'A gust of wind and I could fall,' she thought. 'This is the sort of thing mother would have done.'

It was difficult to hear anything at first, hard to focus in when a very cold wind was blowing noisily in her ears, but then as she was about to withdraw, gripped with cold as she was, she heard her father's infuriated voice come closer to the window. He had clearly risen from his seat and was probably looking out of the window.

'It's not a case of just telling her. I have to think of the consequences.'

The wind was helping with the acoustics today, but Leila could not hear the words being said by the Crow Woman, these were muffled because she was too far from the window.

His voice was impatient now. 'I have to pick the right time, it's not something you can just blurt out. I'm even considering not saying anything at all, ever...I mean, I can only go so far. I can never tell all. You know that don't you?'

Leila could not hear the rest of his speech, he had retreated back into the kitchen.

Imogen reappeared with her coat on.

'Have you heard anything?' she asked.

'Shussshh,' said Leila.

'You'd better watch you don't fall. Here I'll hold your legs. You can hear better than me.'

Leila's hands were stiff from the cold. The next thing she heard was the Crow Woman's authoritative tones, clearly they had swapped places because she could no longer hear her father.

'Well, I think she should be told before she hears it from somewhere else. You know what the locals are like, it's still a minor topic of conversation with them all these years later. Nothing ever happens here, they'll be feeding off this carcass for years to come. Tom, you've got to do it or I will. Don't you see? She may even remember something.'

What he said next sounded cross but she couldn't hear the words.

'But is it right to run away?' The Crow Woman said, suddenly sounding upset.

With that they moved away from the window and Leila heard nothing more.

SIX

'It's peculiar. The forecasters have really got it wrong, there's not been one snow flake, let alone a heavy snowfall. In fact it's rather warm for January.'

Leila's father looked into a book as he spoke, so that she was not sure whether he was speaking to her or the book itself. She sat opposite him at the big kitchen table, where Lio used to sit she fancied, facing him just as ferociously; legs swinging, kicking the table leg. Bang, bang, bang. Her homework book lay untouched in front of her and when she wasn't glaring at him, she was looking meditatively into his fire. He was ignoring her as best as he could, silently barricaded behind his book. She could half hear the cogs turning in his brain. *How to leave unnoticed, how to get away from this annoying, insane child.*

It was two days later when he finally took her aside for the talk that was to reveal almost nothing.

'I'm putting Hafod up for sale,' he said gravely. 'There are lots of reasons why. I suppose it's mainly because I want us to live in a more suitable environment. You are growing up too isolated. You need more friends and you need to stop wandering about on the moors dragging Imogen behind you.'

'I don't drag Imogen,' she protested. 'She always wants to come.'

'Never mind that,' said her father. 'You should see more of the world, more of life.'

'What use are more friends?' said Leila. 'I've got a stepsister. I don't need any more friends. No one else could understand me.'

She didn't believe his reasons anyway. The 'For Sale – *Ar Werth*' sign in the front was real enough, but there was something more than their social life behind all of this.

'I don't want to go,' she said. 'All that's left of my mother is here and I love it here. Why should we want to live in a crowded place with pollution and muggers?'

'It won't be like that where we go, we'll still be in Wales. You *know* Ann won't consider leaving Wales,' said Tom. 'It's just not healthy to obsess about the past. You need more distance. We can still come back to visit. Away from here we all have a chance to live a life based on the present and the future, rather than what happened in the past.'

Leila sighed and put her head into her hands.

'It's all for your sake,' said Tom.

Just as some of the locals were being disparaging about meteorologists, the cold snap came. Oddly, everyone was pleased. Even the old people who complained about the cost of heating devouring their pensions were secretly glad. Winter without cold didn't seem quite right. It had been downright warm since Christmas.

It was not long before the snow had fallen heavily enough to cover the brown moor in an unblemished, pristine whiteness. The wind from the east, which was blowing more snow in with no sign of relenting, was causing drifts to form like huge waves up against the wire fences and stone walls. Leila loved the blinding whiteness. Now everywhere was as white as Hafod, they were set adrift in an endless untrodden, blanched wilderness; even the insolent For Sale sign was wearing a thick hat of snow.

'Look,' she said, face pressed to the glass. 'It's hypnotising.'

She was gazing upwards at the white flakes swirling down from a pale, transparent sky, from nothingness into nothingness. The whole scene was a strange dazzling panorama of spinning white and grey dots and spots and nothingness.

'We've got to get out there somehow,' said Leila. 'Rat hair can't keep us holed up in here forever.'

'I don't like it when you say things like that about my mother,' said Imogen.

Leila was oblivious. 'It's like the world doesn't exist outside of here. You can almost imagine this is the end of creation, the snow has engulfed everything.'

They were able to urge Tom into letting them out. Outside everything was transformed to a pure motionless calm. Only the sheep moved, heads bent down against the easterly breeze and the snowfall, looking like they wore dirty yellow wigs as they trekked downwards.

'It's like the Arctic,' said Leila. 'If you were the first explorer in this land, where would you go?'

'We'll have to stay on the road until we find a way through,' said Imogen. 'There's some big drifts up here. We won't be able to walk them.'

Because she was already cold, Imogen pictured herself wearing a multi-coloured glove that somehow fitted over the whole of her, a big, bright knitted affair with central heating inside. Picturing things well enough could almost make them real; she sometimes pictured herself dancing with dark-eyed Geraint.

They walked on for a little way, treading carefully as the snow wedged into the bottom of their boots, each step growing heavier than the last. The dazzling effect of the pristine snow went on and on and made them feel light headed. Leila thought she might faint over and over with the delight of it, if it wasn't for the bracing cold which was bringing her round. Even the inside of her nostrils felt cold. It was a delicious feeling. As they walked they looked behind at their footprints. The first footprints. They were so well occupied looking behind at their tracks that they did not see Mr Parry approaching until he was almost upon them.

Imogen saw him first. 'Have we got enough time to climb into the field and escape?' she asked.

'We can try,' replied Leila, but she moved slowly because she wanted a confrontation.

He approached them like a stooping ogre, limping more than usual with the hindrance of snow. His red face was squashed into a fur-lined hood and strained forwards, towards the promise of human company. If he could catch them before they escaped. For a moment, Leila felt pity for him. He was a lonely hunchback. Nobody loved him, not even his own dog nor the expressionless faces of his sheep. And he loved only the bottle that filled his days and allowed him to sleep at night. This sudden feeling of compassion towards him was at odds with her supposed hatred of him for his part in her mother's death. Yet for the first time she thought she understood why he followed people. It was just for some human contact and she was sad for him. Sad because she knew no one would ever want his company. So Leila stood and waited, while Imogen climbed the fence so quickly that she ripped her trousers on the barbed wire.

Leila noticed that he had green eyes that day. They were almost hidden under his drooping eyelids, but they were vivid with the distant sea-green glassiness of a person who is often lost in memories and all that which is only kept alive by his own thinking. He looked as if he might cry all over his ruddy cheeks at any minute.

'Hello,' he said. 'What are you up to today?'

They could see there was snow nestling in his thick eyebrows.

'Just walking,' said Leila. 'Tomorrow we might go sledging.'

'The weather will be good for that at least,' said Mr Parry, 'but not for me. I've got to bring the sheep down. I didn't feel this one coming. It's been so warm lately and I don't go in for them know-it-alls and their weather forecasts. Nearly always wrong they are. I must press on now. Be careful, there's some deep snow.'

He leaned into his stick and moved on up the hill, dog at his heels.

Leila had forgotten all the questions and accusations she had pictured herself making at their next meeting. He had not been his usual leering self. He appeared distant and his breath reeked of alcohol, like her father's after the death of her mother. She remembered the smell, it was a miserable smell. It was not so easy to hate this drunken old man who had to face pulling sheep out of the snow alone.

'Do you still think he might have caused your mother's death?' asked Imogen.

'I don't know. He seemed different today, it caught me a bit off guard. He was drunk. But it wasn't a happy drunk, it was a sad drunk.'

'Yes. He was nicer than normal... different.'

They looked behind and saw his hunched figure retreating slowly past Hafod, Euros the sheepdog trotting at his side. Then Leila climbed the fence to join Imogen.

They walked downwards to the stream babbling merrily between its snow-smothered banks, and upwards to the baby plantation. The young trees here had been planted by a local farmer. As they followed the path upwards, they saw someone running through the trees towards them. He was flailing his arms like a madman. At first Leila thought it might be Mr Parry again but the figure was moving far too swiftly for him. As he came closer, they saw that it was a blonde-haired boy in a red ski jacket. He looked a bit older than them.

He stopped running before he reached them and with a wave of a gloved hand, approached them at a more dignified pace.

'Hi,' he said, in a surprisingly friendly manner. 'I was just flying... didn't see you till I'd almost ran into you.'

Leila and Imogen looked at one another and smiled. There was something about him that they immediately liked.

'I'm Jude,' he said.

'You're not lost are you?' said Jude, when neither girl spoke.

'No, I'm Leila,' said Leila, joking, though inside she shook with inexplicable excitement.

The boy laughed. 'It's just I've rescued lost kids before, I suppose I thought my talents were about to be called into use again.'

Leila found herself staring at him. She didn't overly appreciate the 'kid' label but he was another stranger whose face seemed oddly familiar. Something about his pale green eyes and the light, flyaway blonde hair that fell appealingly over them. Only she could not remember him and if there had been any acquaintance, she suspected that again this was long ago, in that time before her memory had begun to serve her well. She was immediately drawn to him. So drawn that in spite of her nerves, she forgot all pretensions and shyness.

'Where are you from?' she asked.

'Near Clocaenog,' he replied.

'Where are you going?'

'Just walking,' he replied. 'I love the snow.'

'I do too,' said Leila watching his breath rising visibly in the cold, looking him in the eye, drawn by him.

'What about you, where are *you* going?' he asked.

'We're just walking too, but tomorrow we are going sledging.'

'You've got a sledge,' he said brightening. 'Is it a decent one?'

'Of course, a proper big, wooden one,' said Leila, smiling back.

'I can show you somewhere brilliant for sledging and it's not far from here. Where do you live?'

'There,' said Leila, turning and pointing to Hafod.

'Oh, there,' he stopped mid-sentence and suddenly looked embarrassed. Then he began to tangle English with Welsh because for him they were almost equivalent. Neither was really a second language and he always mixed them when something bothered him. 'That's a lovely house,' he said, 'I see you're moving... *wyt ti'n gwybod i ble*?'

'I wish we weren't and no I don't know where we'll go,' said Leila, noticing how he had become restless. 'Have you heard anything about us?'

'Oh no, nothing,' he said, but Leila could see how he had become flushed as if he was very excited.

'I'm hoping that no one will buy our house,' she said in order to break the silence that followed.

'Well you're in luck, at least for the time being,' said Jude. 'No one will be able to make it up here soon. The weather forecast said the snow could last for weeks.'

Leila smiled and hoped he was right.

There was a moment's silence then. The two girls faced the boy and all three hesitated since they had come to the point where they could make an invitation or say their goodbyes and they were at a loss for words. But they knew they wanted to see each other again.

'Do you want to come with us?' It was Leila who broke the deadlock. 'We are on our way up onto the moor, hoping to see the wild ponies.'

Imogen gave her a look. It was the first she had heard of it, but she liked Jude too so she said nothing.

'Yeah, all right.'

'They are much easier to see in the snow,' said Leila. 'Last winter we even managed to feed them some hay. We did it every day for a fortnight when the weather was really bad. Do you remember, Imogen?'

'Yes,' Imogen nodded, 'I remember being frozen to an ice block and I remember you nagging me to stop moving because I'd frighten the ponies. As if I could stop myself from shivering!'

'Your teeth chatter too much,' said Leila, wanting to be Jude's favourite.

They only saw the ponies from a distance that day. They looked small and shaggy in their winter coats, a small mare with a dark, curved body, spied them through her long black fringe, which moved when her eyelashes blinked. Then she lifted her head to smell them and gain a clearer view. She tossed her head and turned, whinnying to the stallion, and then together they moved, with a sudden fever, breaking into a trot. All followed with a ripple of movement, their strong hindquarters propelling them, hooves drumming, carrying them. Jude tugged Leila's arm.

'That was good,' he said quietly, standing close to her rather than Imogen. Making her think she had won.

Jude walked back to Hafod with them. He had only ever seen it from a distance, but he loved the look of the bright whitewash and the way it stood alone in an exposed position. There were just a few trees behind the barn and an overgrown hedgerow, all were stunted and hunched by the wind, like thin people in winter gales. Now he felt excited to have come closer to Hafod and its inhabitants. Over the years in rooms full of people he had heard so many stories and so many rumours, but never until now had he met the girl who looked 'just like her dead mother'.

They climbed the farm gate into Hafod's yard and found that Tom had dug a pathway to the door, although the snow was no longer falling and not yet very deep. A few of the descendants of the free range chickens that had come as part of the package when they bought Hafod were loitering by the path, looking hopefully for scraps from the children with quiet clucks that were all at once a kind of cooing and cajoling sweet talk.

Imogen despatched some bread crust left over from the previous day, out of her crumb-lined pockets. She often gave them too much bread with too little moisture, feeding them until bread was wedged in their throats and their beaks were stuck open, a position which required a good deal of vertical neck lunging before they could swallow the sticky loot.

The stepmother opened the door when they arrived. Imogen was blowing hopelessly on her mittens and even Leila was cold by now. They asked Jude in but he declined when he caught Ann's glare. The two girls were reluctant to leave him. They looked back and waved to him and once more glanced at their footprints in the yard and the miles of white snow on the hills, still completely untrodden.

'I hope it lasts,' said Leila.

'Come on,' said Ann. 'Get in, before you let all the warmth out.'

Later, warm with soup in their stomachs, they half-watched a quiz show on the TV. Imogen knew a lot of the answers and was calling the contestants 'thickos'.

'I wonder which school Jude is at,' said Leila.

'I don't know,' replied Imogen. 'That red-haired boy is so thick! He shouldn't be on the telly, he's embarrassing himself.'

'You should be there,' murmured Leila. 'You know it's strange, I feel like I've seen him before, like I know him from somewhere.'

'What, the thicko?' asked Imogen, mouth open.

'No, I mean Jude, silly.'

'Perhaps you've seen him in Llan,' said Imogen.

Leila shook her head. 'No, it's from a long time ago, when I was much younger. Before you were here.'

'We don't even know how old he is,' said Imogen. 'Or exactly where he lives.'

'No,' said Leila. 'But he knew us. Everyone knows us and it's because of my mother. I feel people watching me when we go out. They've always watched me. I thought it was because there was something special about me. I felt superior, until I realised they see me as that strange girl whose mother died when she was only four. Now I see a mixture of pity and a sort of... waiting.'

'What are you on about?' said Imogen impatiently, clearly irritated by the standard of quiz show contestants. 'Waiting for what?'

'Waiting for something to happen. Waiting for me to trip up or act crazy... to prove them right.'

'Right about what?' Imogen drawled, still watching the red-haired boy with increasing irritation.

'I don't know. Right about me being mad or weird. Well they can wait because I was too young to really remember or really be affected.'

'But you are affected,' said Imogen, tearing her gaze away from the annoying quiz show. 'You are always talking about your mother. You might not remember her, but she's far from forgotten.'

'That's a contradiction.'

'Not really. I mean look at the photos you keep of her. You

even have dreams with her in them. You have no real concrete memories, but you are determined to hold on to anything that is like a memory.'

'So what are you saying?'

'Well, don't get cross, but my mother said it's called necrolatry,' said Imogen rather nastily.

'What?'

'It means a morbid obsession with the dead.'

'Oh, I hate your mother, Imogen,' said Leila, standing up in annoyance. 'And do you think she's right?'

'No, not really. I mean I think I would be the same if my mother had died when I was four. I would want to collect and cling onto whatever was left of her.'

There was a hint of sarcasm in Imogen's voice which was not lost on Leila.

'But *your* mother is so horrible, she's not like my mother at all.'

'That's not nice,' said Imogen changing her nasty voice for a wounded one. 'I *was* agreeing with you. And don't you think that your mother had a bad side too? Everyone does. She only seems like such an angel to you because she died before you could remember anything.'

'Don't you talk like that. My mother could never be such a misery as yours!'

'I'm going,' said Imogen, rising from her seat, 'before I give you a good slapping!'

Leila was left alone to reflect, however she was determined she would not be the one to apologise.

Late in the afternoon, Tom roused the girls to go shopping.

'Time to stock up before we're truly stuck,' he said. 'There's more snow forecast, so I don't think the road will be open for much longer.'

Leila smiled, it would be great to be snowed in. It hadn't happened for some years.

'I don't know how Ann and I will get to work,' said Tom.

'Will we be off school then?' asked Imogen.

'I can't say, but it looks likely.'

The van was almost skating down the hill and his foot was on and off the brake pedal.

'Maybe this isn't such a good idea after all,' he said, 'the temperature is dropping and the snow is beginning to freeze.'

'What does that mean?' asked Leila.

'It means we are more likely to skid and get stuck in the bank. Hold tight you two!'

They skidded on the bend near the half-built house, and held their breath until they were round. The van was shuddering in second gear because they were going so slow and Tom had to change down to first. As they approached the Crow Woman's house they saw a man close to the entrance to her driveway and they recognised him immediately.

'Look it's Geraint!' cried Imogen.

He was standing still, doing nothing, looking treacherous. His fair hair seemed to glint with sunlight caught from the glistening snow and he was looking at Leila's father. The expression on his face became hostile and glaring. Leila saw her father was staring back. Between the two men a charge seemed to run, invisible but strong nevertheless. The air fairly crackled with it; a lethal current of enmity. Then Geraint's glare transformed slowly into a smile as he noticed the two girls and waved at them, somewhat mockingly.

Leila waved half-heartedly and Imogen enthusiastically.

'You're blushing Imi,' said Leila, still needing revenge for the necrolatry business earlier.

Imogen pushed Leila but the exchange stopped there as Leila noticed her father tensing dangerously. His foot had gone down hard on the accelerator. The van roared and they skidded slightly on the bend, the back of the van swinging round in the direction of Geraint.

'We're going to hit him!' screamed Imogen.

'I bloody hope so! He's fucked with me one time too many...'

Leila's shock at hearing her father's obscene language froze her and before she could react in any way, there came a dull thud as the van made contact with Geraint.

Tom let the van slide further, hoping to get Geraint underneath it in a sudden, but not entirely unfamiliar escalation of rage, but the rear inside wheel went off the road, the vehicle began to tip sideways and Imogen shrieked in terror. Tom was able to regain the road by accelerating slowly and throwing his weight the other way. He continued to accelerate until they had left the dangerous corner and begun to climb the hill.

'Dad, you hit him!' cried Leila when her father did not react. 'Why did you do it?'

Both girls turned round and looked through the back window. Geraint was there, still standing despite being hit, but only just. He was leaning back against the fence, swaying slightly, putting his hand to his nose and finding blood. Then his knees seemed to go and he fell to them, dripping blood into the snow.

'Dad, aren't you going to stop?' cried Imogen

'No, I'm not,' Tom ranted, barely controlling the adrenalin that had engulfed him. Then he turned on them. 'How do you know him?' he demanded.

'We met him in the forest that day Mum came looking for us,' said Imogen quickly. 'Didn't she tell you?'

'No she did not. I don't want you going anywhere near him. Do you go looking for trouble?' He was very angry but he was also shaking and pale. As if afraid, Leila thought.

'No Dad. He came up to us, we did our best to get away.'

'I don't want you near Clocaenog again on your own. *Ever*,' the van was roaring up the hill and Leila could see her father was shaking all over. He was wild. Full of hatred.

'You must keep away from that man in particular,' he shouted. 'There are things you don't know about and I'm telling you now, he is dangerous. Do you hear me?'

There was no arguing with her father. He had lost control. Leila did not even dare ask what Geraint had done to deserve this tirade, but she half believed it, since she had her own profound fear of him. She twisted round in her seat to look behind, but Geraint was well out of sight by now. And she was curiously glad that he had been hit.

'I hope you heard what I just said,' Tom's tone was still stiff and angry as he changed gear with an unsteady snapping motion.

'Yes,' said Leila, 'I did.' She shivered and looked at Imogen. Imogen looked very worried. Worried for Geraint.

'You mustn't say anything about this little episode, either of you,' said Tom, after he had regained some composure.

'But what if he calls the police?' asked Imogen.

'He won't do that and anyway it was an unavoidable accident.'

They nodded and said nothing. They had seen a side of him they would not argue with.

After a while, when they had all recovered somewhat, Leila revealed where her thoughts had been taking her in the interim.

'Was that his beige car in the Crow Woman's drive? And what do you think he was doing near the Crow Woman's house?' she asked, without really expecting an answer. 'She said she didn't know Geraint.'

'Leave it Leila,' warned Tom, 'I don't want to hear that name again.'

Beyond the hill behind the Crow Woman's house, the road had been cleared by a snow plough which had piled the snow up onto the banks so they felt like they were driving through a great snow tunnel. They caught up with the plough on the main road and found they were stuck behind it for some way, making the fifteen mile journey to the supermarket last more than an hour. When they finally arrived, they found they were not the only ones stocking up. Neighbours, almost unrecognisable beneath thick jumpers, woolly hats and coats, moved like mammoths with overflowing trolleys, followed by trails of sludgy footprints. The supermarket's red plastic sledges were quickly disappearing from the shelves onto the top of trolleys with the guidance of red-faced kids. Tom waved to Ann's friend Bronwen, who gave Leila a funny dark look after she had finished exchanging pleasantries with Tom about the sudden snowfall. Leila wondered whether she should have a fit or burst into tears and throw a tantrum. Was that what Bronwen wanted? Instead she stared back equally darkly and Bronwen soon wheeled her baby away.

'Maybe that is what I should do, stare them out, or even better challenge them as to why they watch me,' she thought. 'Perhaps Ann has been saying things about me to them.'

Even with her hood up, Leila was not safe from the looks. The more polite ones would simply glance, though even they could not resist and only waited until they thought she was unaware, before they looked again. She could feel them watching her as she took things off the shelf and put them in the trolley, as she asked her father what else was needed, as she held on to the side of the trolley in order to guide or be guided. She felt conspicuous, yet her father seemed unconscious of it.

Once the trolley dash was over and they had fought their way through the queues and finally made it out to the van, the snow had begun to fall again and the dimness before dusk was encroaching.

'Come on,' said Tom, 'We need to hurry.'

SEVEN

The dull thud of Geraint's body against the side of the van remained with Leila and Imogen as they tried to sleep that night.

'Your Dad did it on purpose,' said Imogen. 'I think he wanted to kill Geraint. I think he might try again.'

'You think too much,' said Leila adjusting her position under her duvet. 'Dad wouldn't hurt anyone.'

'I'm not so sure,' said Imogen. 'He was very angry.'

'Geraint must have done something awful then,' said Leila. 'Dad wouldn't have been like that over nothing.'

Each lapsed into her own thoughts, and while Imogen thought of Geraint with growing infatuation, Leila found herself feeling smothered whenever she thought of him. As she closed her eyes, she saw a room that she often dreamed of. It had a dirty beige sofa, tattered mustard-coloured curtains and too little light. She felt it closing in like jaws around her neck. As she lay there, a large, dirty blanket seemed to float down from the ceiling of the small, dim room and enfold her in its suffocating, strangling stench. Through the blanket she could see Geraint's face and hands moulded to it and his black eyes burning holes through it.

Leila struggled with the blanket, but her efforts were beaten by paralysis. She was trapped inside an inert body, looking out as if from a sarcophagus, afraid of what her own mind was creating. And then, mercifully, the room's dimensions suddenly expanded out into the universe and everything became dim. She felt herself floating out into a great, dark, emptiness and she felt strangely safe there. Invisible and at peace, looking down peacefully from the immensity of space at a little blue planet far below.

Imogen crawled to the end of her bed and pulled open the curtains to let in the eerily bright twilight and other worldliness of moonlit snow. Snowflakes were falling again, slowly, silently, mesmerising.

'Look,' she said, pointing to the dark shapes of rabbits crouching on the edges of large, black, rabbit shadows. 'I could look at them for hours. Look how still it is. Not that the hills ever move by themselves, but it just seems so still and peaceful.' She sat for a while quietly watching and then turned to Leila. 'Leila are you awake? I think I saw someone out there.'

Imogen saw that Leila was no longer awake. She looked pale and dead in the twilight and had thrown all her blankets off. Imogen shook her head disapprovingly and looked out of the window again. She couldn't see anything now, but if she stared long enough the shadows seemed to move by themselves. Seemed to get up and dance their own hideous dance in the snow.

'No I didn't see anyone,' she thought. 'My eyes were playing tricks.'

She turned to Leila and looked again. She was very still, but Imogen could see she was breathing. Quick, shallow breaths. Imogen covered her up.

'Silly Leila, you'll catch your death like that.'

The next morning found the kitchen in disarray; Tom furiously clanking pots away into the cupboards and Ann staring at condensation on the tiles.

'What's going on?' asked Imogen from the doorway.

Her mother spun around, 'Oh hello dear. I was just listening to the radio and Tom burnt the toast,' she wiped her hands on a tea towel. 'I must clear up.'

'But what's wrong?' asked Imogen, sensing something more.

'They've rescued a man off Afon Ddu,' Ann replied, stepping inbetween Imogen and Tom, who had stopped clanking in order to listen in.

'He fell from the cliffs... where... you know... and apparently he's all right, though goodness knows what he was doing up there in all this snow.'

'Probably skiing or sledging,' Tom spoke unexpectedly and turned to find his daughter at the door. She had heard too.

'Some stupid English bugger anyway,' said Ann, forgetting her English husband for the moment.

'What are you doing listening at the door?' asked Tom, looking at Leila.

Leila ignored him. 'Who fell off?' she asked, walking in.

'No one local – some tourist from the coast I think,' he replied. 'I expect he heard of the skiing potential up by the cliffs and someone forgot to mention the danger. He's lucky.'

'Not everyone is that lucky, eh?' said Leila with a hint of sarcasm.

There was a pause before Tom said: 'I don't think he fell from the highest point and, of course, it's different in the snow, it would have cushioned his fall.'

'Well, maybe this will give people something new to talk about for a while,' said Ann.

Leila crawled up onto her stool to receive her fried egg and toast. The image of the skier going over the cliff kept replaying in her head and she wondered why her mother had not survived when this person who meant nothing to her had. They had always told her that no one could survive a fall from Afon Ddu, but this was clearly not true. Leila could see her mother falling off, backwards, strangely stiff and upright, a creature that was not meant to fly, attempting to swim the air with feeble arm movements, the rest of the body apparently paralysed. And then she pictured the skier going through the air, still upright on his skis. Perhaps that was why he had lived and her mother hadn't.

'If mother hadn't gone down backwards she might have survived too.'

Her father's glasses slid off his nose and fell to the floor.

'It will get better with the new start and everything,' said Ann.

'Ann's right,' said Tom stiffly as he checked his glasses for damage.

'But I don't want to leave here,' cried Leila, putting her head into her hands. 'This is my home, it's all I know.'

'I'll go and get your sledge down now,' Tom snapped, not wanting a scene.

Leila slid down from her stool and ran blindly up to her bedroom. There she threw herself down onto her bed.

She thought that if her mother was there the aching gap would be filled and life would be picture perfect like it was for the fake families in adverts, the ones bought from modelling agencies, with loving smiles all rehearsed and paid for. Only hers would be real. A real model family. She saw them walking over the moors together at sunset with their arms around each other, admiring the view and smiling. She saw them playing in the snow with red, laughing faces and fancy hats and scarves, pelting each other with powdery snowballs.

Leila picked up the photo she kept by the bed. She changed them around occasionally. Since the snow had fallen, she had dug out one of Lio with cheeks red from the cold air and a snowball clutched in one gloved hand, about to be thrown. She thought her mother looked like fun. A person with vigour and gusto and zest and zeal. Somewhere, somebody was responsible for stopping that life and she was going to find out who.

By midday Imogen had finished dressing for the cold and Jude was waiting outside with the sledge.

'Don't be long,' said Tom. 'We'll be snowed in by tonight.'

Leila's unhappiness dispersed quickly at this prospect and Ann gave them a packed lunch and a flask of hot tea each.

Outside the world was bright and fresh with a new covering of snow wiping out the previous day's footprints so that once more they felt they were setting out for the first time. They took turns with two pulling and one riding on the sledge. The narrow lane that led up to the moor gate was pleasantly smoothed out by thick, fluffy snow so light that the wire fencing above them on the high banks seemed to be a creation of snow and ice crystals. This kind of snow made impressive exploding snowballs of which Jude's back bore the brunt. They quietened down as they reached the moor gate because they could see someone there, opening it and walking through with a dog at his side.

'It's Mr Parry,' said Jude. 'He's started drinking heavily again. No one knows why. We thought he'd stopped.'

'You know him?' asked Leila.

'Everyone knows Mr Parry,' whispered Jude. 'He was always a drinker before he was a farmer. He had a wife once, but he beat her and she left him. He never got another.'

'Shall we go before he gets here?' asked Imogen.

'I don't know,' said Leila, reluctant to move. 'I sort of wanted to ask him a few questions.'

'Not this necrolatry again.'

'Necro-what?' said Jude as the strange, earnest looking Euros trotted up to see them.

'I think there's things being kept from me,' Leila continued, 'and I am going to get to the truth.'

'You've been fantasizing again,' said Imogen, sounding like her mother.

They soon caught up with Mr Parry. His face was strained, turned into a pumpkin by alcohol bloating. It had been a quick decline for one who had suffered from alcoholism before. It was not the fur-lined hood that squashed his face, or the wind that made his green eyes water, nor hot aches that coloured his cheeks and hands a deep purplish red. He was drunk and pitiful, and they drew back as he approached. He looked at Leila, almost as if afraid of what he saw. He looked at Jude and raised his hand in a half wave, his lips moving as if mouthing a greeting that required no sound, then he walked past them through the open gate, leaning heavily on his stick and coughing like a phlegm-filled ogre.

'I didn't get a chance to ask him anything,' said Leila.

'Well you'd better ask soon,' said Jude, 'I heard the doctor has only given him months to live if he carries on like this.'

'Wait for me then,' said Leila. Suddenly gripped by a need to do something, she ran awkwardly through the snow, she was afraid and her eyes were blurred by the cold, but she was determined.

'Please, can I ask you a question?' she cried as she caught up with him and stumbled into him, momentarily knocking them both off balance. 'Mr Parry, please.'

She drew back from his hunched figure as he regained his footing and turned to face her. Half of his face disappeared into his coat hood as he looked round. His right cheek was bulging and wet with saliva like that of a baby.

'What do you want from me now?' he muttered. 'You shouldn't be wandering around so much, there's danger for you.'

'I don't know what you mean. What's happened to you?' she asked, but he shook his head and made to turn and walk away, so she shouted at him, the one thing she really wanted to ask. Up into the air she threw her question, with it screaming like a handful of deflating balloons.

'Mr Parry, please tell me, do you know how my mother fell off Afon Ddu? I was told you followed her. Do you think it was because of you that she was there on the cliffs that day?'

Mr Parry stared at Leila in shock for a moment as if she had said something unforgivable. Then he slowly shook his head in a resigned manner.

'I don't know, I didn't see,' he said at last. 'It was an accident. That was the verdict. It wasn't anything to do with me. Maybe there are some who know more than they are saying and maybe that includes me. But I can't because... well I can't.'

He seemed to be on the verge of crying, his voice shook and his eyes filled with tears.

'If you know something you should tell me right now, otherwise you might start to look guilty yourself.'

It sounded terrible and she regretted it, almost as soon as she had said it.

'If it was because of me, I didn't mean it,' he cried, his voice suddenly cracking and rising into an animal-like wail. 'She didn't throw herself off. It was an accident. Now leave me, let me go to my sheep, I have to go. I can't help you anymore, but you must be careful. You are asking too many questions.'

'What do you mean?' asked Leila. 'What might happen to me?'

Mr Parry shook his head and floundered away from her, calling for Euros. The dog went slowly with a glint of mutiny in its eye. Then Mr Parry let out a strange, wretched cry that sank without trace in the muffling quiet of the snowbound hills. This was followed by a desolate sobbing that made his shoulders heave up and down.

'Poor man,' said Imogen as she and Jude rejoined Leila and saw that she was shaking.

'I shouldn't have said it,' cried Leila. 'There is something very wrong with him. He's so depressed.'

'What shall we do?' asked Imogen. 'Isn't there anyone we can get to help him?'

'He has no one,' said Jude. 'Only social services and the hospitals. I'll ask my mother; she's a psychotherapist.'

Leila was silent; she was watching the old man's figure, looking painfully lame yet somehow moving rapidly out of sight.

'I'm sure it isn't your fault he got so upset,' said Imogen. 'He is drunk after all. Come on let's go back. There's a madman loose on the moor and I've got snow melting in my boots.'

They dragged the sledge back, taking turns at riding on it and sliding down the gentler slopes.

'We could still do some sledging,' said Jude, raising an eyebrow at Leila. 'I can show you a good run.'

Leila had been looking at Hafod, admiring its brilliance in the snow. Loving the lamps on in the windows, catching at the gloom and the smoke that curled up from the wood burner and out of the chimney.

'Aren't you coming in?' said Imogen shivering.

'No, I don't think so,' said Leila. 'We haven't done any sledging yet!'

Imogen frowned as Leila and Jude disappeared with the sledge. Then, as she went in through the door, she looked up the lane to see if Mr Parry was returning, but there was no one there.

As they climbed the slope Leila's feelings towards Jude began to take shape and to touch her consciousness. She dragged the sledge with him and the closeness through the shared task took up most of her concentration as they walked up-slope.

'Are your hands cold?' she asked.

Jude smiled at her, 'Yes, but they'll soon warm up.'

Leila's interest in boys had been nonexistent until now. Until the green eyes and blonde hair of Jude. She glanced sideways at him, admiring the structure of his face as they pulled the sledge, loving the raw, headlong energy with which he attacked the upward slog, his breath coming thick and rising like dragon smoke in the cold air. In the numbing snow that day, she felt the beginning of a new kinship and wondered if he felt it too.

'Are we going down together?' asked Jude when they reached the top of the slope. He seemed oblivious to Leila's covert glances.

'Er...Yes. You can actually fit three on this, if you're mad enough,' she replied. 'Shall I go in front?'

This was the kind of life Leila liked. They were going fast, fast down the slope, the wind, cold, was rushing by her ears, noisily, she half screamed, half laughed. The air resistance was pleasantly frosty and sharp and close to painful on her skin as they whooshed downwards. Tears were struck from her eyes, but it was good, like laughing till you cry. Jude was holding onto her laughing too, Jude with his blonde hair and villainous smile was holding onto her, completely unaware, it seemed, of how happy he made her.

'Again! Let's go up again,' cried Leila, weak and out of breath and radiant like the snow when they came to an abrupt halt and were almost thrown into a drift. '*That* was sledging!'

The rush of a sledge on snow and the company of a good-looking boy was all. Even as they were climbing the slope again, pulling the sledge together, Leila was thinking, 'This is perfect. I will always remember this day.'

They climbed the slope several times, until their desire for speed was sated, then they fell into the snow and sat talking because they were warmed up enough to stand the cold, their cheeks red and eyes shining. They were exhilarated. Leila felt a need to touch Jude, just to grab his arms and throw him over into the snow, just some contact, then she would have everything she wanted from this day. So she pushed him back and, catching him unawares, was able to throw snow into his hair, to touch the hair, which was not so fine and silky as Imogen's, but a little darker and thicker and thoroughly flexible. She messed it up more with her hands, he shouted 'Hey!' and struggled violently, like a crazy dog, to sit up again. Something told him she would not mind receiving equally rough treatment. Their play fighting developed into a contest, each trying to do something more hilarious to the other. Leila pushed Jude face down into the snow as if trying to smother him, Jude spluttering snow, laughed loudly at her determined assault and sought to outdo her by pulling her woolly hat off, filling it with snow, putting it back on her head and pulling it, as hard as he could, down over her ears. The hilarity produced by each new and greater violation was crippling and eventually when they could take no more they fell down into the snow to recover.

'You're a nutter,' he said.

'*You* should be sectioned,' she said. 'The first thing I thought when I saw you, was that you look like you escaped from Denbigh.'

'No, but seeing as you know it so well, you can show me around,' he replied.

'Cheek,' said Leila.

'No thanks, I've got four of my own.'

'You think you're so clever,' she said pushing him back into the snow.

'Well I am going to be a psychiatrist,' said Jude.

'A psycho more like,' laughed Leila.

He walked Leila back to Hafod with the sledge in tow. He said he would call again and then he went, head held high with his hair scruffed up at the back. Leila watched him, admiring his posture and smiling because he was funny. She thought then that madness and good looks made an appealing combination and went inside happy, not noticing how dark the sky had become.

'Where have you been?' asked Ann, suspiciously. She was sitting in her armchair with Imogen kneeling in front, having her hair plaited. 'Dinner is almost ready.'

Leila did not argue, she even apologised and then settled down in front of the fire to think about the afternoon she had just had. Outside the snow was beginning to fall again, big flakes falling fast. Falling on Jude.

Imogen asked questions. She was curious but Leila refrained from telling her how she was feeling. Before she fell asleep that night she took the picture of her mother and looked carefully at the smiling face. Was this how her mother had felt when she first met her father?

It was only then that she remembered Mr Parry's words. What did he mean by danger, and what did he know? Who were the others who knew? She knew her father and the Crow Woman had secrets, but was there anyone else involved? She needed to speak to Mr Parry one more time. Something within her, a knowing, intuition perhaps, told her that someone had helped her mother to fall. And now she needed to know about her mother's life before she had died, to discover who was responsible, to have a clear picture in her mind to replace the scrambled, confusing images she clutched at. She would not rest until she could see her mother falling from Afon Ddu on that bright, windy August day, like a film being played out in her mind, the images all crystal clear.

EIGHT

Snow fell on snow, determinedly covering the imperfections that had begun to deface the previous coatings. It snowed so much that the schools were closed, the road was impassable and Hafod was marooned, floating on whiteness. It snowed so much that there was a row.

So Tom took them on the long walk to the nearest shop in Tan-y-Fron, to get some air and some space as much as more supplies. The snow ploughs never came near Hafod, so they could walk two miles before they reached the upper limits of snow plough country, but it was a still, bright day full of sunshine glistening on pristine whiteness. They were well covered in thick coats, hats, scarves and boots and carrying an empty shopping bag each. The two girls followed behind Tom, taking the path made by his footprints. They did not talk but Tom looked behind occasionally to see that they were keeping up, and apart from that he looked around at the quiet scenery, enjoying the still, glacial air. Imogen was looking for birds, she was certain she had seen a snow bunting earlier in the week and was hoping to see it again. Leila walked last, plotting a decoy for her enquiries into her mother's death.

She had a geography project to do for school, which required a survey of local travel habits and she had been planning to make it all up, but it had suddenly occurred to her to use this as a ruse to interrogate people she would normally never dare approach. It was a chance to knock down the barrier that had always been silently there between her and them.

The snow was deep and drifting. It had no respect for roads and thoroughfares and it was difficult to work out where the road and the verge had been. In places the undulating drifts had lifted so high that they covered the fence like great white sculptures of waves. Leila liked the unfamiliarity this gave to the scenery. It was somehow opened out and expanded, brightened and emptied, purified and beautified. The snow on Hiraethog would make her love pictures of the Arctic for ever after, because of that cold, empty, icy loneliness that was so dangerous and yet so dazzling. If she didn't try to concentrate on her transport project she felt she would become drunk on it, that something out there would lure her away from following the canoe-like footprints and rustling waterproof jacket of her father. The lady of the cold snows would sing a haunting song and beguile her away. And she would be lost forever.

They had reached the flatter land where the snowploughs had been. Since it had snowed again, they walked on a path of new snow, in-between the walls of snow pushed up by the snowploughs onto the high banks on each side. Leila could hear their shuffling feet and their raspy breathing, sounding harsh against the muffling snow. Occasionally her father would ask 'Are you two all right?' Less often he would accompany this with a quick glance over his shoulder. It was an effort to answer him with a dutiful 'yes, we are,' as if the serene snow made people quieter too, just like it silenced their footsteps and hushed a whole landscape. Pure polar lullaby. A white shroud covered them all.

When they reached Tan-y-Fron, they were the only people in Mr Roberts's corner shop, but the café next door was half full. Leila looked into the window of the café as they passed and caught the eyes of two women she recognised. As if caught in her icy powers, they stopped talking over their coffee and looked at her. They froze and stared unwillingly. Ha! Now she was the lady of the cold. She turned away and followed her father and Imogen into the shop, smelling the warmth of Mr Roberts's electric fan heater, which Imogen gratefully sat down in front of. Mr Roberts laughed with Tom as she removed her boots and stuck her feet out towards the warmth.

'*Mae'n oer heddiw,*' laughed Mr Roberts. However his smile faded when he spotted the dark child lurking behind her father. Leila could see him struggling for something to say to her so she turned away and walked to the other side of the shop to save him the effort. She felt slightly unnerved. Even with the cover of her geography project she was afraid to meet these people whose eyes reproached her.

'All right, Leila?' her father asked..

'Yes, I'm just looking at these,' she muttered, then raising her voice slightly: 'Dad, could you please buy me one of these notebooks and a pen? I want to begin the survey for my geography project and could I go to the café as I've seen someone I want to interview?'

Imogen was suspicious, but Tom consented, dispensing the necessary change from his trouser pocket without a word, because he did not like to withhold anything material from her. Material was easy after all.

Leila's eyes were on the two women by the window as they entered the café and once again they looked at her. But even with her notebook, she did not dare approach them. They were friends of Ann's. The dull and suspicious looking Rhian Lloyd-Davies was a farmer's wife and the sparkier blue eyed brunette was Sian Pritchard, farmer of a medium sized dairy concern. These women were frightening closer up. Leila was not sure which she found worse; the sharp stare of Rhian or the intelligent, appraising look of Sian. It was easier to turn her back on them and walk towards the counter.

The small, steamy café was run by Mrs Roberts who looked out onto the world from behind thick tortoiseshell glasses. She functioned well enough physically, but mentally she could be as lost as the Marie Celeste. Imogen's friend Gwyneth said Mrs Roberts suffered flashbacks from LSD trips in the sixties and had taken so many drugs that her brain was permanently addled; this explained why she was always spaced out. Whether it was true or not, Mrs Roberts was somewhat vacant and Leila singled her out as an easy first victim. As soon as she had paid for the hot chocolates, she produced her notebook and pen. She could practise on Mrs Roberts, since talking to Mrs Roberts was not like talking to a real person. Imogen hovered, knowing something was afoot. Mrs Roberts replied to the rather inane survey questions slowly as if they required a lot of thought, and when they were only halfway through Leila realised they were already losing her, so she skipped onto the more important subject.

'Mrs Roberts, do you remember my mother, Lio Hughes?'

The old woman suddenly looked Leila in the eye, as if she had noticed for the first time who she was speaking to.

She looked confused so Leila added: 'She was an artist. She lived at Hafod....'

'Oh yes,' said Mrs Roberts with a sudden smile of recognition, 'I remember her. You're her daughter aren't you?'

'Yes, I'm Leila.'

'Ah yes. You are growing up my dear. Time is passing all the time.'

'What do you remember about her?'

'What my dear? Remember? Oh yes. I can remember. She was nice, she used to sometimes come here for a drink after her shopping. It was the year we first opened,' Mrs Roberts paused and then nodded with delight as she recalled. 'She would take black coffee and carrot cake, always liked my cake. She was like you,' Mrs Roberts smiled. 'Now is that all you want?'

'Just a minute,' said Leila quickly. 'Do you know how my mother fell? What have you heard?'

Mrs Roberts looked puzzled. 'Fell?' she said, as if it was the first she had heard of it. Then there was a painful silence, before she seemed to remember. 'Oh yes. Oh yes...yes...it was awful, but of course it was an accident. Wasn't it? Still, if you've heard the gossips, I suppose you might be confused. Just as I am,' she shook her head. 'Malicious rumours, that's all. They should think of the poor child and stop their talking. It's time they moved onto something else…It happened long enough ago…I think it's because of him still being here. Both of them still being here.'

'Pardon,' said Leila, 'what do you mean?'

'What, my dear? Oh, do you know this counter top is never clean and I think the curtains are due for a washing. Still, it's not the washing that I mind, it's the having to take them down and then iron them and put them up again after. Tiresome it is. I used to have fun you know. I know you wouldn't believe it but I did.'

She was rambling. She started to hum with a faraway look in her eyes, wiping around the counter with a cloth.

'Who are these gossips?' asked Leila.

Mrs Roberts looked absently over Leila's shoulder to the two women by the window, who Leila felt were watching her.

'I don't want to lose them, they are good customers,' she whispered.

Then as if waking from a dream phase she opened her eyes wide and raised her voice. 'Go on you two, sit down, you're blocking the way.'

'What are you up to?' whispered Imogen.

'I haven't finished yet,' said Leila, and she carried their drinks over to the table next to the two women sitting by the window. As she approached, they began to get up from the table. Leila took a deep breath but the confidence from her successful interview with Mrs Roberts deflated instantaneously and she was left feeling suddenly panicky. So she sat down at the next table and watched the women head for the toilet.

'What's with you?' asked Imogen with a frown.

'I've got to do this,' muttered Leila through gritted teeth, 'wait here.'

Clenching herself, she headed towards the toilet, notebook in hand. *I have to make myself do this.*

She pushed through the door to find the wash area

disconcertingly empty. They were in the cubicles and a toilet was flushing. All she had to do was wait. At least one of them would be out any second now. *They probably didn't hear the door because of the flushing noise.*

'What do you think of that Leila girl?' said a voice from the middle cubicle.

The question was clearly addressed to the adjacent cubicle. In a fresh panic, Leila moved as quickly and quietly as she could into the cubicle furthest from them and pulled the door to without locking it, gratified that it had not squeaked as the middle one was doing at that very moment.

'She's growing up isn't she?' came the delayed reply from the far cubicle.

A tap was on and someone was out and washing their hands.

'I've heard she's a bit of a weirdo.'

'Yeah. Where did you hear that?'

'From the school.'

Leila's heart was thundering and she was struggling to keep hold of herself, but in the midst of her terror, she felt a small stab of anger. She was sure that it was Sian who had called her a weirdo, which was disappointing because she liked the look of Sian.

'She looks miserable. Sullen piece of work. Ann never says much about her does she?'

Leila clenched her fist. It sounded like Rhian, the sheep faced one.

'Probably for his sake. She's very faithful like that.'

The far toilet flushed and Leila took the opportunity to pull the door further and slide the bolt slowly home.

'Wonder if the girl knows about Geraint and her mother. They would have run off together if she hadn't died like that.'

'Makes you wonder doesn't it? About her death I mean. Accident or not?' said Rhian.

Leila clenched both her hands together, each gripping the other in a white-knuckled vice. Now she was listening with all her might.

'Jealous lovers account for a lot of murders,' offered Sian.

Leila could hear a bag unzipping and one of them was brushing her hair.

'It wouldn't have been Geraint if they were running off together, would it?' said Rhian (nastily, Leila thought).

'I suppose not, though he's the nutter.'

'Was he a nutter then? Or has he gone that way since she died?'

'Always was,' said Sian. 'Do you think the girl knows the full story?'

'Does anyone know the full story?' drawled Rhian. 'Maybe she does know all that she can. That might explain the morose appearance on her. Can't say I liked her mother much either. Fancy piece... didn't fit in round here.'

There is a point where fear of discovery and desire to listen in on secrets are overcome by rage. Leila found that her temper had reached the point where she briefly knew it was not a good idea to burst out of the cubicle screaming verbal abuse at two gossiping women (and that this would only further their theory on her weirdness and fuel more malicious rumours), but she did it anyway.

'Shut up, you pair of bitches!' she heard herself screaming as she noisily clattered out of the cubicle after a brief struggle with the door latch. 'Shut your filthy mouths!'

The two women looked at her in momentary surprise and then the long faced Rhian zipped her bag shut and frowned.

'Nothing good comes to the ears of an eavesdropper! Calm yourself!'

Leila stopped herself short and realised that she was going to cry and that she couldn't stop it.

'I'm sorry,' said Sian, more sympathetic and frightened than Rhian. 'We just got carried away.'

Leila was sobbing now, and aware that she was annoyed at herself with a kind of distant awareness that was overseeing everything with disapproval.

Sian ventured a hand on her back and Leila tolerated it, because she wanted to ask them about Geraint.

'Here's a tissue for you,' said Rhian coldly.

They stood by while Leila blew her nose. She could feel Sian's hand rubbing her back and Rhian's hostility.

'That was a private conversation,' said Rhian sternly.

'In a public place,' said Leila in a choked voice, pleased all the same that she had thought to give such a good answer.

'Are you ok now?' ventured Sian.

'No, not until you tell me what you meant by Geraint and my mother. Was that true?'

'Please don't cry,' said Sian softly. 'I feel so bad. You shouldn't have heard it like this… but, yes it is true. Everyone round here knew.'

'Say the words,' sobbed Leila.

'What do you want me to say?'

'They were having an affair,' said Rhian, rather viciously. 'It wouldn't have been anything particular if she hadn't died.'

'Rhian, really. Have a heart.'

'I've heard enough,' said Leila, breathing deeply to smother the slow, shivering sobs. 'I'll thank you to not talk about my family ever again.'

She pushed Sian's hand away and made sure she shoved Rhian sharply to one side as she pushed past them and out of the door.

The sight of Imogen's concerned look was enough to set her off again into more sobbing; perhaps more of the self-pitying kind than the initial shock had caused.

'What's wrong?' asked Imogen.

'Let's get out of here.'

'But I haven't finished my chocolate.'

'You have now.'

Leila took the cup and emptied it all over the table. But she regretted it even as she saw it spread quickly to the edges and splatter to the floor. It wasn't Imogen or Mrs Roberts's fault after all.

The cold air was a welcome respite to Leila's flushed complexion. The sight of her father approaching with two full shopping bags was not so welcome.

'There's something wrong with Leila,' Imogen was saying. Leila could see her annoying breath rising dragon-like in the cold air. 'She threw my drink all over the table…on purpose.'

'Well that's no way to behave is it?' said Tom with feigned sternness. 'What is it Leila? Are you crying?'

Leila could barely speak to her father, she needed time to think. If all the locals knew of the affair, then surely he must have known too.

'Come on Leila, speak to me.'

'Got my period,' mumbled Leila. 'My first one.'

'Oh, ok,' said Tom, immediately growing taller and more distant. It wasn't true, but she knew it would scare him off.

'We'll speak to Ann about that,' he said, beginning to fumble with the shopping bags.

'Liar,' spat Imogen into her ear. 'You've already had it. You'd better tell me what happened when we get back.'

Leila nodded reluctantly.

Tom had retreated a little and was sorting the shopping into three loads, oblivious to what had just passed. Leila noticed as if for the first time the greying hair on his temples, the lines branching out from his eyes; crying lines. She saw the look of resignation in his grey eyes and she felt sorry for him. If he had known of the affair, he would have suffered.

'He's getting old,' she thought, 'living a half-life without mother. He cannot be very happy, but then I don't really know him at all. I know nothing.'

But now she did know why her father hated Geraint. And why he might want to kill him.

'Dad,' she said. 'You don't need to put so much shopping in your bag and so little in mine, I can carry more. I'm thirteen now you know.'

He smiled and patted her on the head as if she was still a little girl, 'I'll be fine with this,' he said. 'Don't forget it is a long walk.'

There was a more subdued air to the afternoon as they walked back. Clouds were gathering in the east and more snow was expected overnight. Imogen was describing the snow bunting to Tom while Leila trailed behind again, more lost than before. Although her discovery in the café had shaken her preconceived ideas about Lio, she was glad to have found something out. Now at last she could imagine her mother doing things other than smiling as she did in all the photos. Now she could see something of how her mother had lived. But it was a shock too, it was frightening to find that she had not been the only thing in her mother's life, that she had wanted other things too and she had gone out and got them. Would her mother have abandoned her to run away with Geraint?

Leila felt strangely ambivalent, pulled by too many concerns to form an immediate reaction. She even felt some admiration for her mother's strength and independence and the vague suggestion of cruelty. She seemed more powerful now. Yet there was also the pain of knowing that she and her father had not been enough for Lio. Leila found it hard to imagine her father being anything but gentle and caring, especially now she knew why he'd driven into Geraint, so everything seemed to point to her mother. Perhaps Lio had not been so perfect after all.

The snowball in Leila's head continued to grow and she saw for the first time, the possibility of her mother as a really bad person; the possibility that her mother had tired of her, not wanted the baby that had taken up so much of her time. Her imagination bloomed in glorious technicolour as scarlet as any of Lio's grotesquely surreal paintings. Even as she walked up the lane behind her father and Imogen, Leila's vision had darkened and she was briefly in another world. She could feel her mother picking her up and preparing to throw her over the cliff, because she wanted to be with Geraint. She was held by rigid arms, up over that chasm, on the cliffs, the wind rocking her. Tensing, Leila knew she couldn't move because she was in danger. She gave small, dry screams that stuck in her throat and could not be heard by anyone except herself, and clung on with hands like claws. As she looked down at the rocks and the river flowing far below, the long grasses and rushes blown flat by a hot wind, she felt her mother rocking precariously as she tried to regain her balance enough to hurl her down without falling herself. It seemed like forever to Leila. Then suddenly she was on the ground, but she hadn't fallen, someone's strong arms had grabbed her and pulled her to safety. She was held against a rough wool coat with her face buried and behind her there was a long scream that faded down into the valley below. She was held still for a few minutes and she did not try to move. She had not seen the face of her rescuer but she knew it was her father, she could smell the rough scent of herbal soap and aftershave on his coat. Her father had pushed Lio to protect his daughter, and Lio lay on her back far below, in the long grasses, staining them scarlet, her pale face unmoved, staring at the sky, her hair lying out like a fan. Like a witch.

'Come on Leila,' called Tom from somewhere that seemed far away.

He and Imogen were some way ahead now.

Leila suddenly found herself trying to suffocate half sobs in her throat. Her imagination had become her reality. Already she had dismissed Mr Parry as a suspect in her mother's demise. She ran to catch up with the others, her feet sliding in the snow, the shopping bag banging against her legs, heedless of her father's softly spoken, 'Careful now Leila.' She ran to him and looked up at him as if seeing him for the first time. She had spent so much time thinking of the dead, she had hardly had time for the living. If he were to die too, what then?

'Are you all right, Leila?'

'Father, I know. I found out about mother today.'

He seemed to start at her words, the eyes that had been half closed opened wide and white as if someone had run him through with a sword. Then he seemed to realise how this might look because he turned away, hiding his face as he asked: 'What do you mean, Leila?'

Leila did not answer immediately because his look of horror had frightened her and she was watching his profile as they walked, although his face was still averted from her.

'I know how bad she was. I know that she was having an affair with Geraint.'

'Oh.'

There was a flicker of surprise, his whole head jerked towards her and his mouth opened slightly. Was there a vague suggestion of relief there in his brief glance? Then his features seemed to recover into that set, tired look she knew too well. Now she thought she understood his tiredness. She thought he was sad for her, because she was exalting a woman who hardly deserved to be remembered at all. Yet how could he tell her and destroy her illusions, destroy the security fence she had built up for herself?

'Who told you?'

'Two women I met in the café. Everyone knows don't they Dad? Everyone knows except for me.'

'Sian and Rhian,' he paused and then shook his head slowly. 'They're the subject of some pretty rum rumours themselves at the moment.'

'What?' Leila frowned. He had ignored her main point as usual.

'I'll tell you when you are older.'

'Were you going to tell me about Geraint when I got older?'

'I don't know, Leila,' he sighed and wiped his hand through his hair. 'I thought maybe there were some things you were better off not knowing. I didn't know how it would affect you. You have built up your own precious picture of your mother – I didn't want to spoil that. Sometimes I think we should have left here years ago.'

'But I don't want to leave here – this is my home and I want to know the truth.'

'You think you want to know the truth, but sometimes it's not so nice,' he said.

'I want to know the whole story, no matter how bad.'

'I'm not entirely convinced that you will thank me for it,' said Tom with a look that was all at once disapproving and imploring. 'Your mother *was* having a relationship with Geraint, for some time before the accident. I found out shortly before she died. Things were difficult between us.'

'What do you mean by difficult?'

'I suppose I was working too much and she needed more company, more friendship. Of course she had you, but she needed someone to talk to and I was caught up in my work at the time.'

Tom paused, vaguely surprised that he was finding this easier than he had expected. Perhaps it was the unusual circumstances: the snow, the long walk – not at all what he had anticipated.

'Geraint was an old flame of hers, they were in college together. He's from round here originally and he came back when he found out Lio was here.'

'How did he find out?'

'His older brother lived over in Clocaenog. He died some years back of cancer, but his wife and son are still here.'

'Do we know them?'

Tom sighed. 'Yes, you've been making friends with the boy.'

'Jude?'

Tom nodded.

'I wasn't sure about it, but he's a good lad. His mother has brought him up well, and on her own.'

'So Geraint is Jude's uncle,' said Leila.

'Yes, unfortunately.'

'Are you okay about me being friends with him then?'

'Yes, Leila, because I happen to know that they don't have too much to do with Geraint and I trust Jude's mother. However, you aren't to go to Jude's house or anywhere near Clocaenog without my express permission.'

'So why did mother go back to Geraint?'

Tom shrugged. 'She told me that at first she refused to see him, it had been a stormy relationship and anyway she was married to me by then. But Geraint didn't go away, he began renting in Clocaenog, and as you know he is still there. One day when she and I had had a row, she went to see him. I suppose that must have been when it began.'

'Were you upset?'

'Yes, of course I was. But I didn't know for six months. During that time I felt she was moving away from me, but I was so busy, so preoccupied that I didn't stop to ask myself why.'

'Was she going to leave us?'

'I don't know,' he said, then stopped before he was about to say something else. 'No, Leila, she wouldn't have left *you*. No matter what our differences were, she wouldn't have left you. However, I do think she might have left me, if we hadn't sorted it out. I don't know if we would have, I don't suppose I ever will.'

'Was my mother a bad woman?'

'No,' he said slowly. 'She just liked a bit of fun and adventure and I suppose she didn't get enough of that with me.'

'Did she love Geraint more than you?'

'I really don't know. Perhaps she did in the end. He said she did. After she died, he said she was planning to leave me, but he's hardly a reliable source.' Her father sighed. 'As you know I don't like him and I don't want you repeating what happened on the road that day to anyone. We don't need the trouble. He's not right in the head. I don't believe that I would like him even if he hadn't had an affair with my wife. Since she died, he's become well known as a bit of a fruitcake. That's why I want you, both of you, to stay away from him.'

'I don't like him either,' said Leila, 'I thought he was scary when we saw him in the woods.'

'You never should have been there,' Tom snapped, suddenly agitated. 'You *must* stay away from him, both of you.'

Leila nodded, but she was thinking she needed to know more.

'Dad, why did mother leave Geraint that first time?'

Tom sighed; Leila's persistent questions were beginning to tire him.

'She said he was possessive, he wouldn't let her go anywhere without him. So I was surprised when she began seeing him again. She really hurt me, but it was my fault too.'

Leila contemplated all of this for a moment.

'I think I feel hurt too,' she said after a long pause, feeling very depressed for the first time and not really understanding it. 'We weren't enough for her; she didn't love us enough.'

'No, don't think that,' Tom shook his head. 'She loved you more than anything else in the world.'

Leila waited for more, but her father was already becoming more distant, as if the conversation had brought back a horde of images and memories that were coming between them. His last words rang hollow, Leila had heard them before many times, but it would take more than words to prove it.

After a period of silence, Tom pointed out rabbit tracks in the snow, a lone buzzard in the sky, sheep's wool on the fence. His efforts at converting to lighter subject material were too obvious for Leila, but Imogen joined in as if nothing unusual had been said. When they reached Hafod, the lights in the windows welcomed them back. Dusk was falling, Imogen's mother was putting the hens to bed and icicles glittered like a banner of knives strung along the eaves of the storehouse and the barn.

'Hafod,' thought Leila, loving the word, loving the big white house standing like a face in the snow. With an excited but sad bubble rising in her throat she felt the words she did not speak. Hafod is my mother now.

Tom stayed up late that night drinking alone. He had returned from the walk home wanting to cry. As he had thrown together a stew, he had told himself that this was to be expected. Of course Leila would find something out eventually. How could he have blinded himself to this inevitability? Strange how a person could become so deluded; caught up in all the ordinary, small things... He had not really seen that she was growing up, asking questions, sensing in her bones that something was very wrong. There was no chance of moving house while winter persisted, yet that was what he wanted. He felt the urge to pack things even as they all slept in the two rooms above. Lower the price...that was something positive he could do to get them out of there, before it was too late. He glared at the phone, eager to take action but knowing that no estate agent would answer at half past two in the morning. How could he have felt so peaceful yesterday? So caught up in triviality. There was a darkness coming. He could feel it now as he poured the Scotch but would he recall it with the same urgency in the morning?

NINE

Jude came the next day, just when Leila needed him. His gaze focused on Hafod as he walked over the moor towards it. He already loved the sight of that house standing so solid and dazzling with the winter sun illuminating its walls and catching at the crystalline aspect of the snow. The solemn brown of the outbuildings with their low roofing and fringes of icicles contrasted to make Hafod taller and brighter. It wasn't like the pseudo whitewashed cottage look of the newly painted holiday homes with inappropriate windows and doors that ripped the faces out of the original buildings, and it wasn't the converted barn look either. Hafod was old and weathered, yet well preserved. The smiling face of a friend in the astonishing snow.

When he knocked on the door, all red faced and radiant; Leila answered immediately as if she had been waiting. Jude was ready to relay his bit of news, but Leila appeared upset and asked him if they could go for a walk.

'Where is Imogen?' he asked.

'*She's* taken her out,' said Leila. Jude nodded and decided to put the news on hold.

They walked up to the moor and Leila told Jude of her discovery.

'I'm sorry to tell you this,' said Jude. 'But I knew already.'

'And why didn't you tell me that Geraint is your uncle?' demanded Leila.

He imagined she was feeling a little foolish for making so much of the story, at least that would explain her reddening face.

'I'm sorry Leila, but I thought you knew about that. As for the affair he had with your mum, well I had my orders from my mum. It wasn't up to me to tell you.'

'No, you're right,' said Leila, now looking furious rather than embarrassed. 'It was my father's job and he didn't do it. But they were talking about me last night and this morning Father was onto the estate agent about lowering Hafod's price, without even saying a thing to me. Then Ann takes Imogen off to visit Bronwen. They just leave me like this. Everything feels so wrong. There are still things I should know but no one is telling me.'

'What sort of things do you think they are not telling you?' asked Jude.

'I just know that there is more and my father won't tell me for some reason.'

'But he told you about the affair, didn't he?'

'Yes, but I had found out anyway and today he seems distant again, like he doesn't want me around.'

'He probably just wants to protect you, but doesn't know how.'

'I really need to speak to your Uncle Geraint. He is the one person who can tell me about my mother. But I'm not allowed near him and... well... I'm scared of him.'

'He is a bit strange,' Jude agreed, 'but not as bad as your father has painted him. He's always been fine with me. He makes an effort to speak. If you want to see him I'll come with you. I'm not scared of him.'

'Suppose my mother did want to throw me off the cliff? Why did I think it, if it's not true?'

'You think a lot of things – they can't all be true. I'll look after you, anyway. Come on, we need to put these demons to rest.'

'Will we get there with all this snow?'

'It's not far from where I live. You can come and meet my mother first.'

'Ok, but we need to plan out what I will ask Geraint.'

'We can do that on the way,' said Jude.

Jude turned around and smiled at her as he led the way. She looked a little scared, but she wasn't going to admit to it. She must want to impress him as much as he wanted to impress her. It was a good thought.

Leila followed Jude uneasily into his home in the forest. He was keen for her to meet his mother but she had grown to expect an unenthusiastic welcome wherever she went. It had gradually become less to do with Lio and more to do with her. At first it all went well. She was surprised to find Jude's mother petite, with dark cropped hair and pleasant freckles. When she politely addressed her as Mrs Noon, the woman shook her head and asked to be called Celyn.

Jude made mugs of tea and they sat down and it was all going nicely with Jude calling Leila 'Lai' in an affectionate way, until Celyn asked what that stood for. And then the mood changed like a sudden chill breeze on a hot day.

'Oh,' said Celyn, pausing for far too long. Leila felt the scrutiny even before it came and retreated in her usual way, sliding backwards, her eyes going down, her index finger slowly skimming over a few drops of spilled juice, spreading it quickly from side to side.

'Well, what are you two doing today?' asked Celyn briskly and Leila was grateful that the question was directed at Jude.

Jude told Celyn of their intention to visit Geraint while Leila clenched her fists under the table. It seemed a lot of trust to place in an adult, but the expected prohibition did not come. Celyn merely said they should be careful in case Geraint did not want to talk, maybe Jude should approach him alone first.

'Jude gets on quite well with Geraint,' said Celyn, as if she had sensed Leila's misgivings, 'and you do deserve to know all you can about your mother's life. You are at that age when you have a lot of questions that need answering.'

Leila nodded, but could not bring herself to speak. She was not used to adult women speaking openly to her (if she didn't count the Crow Woman) and she felt strangely intimidated.

'Do be careful in the snow,' Celyn said just as they were leaving. 'Did you hear about Mr Parry?'

'Ah, yes,' said Jude before Leila could reply. 'I was going to tell you Leila, but you had so much of your own to tell me today.'

'What about him?' asked Leila.

'He's missing,' said Jude, 'they found seven of his ewes killed and no sign of Mr Parry anywhere. His dog was running around the farm as if deranged. It was covered in blood, so it seems to be responsible for killing the sheep.'

'Has the farmhouse been searched?' asked Leila, suddenly afraid.

'Yes, I think so,' said Celyn, 'on account of the dead ewes, they feared he might have had an accident and be unable to reach the phone, but the house was all locked up and empty. It's almost certain that he went out somewhere and hasn't made it back.'

'Oh, we saw him didn't we!' cried Leila. 'When was it? Remember, we saw him going up onto the moor with his dog!'

'Two days ago I'd say,' replied Jude. 'In the afternoon. Like I told you Mum, I think he said he was looking for lost sheep. But perhaps he wasn't after all,' he said with a sudden morbid look on his face.

'What do you mean?' asked Leila.

'Perhaps he wanted to die out there, who knows.'

'That's enough Jude,' said Celyn.

'Is anyone looking for him?' asked Leila.

'Yes, they were up there. They have found nothing so far, but the snow is deep, so we may have to wait for it to melt,' said Celyn.

'Did they find any tracks?'

'I would expect the snowfall has covered all tracks,' said Celyn, 'but they will find him, and make sure you don't go wandering up there. Stay with Jude.'

'If we were the last people to see him the police may want to talk to us,' said Leila.

'I've already spoken to them this morning,' said Jude, 'but they will probably want to ask you and Imogen the same questions.'

Jude's mother left them while she went to wash up. Leila grew more despondent.

'Why didn't you tell me earlier?'

'You had big news about your mother and Geraint, I could hardly get a word in. I was going to tell you, I just got sidetracked,' he smiled in a brotherly way, 'I got caught up with all your problems and forgot.'

Leila sighed, 'All those things I said. The way I was towards him.'

'Don't worry,' said Jude, 'you had good reason to feel the way you did. He might be all right. Just remember no one round here liked him, so if he has gone crazy, perhaps we all had a part in it. At least you spoke to him, that's more than most did.'

'Why don't you two stay in for today,' said Celyn, putting her head around the kitchen door. 'I've had a little think and I'd rather get Leila's father's permission before you go to Geraint, especially with Mr Parry and everything.'

'Don't worry, her dad said it's okay,' said Jude, lying easily.

'All the same, maybe not today,' said his mother and then the phone rang and while she was answering it, Jude led Leila outside.

'Jude, what are you doing?'

'Come on,' he said taking her arm and grinning. 'She'll be all right. Besides we're not giving up now, I want to see this through.'

Geraint's home was a beige-coloured dormer bungalow in the middle of Clocaenog. Behind it was a clearing with a small garden and a paddock where he kept a few mangy looking goats. It was tucked into a bend in the forest road and the snow that hadn't been cleared was dirty from the passage of vehicles. They approached the front door along a concrete path that was treacherous with ice.

'It looks like no one is in,' said Leila skidding to a halt. Her voice gave away her nerves. 'Jude, I don't know what I'm going to say.'

Jude smiled and produced a notebook and pen. 'Don't forget your project. I thought it was a great idea.'

He knocked on the door and Leila looked behind onto the forest road, wanting to escape. But the trees appeared to be closing in, walking inwards in an unbalanced fashion, tipping forwards like cardboard toilet rolls with legs. Now that she was there on the slippery path, she was very afraid.

'Come on, he's not here, let's go,' she said, already halfway down the path, going towards the walking trees, her throat constricting. That again.

But there was a shadow behind the frosted glass, and the latch was being undone. A dark fiend was unpadlocking the way into the crypt. Geraint, his eyes black, opened the door and looked at Jude with mild surprise.

'Hello Jude, my goats haven't got out again have they?' he asked politely.

'No,' said Jude, 'it's for our geography projects, can we ask you a few questions?'

Geraint's face seemed to tense when he noticed Leila. He stared at her for a moment as if startled by her presence.

'It's good to see you,' he said quietly.

'Can you answer some survey questions?' Jude repeated his question in attempt to draw Geraint's attention from Leila.

'Geography?' said Geraint quizzically. 'Well I'm flattered that you thought my opinions were worth coming out through all this awful snow for.'

He looked at Leila again, standing wavering halfway down the path and she knew that he knew that they were not here for geography projects at all. He smiled beguilingly and opened his door.

'Come in. I've got a lovely fire going.'

Leila was almost overcome by nausea as she stepped over the threshold onto a grubby 'Welcome' mat, with a faded 'l', so it looked more like 'We come'.

She paused on the mat and Jude beckoned her further in. Slowly she followed him into the narrow hallway with a dirty carpet and the smell of unclean cats. She was revulsed, everything was grubby, even the turquoise chenille polo neck jumper he wore. Yet in the dimness, he looked younger and more handsome than before, his face was thin and angular, the eyes dark and strange in contrast to the straight blonde hair. She could see that it wouldn't be difficult to find him attractive, and he had been younger at the time of the affair with her mother.

'Would you both like a drink?' asked Geraint as he brushed cat hairs from his jumper. It was a woman's jumper and she wondered why he was wearing it. Perhaps it had been her mother's...

Before Leila could refuse, Jude had asked for orange juice, so she nodded in assent. Jude sat down on one of the worn out sofas, which looked familiar and sent an ice slither up Leila's back, so she sat on the edge of it. That way only the bony seat of her bum had contact with its nasty beigeness. When Geraint went to the kitchen to pour the drinks, she breathed a temporary sigh of relief.

'I haven't got the questions with me,' she whispered urgently to Jude.

'Don't worry, we'll improvise,' he whispered back. 'Just make them up if you can't remember.'

'This is awful, I wish we hadn't come.'

'But at least he seems all right today,' said Jude and Leila frowned at him.

Geraint re-appeared with two glasses of orange. Leila noticed his nails were black and there was a dirty smudge on the glass he had given her. She turned it around and checked the other side before taking a sip.

'So, how I can help you with your geography projects?' asked Geraint with a hint of amusement.

'I've got a transport survey to do,' replied Jude, and Leila listened with amazement as he improvised on the spot. Geraint kept looking at her, even though Jude was talking to him and she began to feel uneasy. When it was her turn, she was surprised that she managed to talk at all, such was her tension. Yet she maintained a level voice and remembered some of her questions, and even managed to mark down Geraint's replies in a legible hand despite the fact that she was shaking.

'And is that all?' asked Geraint when she had finished.

Now he was asking her what she had really come for.

'No,' she said, taking a deep breath, 'I've been wanting to ask you about my mother.'

He sat back in his chair and smiled grimly.

'I knew you would come one day,' he said, slowly drumming his fingers on the arm of his chair. Small, smooth hands and dirty fingernails. Drumming. She felt she might scream.

'One thing surprises me,' he went on, 'that your father let you come here, even after he tried to run me off the road! That was a very dangerous thing to do. I had quite a nose bleed after.'

Leila shivered. 'Yes I'm sorry about that. I don't think he meant to do it.'

Geraint laughed dismissively. 'As I said, I'm very surprised he let you come here today.'

'He didn't,' said Leila.

'So he doesn't know you are here?'

'No. But Jude's mother does.'

Geraint glanced at Jude, as if he had forgotten him for a moment. Jude was frowning. He was missing something. He did not know of the incident on the road.

'What do you want to know?' asked Geraint.

'About your affair with my mother.'

'So they've told you.'

'Yes, I know now. But who do you mean by "they"?'

'The village gossips I suppose,' said Geraint, a faint sneer on his face. 'Well, I certainly didn't think *he* would have told you.'

'No, you're right, he didn't,' said Leila uneasily. 'What I really wanted to know is whether my mother was happy before she died.'

Geraint laughed to himself as if she amused him, 'I would say she was happy enough. She wasn't happy with your father, but she was happy with me.'

'She wasn't depressed or anything?'

'No. If you're thinking she wanted to die, you are wrong. She had a lot to live for. It is true that she was not perfectly happy, but is anyone? No one can ever be perfectly happy just as no one can be perfectly miserable. There is always some little thing that could save the unhappiest person and something that could doom the most happy, joyous person. Your mother was a bit down about her marriage and all the sneaking about wasn't ideal. She was coming to realise she had to make a choice between me and him.'

'And do you know what she was planning to do?' asked Leila.

'The last time I saw her, she had decided that she would have to leave your father,' said Geraint. There was a cruel edge to his voice, his eyes were intent on her.

'What was going to happen to me?' said Leila.

'I don't know. She didn't say what she planned for you.'

Leila was disappointed by this answer, but she pressed on.

'When was the last time you saw my mother?'

He sighed and shifted in his seat.

'It was the day before she fell from Afon Ddu. We had not arranged to meet, but we met in town that day. She was upset because Tom had found out about our relationship before she had had the chance to tell him herself. He was very angry with her. It turned out that he had known for some time and had been spying on her.'

'My father?' said Leila in surprise. 'What do you mean by spying?'

'I suppose he had followed her, she didn't really know herself, but he had said things…things that he could only know by watching, or spying, or whatever you want to call it.'

'He didn't tell me this,' said Leila sceptically.

'Well, can you blame him? It's not the sort of thing you admit to your own daughter.' Geraint laughed again, as if he was just tolerating this inquisition.

'Tell me about that last time you saw her. Was I there?' Leila was nervous, but the questions were piling forwards, climbing her constricting throat, forcing their way out.

'No,' said Geraint. 'You were with him. You were sleeping when they had the row and she ran out of the house. As I said she was upset, so we drove back here and had a long talk. She was confused, she had been thrown by the row, by Tom knowing and wasn't sure what to do. He had made threats, about getting custody of you. She now realised that it was not going to be easy to end it with him. Whatever she did, someone was going to be very upset.'

'And what happened then?'

'After two hours she decided to go back; she said you would be missing her. I told her to be by the phone at five and I rang her then to make sure she was all right.'

'Was she?'

'Yes, they had had a few words on her return. He had told her that she had to stop seeing me, she had told him she needed time to think. Then he went out.'

'Where?'

'I don't know.'

'And did you arrange to meet again?'

'Yes, I had told her I would be in all of the next day if she could get over.'

'So you were in your house when she fell?'

'Yes, as I said,' a look of irritation suddenly flickered into his eyes. Up until now he had spoken in a calm monotone. Now he was aware of her again and she seemed to annoy him.

'So you didn't see her fall then?' She knew she was pushing her luck.

'Look out of the window,' he said impatiently. 'Can you see Afon Ddu from here?'

She looked, knowing that she would only see the dark pines splashed with a covering of snow.

'No.'

'Of course you can't. But she was coming here that day,' he said, leaning forwards and staring at her in an unsettling way. 'Lio was coming here and I'll never know what she was going to say.'

Geraint looked angry, his face was changing colour and a murderous shadow seemed to cross it while his eyes were intent on Leila.

Jude had noticed the change in Geraint and was surprised by the subtle sneering at Leila's questions. Jude's own nosiness was not quite satisfied but it was a toss up between risking a scene for the sake of his own curiosity or looking after his friend, Leila. Clearly he was being ignored by his uncle today, although he considered himself Geraint's only friend. And it was oddly exciting trying to decipher what was going on. There was an obvious charge in the atmosphere. Geraint was volatile – he knew that much – and Leila was pushing her luck. The man would not take much more questioning.

'Well, thanks for the information for our projects,' Jude said, 'We'll let you know how we get on.'

Geraint sat back in his chair and regarded them with a curious look.

'Are you two going out together or something?' he asked in a tone that was mocking.

'We are just friends,' said Jude quickly. 'Leila is younger than me anyway,' he added looking embarrassed.

Leila had one final question she wanted to ask, she *had* to ask. But Geraint was up out of his chair, leading them to the door. He was silent, his face tense, an errant muscle in his jaw twitching. He looked at the orange juice, which she hadn't drunk and then looked at her with something she could only interpret as intense dislike.

'Do you think that it is possible that my mother's death was not an accident?' she blurted. 'Could someone have pushed her?'

He gave her a look loaded with meaning which then evolved

into a strange little smile.

'I wouldn't say it's impossible. But if that's the case it appears the murderer has got away with it. I suppose we have to think who would have had the motive.'

'So you think someone might have pushed her?' said Leila.

His eyes rested heavily upon her. With a look of hostility.

'Its not impossible is it?' he said. 'But I really don't think this line of questioning is a particularly healthy one.'

'I think we should be going... Thanks for all your help, Unc,' said Jude and taking Leila by the elbow he guided her into the dimly lit hallway. 'See you again.'

Leila looked back as she was ushered out. Geraint lifted his hand in a dismissive wave and then shut the door.

'You need to be careful what you say,' said Jude, sounding annoyed.

They walked on in silence, Leila watching her feet trailing in the snow.

'Are you all right?' asked Jude after a while.

'I think so. He seemed to get quite annoyed with me, yet it started off all right didn't it?'

'Yes. I think maybe it brought back painful memories for him.'

'I don't know whether to believe the things he said about my father. Do you know my father said he's insane?'

'I think that is a bit of an exaggeration. Though I'd agree that Geraint deludes himself,' said Jude. 'The thing is, they hate each other, so they aren't going to paint the other in anything but the worst light. You should have told me about your father hitting him on the road. When I heard that I wasn't sure that it was such a good idea for us to be there.'

'I'm glad we went – I needed to hear his side of it,' said Leila. 'I just can't understand why my mother went back to him. He's so creepy.'

'Don't forget he is my uncle.'

'Sorry, but that's how I feel. Maybe my mother forgot what he was really like. I suppose if she was lonely and unhappy and he was there for her...'

'I don't really know him very well,' said Jude. 'Mum says that he's not like my dad except in looks. It's just recently that I've started to get to know him. He's not so bad, but he likes to be alone. I suppose he's a bit of a hermit.'

'He seems to think my mother might have been pushed,' said Leila, 'I would have liked to have asked him more about that. Why did you make me leave just as it was getting interesting?'

'Well, I felt responsible for you and I hate to say it, but I don't think he likes you much. You could see he was getting edgy. He's all right most of the time, but he has mood swings.'

'I really think my mother was killed,' said Leila.

'Didn't you get the impression that he was encouraging you to think that? And how can you prove it anyway? There are no known witnesses, only gossip and rumour.'

'Well, what did he mean about finding someone with a motive?'

'I think he was trying to cause trouble,' said Jude.

'How do you mean?'

'You mustn't take this to heart,' said Jude seriously, 'I just got the impression that he wanted to point the finger at your father. They hate each other enough don't they? How better to get at Tom than through you? I should have thought of this before I took you to him. You see, the story I've heard is that when it all happened, Geraint claimed that Lio was on her way to him, that she was leaving your father for him and that your father followed her to try and get her back. According to Geraint, she was pushed by your father when she refused to go back with him.'

'That can't be true. My father was at home with me. He wouldn't have left me alone.'

'Geraint was upset when he said that and it probably wasn't the only thing he said; he raved a bit back then. It was all a long time ago, but you can see how he might have started the rumour mill, as if it needed starting. He's still bitter, so you shouldn't take everything he says as gospel,' said Jude, 'and of course, no one believed him. He lost all credibility through his ranting. Then he just seemed to shut up and practically became a recluse.'

'It seems that everyone knows more than me about this,' said Leila, frowning. 'And I still don't think it was just an accident, Jude. I think that someone knows something. Something is *not* right.'

'Then we will continue with our investigations until you are satisfied.'

'I need to talk to my father again.'

'Well don't let him know you were at Geraint's, whatever you do.'

'I'm not even allowed to go to your house,' said Leila with a wan smile.

Jude walked with Leila until they were in sight of Hafod.

'Be careful of what you say to your dad,' he warned her again before he set off back to his own home. Leila watched him go, realising she had forgotten to thank him for helping her. Then she turned towards Hafod. Dusk was falling and the air was very still and quiet. It did not feel as cold as it had and she had the faintest feeling that the snow was beginning to melt. Up on the moor a lone buzzard was mewing, flying slowly up towards the ruin on the hill. There appeared to be nothing else out there, but she could not help thinking of Mr Parry. Where was he? For a second an insane idea took hold and she wished Jude were there to hear it. She would go and look for Mr Parry, she knew the direction in which he had been headed that day they'd talked, and she was confident on the moor, even in the snow. But what if she found him? She had never seen a dead body before. Maybe that was what she wanted, to be the one to find him. She looked back at Hafod. A light had come on in the lounge and the stepmother was about to draw the curtain but had stopped and was looking out. Leila realised she had been seen. It was getting dark already and she knew she had some explaining to do.

They seemed to accept her story of following the wild ponies and forgetting the time. They were more interested in the disappearance of Mr Parry. The police had been to speak to Imogen and they wanted to talk to Leila.

'An officer is calling round tomorrow, so you can stay in all day,' said her father. 'In fact, I don't want you out all day again while there's still deep snow. If you fell out there, we'd have a job finding you. There have been a record number of accidents this year – we've heard there's been another fall near the Afon Ddu cliffs.'

'Who?' asked Leila.

'One of the Pistyll farm boys. He was lucky his friends were able to go and get help.'

'Was he hurt?'

'No, he didn't go far. Apparently he was stuck on a bit of an outcrop, silly fool.'

'Those cliffs must be cursed,' she said, and looking at her father she wondered if he really could have pushed her mother in a jealous rage.

All through dinner she considered how she might ask her father about Lio's fall, without giving away where she had been that day. At last she thought of a way.

'Father,' she said, pausing to clear her throat properly. 'I need to know more about the time around my mother's death as well as the day she died. I want to have a clear picture of those two days in my mind so that it will stop bothering me all the time.' She had sat up straight in her chair and asked in a clear, cold voice. A grown up voice. A voice that demanded an answer.

'Why does it bother you?' he asked after he had taken a moment to consider what she was saying.

'Because I don't know much about those two days. You've told me that on the day she died Mother went for a walk and did not come back, but I need a picture in my mind of that day and the day before, then I can have peace. Can you tell me what *exactly* happened on those days?'

He sighed and looked across at Ann, who rose and began clearing the plates.

'Well, I can hardly remember the detail,' he said as he watched Ann retreating to the kitchen. 'But the day before, Lio went into Llan to do some shopping and was gone most of the day while I

108

was home with you. You were sleeping when she went but then you woke and kept asking for her. She came back late in the afternoon and I suppose we had a bit of a discussion, because I was meant to be going to a friend's and she had come back much later than she said she would.'

'What friend?' asked Leila.

'Oh, no one you know, just an old acquaintance… someone I used to work with,' he paused and sighed. 'Anyway, I did go and I was back by midnight. By then you were both in bed asleep. The next day was just like any other day. We were both on holiday with no plans to do anything other than relax. Lio had made a packed lunch and as it was a lovely day she said she would go for a walk. You were having your daytime nap, so I said I would stay behind with you. It was just a normal summer's day, a beautiful day, not the kind of day you expect a terrible thing to happen. When she went out of the door, I had no idea that I would never see her alive again.' He paused, to think if there was anything else, then shook his head. 'The only strange thing was the heat that day. It isn't often we get such hot weather up here. It was quite windy and even the wind was hot.'

Leila waited for more, but that was all he was prepared to say. There was no mention of the supposed row between her father and Lio when (according to Geraint), he had revealed that he knew of the affair. No mention either of Lio running out of the house, though he had admitted that she had driven into town and she had been late, which would account for her time at Geraint's bungalow. And her father was not about to admit to being a spy, if that part was also true. What her father was giving her was a vague, sketchy outline of her mother's final hours, omitting most of the words spoken, the feelings felt and the actions taken. He wasn't going to tell her now and perhaps not ever. She was almost angry enough to tell him that she had been to see Geraint. That would force his feelings out. But she had not forgotten his fury when he had run Geraint down. He would be even more enraged if she told him she had seen Geraint again. Then what? She would probably never be allowed out again. Maybe he would kill Geraint too. So it seemed that she could not make him tell her the complete story.

'What's with all these questions now?' said Ann as Tom helped with the clearing up.

'She's at that age I suppose,' he replied. 'And your two so-called friends didn't help with their yapping in the toilets the other day.'

'Yes. But Sian has apologised and you know I have never spoken about Leila with them.'

'With a bit of luck we'll start getting some viewings as soon as this snow clears up.'

'Hmm, I'm just a bit worried that if Henri Parry really is dead on the moor it won't help us to sell.'

'That sounds selfish, but it's a valid point.'

Tom smiled grimly as she left the kitchen and then sat down at the table. Leila was on a mission, he could sense it. She was like her mother in that way; she would not let go. They were not safe anymore. If only he had moved them a year earlier. It had all been so much more innocent then: picnics on the moor, toy people and animals climbing the rockery, horse jumps built from driftwood and bricks, Leila and Imogen the horses jumping them. All that whinnying and shouting, laughing and shrieking. Why was it so quiet this year? He had taken it for granted that they could go on like that forever. They needed to get away, far away from Geraint and Arabella. Somewhere safe, where no one knew anything. Brush the past away. It seemed foolish now to have even tried living with the past all around him. Waiting. But he knew why he had done it. Maybe even poor Ann knew; after all she had tried to make him move before. She had not wanted to live in the shadow of his dead wife. He had been selfish in that way, forcing her to live there while he fought his own secret obsession with Lio and her death. By staying he had punished himself and everyone else. He had drowned and resurfaced, only to drown again. As if he wanted it. He had relished the irony of the staid man, the sedated man (as Lio had jokingly called him once) becoming the passionate man. And he had felt it all, love, desire, nostalgia, hatred, grief, revulsion and bitter yearning until at last he had found a refuge of a kind under a haze of ignorance and numbness. If only Lio had been there to see it. Now it was time to wake up. He was close to tears again as he closed the kitchen door and headed for the glass that he always used when he was drinking.

Leila did not speak to Imogen about her day, and said so little that in the end Imogen pulled her duvet over her head and went to sleep. Long after, Leila lay awake looking at the waxing moon through the gap in the curtains. The room was immersed in the ghostly, silver twilight of an almost full moon mirrored and amplified by the still, quiet snow. She was angry with her father. He would only tell her if he was forced and one day she would do it, she would make him tell the truth, but now, in defiance, she was thinking of something else. If only she could make herself get out of her warm bed and face the cold, she would go outside, and if she dared she would go up onto the moor and find Mr Parry. It was a ridiculous idea of course and normally she would not have acted on it. But she wanted to find out more about her mother. After all there was half of herself that she didn't know. Perhaps her mother was in the adventurous, crazy side of her. So she wouldn't stop herself from being reckless. That way she could get to know herself and her mother. And she wanted to defy her father

'Perhaps,' she thought, 'this is the sort of thing my mother would have done.'

She found herself tiptoeing about, pulling on thick socks, leggings, jumpers, her coat and scarf. It would be cold, but somehow she needed even more layers of clothes than normal, clothes to be her armour against her fear and whatever she was going to see. When she was dressed, she found it difficult to move, but she felt bigger, like a fat bird that had become even fatter by huffing its feathers up against the cold. Imogen was tossing and turning and breathing noisily, and Leila watched her quietly until she settled again. Then as she crept like a sprite towards the door, trying to leave the room unnoticed, the duvet on Imogen's bed suddenly rose up pale in the moonlight and Leila jumped with fright before realising that it was Imogen and not a ghost. Imogen removed the duvet and saw Leila standing at the door with a finger to her lips.

'Where are you going?'

Ten minutes later, both girls emerged from the house with their boots and coats on... Two small overdressed figures with long shadows trailing them up the lane towards the moor.

'They say the snow will begin to melt soon, it will be completely thawed in two weeks,' said Imogen.

Leila was silent, she'd been surprised that Imogen had wanted to come, but had encouraged her because she was afraid of going alone.

'Do you think we will find him?' asked Imogen.

'I don't know,' said Leila. 'It won't be easy if the search and rescue haven't, although we have more idea than them of where he went.'

'I'm just worried about his eyes,' said Imogen. 'If we find him, I won't want to look if his eyes have been eaten by the birds.'

'Perhaps he isn't even dead anyway,' remarked Leila. 'Everyone seems to be taking it for granted, but he could have gone anywhere, he might have just decided to disappear.'

'It's a bit cold,' said Imogen, hunching her shoulders forward.

Leila had been thinking the opposite, the effort of walking in the snow in all her layers of clothing, was warming her up rapidly. The night was still and there was a definite hint of warmer weather on its way, already she suspected the snow had reduced by the tiniest bit – it was not so fluffy and new, but more compacted and crunchy as it shrank in upon itself.

'Here take my scarf,' she said, wrapping it around Imogen's neck. 'And let's hold hands.'

Imogen accepted. She looked pale and groggy and Leila wondered if she was fully awake.

'This is really eerie,' said Leila, 'look at our shadows, so big! It's scary, though really there is nothing to be scared of.'

'Except for *him*,' said Imogen.

'Mmm,' Leila mused, 'maybe we should just walk the way we

saw him go and then turn back. We don't want to end up stuck and lost ourselves.' She was thinking of how the little plans hatched in her fantasies were bigger and more frightening in reality.

She looked behind at Hafod's face, wan in the snowlight, and thought of their warm beds. Ahead the moor was a huge and ghastly blue-grey wasteland. She missed the sheep now they were gone, their constant baa-ing, and the way they peopled the hillsides with their simple lives.

They had reached the five bar gate and while Leila hesitated, Imogen climbed automatically, like a zombie. Leila followed. Her self-imposed task seemed colossal now; the moor was a dangerous place at night and even with the light afforded by moonlit snow, there were still large areas of blackness, like voids of nothingness. Leila was about to ask if they should continue, when Imogen lurched forwards onto the path Mr Parry had taken that day, pointing ahead and mumbling, 'this way.'

They walked slowly along the path, noticing tracks here and there, some slurred by the most recent snowfall, many clearer. Other people had been looking, and the task seemed hopeless.

'The standing stone,' mumbled Imogen. 'That's where he was going.'

'It was half buried in the snow,' said Leila, 'and it's near the edge of a steep slope.'

It did not take them long to reach the standing stone – it was not far. Even in the moonlight they could see how the snow was badly disturbed. There were large adult footprints everywhere, the snow was dragged this way and that by boots, a sledge and some kind of all-terrain vehicle. In the moonlight these disturbances looked like dark blue pools in the silvery snow, disorder that looked somehow violent, like large, bleeding wounds. The standing stone stood as always, casting a long warped shadow over the disarray, a calm monolith in spite of the circles that had been run about it. Hundreds of small demons with huge feet had popped out of holes in the night and stolen the corpse and, before anyone could stop them, they had jumped back into the black voids and disappeared. Leila was half relieved, half disappointed.

'I've never seen a dead body,' she said. 'I so wanted to see a dead body all to myself.'

'It looks like he fell down the slope,' said Imogen dozily, 'they must have had climbers and ropes to get him out.'

'I wonder what he looked like, dead,' Leila continued, morbidly shuffling through the disturbed snow and the slicks of mud which had bled through from underneath, in order to peer over the edge of the ravine.

'Be careful,' said Imogen. 'It looks slippy, you might fall too.'

'It's not exactly a deathfall though is it,' said Leila, and she peered over as if she expected to see Mr Parry still lying there, undisturbed, staring up at the almost full moon with sightless eyes.

'Come away from there,' Imogen said less dozily. 'It's your necrolatry again.'

Leila reluctantly backed off, feeling strange, because instead of seeing Mr Parry down there, she had seen her mother, Lio, lying there, dead, like she had imagined her, just staring up at the sky with her hair all spread out. She had not even been thinking of her mother, she had been thinking of Mr Parry, but it seemed she could not see him at all.

'Let's go back,' said Imogen, 'he's probably been rescued, but maybe we will be told he is dead.'

They half walked, half sleep-walked back, their shadows reaching ahead of them like long fingers stretching hopelessly to reach something. They were cold now, and the stillness of the moor weighed on them like a mausoleum. There were no screech owls nor any tawny hoots rising from Tan-y-Du, just an appalling silence.

TEN

Arabella rose with the first light. The sky was a wintry pink; a weak sun filtered through scudding clouds and darker clouds gathered in the west. She put on her clothes and ventured out to feed her animals, glad of the milder air, though the wind was blustery. She was cheered to see the snow retreating; it saved her the bother of digging paths and worrying that the hens' shed needed re-insulating. The jobs were endless, always something needing repairs and usually something outside.

This winter she only had the energy to think. The trouble with thoughts was that they turned into thought attacks. Big stories, emotions and varying scenarios running through her head, some real, some imagined. She could spend an hour in her armchair feeling every emotion from joy to anger all because of thinking. The past rising up like an airy dragon…

Why did she always miss him at this time of year? Was it the lack of light that made her sad and introspective? She was alone too much, she knew that. It was, of course, pitiful to miss someone this way, year after year, when she had meant so little to him. Now she was counting the days to her death. But that was too morbid. No, she was counting the days until the snow melted and the two girls could visit again as Tom had promised. She had already planned some art activities for rainy days.

It didn't seem fair that Tom had forsaken her like this. How could he be so sure that she could cope with the secrecy all this time? With no one to talk to? No one to reassure her and remind her that she was not alone? Sometimes when she was angry she thought of blackmailing him. Forcing him to come to her because she knew he would do anything to keep Leila safe. But where was the good in that? He would only be angry and revulsed. Anyway, it would be spring soon and by then she would feel better.

'I had a strange dream last night,' said Imogen. 'Leila and I went on the moors to look for Mr Parry.'

The cold sunlight slanted through half opened kitchen blinds and she twisted her yellow hair into a rope as she spoke.

Leila watched her intently but said nothing. Did Imogen really think it was a dream? It seemed like a dream now, but she knew it wasn't because she had woken up sweating inside three jumpers, trousers with leggings underneath and two pairs of socks. If they all thought it was a dream, it could do no harm. Now she was waiting and watching for the police to come and tell them that they had found Mr Parry, just like someone had once come to tell them they had found her mother.

She looked at her father. He was busy cutting up toast soldiers for her. Frantically cutting, barely missing the ends of his fingers. He was tense. He had never told her about who had found her mother. Yet someone must have. And he hadn't told her for how long her mother's body had lain near the fast moving waters of Afon Ddu. Had anyone seen it and looked at it, thinking it was all theirs? It made her suddenly furious with her father for not telling her, and at whoever had found Lio.

'Do you know how long some religions prefer a body to be left undisturbed after death?' Imogen was asking, swivelling her head round to look at everyone in turn as she always did when she was about to come up with something intriguing.

'No,' said Leila's father, looking sideways at Imogen, 'but I do believe you are going to tell us.'

'Three days,' she said. 'It's so they can begin their journey after this life without disturbance. And they also say when someone is near death that it is sometimes better not to disturb the body with needles and machines and drugs and if a person is resuscitated, they might miss their natural death and be forced to live on for weeks, like a zombie. They might not really be there anymore after being forced back from the dead.'

'That's not always the case,' said Leila, 'that only applies if a person is ready to die. Meant to die. And we can't tell that so we can't make that decision.'

Imogen frowned. 'Well, there are cases when death seems to do more good than staying alive. That's why some people believe in euthanasia.'

Tom sighed heavily.

'What's with you two this morning?' he asked. 'Is this really the kind of thing we need first thing, at the breakfast table? And as for Mr Parry, can we stop all this conjecture? I'm fed up of village gossip, and here are my own daughters, doing the same thing.'

They watched him rise angrily from the table and leave the room.

'Right, that's enough,' said Ann.

They were sent to their room.

At midday, with noses pushed against glass, they saw through their own breath on the window a policeman approach. He was trudging red-faced in the snow beneath Hafod.

'This is it!' said Leila, un-squashing her nose. 'They are going to tell us they've found him.'

'No,' said Imogen. 'Remember, they were sending a police constable round to speak to you, to ask you what you remembered about the last time you saw Mr Parry.'

Subdued, Leila sat down and wondered what she would say.

When the policeman had been let in, they ran to their own door and with ears flat against it, tried to listen. There was nothing but a quiet murmuring, even with Leila's special hearing. The lowered voices reminded Leila of undertakers. She could imagine them all standing round in black whispering. After a few minutes, the stepmother's shrill voice summoned them down.

'Mr Parry's been found,' she snapped, enjoying the moment of drama as they both held their breath and gasped.

'What…is he dead?' cried Imogen.

A smile seemed to flicker on the stepmother's lips as it always did when she was relaying grave news that wasn't too close to home.

'Yes,' she said. 'PC Roberts is here to ask you a few questions.'

'But what do *we* know?' asked Leila, looking red-faced.

PC Roberts stepped forwards as the girls reached the bottom stairs, smiled warmly and seemed affable.

'Come into the lounge,' said the stepmother, 'I've got the fire lit.'

'I only want to ask you to tell me what you saw that day,' said the policeman. 'There is no pressure or blame on you, but we need to build up as good a picture as we can of Mr Parry's last movements. We need as much information as possible. You are witnesses, if you like.'

'How did he die?' asked Imogen.

'We won't know for sure until we get the results of the post-mortem. What I need to know is what you thought of his behaviour when you saw him.'

'He was drunk,' said Leila. 'Jude pointed out a bottle of whisky, almost full, in his coat pocket, and he stank of it.'

'Did you notice anything else?'

'His eyes were all glassy; he seemed different, not himself at all.'

'How do you mean "different"?' asked PC Roberts, stepping towards her.

'He seemed sad, like something bad had happened to him.'

'Do you know what could have made him sad?'

'No,' Leila spoke hesitantly. PC Roberts was bearing down on her, staring her down like a large snake, poised to strike. She could see the blackheads on his shiny nose. He was trying to stare a confession out of her. She could distract herself by playing join the dots on his nose. She was guilty until proved innocent. Perhaps he had seen her footsteps in the snow. Wondered why had she been out there, corpse hunting in the dark?

'Think carefully,' said PC Roberts. 'What else did you notice about him?'

PC Roberts had certainly picked up on her hesitation.

Leila chewed on a fingernail. She recalled how she had ruthlessly questioned Mr Parry and felt that his decline had begun when she had started suspecting him of involvement in her mother's death. After the Crow Woman had let it slip that he had been a stalker...

'I don't know any more,' she replied after a long pause. 'Do you know that he used to follow my mother?'

PC Roberts was reluctant to be sidetracked.

'Is there anything else you can tell me about that day? Did he say where he was going or what he was doing?'

'He just said he was going to his sheep. We thought he was looking for strays – he's been up on the moor before doing that.'

'Did you see anyone else?'

'No, just him,' said Leila, frowning as much as she dared. 'He was having such a struggle walking...he was really leaning on his stick.'

There was not much more to be said and Leila waited to be handcuffed and carted off.

'Do you remember anything else?' asked PC Roberts, turning towards Imogen.

Imogen shook her head.

'Well there is no need for nightmares. Now we've found him, he's at peace. He wasn't well, you know. We spoke to his doctor – he was recently diagnosed with cancer of the stomach. That may well explain his decline. He seemed to just give up.'

PC Roberts retreated to a safe distance and put on his hat. The stepmother had gone out of the room to look for Tom who had been absent from the proceedings and now, since she had not been arrested, Leila stepped forward and took her chance.

'Sir, were you involved in my mother's case?'

'No…' he replied, and after some hesitation he added, 'it was before my time.'

'Do you know who found her?'

He looked at her blankly, 'No…not offhand.'

'Was there ever a suspicion that she might have been pushed?'

'No, most certainly not,' he suddenly sounded quite sure. 'What makes you ask such a question?'

'I don't know,' she replied, 'people talking all the time, still; all the things that I feel I haven't been told.'

'You should ask your father, he is the one to tell you. Can you talk to him?'

'I've tried,' she said, 'but he never wants to say much.'

He looked down at his feet as if he had expected this. As if he knew. 'I'll see if I can have a word with him.'

Leila swallowed hard, 'Oh no, there's no need.'

'Don't worry, there was something I had to discuss with him anyway.'

With their talk over, the young policeman went into the sitting room to speak with Tom. Leila followed without being seen and stood on the bottom stair ready to begin climbing if necessary. She strained to hear, but only got the faintest murmuring of low voices. She waited, focusing in, her eyes closed tight, hands gripping the door lintel. She was almost sick with the effort of concentrating her hearing. What was he saying? Why couldn't they speak up a little? She waited, knowing that she risked being caught, until just as she was about to give up, the nugget was given. The voice of PC Roberts raised for a moment in exasperation, her father always an inaudible murmurer.

'You will have to tell her Tom, because she could hear it from someone else! I'm surprised she hasn't already. If she looked back at old newspaper records, she could find out for herself. Aren't you worried?'

*

She waited for her father to tell her. She waited all evening, watching him from behind a book that she wasn't really reading and she lingered at breakfast the following morning, but he hardly looked at her. So she began to think about the newspapers instead.

Outside the sun was shining and the snow was slowly melting. It had a rather ugly, packed look now. Dirty trails of slush swirled around Hafod's large front yard where Tom had been digging and feet had been walking. Leila was glad the thaw had come at last. She wanted to go to the library in search of ten-year-old newspapers.

She did not have to wait long. The next day her father announced that they were going back to school. As they stood next to the van waiting to be let in, she noticed the music of the fast, clear melt-waters flowing down each side of the pale lane and thought how much she wanted to see the brown moor again. She wanted to see the mosses and grasses, the blots of lichen on rocks and to touch the heather once more. She longed for the rebirth that came with spring.

It was now more of a slushy ride on the road and it did not take as long as it had weeks ago when the snow was new. Leila listened quietly to the wet swishing and swoshing of the tyres in the slush, with a growing, nervous excitement. What would she discover today? At the school gates she and Imogen waved to Tom and went off to find their friend Gwyneth.

At half past three they told Lisa, their minder, that they wanted to spend an hour in the library studying history and they liked the fact that they weren't lying. Lisa agreed to meet them at five. They nodded and watched her go. Then they pushed through the swing doors and found Jude waiting.

'I've got the goods,' he said, though he looked apprehensive. 'We're over here. It's on microfilm.'

'You haven't looked already, have you?' asked Leila.

'Of course not,' he said firmly, pulling the chair back for her.

'Imi and I can look in the nationals, if you like.'

'Ok.'

Leila didn't quite know why, but she went back to the day she was born first. The thirtieth of April 1974. The format of the paper looked dated by modern standards, not least because there were pictures of locals she knew looking much younger. Mr Parry was pictured on page three looking disgruntled after ramblers had staged a mass trespass over his land.

'Why are you looking at that?' asked Imogen. 'That's the wrong date.'

'I know,' she said.

She was glad of Jude and Imogen by her side, suddenly aware and grateful for their friendship. Then she searched the date her mother died. The seventeenth of August, nineteen seventy-eight.

There was nothing. She should have known it would be a week after the incident before it appeared in print. She looked again. And she held her breath while she read it. There… headlines in the next paper. Bold black letters. She was sick with excitement and fear:

Mother Falls To Death

This must be it. Now Leila was gripped from the throat down, her heart was struggling with mounting fear and dread, her twisting hands cold and damp, whole body leaning forwards closer to the screen, taut, intent. This was it. There would be something here. The something that had always been wrong would be made right. She was almost afraid to read the words. They seemed to jump out at her and dance around the page, mockingly, refusing to be taken in. These official-looking, printed newspaper words were about *her* mother.

She put her finger on the lines and purposefully moved it along, guiding her eyes along each sentence. There was the date of the fall, the seventeenth of August, nineteen seventy-eight. Lio had fallen to her death; there were no witnesses to the accident (it was presumed to be an accident, who on earth would push her?).

It was a fine hot day... no one knew how it had happened... they were not looking for anyone else in connection with it... a tragic accident... she was found by husband Tom and friend Arabella...

Leila stopped reading and stared blankly. *They* had found her! *Why* had *they* not said?

But there was something else, some more words. Words that should not have been there and demanded to be read. Something had gripped her, was rushing through her. She was tensing up, her throat constricting, she wanted to cry out, to shout the words that shouldn't have been there.

GIRL ON THE EDGE
Lio Hughes was found lying dead at the bottom of the Afon Ddu cliffs after what appears to be an accidental fall. Her four-year-old daughter Leila was found distressed but unharmed on the edge of the cliffs. Lio had been out walking with her daughter...

There were no further details at the time of the report. Leila sat and stared without breathing. She wondered how long she could sit and not breathe, feeling and encouraging the tight constriction in her throat, as if she was being choked and wanted to be choked. For a while, she couldn't even think, couldn't think of what this all meant. But then she began to breathe again, slowly and quietly and she knew that she would have to cry the shock out at some point. Even at that moment she could feel her eyes filling and then the warmth of tears, slicking down her cheeks. At least now she knew something of the lies that she had been told by those she had trusted.

So this was what her father had refused to tell her. She had seen her mother die. She was the only witness and she thought she could see herself there on Afon Ddu, wondering where her Mother had gone. But she only had fragments, nothing coherent and a sudden dread of delving further seemed to appear like a seed and root itself.

'Are you all right?' said Jude, noticing her paleness.

123

'Did you know?' she said, looking at him.

'Did I know... what?' he looked afraid.

'About me being there when she died. You did, didn't you?'

Jude looked away.

Leila looked at Imogen. 'You too?'

'Me what?' said Imogen. 'It's not your necrolatry again is it?'

'Shut-up about necrolatry,' snapped Leila, 'I'm asking you if you knew that I was there on the Afon Ddu cliffs when my mother fell.'

Imogen's expression told Leila that Imogen had not known. That at least was something.

'Is that what it says in the newspaper?' said Imogen. 'Let me see.'

'Yes. They have all been lying to me,' said Leila. 'Everything is lies. My father and Arabella found me alone on the cliffs. Yet my father has always said that I was at home with him and that Lio went out on her own.'

'Don't you think he said it to protect you?' said Jude.

'I'm nearly fourteen Jude. I should've been told. My father is a liar. I wonder now, what else he has lied about. How can I trust him ever again?'

'You'll have to talk to him about it when we get back,' said Imogen.

'I don't feel like *ever* talking to him again,' said Leila and then she turned on Jude. 'Why didn't *you* tell me?'

Jude looked upset.

'It's a big thing Leila,' he said slowly. 'I haven't known you well enough for long enough. I only recently realised that you did not know and my mother said I was not to tell you. She said it was your father's job.'

'Well, I knew nothing,' said Imogen. 'It's all very strange. Keeping it secret has made things worse. I wonder if my mother knows?' She pondered this and decided she must know. 'Do you still suspect foul play in your mother's death?'

'I don't know,' said Leila, 'I can't think straight.'

'It means you are the only witness,' said Imogen. 'How strange

124

– you have been questioning people trying to find something out, yet you are the one who was there, you are the one who knows. It's just that you can't remember.'

'It's all in there somewhere,' Jude tapped her head with his index finger in an attempt to be humorous. 'We just need a spade to dig it out.'

'Or we should leave it alone,' said Imogen.

'Hypnosis would do it,' said Jude, ignoring Imogen's disapproval.

'I've heard that hypnosis can make people remember things that never happened,' said Imogen.

'Only five percent of our mind is conscious,' Jude continued regardless. 'Ninety five percent is the unconscious.'

'I'm going to visit my mother's grave,' said Leila.

Imogen glanced at her watch. 'We've got half an hour still, do you want me to look for more? There'll be more coverage on the case in the locals I should think.'

'Another time,' Leila mumbled and began to walk away.

She had not seen the grave since before Christmas. There were some fresh daffodils, she did not know who from, sitting in the small urn, and all around patches of sad looking grass were poking through the snow. Lio had once said to Tom that she wanted to be buried on the moor, but that had not been possible. The Llan churchyard had a view of the moor, a rather distant view, with the ruin of Gwylfa Hiraethog looking darker and more conspicuous than usual in the snow.

> *Lio Hughes, young wife of Tom Hughes*
> *and devoted mother of Leila Hughes.*
> *Sadly taken from us on 17th August 1978*
> *at the age of 29.*

Leila had always thought there was something missing from the gravestone. Now she saw what it was, at least part of it. It did not say 'beloved' or 'dearly loved' wife, just 'young wife.'

And it sounded unfinished, as if there should be more, as if there should be a third line like: '*She will be greatly missed but never forgotten.*' The words were almost as cold as the lichen-covered stone they were carved into. It sounded as if her father had not loved her mother at the time of her death. But could she blame him? Surely her father was responsible for nothing more than this. Surely he would have been more likely to kill Geraint than Lio.

If I saw it, I might know. She was thinking of the dark reservoir of the unconscious and looking at Jude as if he might one day have the key to unlock it.

'I don't think there's much of my mother here,' she said aloud, 'This is where her body lies, but her spirit is up on the moor. It's too shady and damp here, she didn't even want to be put here. She would have wanted to go to sleep in the sweet heather.'

'The soil on the higher parts of the moor is mostly too shallow for burial,' said Jude. 'Of course she could have been cremated, that would have allowed her ashes to be scattered on the moor.'

'Or you could have buried her in a bog. They're deep,' said Imogen.

'We had better go and meet Lisa,' said Leila, shivering. 'It's almost time.'

Before they parted company, Leila told them of her plan to visit the cliffs.

'I'll come with you,' said Jude. 'You can't go alone.'

Leila wanted nothing more. She wanted Jude all the time now. There was a light that seemed to follow Jude like a halo attached to his hair. He was shining bright and she was light-headed in his presence. Nervous, joyous and scattered. It was a bit like falling apart every time she saw him.

'Goodbye,' said Jude and Leila swallowed hard, feeling pulled but standing still.

'What a week it has been,' said Imogen as they watched the figure of Jude walking away. 'First Mr Parry and now this. You shouldn't go up there you know, it's dangerous.'

Leila was looking at Jude's fair head, he seemed to be walking a little self-consciously under his halo, as if he knew he was being watched.

'I must go up to Afon Ddu, because then I might remember,' said Leila, as Lisa appeared, puffing slightly and laden with shopping.

Leila's father did not sense any change in her as she had hoped. She had long known that they were separate entities, this she had learnt in infancy around the time when on waving her arm in her cot she had realised she had control of her arm but nothing much else. When she waved, the cot did not move, the walls did not wave back, the ceiling stayed where it was, the world did not wave along. Yet at the age of thirteen, she sometimes found the separateness of her only parent too much. There was little she could do to gain his attention; there was no way to give him a hint or a clue as to her suffering. Only a head-on confrontation would do, but Leila was tired, too tired to confront anything. Instead she went to bed early, watched suspiciously by Ann as she went over to say 'Goodnight' to her father.

'Yeah... night,' he said, glancing quickly, somewhere towards her left shoulder, his eyes never meeting hers. He clearly could not feel the gravity of her stare. She had no power, her father did not quake in his boots at what she thought was her coldest glare. But she was tired, deathly tired, so she said nothing and went.

Tom watched the back of Leila as she left the room, sorry that he had not been warmer with her. He was looking through the property section of the local paper, comparing prices. Hafod was now under-priced but there was still no interest. The cursed place would probably not let him leave. Someone had cancelled a viewing after the dead farmer story had hit the papers. It was understandable, Hafod being the last house on the road up to the moor was too isolated for most people. One of the highest houses in Wales. He walked to the window and looked out at the view that Lio had fallen in love with. He tried to trace the path Mr Parry had taken and wondered what that would be like. Too drunk to care or know what you were doing. These thoughts of escape were coming more often. The view was a sour sweet alliance of tranquil and deadly. It stirred him with a pleasing melancholy. Why was he feeling tears pricking his eyes? Numbing snow, blue in the moonlight slowly withdrawing from the moor. A faint blueness, like the tinge in a cold, dead body. It was not like him to notice the view much anymore. He just wanted to leave this place, but he took a seat by the window and leaned across the deep sill, just looking. What a place. How dark and hypnotic; the only thing that stayed the same was its eternally everchanging nature. Changing with the light, or the dark, with the seasons, even with moods. He fancied now that it was dead for him. That was why he noticed it now, when it was still and blue and cold. He would bury it and save his daughter. But even as he looked, a sudden breeze whistled around the eaves and blew a brief, pan pipe sound through the hilltop ruin, rattling the For Sale sign as if in mockery before it died and all was serene once more. He sighed and turned away. The fire was all ash and Ann had gone to bed feeling unwell. His college papers were scattered hatefully on the coffee table and there was an expectant air about the furniture, huddled around, waiting for the verdict.

He could not tell Leila what she wanted to know. She was becoming hostile and there was that look of sedition in her eye. She was up to something and there wasn't much he could do to stop her. Ann had asked Imogen to keep an eye on her, but Tom knew that Imogen would heed Leila first. He would speak to Arabella again, maybe she could help, though he hated having to ask her. What did Leila want? The whole truth? She would not quit until she was there, but he was going to try and prevent her from getting to such a terrible place. He stopped himself halfway to the kitchen, his eyes on the cupboard where the Scotch was and with an effort turned around and gathered up his college papers instead.

It was a hot day on the moor. The skylarks were rising with the heat and a golden plover's plaintive piping ascended from the marshes. Lio was walking too fast and Leila couldn't keep up. Her eyes moved from the stony ground she was stumbling over to the back of her mother's legs, marching purposefully ahead. Lio had forgotten to tie Leila's sunhat on and Leila could now feel it falling forwards. It was hot and there was dust on her knees from the numerous falls she had already had. The climb was steep and Leila didn't want to go up but every time she tried to speak bubbles came out of her mouth instead of words. Something was wrong. Lio was clumsy and had fallen twice herself. Leila watched her boots scuffing and stubbing against the rocks on a path she should have known well by now. On a walk Leila was sick of.

'Be a good girl for Mummy, Leila,' said Lio. Her voice was distant because she was pulling ahead and didn't look back as she normally did.

Now Leila knew all was not well with her mother because she could hear her crying at intervals, though she was trying to suppress it. She was sniffing a lot too, and Leila knew that her mother and father had just been fighting, but though she recognised the path, she did not know where they were going.

'Where are we going Mummy?' she asked, more than a few times, but all Lio said was, 'Just for a walk'. She sniffed as she spoke and then raised her voice, forcing it to be cheerful. 'Isn't it a beautiful day darling? The sun's out and the birds are singing and the air is so hot. We're going to have a lovely time…'

Leila stooped to pick a sprig of one of the pretty heathers that grew by the path. Lio had slowed down a little so Leila offered the heather because she knew her mother liked heather but an angry, hot gust of wind blew it away and Lio didn't see the gesture. Now there was someone else with them – he had just appeared on the path ahead of Lio. It was Mr Parry. There was a short exchange of words, Lio sounded agitated, like she had for most of the day so far. Leila tried to catch up with her and caught sight of her face for a moment as her mother turned to look behind. But she was not looking at Leila, she was looking over her shoulder. There was a grim set to her mother's jaw and then she was walking hard again, leaving Mr Parry behind. They had been heading over the moor, but now Lio turned towards Afon Ddu, tripping roughly over whatever stones lay in the way. It was so hot and windy.

As Leila fell further behind, she watched her mother's walking figure intently. By keeping her eyes on her she would not lose her. Lio could not disappear. But it got harder as they began the steep ascent to the cliffs and finally Leila lost Lio, though she kept walking onwards to the spot she had fixed ahead. The place where she had last seen her.

When Leila reached the top, at first she thought she was alone. There was a constant wind at this height and the bubbling cries of a curlew lifted from the heather, whose fragrance was made exotic with the heat. Leila spun around twice, because in spite of her fear she was intoxicated by the high point. Then she heard her mother's voice.

'She's here,' Lio said and she appeared in front of Leila with a smile.

'Let me take a photo of you both,' said a man's voice, 'stand back against the cliff.'

Leila looked at the man. The sun was in her eyes but she could see that he was hidden behind a hat, a pair of sunglasses and a camera. There was something familiar about him. Her mother turned her back on the cliff edge and the man said 'Cheesy smile please,' to both of them. Leila did not smile. The sun glanced brightly off the camera lense and a slight breeze blew a little of her hair over her eyes. The hair looked bright in the sun. It turned into magnified brown and red strands before her eyes like a beaded curtain. She looked through the beaded curtain, which she felt hid her from the man and refused to smile at his big black plastic eyes, though he continued to try and encourage her to smile. She blinked at the sun and then it was over, she was on her own again. She stood there for a while watching a small confused moth flitting around the brambles at the edge of the cliffs. Then suddenly she heard a scuffle behind her. She tried to turn around to look but found that she was paralysed. It was terrifying. There was terrible danger nearby, something awful was happening but she could not move or speak. She tried to scream 'Help me!' but only a strangled breath came out. And then a long scream came from behind though at first she thought it was her own. It was a bit like the screaming of the peacocks on Pistyll farm. It faded quickly, as if whoever had screamed had gone away quickly. Leila knew that it was her mother.

'Mummy,' she said, over and over, but there was no one. Even the man with the black plastic eyes had gone. There was nothing but Leila standing frozen near the edge of the cliffs. The grass all around her rustling and flattening in the hot wind and from not far off, near the ruin perhaps, the melancholic cries of a lone buzzard.

Then she felt sadness, a terrible, deep sadness that sent her reeling towards the cliff edge herself. She knew beyond all doubt that she was all alone and that her mother was dead.

'Mummy. Where are you?'

As she approached the edge she noticed, through vision blurred by tears, something white fluttering vigorously in the breeze. She rubbed her eyes and stopped. It was her white sunhat, the one she had been wearing earlier, and for a moment this sight distracted her. She had not noticed it fall off but here it was fluttering happily in the breeze like a sail at sea.

The cliff edge was close now. If she could get there and look over she would see. The cliff suddenly seemed higher, as if it had risen faster than an elevator into the sky, higher, higher. She was bilious with vertigo, the wind was pushing her or was it fingers and hands? She fell to her hands and knees, almost sick, head spinning, eyes blurring and crawled to the edge. Pulling up tufts of grass as she gripped, claw-like, she pulled herself to the edge and looked over. The tough clumps of grass near the edge made good hand holds, but still her whole body swayed and the ground seemed to fall away beneath her. As if the elevator was going down now, really fast. To her left, the hat fluttered cheerily and in front of her a skylark launched from a perch on the cliff somewhere below and flew up, pirouetting and singing sweetly. And then she saw Lio below. Far away, she lay like a doll, looking skyward, not moving, not doing anything. Her dark hair spread out as if someone had arranged it, one leg twisted upwards, her arms out flying, like a star that had fallen from the sky. And not

131

a mark on her. Nothing except a crimson stain on the long grass which was bowing around her, a royal pillow of reddened grass around her head and rays of sunlight glancing off her. Lifting her flittering, jittering soul from her while it struggled and flipped as bright silver fish do. And it rose as Lio was lowered, flew upwards like a climbing, singing silver skylark, brushed against Leila as it went, went through her like a dart, bringing alive something inside her, something that jumped and flipped too as if it wanted to follow that silvery thing that was too quick to catch. And far below she found that her mother had disappeared, so Leila whimpered, backed away and stopped. There was nowhere else to go.

So that was how it had happened. Almost ten years later, Leila woke quietly in the night, very afraid, half expecting to see grass stains on her hands. Someone else had been there; someone had pushed her mother from the cliffs. If she could find the man behind the black plastic eyes, then perhaps she would find her mother's killer. And even as she thought of it, she sat bolt upright, because in her dream, his identity had been revealed. And now she was more confused than ever. He had not been the same person for the whole time. He was in fact both her father, Tom Hughes, and at the same time, Lio's lover Geraint Noon.

ELEVEN

Leila had been to see the grave of Mr Parry. As she stood looking at the small but new headstone, somewhere down-slope of her mother in a cheaper plot, she began her first real comprehension of the finality of physical death. Her mother's death had been so long ago, too long to really understand. Now she knew that someone she had seen walking on the earth was gone. She wouldn't see him walk again.

The snow lingered on the moors long after it had disappeared from the coastal plains and the green hills and valleys below Hiraethog. From school in Llan, Leila would look up at the snowbound moors, distant against the green of the nearer hills and somehow as faraway as the mountainous cumulus that folded and billowed over them. Whenever she thought of Mr Parry's death, she sensed a secret cove of grief and guilt within. Jude, less helpful than usual, spoke of how suicide might arise from that final push that all the world's burdens and cares could not achieve. Just a few badly chosen words from a friend or acquaintance, as if they had ever so gently poked a finger in the back of one on the brink.

'Do you think that I am in any way responsible?' asked Leila.

'No, don't be silly,' said Jude. 'You hardly knew him. No one really knew him, and I expect he knew himself even less.'

'How are they saying he died?'

'Accidentally. He was letting go of life bit by bit,' Jude said, though his voice carried a hint of patience coming to an end.

'You seem to be taking on too much responsibility for things,' he added, sighing heavily.

'I just wish I had been nicer to him,' said Leila.

Jude smiled weakly and tried again.

'Mr P's last days were a slow suicide, whether he was conscious of it or not. He was living in a drunken haze and then I think something must have snapped in him and he went off up onto the moor in the snow. There was no other reason for him to be out there.'

'But I'm sure he told us he was looking for sheep,' insisted Leila.

'He did, but they accounted for all of them at his farm. He was taking his last walk, but of course he would not admit that to us, and he might not even have been sure of it himself at the time.'

'So he died from a mixture of his fall and from freezing?'

'Yes and I don't expect he knew much about it. His body was carrying enough drink to kill you or me outright. And mother said the cold makes you sleep before you die.'

'I don't think he really caused my mother's death after all,' said Leila. 'It wasn't him who pushed her.'

Jude nodded.

'What if I was the last straw for him?' said Leila. 'What if I killed him?'

Jude shook his head and tried not to laugh. 'He had advanced cancer and hadn't been given long. It would have been that which killed him more than anything. Don't keep blaming yourself for things that were always beyond your reach.'

It was cold but sunny in Llan, and the roads were dry. They had met after school in the street outside the library and now Leila was crying and Jude for the first time was holding her. From the greengrocer's further down the street Arabella was shopping with her basket and when she saw Jude hugging Leila, she tripped on the curb and fell to her knees.

Whenever Leila looked at her father, she saw a man who kept secrets and thought he could get away with it, a man who could not look at or talk to his own daughter and a man who might have pushed his wife off Afon Ddu. She had seen his rage when he had hit Geraint with the van. Perhaps that was not the first time his rage had hurt someone. Her pity for his suffering over her mother's affair had long since departed. While he carried on as normal, she waited for him to approach her and speak to her. She gave him angry looks, made hostile remarks, even hinted that she knew something, but he failed to notice. So in the end she told him that she knew.

'Dad, I'm angry with you because I have been waiting for you to tell me the truth and I think I'll have to wait forever if I don't force you.'

'What *do* you mean?' he asked, his hands submerged in the washing up bowl.

Leila glared at his back and the side of his face as he half turned. She avoided his eyes though; it was easier to mount her attack from behind.

'I know that you lied to me. I know that I was there when my mother died.' Her voice shook as she spoke, too much rage rushing upwards to her head all at once. Tears threatening.

'What?' Tom scowled as he spoke, as if he was irritated, as if she was talking nonsense and he was barely tolerating this.

'I also know that you found my mother. You and Arabella.'

'And how do you know, Leila?'

Her eyes opened a little wider as he turned aggressively, dripping suds onto the floor. There was a flash of anger in his eyes that was reminiscent of the incident with Geraint. She was momentarily disarmed. Was this the rage of a killer?

'Who have you been talking to, Leila?' the repetition of her name probably meant that he was furious. There was certainly a transformation in him. His stance was gorilla-like. She found herself taking a step backwards.

'No one,' she muttered, dropping her shoulders. Her own anger diffused by his. 'But I had a dream and I *know* it's true. I just know in my bones.'

'Dreams,' he laughed then with a slight sneer, 'mean nothing.'

Leila looked at him a little quizzically. She felt that sometimes she did not recognise him; there was a man she didn't know under the calm, canoe-shod father figure. Still she could sense that he was becoming less dangerous because he was relieved that it was a dream and not a person that had told her. Now it was her turn to be angry again.

'I checked on the microfilm in the library.'

His face fell.

'So I know it is true.'

'How did you think of that?' he asked quietly, looking down at his canoes. 'Are you sure you weren't listening at doors, Leila?'

He was right of course.

'We used it at school in history.' She was disconcerted, but still lied easily.

There was silence and his face seemed to fall further. Then he looked at her with tired eyes, but at least he was looking at her. That was something.

Finally he said, 'I'm sorry.' Then without a word he took the van keys and walked out of the house, leaving her alone.

She watched from the window as he drove the van out of the yard and vanished down the lane. The tight feeling was growing in her throat again, as if someone was strangling her. Why was it happening more and more? She lifted her hand to touch her throat, half expecting to find another hand already there; a thin white hand, choking her. Yet there was nothing. She could find no obvious, physical problem, but while her throat remained in this terrifying, constricted state she felt paralysed by it. So she stood at the window, hardly breathing, except for irregular, shallow controlled breaths which she took while she clutched at the invisible force that held her by the her throat. It was then, while she was incapacitated and just after her father's van had disappeared, that she heard the noise from the kitchen at the back of the house. Just something falling. A plate on the draining board perhaps not stacked very well. She stayed very still and listened intently. She knew that her father had been chopping wood outside the back door that morning and it was possible that he had left it unlocked before his unexpected departure.

Something told Leila that there was someone outside. Fear seemed to make the feeling of being choked worse and with the rising thunder of her frightened heart, a feeling of nausea fountained upwards. She listened, not daring to breathe, still clutching her throat; she listened intently for a sound to prove her suspicion. It was hard to move; she felt rooted by fear. If she did move, what would she do anyway? It occurred to her that she should check the back door was locked, but the thought of going into the kitchen if her enemy was already there took away her will to move. She was still standing at the window where she had watched her father go, listening as hard as she could, when she heard something moving. Imperceptible at first, so much on the edge of hearing that she could not be sure she had even heard it at all, but then immediately after there was a definite sound.

In the high winds of winter some tiles had been removed from Hafod's roof and they still lay broken on the concrete path that ran around the perimeter of the house. What Leila heard was someone stepping on the broken tiles; someone who was trying to walk very quietly. As she stood transfixed, the footsteps drew closer to her window.

Leila moved stiffly aside from the window towards the curtains in order to conceal herself, and not a moment too soon because as she moved, the intruder was at her window. She drew back against the wall, clutching the end of the curtain, holding her breath, just about hidden from view. Someone was looking in through the window. She could see their shadow on the floor, quite still, and waiting. A man's shadow. For a long time, Leila remained frozen against the wall, barely allowing herself to breathe. Then at last the intruder moved on, taking his shadow with him and she took a deep breath. Immediately she stepped towards the window and she saw that the intruder had paused as if listening and before she ducked back against the wall, she saw the back of him and his pale, blonde hair. Blonde hair like Geraint's. Or Jude's. She stopped breathing while she contemplated this. Surely Jude would have knocked on the door? Yet what would Geraint be doing out there? It was then that Leila ran to the kitchen.

Just before she opened the door to the kitchen, she felt a cold draught on her legs and the door handle rattled in her grip. She turned it and as it opened felt the full force of a strong cold breeze lift the door out of her grip and slam it back against the wall. The back door was wide open, she could see the remaining patches of snow outside and a strong wind was thrusting loose papers from the morning post around the kitchen. It took Leila a long, alarming moment to assure herself, in the midst of the rattling of flying papers and the sound of the wind blowing noisily through the door, and the banging of that door against a kitchen unit, that she was indeed alone. As she stood there trying to work out what had happened, she felt a sudden fearful urge to get out of the house and instead of locking the door she ran right out of it and with just a quick glance around, took herself up the slope behind Hafod.

She did not stop running until she was well clear of the house. She had often thought of what she might do in such a situation as this and almost always it seemed to be to run away, to run away outside (if she was alone). Her fear of being stuck indoors was greater.

She went to the viewpoint near the babbling spring. From there she could look down on Hafod without much chance of being seen herself. With the spring running cheerily below, she sat on her knees in the heather, shivering from the chill edge that still lingered on the moor. There was nothing to see. She could see the open back door, but no sign of the intruder. She supposed it was possible that her father had left the door open, or that the door had blown open. But who had been there without knocking?

Then she set off for Jude's. It had crossed her mind that the strange visitation could have been him and she knew that part of the reason she now headed to see him was to make sure it was not.

That and the fact that she was as in love as a thirteen-year-old can be, brimful with a heady mix of infatuation and devotion. Jude was constantly on her mind. In a short time he had become the most important person in her life, her best friend. His face was etched into her unconscious, whenever it surfaced she saw it clearly. Yet in spite of this, there was deep within her a barely acknowledged fear of Jude. Perhaps it was his jokes about murder, the time when he had said he would kill someone one day, or perhaps it was his impish smile and the fiendish laugh that accompanied it. There was a shadowiness to Jude that was part of his attraction; the sober, sensible Jude, the boy who seemed wise beyond his years was unbalanced by this occasional darker side. Was it a conscious performance to make him more alluring? Was he only joking when he asked her to race him through one of the larger bogs on the moor (knowing that she would refuse?) and when he suggested they could break into his Uncle Geraint's house to look for evidence, did he really mean it? Or had he sensed Leila's terror of that revolting beige bungalow in Clocaenog? She would ask him when she reached his house. Perhaps she would call his bluff. She could pretend she wanted to do the break-in. But what if he wasn't joking? Would she actually go along with it to save face? She had to find out what Jude was up to and so she walked to his house. She needed to know if he had been the intruder and if so, why.

Before she disappeared over the hill she looked back at Hafod. Would her father return? Where had he gone? If she had not brought up her newly-acquired knowledge, she would not be here now, running away, alone. Then there was the intruder. If it had been Geraint, it was alarming to think he had got so close to her while she was alone with the door not even locked. And just what did he want? Had he been after her? If he had known she was there alone would he have come for her? This brought a lump of fear to her throat. And why was Imogen so long out shopping with her mother? Not for the first time, Leila imagined them all in some elaborate conspiracy against her.

She reached Jude's home and stopped for a while, looking

down on it from the top of the slope that skirted around it. She was greeted by the rough smell of wood-smoke drifting from the chimney and the sight of orange lamps in the window, turned on to light the dusk that advanced more quickly in Clocaenog than anywhere else. She sat down, though it was cold, and hugged her legs against her. Behind the house was the forest, the dark gloom of Clocaenog. Jude's house was like the last beacon of warmth fighting against the shadow, and at this moment she would have happily forsaken everything for the warm glow shining from its windows. She could see Celyn wiping the table and outside Jude's bike against the wall next to a pile of neatly chopped wood and the hens his mother kept, pecking and scratching outside the hen house. She could not see Jude, but she was now sure that he was there in the house. She stood up and began to descend the slope, avoiding as best she could the last of the snow. Perhaps what she was doing now made no sense, yet she brushed her doubts aside and continued, shivering all over and gingerly stepping on her cold wet feet. She had to know if she still had Jude.

Leila was half way down the slope when the front door of the house was flung open and Jude ran out, but before she could speak, she realised someone was attached to him. A girl followed, holding Jude's hand and laughing. She was an older girl, about Jude's age. Leila did not know her, but suddenly she became fearful of being seen and she froze where she was, shrinking back against the long dead grass on the slope as best as she could. The girl kissed Jude's cheek and he smiled at her before they proceeded together, holding hands, in the direction of Clocaenog. It looked as if they were going for a walk.

It was as if Leila had been shot. She sank to the ground without uttering a sound. Numb, unable to follow a single coherent line of thought. There was only one thought, that she had been betrayed again. Jude was also lying to her. Had their friendship been nothing more than a trick? Had Geraint put Jude up to it? There was no one left then. Shaking, she climbed back up the slope as quickly as she could and with the dreadful realisation that there was nowhere else for her to go. She felt that the bottom had finally fallen out of her childhood.

Reluctantly she turned her steps back towards Hafod, but walked slowly, weighed down by a feeling of dread. Jude did not like her or care for her in the way she had hardly dared hope, her father had walked out on her, perhaps never to return and the stepmother was purposefully separating her from Imogen and poisoning Imogen with words like 'necrolatry.' And there was Geraint, who appeared to have been lurking about outside. It had to be him. What did he want? To kill her? With Jude's help? Well he was welcome to it.

She had begun to whimper self pityingly when she slipped and fell with a breathtaking thud. Crying all the more now, she pulled herself up and floundered hopelessly in a small, snow-filled dip, missing the easier path in her grief. She had no one, but she knew at the back of her mind that there was another option; she had not thought of everyone. There was still her mother. There was still the possibility that someone had loved her once. She paused to ponder this and then changed her direction away from Hafod. She was going to see her mother, on her own, for the first time. She was going to see her. She was going to ask her mother what to do now. She walked quickly, forgetting how cold she was, feeling the breeze brushing her hair and the mist kissing her cheek with its damp vapour. The brown hills were reappearing through the snow, welcoming, reassuring and loving her. Like a mother.

She was hungry and tired, and her feet were frozen when she finally reached the top of Afon Ddu. It was not like it had been on that August 17th, almost ten years before. Nor was it the way it had been on every August 17th since, when she had come bearing flowers with her father. Now the dusk was falling, and the snow still clung on to the cliffs, though her footprints revealed dead grass beneath. It was like the dead of winter. April was barren with an empty womb and a sky like a morgue. And it felt different being there without her father; she could be herself and savour it, without being dragged away in the middle of a prayer.

'Mum.'

The name fell flat. She was not used to it. Once she had called

Lio Mummy – a long time ago. Then after she died, for many years she had referred to her as Mum, probably because that was what the kids at school called their mothers. She didn't quite remember when she had begun to think only of her as Mother. Perhaps it was because Lio had become more distant with time. She knew she had forgotten things over the years. It seemed that she only had two clear memories now. Both of her walking in Clocaenog with her mother, holding hands with that vague shadowy figure at her side. She seemed to remember a kind voice talking about different kinds of trees in the forest and the red squirrels that thrived there. But that was all. She could not remember how her mother's living face had looked or exactly how her voice had sounded. She thought she could remember a red coat and the lipstick that matched it. If she pressed herself to remember, all she got was a shadowy outline of the woman who had given birth to her. She had the photos but not the memories to go with them. How could her brain do that to her? How could she not remember?

'Mother.'

She reached out for her mother's hands, for cold, white hands in the mist and clutched handfuls of nothing, of water and vapour. Her eyes were closed, the mist was crying on her face mixing with her own salty droplets.

'Can I come with you?' she asked.

She began to walk slowly towards the cliff edge, with her eyes closed and her hands reaching out into the airy space all around her. Her crying was liberating her throat from its strangling tightness, her tears warm and splendid in the mist, washing her away. She had been drawn to walk to the edge and over it, wondering how it would feel. But when it came to it, she was too afraid to walk all the way, the sensation of falling so familiar from dreams was a terrifying prospect in real life. She was not brave enough and there was no one behind waiting to push her. Or was there? She turned around with a sudden, prickling fear, a lurch to the stomach telling her she still wanted to live. There was nothing there but the mist shrouding out the scenery. The realisation that she could not do it, did not want to do it, brought despair and a drowning of tears.

Why was it so hard to live? For a short while she was paralysed by a hot face and streams of smothering warmth running from her eyes and nose, yet also released. To walk off the cliff would be the ultimate act of hostility. That was almost reason enough to do it. Yet if they did not care for her, then it would not hurt them. And if she did it to join her mother, how could she know that her mother would be there on the other side, waiting for her?

She took a deep breath of the cold, cold air over Afon Ddu, filling her lungs. She was glad to be out there, feeling the spinning height and the chilling mist. The dense whiteout removed all of the panoramic view and replaced it with an eerie whiteness compounded by the pale reflection of the snow from the ground.

'I'm like a ghost,' she thought. 'Hidden from everyone.'

She kneeled next to the small memorial stone that marked the place where her mother had left the cliff. It was covered by lichens and cold to the touch. Then she walked carefully to the edge. Her father had never let her do this, and with a strong sense that she had indeed done this before, she looked over.

Lio was not lying there.

She had half expected to see her again, like the night she had looked for Mr Parry. The mist just allowed her a swirling view of the spot where Lio had lain in her last moments and she wondered if her mother had died immediately. Or had she looked up and been able to see her daughter with the last of her fading vision. What was it like to die? Here on Afon Ddu, Leila felt that it might be peaceful, like Jude and Imogen had said it could be. If fairy tales were real, she thought there should be a beautiful flower growing where her mother had died. A fairytale rose bush perhaps, nourished by her mother's spilled blood and brain.

'Love you.'

Leila felt her soul flip. She looked all around. She was alone, yet the words, quietly spoken, a playful whisper almost, had not been from her own thoughts. She felt the silver past shining within her, but did not know what to do with it, to keep it alive. Someone had spoken; those words had not been in her head; she had been thinking only of blood-nourished rose bushes. The words had instead brought back a lost memory from her subconscious; the memory of how her mother had daily said 'Love you,' and only occasionally said, '*I* love you.'

She spun around, thanking the voice, suddenly elated, suddenly glad to be alive. The soul fish was flipping.

'Was that you talking to me, Mother?'

But no answer came and after a while all she heard was the possible answers, the ones inside her own head, making a commotion, clamouring to be heard. Perhaps she had imagined her mother's voice too. She stood listening quietly but there was nothing more, just a feeling of peace. So she stayed for a while, knowing that she would return to Hafod and that someone would be there by now. She would face whatever was lying in wait for her and then stop dwelling too heavily on the past. Before it became too dark she began the descent down the steep path and the walk back towards Hafod.

It was dark by the time Hafod came into view, but it was easy enough to see her way with the luminosity still provided by the snow. Hafod's lights were on, shining out onto the snow and she felt hugely relieved. The car and the van were both back in the front yard and she was glad to see that everyone had returned. It occurred to her only now that they would be wondering what had happened to her. As she drew closer she could see Imogen sitting on the window seat. Imogen, who she had hardly seen lately, who she had neglected in favour of Jude. She began to run through the dark, towards Hafod and the peaceful image of Imogen.

Inside the warmth and indoor smells hit her like a wall after her long afternoon outside. All at once she could smell the curry they had eaten for tea, Ann's perfume, Imogen's bubble bath and the slightly smoking fire.

'Hello' she cried, 'you're all back! Where did you go?'

'I need to talk to you Leila,' said her father.

'I can explain everything,' she said quickly, 'there was someone outside and then I found the back door open...'

'Yes,' he said, without really listening. 'I mean I need to talk to you about earlier and I need to apologise for walking out the way I did.'

'But Dad, didn't you notice anything wrong when you arrived home?'

He frowned. 'Well, you left the back door unlocked. Why what should have been wrong?'

'Wasn't the back door wide open?'

'No. Did you leave it wide open?'

'Oh, the wind must have blown it shut.'

'Look, sit yourself down. It's about your mother's accident. I am ready to tell you now.'

Leila gave in and sat down. She was tired and it seemed a long time since she had seen the intruder outside – it was almost as if it had never happened.

'I've been thinking about what you have discovered all day,' said Tom. 'I realise I made a big mistake in thinking you would never find out. To be honest, I originally meant to tell you when you were eight years old. I thought that was a good age, but for some reason I never did, I kept on putting it off just like I did with the Geraint business and now it has all come out in the worst way possible. So I would like to say that I'm sorry for not talking to you before now and sorry for walking out earlier. I'm afraid that I haven't been much of a father.'

As soon as her father took the time to talk to her, Leila felt all of her anger and hate for him slip away. If only it could always be like this. But even as he began to tell her she was afraid that after this, he would go back to being as distant as before.

'We argued,' he said. 'I didn't want you to know because you seemed to have such an idyllic view of our family life, short though it was. I didn't want to spoil that, but now, since you have found out about the affair and you know that you were with your mother when you died, you know everything.' He paused there, in order to remember his seemingly rehearsed speech.

'Lio and I were going through a difficult patch. I found out about the affair and I was very shocked and upset, although perhaps I had it coming. I had become so distant towards her without even realising.'

'You still are distant and you still don't realise it,' thought Leila, but she just nodded to show him that she was listening.

'I made things difficult for Lio. I demanded that she stopped seeing him and for a while she consented, but then she told me that we could not go on the way we were. I had to cut my hours on my job or she would leave me, but I told her that I couldn't cut my hours just like that and that I suspected she might still leave me. It was all a bit of a mess, I wanted to discuss it like a mature adult, but seemed to keep losing my grip.'

He stopped talking and readjusted his position on his chair, as if this talking was making him uncomfortable.

'We argued that day. The funny thing is, I don't even remember what about. It was one of those arguments which started off being about something, but it went off at a tangent and ended up being about everything... and nothing.'

Leila noticed for the first time that her father's eyebrows were tinged by grey. She felt that he was still holding something back. He spoke as if there was a burden that must somehow be juggled around the truth.

'She was upset and the row had woken you up. She went upstairs to get you. That gave me some time to cool down. By the time Lio came down and put your coat on, I felt ready to talk like a civilised adult. She was on her way out with you when I approached her with the intention of talking. She said she didn't want to in front of you, and that it would probably only end in another row anyway. I asked her where she was going, she said she didn't have to tell me everything. She asked me why I was suddenly so interested anyway. I became angry, I shouted at her, I said that she was going to see him. Then I got hold of you and said she wasn't taking you to him. I suspected her of planning to run away and threatened to fight for custody of you. I really lost it. Then you began to cry and Lio said, quite calmly, that if I cared at all for you I would stop upsetting you and let go. So I did.'

Leila's mind wandered even as she listened intently. She noticed the way her father sat with his long, thin legs crossed in his black cords and how he periodically uncrossed them before re-crossing them the other way round. Apparently random movements needed by the subconscious in its work of repression. His feet were too big; his brown slippers looked ready to set sail.

'I watched her walk out with you,' he continued, 'I noticed she had no luggage; that at least was something. I ran upstairs and checked her things; no packing had been done. Of course I was being irrational. Lio was not the kind of person to have left without a word. I watched you both growing smaller from the window. I had calmed down again, but the thought of her going to Geraint was more than I could bear. So I followed you both. Lio had adjusted your route towards Afon Du, which meant that if she was going to Geraint's, she was taking the longer route. It gave me hope that she was not going there after all, but I suppose we will never know now will we?'

He looked at Leila a little strangely; a look she could not fathom.

'But where did Arabella come into it? You haven't mentioned her. She was there too.'

'Ah... yes,' he said and a redness rose in his cheeks. Was he blushing? She had never seen her father blush so she did not know.

'Arabella was just coming up to pay a friendly visit as I was going out. She saw I was worried and said she would join the search, even though I did not really want her there.'

He glossed over Arabella as quickly as possible and Leila suspected there was more to her part in the day than he was willing to discuss.

'Did you see Mother fall? And where was I when she fell?' she asked, unable to wait any longer for the crucial bit.

His shoulders sank and he looked away for a moment as if he needed to remember, yet how could he not remember?

'No. I didn't see her fall.'

'Did you hear her scream as she fell?'

'No. What makes you think she did scream?'

'I think I remember,' said Leila, 'I dreamed it.'

'Then it was a dream and nothing more. You can't possibly

147

remember, but you want to, so your mind creates things. Now listen to me and I will tell you what *really* happened.'

Leila visibly shrank back into her seat, silenced by the sudden stern note in his voice.

'Arabella and I followed your mother up onto Afon Ddu. We saw her ahead of us, but she was too far ahead to hear me calling, or else she was ignoring me. We couldn't catch up, but I became concerned as she went up onto the cliffs. I never liked her going up there and that day I had a bad feeling about it.'

'Did you see anyone else? Mr Parry or anyone?' Leila could not help but interrupt.

'Well...' her father paused, annoyed at being thrown off the track again, 'as a matter of fact, Mr Parry was on the moor that day with his dog. Your mother passed him on her way. But as I was saying, I became concerned and began to run after her. I wanted to sort everything out with her.'

He stopped and grasped for what he wanted to say next. It was not coming out as smoothly as he might have hoped; he was trying to avoid some little snag.

'Did Mr Parry say anything to my mother?' she prompted him.

'I suppose they must have exchanged a few words. You know the kind of thing, small talk about the weather.'

'Was he following her?'

'No. She had turned towards Afon Ddu and he had gone off over Hiraethog.'

'Did you see anyone else?'

'No, there was no one else,' her father's irritation was increasing. He had wanted to tell the story he had spent hours rehearsing and now she was interrupting and messing it all up.

'I ran all the way up to the cliffs,' he said. 'Arabella got a bit left behind. I was hoping to catch up with Lio down the other side, but when I got to the top I saw you. You were near the edge; you were alone.'

'Was I crying?'

'Yes, you were,' he said. 'I was angry with Lio for leaving

you there, but only for a moment,' his voice faltered, sounding suddenly strangled. 'Then the terrible realisation dawned on me. There was no sign of Lio, and I was sure then that she had gone off the cliffs. I grabbed you first, held you and carried you with me; I remember you held on so tightly your grip hurt. Then I walked to the edge, hoping that what I suspected would not be true, hoping that if it was, that by some miracle she would still be alive.'

His face became a grimace and he looked away. It was a long time since she had seen him cry, though he hid his face. Leila felt her own tears welling up in response to his. She was about to go over and put a hand on his shoulder when he rose from his chair and walked towards the window.

'At first I thought she was still alive,' he said, not looking at Leila, looking at his reflection in the window instead. 'The way she was lying, she could have been just daydreaming, just lying there looking up at the sky like we used to when we first met.'

Leila turned around and kneeled on the armchair, looking over the back at him. 'So she was lying facing upwards?'

'Yes,' he said, his voice coming quietly over from the window so that she had to strain to catch every word. 'Her hair was all spread out as if she had floated down, and her arms were out as if she was stretching. It didn't look like she had fallen, except for her leg.'

'Was it twisted in a funny position?' Leila felt herself tensing.

'Yes, it was broken I expect. She looked like a dancing doll with one funny leg. She didn't look dead at all. She looked peaceful, serene,' he paused. 'She looked beautiful. I was transfixed, looking for a sign of life, but there was none. The longer I looked, the more I realised she was gone. There was a stiffness to her face, her eyes were still and staring and her neck was a little arched; it was broken.'

'How did you know it was broken?' asked Leila.

'I didn't know then, but we found out later. She would have died instantly. That was the one thing I always told you, and that was not to spare your feelings, it was true. It happened so quickly.'

'Was there any bleeding?'

'A little around her head where it probably hit the rocks as she fell. Her head was nestled in the grass. It took me a good half minute to notice the blood.'

He moved away from the window and returned to his chair, his composure regained.

'How did she fall?' asked Leila. 'If you didn't see, how do you know it was an accident?'

His eyes fell away from hers and he said, 'I can't be one hundred percent sure, but there was something which pointed to an accident.'

'What was that?' asked Leila leaning forwards.

'A white hat caught on the brambles just over the edge of the cliff... your hat.'

'I do remember it then; everything you have described is in my memory and the dream I had, everything and more.' Her eyes were shining as she spoke and, across from her, Tom looked strange and frightened.

'There was someone else there,' she continued, 'the person who took the photo of mother and me. He had sunglasses on. Did you not see him?'

'There was no one else there, Leila. Your memory or dream may have some of the details right but there wasn't anyone else up there. I would have seen them going down the other side – the landscape is far too open, you know that.'

'But he might have been hiding,' said Leila.

'There isn't much to hide behind up there...'

'He might have climbed part of the way down the cliff and hidden behind some rocks,' Leila said imagining Geraint walking imp-like backwards down the cliff with his hands and feet gripping the rock like an insect man.

'No, Leila, I was there and my memory of it is clear. Yours is the memory of a four-year-old. There was no one else there. I understand that it is very hard for you to accept that your mother died from a freak accident. You want a murderer because you can't believe that she could be taken from you just like that, through her own carelessness. Maybe deep down you think she couldn't have loved us much if she was careless enough to fall, careless enough to throw her life away like that. But it wasn't murder and it wasn't suicide either, it was a freak accident, there was a gust of wind, she lost her footing.'

Leila swallowed hard against the hard lump in her throat, she was subdued but she could not help but notice the discrepancy.

'Father, if you didn't see, how do you know a gust of wind helped her to fall?'

'I didn't see, and can't be sure,' he said, looking at her levelly for once, 'but I felt it going up there, and I remember hoping you weren't near the edge of the cliffs.'

He sighed. 'Leila, you must come to terms with your mother's terrible, tragic accident. It is so unfair that she was taken from us, but she would have wanted you to go on living and to be as happy as you could. She would not have wanted you to spend your life agonising over her death. You know it all now, I have told you everything.'

Yet even as he said it, Leila saw the man with the black plastic eyes clearly and it seemed to her that there was great significance attached to him. She only knew that she had to cling onto this image. There was still more to know and her father knew more than he was telling.

They sat quietly for a while, both immersed in their own thoughts. While Tom was thinking that he must now pay an unwanted visit to both Arabella and Geraint, Leila was looking at a pattern on the carpet that looked like a twisted dragon. Then Arabella popped into her head and she looked again at her father.

'What about Arabella, she was with you wasn't she?'

He looked at her sideways. 'Yes. She got left behind. I had picked you up and moved you to safety when she reached the top. I told her what had happened and she offered to look after you while I went to call an ambulance. So that is what we did. I ran over to the Sportsman's Arms on the turnpike road. The pub was actually closed, it was being refurbished at the time, but there is a payphone there, as you know. The one thing that has always bothered me, is whether I could have made my way down the cliff and attempted to resuscitate Lio. The ambulance men told me she was killed almost instantly, that nothing could have saved her, yet I sometimes can't help but think I should have tried, and in that sense I am like you. I am unable to accept that there was nothing else I could do, just like you cannot accept it was an accident, that it was no one's fault,' his voice faltered again, and he was overcome.

Leila watched him for a few seconds, and then she said. 'It's all right Dad, I will try now. Thank you for telling me everything.'

She believed him as far as she could. This man would not have pushed her mother off the cliff. Her thoughts, she was aware, were increasingly fickle and turned now towards Geraint. In her dream she had seen both men, perhaps because both men *had* been there. But somehow, she had muddled them up and they had become one, when in truth Geraint must have been there before her father and must somehow have made his getaway before her father had reached the cliff top. Her father had probably saved her life even if he had not managed to save Lio's. He was a hero then, not a villain and he was punishing himself unnecessarily. She might have said this there and then, she might have told him he was a lifesaver, that he had no reason to feel guilty, but the words choked and died in her throat. Because she knew there was still something he was hiding; felt there was someone he was protecting.

TWELVE

The more she thought about how much she needed to sleep, the less likely it seemed that she would. Leila was lying on her stomach in bed, her hair sticking to her face like a pony's forelock in the rain. She brought her knees up, breathing through the pillow and burrowed her way into the foetal position. She wanted her mother to carry her around, as she had once done. A sharp yearning for something like hot tea in her throat struck her, making her faint, but it wasn't really hot tea she wanted, she couldn't fathom what the yearning was for. Perhaps it was amniotic fluid. Under dark water she would sleep and sleep.

From the next bed Imogen's quiet snores were reassuring. Leila was still suspicious of her father; sure that there was something more. Had he really loved her mother? He was confusing. He had spoken more freely than ever before, but he had also very obviously rehearsed his speech.

Gradually, somewhere in the penumbra between consciousness and unconsciousness, the full events of the day came back to her. There was another cause for her tired, wounded feeling. Jude was a liar. He had led her to believe that she was the only girl in his life, that she was really important. He had never mentioned a girlfriend. Was this the end of their friendship? Perhaps she was nothing more than a curiosity. The girl whose mother fell off a cliff. The girl who *saw* her mother's death. Even worse, he might have been in some kind of conspiracy with his creepy uncle. This did not sound like her Jude, but she had come to realise that the important questions in life were the ones that could never be answered for sure.

As she began to slip away she found Geraint on the edge of her dreams, smiling in his sunglasses and waiting. His small smooth hands had pushed her mother off the edge. When she asked him if he was the intruder at Hafod, his smile broadened. It seemed the answer was, 'Yes.' And he had not been in his bungalow at the time of her mother's death as he had claimed. It was almost certain that he had been on the moor. He was often on the moor; he had learnt how not to be seen. He liked frightening people. He had frightened Mr Parry, but no, he shook his head; he had not killed the old man. Mr Parry had done that all by himself. Then he laughed, he was sitting in a tree, like an elf. Everyone noticed and forgave him because he was a pale, delicate alien. What was he going to do to her? He did not answer but removed his glasses. His eyes were dark holes.

Leila opened her eyes, sweating, afraid and paralysed. There was an evil shadow behind a black tree. There were two small, pale hands pressing into the tree. Above it the moon was shining. The moon moved round and as it shone on the tree it revealed a wicked face. Someone was after hurting her.

Jude had said that depression was a symptom of a bigger process, often a change or a signal that change might be needed, a change in lifestyle or perhaps a change in a way of thinking. But then Jude said many things and Leila was irritated at herself for treasuring everything he said. It was likely that he was only misquoting his psychotherapist mother. Still, if she could understand why she felt the way she did, it might be easier to deal with.

Over the next few weeks, Leila's father made the occasional effort to talk to her and he was pleased to see that she seemed to be satisfied with his version of events. Now that she knew, he felt a burden had lifted from his shoulders and a shadow had departed from his mind. Leila knew all she needed to know and as far as he could tell, she was content with it. She was leaving it alone.

He was almost right. Too much darkness had closed around her mind. However, Leila had begun to visit the Afon Ddu cliffs regularly and had even taken Imogen with her on one occasion. She felt oddly peaceful when she visited the place where her mother had died. Since the day she had spoken to Lio, she had been compelled to visit the cliffs to think and pray. She had only seen Jude once since that day outside his house. He had been waiting outside her school at home time, alone, looking despondent. She had left by the back way, reluctant to talk to him although she was almost sick from excitement at seeing him there. Waiting for *her*. Imogen spoke to him and at Leila's request told him that she was not in school. He did not ask any questions but left quietly...

May brought some good weather and after the snow in April, it appeared that summer had finally arrived. The evenings were light and the later sunsets were glorious. The moor was full of the bubbling song of hidden curlews nesting in the heather and skylarks filling the air with their high ecstatic song. Imogen was spending more time on her homework and Leila was spending more time on the moor. She had begun to feel that she was being watched. She was, of course, well used to being watched. Since almost everyone knew that she had seen her mother's fall off Afon Ddu, she now understood why she had become the local oddity. Some argued that she could not possibly be expected to remember anything, while others disagreed, claiming to have memories of their own from their early years and suspecting that she too might be harbouring a secret. Could she hold the key to her mother's death? They longed to ask her what she remembered of that day. The verdict had been accidental death; it was in the old newspapers that Leila had been reading after school in the library, it was on the death certificate and the police records, yet still her suspicions remained and the townspeople persisted with their own dark rumours.

Leila was leaving it all alone for the moment; but nothing could take away the creeping feeling that things were far from wrapped up and that someone was watching her. She had no tangible reason to believe that she was being watched; whenever she turned around to look for the source of her fear there was never anyone there. It happened on the moor, outside school, in Llan library and on the streets, when she was with Lisa and Imogen and when she was alone. It was always a sudden unease that crept over her like an instinct. She would look about with a growing feeling of panic and finding nothing would not be reassured at all. On these occasions she found herself shuddering with a chill feeling prickling her skin and the instinct for flight gathering within. Once it had happened on the sunny streets of Llan when she was with Imogen. They were on their way to the library when Leila felt it and she turned to look around. Everywhere people were on the street, walking from shop to shop, gossiping, preparing for the end of the day and a few looked at Leila a little longer than they might at any other school girl, but it was more than that. On this occasion, she grabbed Imogen's arm tightly in momentary panic.

'What is wrong Leila?' asked Imogen.

'It's that feeling again,' said Leila, still looking around with a fear that Imogen found alarming.

'You're being scatty,' said Imogen, though her own voice faltered as if something had communicated itself from Leila's hand into her arm. 'There isn't anyone watching you.'

'No, I know. I must be going crazy.'

At five o'clock they met Lisa and behind her they saw the Crow Woman, hurrying towards them with her shopping basket.

'Girls,' she cried, 'I'm so glad I caught up with you. It's so long since I've seen you. I was thinking of making us a lovely dinner this weekend if you want to come to visit,' she flapped her shawl around her, 'and I have great news. The Peregrines are back. I have seen a nest on the hill behind my house, which I've been watching and I thought to myself, wouldn't my girls love to see that!'

Lisa appeared taken aback by the Crow Woman's overbearing manner. She glanced at the two girls to see if they needed help. Leila was unusually reticent, but then she had been like that recently. It was probably her hormones kicking in. Imogen was nodding vigorously.

'Yes, it would be great, what day do you want us?' said Imogen.

'Sunday,' said the Crow Woman, 'I will come and collect you.'

'We can walk,' said Leila. 'Mr Parry is dead now, he won't harm us.'

The Crow Woman stopped fluttering and saw the dark look on Leila's face.

'Well, I can come and collect you anyway, to save you such a long walk,' she said.

'Ok,' said Imogen, 'that would be great.'

After the Crow Woman had turned and left them, Lisa asked Leila why she had been so rude.

Leila hunched her shoulders in a shrug.

'She was up on the cliffs just after my mother fell,' she said, vaguely, as if only partly present in the moment. 'She stayed there with me while Father went for an ambulance, but she *never* told me.'

Lisa put a hand on her shoulder.

'They only wanted to protect you,' she said, 'I suppose they carried on with it for too long. Everyone makes mistakes. Anyway, what's happened to your friend Jude?' She noticed how Leila visibly jumped at the name and how the blood seemed to jump into her cheeks.

'He's got a girlfriend,' said Imogen, 'and now Leila won't speak to him.'

'Well,' said Lisa, 'I don't think he will last with that girl.'

There was a pause and then Leila asked, 'What makes you think that?'

They were at the car and Lisa was unlocking the door and watching them with a sly smile. 'Tell us!' cried Imogen.

Leila could not speak, she found her fist gripping the contents of her pocket: crumbs and a wrapper.

'The girl and her family are moving soon. I know because she is my second cousin's friend,' said Lisa. She waited until they were sitting in her car with their seat belts on, before she continued.

'Jude is the third boyfriend she's had in as many months. It's like she's just woken up to boys and wants to fit the whole school in before she leaves.'

'Does Jude know?' asked Imogen.

'I should think so,' she said. 'Of course he probably doesn't care overly much. She does most of the running and decides when it is over. They all know what she is up to.'

'She sounds like a tart,' said Leila bitterly.

Lisa smiled. 'Maybe so, but she hardly cares since she'll be in another country soon. Anyway Leila, I can't guarantee he'll ever go for you. Why don't you look at the boys in your own school?'

'I'm not really bothered,' said Leila, fighting back tears and annoyance at Lisa for building her up and then knocking her down without a thought. She was only interested in Jude, no one else would do.

Back at Hafod, Leila put on her boots and slipped out, leaving Lisa to plait Imogen's hair. She headed out to Afon Ddu, drawing her coat around her and breathing in the cool, damp May air. The morning mist, which had persisted through most of the afternoon on Hiraethog, was now finally lifting and she thought she might see the sun shortly before it set. As she climbed the stony path to Afon Ddu, she found herself shivering again, shivering with the feeling of being followed. She turned around, but there was only the path curving around a rock below her and fronds of bracken nodding on the verge. There was even a pied wagtail behind her, cocking its head and jerking its tail at insects spied between stones on the path. If there was anyone behind her the wagtail would not be there; she was being foolish. She stopped to watch the bird for

158

a few moments as if waiting for it to tell her something. Then, just as she was about to move, it cocked its head, appearing to listen and with a sudden, quick skidding over the smallest stones the bird fluttered away. It had seemed startled. Leila watched its rapid, bounding flight and envied the quick escape.

She stood still and listened, stiffening, afraid to move. What was she doing here, alone again? Did her personal cargo of genes include an inherent suicidal tendency? There was no sound, but she felt cold and weak with a sudden self-loathing brought on by her own stupidity. The familiar metamorphosis was taking place as her throat began to constrict and her whole body stiffened with a paralysing fear. Whatever it was, she could not control it, as it built up in spite of her efforts to calm it. Struck by inertia, it took much effort for her to shift herself and turn. But when she did, she found her feet and began running up the path. Running in terror, as if she expected someone to be right behind her and about to grab her... Running clumsily, not nearly fast enough away from a man with black plastic eyes, falling on the stones, crying out at the pain of her scraped knees, looking behind with dread, expecting him to be there, closing in on her with his smooth hands.

But there was nothing. There was no one there. Nevertheless, still afraid, still tight-throated, she ran on up the path, until she reached the top and was unable to hear anything other than her own hoarse breathing as she sank to her bleeding knees. She continued to look all around, checking all sides for the enemy and still visualizing smooth hands gripping her throat.

'Go away,' she thought, 'I don't want to think about you anymore.'

But in spite of her conscious efforts to stop thinking about the strangling hands, they always returned. She would have to keep still as her world fell inwards. In a few minutes it would be over.

The mist was clearing quickly, soon she could see all around. She sat down to recover on the damp grass not far from the edge and watched it blowing in the breeze that was almost always brisk on the cliffs. She looked at the tangle of brambles that grew over the edge and wondered if this was the same plant that had caught her sunhat almost ten years ago. Was it really because of a bramble bush and a hat that her mother had died? She now knew that she would feel very disappointed if her mother *had* died in a freak accident. It was such a waste and if she really had to lose her mother then she should at least gain something from it, even if it was only a bit of drama and mystery. She had found out about Lio's affair with Geraint and the fact that she herself had been a witness. But since she had found out that much, even more mysteries seemed to have surfaced.

Today she was not comfortable on the cliff, she was edgy, looking around as if she expected Geraint to suddenly appear behind her, saying nothing, just pushing her, pushing her off the cliff after her mother. Why *was* he following her? She was sure it was him. If her mother had gone to meet him on the cliffs in order to finish with him and return to Tom, Geraint might have pushed her in a jealous rage and made his getaway just before Tom had appeared on the scene. It was possible that her mother had made a choice that day; she might have chosen Tom after his threat to fight for custody of their child. Of course, it was also possible that she had decided to run away and Tom had run after her and caught her. Leila could see him trying to drag her mother back, struggling with her near the cliff edge, both of them angry, forgetting all about Leila waiting quietly behind them. Perhaps her father had forced a confession from Lio, a confession that she was leaving him for Geraint and had pushed her over in a fit of rage. Leila had seen the quality of his rage, that time in the snow with Geraint, and she knew it could be deadly. He would have regretted it immediately, but what could he do in such a situation? He had to protect his daughter and therefore he would have lied, because having robbed her of one parent he could not rob her of the other. So he lived a half-life, a miserable existence where he carried the burden of his guilt every day and as a consequence had not been much of a parent. Leila sighed, unable to be convinced by anything. Perhaps she should just leave it. Her mother was lost and nothing could bring her back.

Before she set off for home, Leila said a short prayer for her mother, wherever she was now. Then she picked herself up and began the walk down the path. But she had only gone a short way when the feeling of unease returned. She stopped and looked all around, listening intently. There was nothing. But the feeling persisted. She continued, walking as quietly as she could and taking pains not to dislodge any rocks or stones, until she reached the bend in the path where she had seen the wagtail. Now she wanted to get away from Afon Ddu; it really was not a safe place to be alone if someone was following her. No one could hear a scream from Afon Ddu. No one except the gallivanting winds. She hastened on. As a matter of recent habit, Leila looked over her shoulder continuously wherever she went, and she did this all the way back to Hafod, not seeing anyone.

THIRTEEN

When Tom had appeared at her door after the brief phone call, Arabella's heart had lurched in her breast, even after all the years that had passed. She had bathed and blow dried her hair for his visit. But he had only wanted to check that he still had her allegiance. He had explained Leila's brooding and warned her not to let herself to be tricked into anything. He was as distant as ever and if he hadn't looked so careworn she would have been angry at his patronising; angry enough to defy him. But with a shiver of dark pleasure she saw that he too was suffering. From a distance he had appeared to be doing very well with his lecturer job, second marriage and two daughters. He had appeared to belong to that great clan of happy families, living day by day, not too concerned with the past or future. Now she knew that he was not okay, he avoided her eye like an inferior (was her gaze too hungry and intense?), looking down into his coffee or at his hands; old looking hands, rough like a farmer's. He was pale and drawn and she caught the scent of something alcoholic with her keen nose. Something like vodka, that she was not meant to smell. Was it Dutch courage or was she looking at a drinker? She knew he had turned to drink after Lio's death. She didn't imagine that he had loved Lio much; he probably suffered with guilt more than anything. She knew that was why they could never be. And now he was moving on, determined to leave.

'I'll admit I've got frightened,' he had said, 'I think something will happen if I don't get my family out of here.'

She had tried to ask him what he had meant but he was putting his coat back on and standing up with his eyes averted. He had his family to go back to and she would be alone once more.

It was only a few days later that she found herself driving towards Hafod for the two girls, but hoping to see Tom first. He was cooking lunch and sharing a joke with the stick insect, Ann. He looked different, still tired but more cheerful and when he looked at her it was with the brief glances that seemed to suggest disgust. He didn't want her there. He couldn't bear her and wanted to get away from her. Indeed he was quite rude and she was so thrown by this that she retreated outside to await Leila's sulky exit. Imogen was already at her side, blithering on about red grouse, but she was swaying and only half able to hear. Why should she carry this burden? She was angry and at that moment consumed with sufficient hate to give up some secrecy without a care for the consequences; to a degree that was what she was preparing to do.

She drove the girls back to her house in her old Land Rover and all the way she answered Imogen's questions about the Peregrine's nest, without more than a few words or glances in Leila's direction. She had missed them so much and lived with the painful knowledge that they missed her less, but Leila's morose refusal to speak was agitating the anger that had not yet subsided.

Outside it was raining. They were well over the rainfall average for May, and still it poured. Cold rain. The windscreen wipers were worn out and juddered across the window, wailing in protest. Arabella swerved into her driveway and the tyres slithered up the muddy track towards her house, which stood dejected like a tall person in a raincoat. It was not a good day for looking at birds' nests.

'Good job I lit the fire,' said Arabella in a strained voice, because she was not enjoying this as much as she had hoped. 'I know how you girls like a nice, warm fire.'

Once inside the house they found they had to open the window in order to see something more than the blur of rain on glass. With the binoculars directed up the steep, wooded hillside that clambered up behind Arabella's house, they could spy on the nest. There was no sign of the two chicks today; the bedraggled hen was sitting tight, ogling them with eyes bright as amber in the rain. Arabella made them tea and Welsh rarebit ('It's got ale in it today,' she said, 'so don't tell your parents!'). This was what she really liked, sitting in front of the fire with them. But there was an edge of sadness to such moments because she knew they were not really *her* girls and all too soon they would be gone. When they had finished savouring their hot rarebit, Arabella, though still a little agitated, decided to tackle Leila's sullen silence.

'I hear you found out a few things,' she said.

Leila looked at her sideways and nodded her assent.

'Your father mentioned that you discovered you were the only witness to your mother's accident.'

Leila moved her head slightly, a half nod perhaps.

'You know that you were present and that I too was there,' said Arabella, trying to keep her stirred up state out of her voice. 'I'm sorry you weren't told earlier, but it wasn't my decision. Now I think I should have done it, regardless of what your father says, because I don't think he has handled things very well at all.'

She stopped as Leila looked at her with a softer, less sulky expression and encouraged by this she decided that she knew better than Tom and would act in accordance with her own judgement from now on.

'I arrived some time after it had all happened. I picked you up and held you. You didn't know me very well and you tried to push me away. You were crying for your mother...' She stopped, 'I don't know if you want me to tell you this...?'

The latter was asked in the tone of a question, she was not

prepared to tell Leila anything more unless the girl made the concession of speaking to her.

Leila gently rested her feet against the sleeping form of Boadicea.

'Tell me everything you know,' she said.

'I only know what I saw,' said Arabella. 'I cannot tell you how she fell, but as your father has probably told you, we suspected it was in retrieving the sunhat from the brambles that she somehow came to lose her footing.'

Arabella saw Leila frown, perhaps she didn't want to hear this. Tom had mentioned that she had convinced herself that her mother was murdered.

'Did you see my mother lying dead?' asked Leila in a small voice.

'Well, er… yes I did,' Arabella's voice became softer, 'but she did not look dead at all. She looked as if she were lying there, looking at the sky. She was like a fallen star, her arms outstretched, her hair spread out and her face peaceful.'

'Do you think there was a chance of saving her?' asked Leila. 'Say, if a medical team had been at the bottom of the cliff when she fell. Could they have saved her?'

Arabella shook her head. 'Her head and neck injuries were so severe her death was instant. If you've ever been up on Afon Ddu, you'll know it's quite a drop.'

'So what was the first thing you saw when you reached the top?' asked Leila.

'Well, as I came puffing and panting around the last bend in the path, I remember feeling somewhat faint. It was probably a combination of the heat and the exertion, which I was not used to. I had a strange bout of double vision, I think, because at first I thought I saw two adults up there. Then I came to and saw that in actual fact it was just you and your father. He was looking over the edge and clearly very distressed. His hands were clasping his face and he was crying out, "No!" over and over. It was then that I noticed you standing behind him. You had begun to cry too.'

Arabella stopped and took a breath, realising that the double vision lie had been quite daring for her. A subtle way of revealing a truth.

Leila was looking puzzled.

'I ran over, suspecting that someone had gone over the edge and it was a horrible moment when I saw Lio there, a terrible surprise. In the first instant that I looked at her lying down there, looking so comfortable and peaceful, I actually thought she was fine, I thought she was looking up at the clouds or else it was a joke. Then after a few seconds I realised she was dead and I didn't doubt it because of the distance that she had fallen. It seemed like an age that we stood there in a real distressed state, wondering what to do...'

Arabella paused as she thought back. She remembered how she had stood by the side of the man she loved and saw Lio dead. And she remembered feeling glad that Lio was dead.

Leila was waiting for her to continue, an earnest look on her face, so Lio-like and yet not.

'After some moments of discussion,' Arabella continued, 'Tom said he would run to phone an ambulance, while I stayed with you and tried to placate you. He screamed at me not to let you out of my sight as he ran off. I waited with you for what seemed like an age, then suddenly everyone seemed to be on Afon Ddu: police, ambulance crew, mountain rescue and local people coming to see what was going on and everything became confused for me at that point. I was feeling the shock, so Tom stayed while the police took you and I back to Hafod where I put you to bed. You were tired and you had fallen asleep long before we got back. I of course had to answer their questions about how it all happened.'

'Is that everything you remember?' asked Leila.

'Yes, I think so. That is it really.'

Arabella shifted her position and lifted herself from the sofa in order to put more coal onto the fire. She thought of the secret painting she had made of Lio, conceived from the sketch she had taken as she stood looking over the cliff at the dead woman. Leila, who had stopped crying by then, was occupied by picking small flowers and heather sprigs to make a bunch of flowers for her 'sick' mother. The painting accurately depicted Lio as she had seen her that day. She did not know why she had done it nor what to do with it. Sometimes she had nightmares, where Leila as a grown woman found the painting and turned on her in a rage. It was risky keeping it. It had been risky taking the sketch. She supposed it was a nauseous, low act really, but she could not bear to throw it away. It was a fine piece of work. She looked furtively at Leila, half-expecting the green eyes to be watching her, seeing through her. But Leila was looking down at her hand, which was picking at a pulled thread on the sofa.

'Do you want to talk anymore about this today?' asked Arabella.

'Yes,' Leila replied, 'if you don't mind I would like you to tell me about the kind of person my mother was.'

Arabella gave a heavy resigned sigh. Why did the world still have to revolve around that woman? She'd been dead for over a decade. There was only one thing she liked her for and that was the affair with Geraint. The affair that had led to Tom putting his arms around her that day when they had both been in the Sportsman's Arms drinking themselves numb. Her husband had died somewhere far away and Tom's wife was with another man somewhere nearby. They had been united for a few weeks. Had he seen some similarity in her? She was not as young and had never been as good looking as Lio, but she was just as passionate, artistic and brunette as the other. Had she just been a poor facsimile of his wife? She didn't know because he had never told her anything. Perhaps that was another thing she had in common with Lio, annoyance at his lack of communication. They might have been comrades had Lio survived. She smiled slightly as another voice in her head, quietly said: 'unlikely.'

'You must have known her a bit?' prompted Leila.

'Well, I am not the best qualified,' Arabella said slowly, wishing they could talk about something else instead, Tom for instance. She always wanted to talk about Tom, but rarely got the chance.

'I will tell you what I know, or at least what I think I know, because she was your biological mother and you are bound to be curious. You want to know if you are like her don't you?'

'Yes,' said Leila, eyes shining.

Arabella was a little disappointed in the fervour of the child and was aware that her answer would attempt to dash some of that fervour to the ground, just as its object had hit the rocks.

'You look a little like her, but in personality I would say you are more like your father, Tom. You have a look of him too, though most people do not see it. It takes a discerning eye. And in your mannerisms, you are every inch your father.'

'Really?' said Leila, but the question was rhetorical, the light in her eyes a little dimmer. Silly girl wanted to be the glamorous image of artistic ardour and death by cliff fall. Red lipstick, red coat, pale skin, green eyes, loud, ringing laughter, cold angular features like a beautiful mask one would wear only for special occasions. That was it! The mask. Arabella had almost forgotten it. It would keep Leila interested in visiting until they were closer, until Leila started to imagine that Arabella was actually rather like Lio. Until maybe Arabella became the mother figure the girl was looking for. She had done right in disappointing the girl a little, it wasn't wholly selfish, because she had to keep her safe. Then she realised in the midst of all her calculating that she hadn't answered Leila's question and Leila was beginning to look sulky again.

'I suppose that your mother was many things; a person who remains a mystery to many people. Your mother wasn't perfect, you know that by now. She was cruel as well as kind, sweet and bitter, clever, yet also stupid enough to think she could get away with having an affair quite publicly, in a small community. She required more excitement and adventure than her chosen life could bring her; a bit like me really,' Arabella paused, noticing Leila's distrustful frown. 'But there are many more good things I can say about your mother. She loved you and she took you almost everywhere with her. I would be the same if I had a child. I understand your mother's love of Hiraethog because I feel it too. I'm an artist like her and that is the way you are like her too. You have that soul.'

Leila nodded and looked at Arabella as if noticing her for the first time. Perhaps Leila was wondering about how much alike the two women were and, as if to encourage this, Arabella ran the hand which was wearing a big, ruby ring through her dark hair.

'I like your top,' said Leila quietly, 'it's so shiny and the red goes well with the black.'

'Do all artists wear clothes like that?' Imogen asked. She was looking bored, half lolling on the couch, but Imogen didn't matter as much. She was lovely, but she had a mother.

'I don't think we have a particular uniform,' Arabella answered with a light, laughing tone in her voice as she lifted her shawl to reveal more of the shimmering red dragons and their black, curling smoke. She was feeling quite light and airy, almost like someone else.

'This is a Chinese tunic. I wear it for inspiration.'

Leila smiled up at her, her face warm and glowing in the firelight. It was still raining outside and the fire was the heart of the dim room. Imogen, always cold, was in its sway. Leila for the moment was in Arabella's power. Her eyes had regained some of their glitter. This time for a living person.

'Girls, would you like another sandwich?' Arabella handed Leila the plate first, feeling a little flushed with her victory. 'What else would you like me to tell you?'

'Can you tell me about Geraint?' said Leila after some thought. 'I know you said you didn't know him, but I think you do.'

Arabella looked at her for a few seconds. Forget Tom. She was building a relationship with his daughter now. No more lying.

'Okay,' she said, 'you're right. First I will tell you why I denied knowing him.' She sat back onto the sofa and straightened her skirt. 'At the time,' she began slowly, 'I couldn't really talk about him. I made a promise to your father not to mention him and to say nothing if you ever asked about him. Your father was going to tell you in his own good time, though I warned him not to take too long. Now that you know about your mother's relationship with Geraint, I will tell you what I think of the man.'

As Arabella paused, Leila began to swing her legs subconsciously as if to hurry her up.

'Geraint is not a well man. I don't know if he ever was a well man. He came up here looking for Lio some time after she had married Tom and had you. I don't know him well enough to know exactly what is wrong with him, and I'm not a psychiatrist, but it seemed to me that he was obsessed with Lio and had become in some way dependent on her for his own happiness. This dependency meant he could not allow Lio to be her own person; her independence frightened him. Your father may have told you how he tried to own and control Lio. He was very possessive and incapable of seeing beyond his own needs. Basically he only cared about what he needed to make him happy.'

Leila remained silent. Clearly she was anxious about Geraint and was right to be. Imogen, meanwhile, was probably looking worried for other reasons. 'Don't worry Imogen,' she said, 'everyone is keeping their eye on him and on the way he treats those animals he keeps. He won't get away with much now. But you must still keep away from him.'

'What do you think my mother would be doing if she were still alive?' Leila asked.

Arabella mused slowly on this.

'It isn't easy to say. I didn't know her very well, and even those who did said she was often unpredictable. How can I describe her to you? It was like she had this outer skin of sweetness and that friendly, warm smile that you see in all those photos you have. A woman who looked approachable, a wonderful mother, full of life. Yet there was something else. Sometimes there was a cold edge, an unreachable aloofness and a hard glint in the eye, a look that said: "I don't care if you die." At other times, an itchiness, like she wanted to be removed, somewhere else. Like she was treading a tightrope between domesticated bliss and exodus. Like at any moment she was going to take someone by the throat and throttle some sense into them.'

Arabella paused and her careless words caused a sudden tightening in Leila's throat.

'But not you,' she added, seeing the distressed look on the girl's face. 'With you she was always loving, as a mother should

170

be.' She sighed and wondered if she had gone too far. Then she began to gather the plates up from her coffee table.

'With Lio you could be sure of nothing,' she said furtively, though the implied contradiction of what she had only just said was not consciously intended.

They were quiet for a while as Arabella washed up and boiled the kettle for another pot of tea and Imogen took another look at the Peregrine's nest. The rain was abating, Leila seemed to be rubbing her throat and swallowing a lot. At times she looked almost as if she was in pain, but when asked replied that she had a sore throat, it was nothing.

The weather was not hospitable enough for a walk in the garden, so Arabella took them up to her workshop, a small dusty room with bare floorboards and a window looking out over her vegetable plot. She showed them some of her sculptures, one with a young woman emerging like a butterfly from an old woman's dejected, beaten figure embodying the agelessness of spirit, and her latest works; small animal ornaments for the local market.

'They are a bit like the ones my mother used to do!' exclaimed Leila.

'Are they?' said Arabella in mock surprise.

'Have you ever done a full size human sculpture?' Imogen asked, 'I have seen some exhibited in the Llan library.'

'Not a full size figure, but I did sell a few busts when I was hard up. Shame because I rather liked them. In fact, you've just reminded me of something,' she said. 'I have a confession to make.'

The two girls stood on the dusty floor, looked at her and waited.

'I once did a rather lovely life mask. Quite fragile. I made it by taking a mould from a real woman's face. Lio's face. She came to me that year, not long before she died, probably July. She wanted it for a present, I presumed for Tom's birthday in September, but she didn't actually say. It was all her idea, but she couldn't do it by herself so she asked me.'

Leila had brightened at this, her mouth opening with surprise.

171

'So you made a mould of my mother's face?'

'Yes, I did. It was an interesting thing to do.'

Arabella remembered how she had only accepted the work because she thought she might discover something about the likely fate of Tom and Lio's faltering relationship through it.

'Why didn't you tell me this before?' Leila asked. 'Have you still got it? Can I see it? Please let me see it! I've always wanted to know what she was like in real life.'

Arabella made her face fall.

'Oh dear,' she said, 'I *am* sorry. I should have thought it would mean a lot to you, my poor dear. I should have said first.'

'What?'

'I'm afraid I sold it dear,' she shook her head, 'I sold it to Geraint nine years ago.'

Leila's brief happiness was quickly crushed. 'Why *him*?' she demanded, her euphoria collapsing into tears so quickly she could hardly stop them. 'I *hate* him.'

'Oh Leila, I am sorry. Let me explain,' said Arabella and she tried to put her arm around Leila, but Leila shifted away.

'I had presumed it was for Tom's birthday,' said Arabella, 'and I thought of giving him the mask, though I admit I was loath to part with it. I had grown rather attached to it. It would shine in the moonlight with a kind of beautiful, luminous light of its own. Since Lio had died the mask seemed all the more precious.'

Imogen was sucking her index finger as she often did when disturbed. Arabella sighed heavily with the realisation that she was not doing well. She would lose them if she continued to blunder so severely.

'I was going to give it to your father, when Geraint came knocking at the door, claiming that it was for him. I had to believe him, because I couldn't think how else he would have known about it without Lio telling him. Yet I was puzzled, because she had said it was to be a surprise. Anyway, I told him I did not want to sell it. However Geraint offered me one hundred pounds for it. He said he would go and get the cash right away and I accepted. It hadn't actually been paid for by the time of Lio's death, you see, and I was rather in need of the money.'

Arabella paused to look at Leila and saw that she was really distressed. Misery turned her stomach.

'I wish I hadn't sold it. Even back then I had to stand on the doorstep for quite a time, wrestling with the idea. I had a feeling its rightful place was with Tom and you, but I was also afraid of upsetting your father in his bereavement and was thinking it would be better for him not to know about it. It was a cowardly act, but here was Geraint offering me one hundred pounds, money I needed, desperately, so I caved in. I told him to be careful with it, he said he would guard it with his life. That was the last I saw or heard of it.'

Arabella sighed. It was not complete lies, although she had been more willing than she admitted to offload the thing onto Geraint, because she did not want Tom to think Lio had wanted him before her death. She had still reserved hopes of getting him for herself.

'Does Geraint still have it?' asked Imogen.

'I don't know, but I expect so. I think he would have taken good care of it. I had a thought that I might ask him if he could let me borrow it back to show you.'

'Yes! I must see it,' wailed Leila suddenly. 'I must see it!'

'Well, come and visit me soon and perhaps I will have news of it. But don't tell your father. Promise me.'

'We won't.'

'Perhaps if he won't let you borrow it, we could maybe visit him to see it,' said Imogen furtively.

'Well, I suppose that might be possible.' Arabella mused on this for a minute and then shook her head, 'No, I'm afraid I don't think it would be a good idea.'

'But you could still get him to lend it to you,' cried Leila. 'You are the artist, you are in charge!'

'Yes, of course,' Arabella replied, though her voice faltered a little. She hadn't thought this through very well. Did she really think she could convince that creep Geraint to lend the mask to her? It could backfire on her if he refused; she would look weak and not at all like Lio.

'Maybe you should ask him to give it back,' said Leila, her voice passionate, her face determined. Arabella realised that it had been a blatant lie to tell her she had her father's personality and mannerisms.

'I can't do that – he paid for it,' she said more humbly.

'Why not?' asked Leila. 'It should be in my family. You said you thought it was for my father. She was *my* mother. I hate the thought that he has got it. I can't bear it!'

Arabella dropped her hands into her lap. 'But would it be enough just to see it Leila?'

'Yes, to see and touch it. I think so.'

'You would want to have it, I think,' said Arabella, 'but what worries me more is that you might try and approach Geraint yourself, perhaps through his nephew Jude. You look so like Lio; I'm worried about how Geraint would react to you. I think it would be better if you kept away from him altogether. As I have said, there is reason to be concerned about his mental health and as you get older there is even a danger he might think you are her. He once or twice mistook me for her.'

She winced at the lie. It sounded ridiculous even as she said it.

'You must leave this to me,' she continued firmly. 'No telling your father and no going to Geraint.'

'I promise.'

'Maybe you could ask Geraint to let you take a photograph of it, which you can then let Leila see,' suggested Imogen.

Leila shook her head. 'It's not the same. I need to see it for real.'

'Then you must keep in touch with me and I will do my best for you,' said Arabella, feeling that she had drawn much closer to Leila that day and yet had also put herself on a knife edge. The thought of having to talk to Geraint was nauseating.

'Don't get too excited now, I haven't even got his agreement yet.'

'It will be all right,' said Leila. 'I have spoken to him before.'

'I know, but you must leave this to me,' said Arabella firmly. 'If no one else will warn you about him, I will. No one can tell if he would try to abduct or harm you.'

Leila assented, but her eyes did not. Arabella frowned at her, she was going to be tricky.

God knows he has reason enough to abduct her, she thought, but she knew she could not say this aloud.

The rain outside had stopped. They sat back around the fire with Boadicea at their feet. It was cosy, but their mood was not as relaxed as usual. Leila was excited about the mask and probably resentful over Geraint having it. Arabella was victorious and yet unnerved by how far she had gone. Time was short, so it was good that she now had them in her confidence; dare she also hope that Leila had, for the first time, begun to see her as a potential mother figure?

FOURTEEN

It was as she agreed to the unthinkable that Arabella recalled Tom's words: *'Don't allow yourself to be tricked into anything.'*

But she had no choice. Geraint had refused to let her borrow the mask, so she found herself asking if she might visit him with Leila, so that Leila might see it (as she was determined to). Though this gave Arabella misgivings, it was better than the alternative. She suspected Leila might recklessly attempt to approach Geraint by herself.

Geraint was hesitant at first, then his mood changed and he agreed readily. He became disconcertingly eager. She suspected he liked the idea of seeing Leila again. The thought made her skin crawl. Yet her ego could not take the alternative; she would not admit to Leila that she had failed.

It was the middle of May when she rang to tell the girls of the arrangements. Leila refused to back out of it but was nevertheless filled with an unaccountable dread. Arabella would pick them up the following Saturday, on the pretence of them spending an afternoon at Llyn Brenig, the reservoir and the recreation centre in Clocaenog, not so far from the dingy bungalow they would actually visit.

They had spent almost a week shrouded in cool mist, though from the weather forecast they knew the coast was enjoying rays of sunshine. Imogen and Leila decided to wait outside.

'The swallows aren't here yet,' said Imogen vaguely. 'It won't really be summer until they come. Are you scared Leila?'

Leila was feeling tense. 'Yes, a bit. Are you?'

Imogen nodded and then shivered.

'You don't have to come,' said Leila. 'I'll be alright with Arabella.'

'No, I'll come.'

Leila looked away impassively. She suspected Imogen still held Geraint in her affections and this annoyed her.

They waited and quietly watched the mist drifting down from the moor. The moor itself had disappeared into the whiteness, though the lonely piping of a golden plover assured them it was still there. It was not long before they heard the clamouring of Arabella's old Land Rover as it climbed the hill towards Hafod. Imogen ran inside to tell her mother they were off and Leila went over to the gate. She clutched both hands together and took a deep breath. If she could clear the obstacle of her fear of Geraint, she would see her mother's face.

'Are you sure about this?' Arabella asked three times on the drive to Clocaenog. She appeared concerned.

Leila nodded each time and thought: 'She's not like Jude. Jude was not at all afraid of Geraint.'

Arabella drove slowly over the moor road. The mist had reduced visibility to a few yards and the air was warm and damp. The Land Rover rattled precariously over a cattle grid and they made a tight bend before the descent to the penumbral shadow of Clocaenog. Leila was feeling sick. She had wound the passenger seat window down and was inhaling the soggy air and the gentle scent of dewy heather in an attempt to calm herself, but she withdrew and closed the window as they approached the shadow of Clocaenog. They entered the cold shade and its silence descended on them. No one spoke.

To all three, there was an inescapable sinister air to the old beige bungalow that crouched on a bend in the southern part of Clocaenog. Despite this being the more pleasant part of the forest, the bungalow was built in a heavily planted section where the air was as cold and the light as dim as in the north of the forest. All of them shivered. It was something to do with the dank evergreens and the old blue paint peeling off the bungalow's wooden framed windows, the dirty terracotta pitched roof which sat like a tall hat on a small, boxy head, the cracked concrete path padded with muddied moss and the dark patches of mould decorating the window edges from the inside. As they walked up the path Arabella pushed them behind her and told them to wait a little way back from the door. They stood halfway down the path and looked around at straggling, light-starved weeds growing tall and puny about the place. Behind the dirty net curtains they saw a shadow move.

Arabella knocked on the door rather lightly, as if she did not really want anyone within to hear. Leila and Imogen found themselves holding hands, something they rarely did nowadays.

The door opened and Geraint looked out, with a strange intense paleness – as if a stone had been lifted and he was a creature of the underworld that shrank and writhed from the light. His strange eyes looked straight past Arabella at Leila and she recoiled from within with such a force that she had to take a step backwards. Arabella looked at Leila too. She looked afraid. Then, suddenly Geraint withdrew his glare, blinked, and said: 'Will you come in?' in a muted but civil manner. As if he was restraining himself, almost. Leila went last, pulling her shoulders inwards like a protective shell. The dirty carpets exuded the fetor of Geraint's invisible cats while the clammy walls quietly exhaled mould spores and rot. Geraint's brown cardigan gaped with holes, he looked thinner than before and his trousers were too big around the waist, his silky, pale hair ruffled by restless sleep. He looked smaller than the first time they had seen him, on that November day in Clocaenog. Like he was wasting away...

As Geraint led them into the lounge, Leila's throat constricted painfully and she had to gasp for breath. She recognised the room. It was the small dim room that looked out onto the road and the pines, where she had been before with Jude by her side, in what already seemed like an easier and happier time. But she was sure that she had seen the room before that; when she was much younger.

'Would you like a drink?' Geraint asked Arabella. 'Tea? Coffee?'

'No thank you,' she replied, 'we've all just had one not so long ago. We really only came to see the mask, if you don't mind…just a flying visit.'

There was unease in her voice that they had never heard before and she moved in front of the girls as if shielding them. Geraint had to look around her to see them, which he did leaning to one side, but he decided not to bother asking them if they wanted a drink.

'Right,' he said, moving himself to a position where he could see all three of them, 'before I show you the room, I have to say that I want you to treat it with respect.' He ran a hand through the flexible hair and his jaw tightened. 'No one else has ever seen it before. I am only allowing you in because one of you is related.'

Imogen nodded. 'We will be careful,' she said.

Leila looked at her, Imogen's eyes were intent upon Geraint and they shone with devotion, even in this foul den.

Geraint led them to the back of the bungalow and opened a wobbly pink door. With his back to them, he paused when the door was half open, just stood still, leaning on the handle as if having second thoughts. He did not look behind. Arabella appeared to brace herself, but then he pushed the door wide and walked slowly and reverently into a small dim room. There was a patch of yellow light on the floor, which had filtered in through the thin curtains on the only window in the room.

Geraint reached for the light switch. The light clicked on with an audible whirr of electricity. The room was brightly lit by a fluorescent tube. The shock of what she saw paralysed Leila and set her heart racing with panic. The walls were plastered with photographs of her mother as well as examples of her paintings and poetry. Lio looked out from hundreds of photographs, a smiling face, but not always smiling, sometimes serious too. Geraint had taken photographs of her when she appeared to be unaware, photographs of her sitting on rocks on the moors, pictures of her walking through Llan with her shopping and as a small figure caught on the skyline of a fervent sunset, but nearly always alone. There were others that looked like the work of a photography student, black and white photos of her leaning against a tree, walking in Clocaenog, pushing a pushchair. Some of the photographs were more haphazard, these appeared to have been cut out and were not as well placed and carefully arranged as the others.

'Who has been cut off?' Leila heard herself ask nervously, pointing towards the photos.

She shivered and lifted her shoulders to combat the cold knives that ran up her spine when Geraint looked at her. His look was full of disdain, she noticed dark shadows under the dark eyes, and then he looked at the photos that she had pointed to.

When she thought he was not going to answer and had turned away, she heard him quietly say: 'Who do you think?'

She looked back at the photos. In one of them her mother's arms were extended, holding a handle, the handle of the pushchair. The pushchair was cut off, the cut was jagged as if it had been done quickly. Stiffly she stepped closer, feeling Geraint's eyes burning through her, hearing Arabella's fast, nervous breathing. In another she saw her mother's arms cut off, arms that were holding a baby, a small piece of white woolly bootie remained, dissected and floating on the edge of the jagged cut. Another quick cut. She now saw that it was she who had been chopped off.

'Why me?' she thought. 'Why does he *hate* me?'

But then it was right that he should hate her. It was the only way.

As I hate him...

'Where is the mask?' asked Arabella from behind, her voice

wavering in the room that was silent except for the whirring of the light.

Leila had found one picture with her still on it. She froze on the spot and went cold all over. It was *the* picture, the one she remembered. There they were on Afon Ddu, a sunny day on the cliffs, her mother was holding Leila at around the age of four; she was holding her against her hip and smiling. Crimson highlights, picked out by the sun, glinted in Lio's hair. She was squinting in the sun, but she looked lovely, as always. In her arms Leila sat slumped, a little too big for holding, looking reluctant. There was a frown on her face and her green eyes looked out of the photograph with suspicion. Leila turned around and her eyes met Geraint's. A small smile formed on his face; he had seen her looking at the photo.

'Where is the mask?' asked Arabella again. 'We really must go soon, Geraint.'

Geraint walked forwards, towards a wonky desk, which apart from the chair in front of it was the only piece of furniture in the room. He opened the top drawer and looked inside. He stayed still for a moment, just looking, and then he carefully put both of his hands in and lifted it from its blanket bed.

Leila stepped forwards and saw a luminous, white face rising like a moon.

'There she is,' he said, holding the face in front of him with outstretched arms.

My mother, thought Leila. 'Can I hold it?' she said.

He looked at her distrustfully.

'Be very careful,' he said. 'Don't move from where you are,' and he reluctantly handed the mask to her.

She held it carefully, afraid even to move it around in her hands with Geraint standing over her, so close that she could smell the pungent odour of recent coffee on his breath. At first she was disappointed, not able to relate the bland, perfection of the unsmiling white mask to the living, smiling face she had seen in photos. Then as she looked, she began to recognise the clean cut features of the mask that had been a beautiful face. The eyes

181

were closed, as if she was sleeping or dead. It was a cold thing, the mask, but she wanted it all the same. It was perfect.

From behind, Arabella saw the figure of Leila, standing stock still, hardly daring to breathe, her head bent over the mask, her hands still with palms upward, the girl as fragile as the mask. A well of feeling bubbled up in Arabella's large abdomen, she felt weakened by it, and she felt lost, way out on the perimeter, nobody's mother and nobody's daughter.

'Can I touch it?' asked Leila quietly.

'You may, but gently,' said Geraint, moving even closer. 'She was lovely, wasn't she?' his voice was almost kind.

Leila nodded and used her right index finger to trace the contours.

'And this is life size, isn't it?' she said turning to Arabella, glad of the excuse to shift slightly away from Geraint.

Arabella nodded, looking sad.

Leila turned back to the face. She was holding her mother's face in her hands. Or at least a mould made from her mother's face. This was the nearest she could get to the woman, a poor substitute maybe, but a thing of beauty nonetheless. It was the biggest tangible thing that remained and she did not want to give it back.

'It's very special,' she said, more to herself than to anyone. 'I wish I could keep it. This face is gone now. It was unique.'

She tightened her hold, not wanting to give it up. Imogen was looking quietly over her shoulder, Arabella impatiently shifting her feet, wanting to go, thinking now that it was too late, that if there was ever a way to make Leila love her, it would have been to give her that.

Leila seemed to remember looking up at her mother as a baby, pulling her hair for attention, making her say 'ow!'

'Don't cry on it,' said Geraint sharply, when he noticed Leila's eyes filling up, her nose growing red and sniffy. There was no compassion in his voice. 'I'll have it back now.'

Leila stubbornly held on for another few seconds, the face had become a white blur through the underwater vista of tears. She wanted to keep it forever; it was hers by right. Then it floated away. Geraint took it back.

'It should be mine,' she choked. 'She was my mother, she never belonged to *you*.'

Geraint visibly shook as he carried the mask back to the drawer. Then he twisted around aggressively and faced Leila with flashing eyes.

'You never really knew her,' he spat, his voice a furious whisper. 'Not like I did. We were so close...'

He let the sentence hang and swallowed hard. His face had become blanched, pinched. Like he was losing control.

'Please leave now,' he snapped. 'I will show you out.'

'We're leaving,' said Arabella, nervously moving towards Leila. 'There's no need to get upset now. Come on girls, let's go.'

Leila became desperate, sensing that she was unlikely to be allowed into the shrine again. She thought of pulling the drawer open and taking her mother's image. Against one, three of them could manage it. He looked so thin, she was sure that with a blunt object she could even deal with him alone, if she could get him unawares. She looked around the room, but there was nothing to use. The other two would not stand for it anyway. Imogen was still looking doe-eyed and Arabella was ushering her out of the door. But she had to salvage something from the situation.

'Why are you following me?' she asked, not really expecting him to answer her. 'And why did you come to Hafod that day when you thought no one was in?'

'What's this?' asked Arabella.

'Nonsense, by the sound of it,' said Geraint contemptuously. 'She needs therapy.'

'Never mind that,' said Arabella. 'I'll get to the bottom of this. Thank you for your hospitality. Come on girls.'

It took both of them to guide Leila out. Her world was awash; she couldn't see a thing and she could hardly walk for the feelings of weakness and misery that had overwhelmed her. She wanted to collapse and her legs dragged as if she was walking through a tunnel of water.

'I shouldn't have said that,' she thought hopelessly. 'I should have kept my mouth shut.'

'Pull yourself together, Leila,' snapped Arabella.

Arabella decided to take them back to her house first (Leila was in no state to be presented to her father). If she could have taken her foot off the accelerator, she would have given herself a good hard kick for mentioning the mask in the first place. She was tempted to head butt the steering wheel, but as this was likely to result in her sounding the horn and driving the vehicle off the road, she gritted her teeth and drove on through the mist instead.

When they were sat down in her lounge with a pot of tea and Boadicea watching from the hearthrug, Arabella asked Leila what she had meant when she accused Geraint of following her.

'I know I shouldn't have said that,' said Leila. 'I realised almost as soon as the words left my mouth.'

'Yes,' said Arabella, 'I thought I made it clear to you that you were to stay in the background and not say anything unless necessary. I was doing you a big favour today, but you seemed to forget this entirely, just like you seemed to forget that Geraint bought the mask, and it is his. I saw the way you were hanging on to it; I thought you weren't going to give it back.'

'Well, I didn't want to,' said Leila. 'It doesn't seem right that he has it; my father and I should have it. You don't understand how I felt when I saw it, and felt it.'

Arabella nodded slowly. 'I know, but it belongs to Geraint now. You agreed just to look at it and hold it and that would be enough, and you still haven't answered my first question. What did you mean by Geraint following you?'

'Oh, it's just a feeling. I was silly to make such a big thing of it. I thought I saw him outside Hafod one day and there have been other times when I've felt uneasy, but as Imogen said, I am probably imagining it.'

Arabella looked unconvinced. 'Describe to me exactly what has been happening. I may have to tell your father about all of this, after all.'

Leila's eyes widened. She did not want that. So she told

Arabella about how she thought she was being followed and how she thought there might have been an intruder at Hafod. She omitted the fact that she had actually seen a man outside Hafod. She played it down as much as she could, because she did not want her father alerted.

'I think I'm just being a bit paranoid,' she said meekly. 'A lot has happened lately, I've had a few bad dreams.'

When Arabella was satisfied that everything was as normal as it could be, she drove them home to Hafod.

Lio was holding Leila against her, while talking to the man in the black sunglasses. It was hot and sunny. They were all sweating. Leila frowned, not just because of the sun but because she could not tell if it was him. The man she did not like. She moved her hand up and felt her neck, it still felt slightly sore and sometimes when she was afraid it went tight. She decided it was him; something about the smile underneath the glasses, something about the blonde hair blowing in the strong breeze on Afon Ddu. Something about the pale hands that held the camera and pressed the button... CLICK. Geraint took off the sunglasses and smiled at her mother and then he smiled at Leila, smiled with a glint in his eye like an eel turning in a polluted stream. Leila cried and turned away, reaching her hands up to her mother's shoulders and holding tight onto her T-shirt, she buried her head in the warm material.

'Leila, what's wrong?' said her mother. 'What's the matter?'

Then it was dark, the air cooler. She lay on the worn sofa.

'I'll be back in a minute,' said Lio. The door shut. Leila was tired, she whimpered.

'Its all right,' said the man. 'I'm your Daddy now. We are all going to live together happily ever after. Would you like that?'

Leila stuck her chin into her chest and looked at him leaning over the other end of the sofa. She shook her head and said 'No,' softly.

'Oh yes you would, wouldn't you?' he reached his hands out as if to tickle her.

She rolled away, pushing herself against the back of the sofa.

He was hurting her, he was too rough.

'Tickle, tickle,' he said, putting his hands around her neck.
'Tickle, tickle.'

The hands tightened. Leila could not move or breathe. He was
pushing her head down into the crack between the back of the
sofa and the seat cushions. It was smelly, there were crumbs and
hairs and bits of food. Leila could feel them on her tongue. Much
stronger she felt the hands on her neck like a vice, squeezing. Then
they let go. She did not cry, or scream, she took careful breaths
and stayed where she was with her head down the back of the
sofa. If she stayed still he might go away, then her mother would
come back.

'Come on,' he said lithely. 'I've got some ice cream in the
freezer. Come on, let's have some ice cream.'

It was just another dream.

After school, Leila and Imogen decided to look at Lio's things in
the spare room. It was over a month since they had last been in
there. It was almost a year since she had looked at the things that
were carefully packed away in boxes.

'There was a book somewhere,' said Leila. 'Father said he
showed it to me once.'

'What sort of book?' asked Imogen.

'A baby record book. My mother kept a record of me; she was
still keeping it when she died.'

They found the book at the bottom of a box of Leila's old baby
clothes and a few toys. It was a thick, vinyl-covered book, adorned
with faded cherubs holding hands and harps. It was fastened by
a clasp, and had sections for records on milestones, vaccinations,
weight and growth.

'What exactly are you looking for?' asked Imogen after
observing the way in which Leila was feverishly turning the
pages.

'I'll know when I find it,' said Leila. 'If I find it.'

There was nothing much to be found for when she was four
years old, but in the back she discovered a small notebook which

seemed to have been kept like a diary of Leila's progress. She flicked through it. There were entries right up to the day before her mother's death. The entries focused on what Leila had done each day. There was very little on what was actually going on in her mother's mind.

Leila took the notebook to bed, to read alone.

Leila's 4ᵗʰ Birthday 30ᵗʰ April

We gave her a party. Tom's mother came. Every time she opened a present, she gave a loud laugh.

We let her stay up late to watch her video (three times over!).

29ᵗʰ June

Something strange happened tonight. Leila has been a bit off all day, but tonight she wouldn't let me turn the light off or leave her room without screaming for me. At first I thought she was playing up, but she was really frightened. It isn't like her at all. In the end, I sat with her until she went off.

11ᵗʰ July – 18ᵗʰ July

Leila has suddenly become prone to waking in the night as if having nightmares. Often she is very upset, other times I hear her crying, but having not woken properly she goes back to sleep. On a few occasions she has woken screaming. I think it is my fault.

21ˢᵗ July

The doctor cannot find any physical problem with Leila's neck. It is a little sore, but he says that is probably from her continuously touching it. He thinks that perhaps she got something caught around her neck, or had some kind of painful experience that she has remembered clearly. Now whenever something happens to upset her, she puts her hand to her neck as if expecting the pain she felt to return. I wish I knew how it had happened. The doctor also said (like everyone else), this is just a phase. But Leila isn't like other four-year-olds anymore. She seems to have a mortal fear of   something she can't or won't articulate. I have started to sleep in her room.

I have hardly been out of the house this past month, but at last Leila seems to be improving so perhaps it has all been worth it. However, she is not that happy little girl who celebrated her fourth birthday three months ago.

It seemed logical that a young child might be threatened by another love interest in her mother's life (just as she had been later by her father's new love). So why had her mother exposed her to Geraint and created this fear that was still with her? Leila knew what it was now, where it had begun. She read on a little and found something else. The day the photo was taken on Afon Ddu was not the day her mother had died, but two weeks before:

3rd August
Geraint took a photo for me, of Leila and myself up on the cliffs. But Leila was unhappy with his presence and recoiled from it. I have to record this now.

'I have to record this now…' What did that mean? Did Lio suspect that something had happened or did she have a foreboding of things to come? She had recorded Geraint's identity because Tom now knew of the affair, so there was no point in being cryptic anymore. What was the point of this record? Evidence of some kind? Did her mother feel threatened, and did she believe that Leila was also under threat? It was hard to tell. Leila was somewhat disappointed that the photo session on the moors had taken place two weeks before her mother's murder, it meant she had no proof that Geraint had been on the cliffs that day. Not yet anyway. But she was becoming sure that the origin of her choking attacks lay with him. He had wanted to kill her and he had tried to. But who would believe her?

It was not late, only a quarter past eight. Leila put the book under her pillow and went downstairs and out onto the patio at the side of the house. A whitewashed wall covered by ivy concealing a trellis sheltered it. Imogen was already there, looking dreamy. Leila joined her on the bench. The sun was feeding the moors with its elusive fire as the world moved round and slowly shut it out.

'I love the long dusks of summer,' said Leila, resting her hands on her knees.

'Yes,' Imogen nodded, then looking out beyond, she gave a sudden gasp. 'Look, the swallows have arrived!'

They had. The unmistakable chip chip, chatter of the swooping, fork-tailed comets filled the evening air. The shiny, blue-black cutthroats had returned for another summer on Hiraethog. Leila smiled, she wasn't the twitcher that Imogen was, but swallows were her favourite birds. So optimistic, so ecstatic, intoxicated by their aerial life… High spirits incarnate.

Chip, chip, chip, somersaults swoon, whirligigs whistle, cartwheels crack. Chink, chink, chink, the swallows are back.

'While we've been just here, they've been to Africa and back,' said Leila.

'I hope our pair have returned,' said Imogen, 'and that they nest in the barn again.'

They sat quietly for a while, watching the swallows gorging in the sky, feeling the coolness and the gradually approaching night, the imperceptible thickening of greyness. Slowly, Leila's thoughts returned to Geraint.

'Imi, can I ask you something?'

'Yes,' said Imogen vaguely. 'Ask away.'

'Tell me what you think about Geraint. After last weekend, has your view of him changed at all?'

Imogen tilted her head to one side, away from Leila, then looked sideways at her.

'I felt a bit sorry for him,' she said. 'He didn't look very well. He must have really loved your mother, the way he has kept that shrine to her. He doesn't seem to have much of a life without her – it's like he's wasting away.'

'So you just think he is besotted?' said Leila.

'Sort of. I don't think he would hurt anyone.'

'Well, I think he is deranged. I don't think he ever really loved my mother at all. Didn't you hear what Arabella said? He was dependent on my mother, he made her responsible for his happiness but he didn't bother to think what would make *her* happy.'

'How do you know he didn't try to make her happy?' asked Imogen.

Leila paused and thought to herself: *Because he wanted rid of me and that would surely not have made her happy.* But she felt unable to say this aloud, so she shook her head and said: 'He only thought of himself; he wasn't capable of seeing things from anyone else's point of view.'

'You don't know any of this,' said Imogen. 'We've only got Arabella's word for it and much as I like her, I think she has got it in for him and I also think she is trying to build her relationship with us.'

'Why would she want to do that?' demanded Leila.

'Because she hasn't got any children of her own.'

They had reached a dead end and sat in mutual silence. Leila knew now that she could not tell Imogen of how she believed Geraint wanted her dead and had tried to choke her when she was only four. And she could not tell her how she suspected that he might have killed her mother. Imogen would not believe her. She would cry 'necrolatry'.

'I think I'm going to go in now,' said Imogen. 'It's getting late.'

The swallows were still carousing, swimming fast through the dusk, their closeness emphasising the airy warmth of another summer – maybe their last summer on Hiraethog.

The final entry was the day before her mother's death:

16ᵗʰ August
Although things have been difficult at home and Leila picks up on tense atmospheres, she seems to be getting better. She wouldn't let me wash her hair today and spent most of the morning disagreeing with everything I said. I thought, 'Yes, that's more like it!' It was nice to hear her speaking again. Now it's time to straighten out my

own life. I will do it tomorrow, I have decided.

What had she decided? Leila wondered, but there was no more.

FIFTEEN

It was a windy night on Hiraethog. The ruin was booming across the moor and tonight its song was desperate. Leila lifted the curtain aside to see its black, skeletal form against fierce clouds that were illuminated to pale greys and wispy whites by a hidden moon. Leila pitied the ruin; ill-fated, lonely lodge, playing its dirge in the wind. It had not known human habitation for long; built around 1908 and deserted by the 1950s. The years of lighted windows, conversations, laughter and music had been brief. Was the ruin lamenting its loss? Or crying for attention? There was only a lonely girl to listen. Could it be that the life that had lived in the walls had conferred onto it that dark sadness; or was it a coincidence? Was it somehow given its character by the fates of its occupiers' dreams and could it be partly alive? Leila was sure that Hafod was, to a degree, a living organism. But Hafod's face was beaming, bright, steadfast, a smile and beacon... A loving look. Gwylfa was organic in the literal sense with its garnish of mosses and lichens, with weeds and grasses and the small world of mammals, birds, bugs and bacteria that were in various ways nourished by it. But this was not enough to make it smile. Its face was a horrific accident, leering, glaring, hollow, broken. A vision from a nightmare.

Leila let the curtain fall back into place with a shudder. As she lay down she heard it resound like a giant pan pipe and she wondered if it was sad because no one was looking now.

In the next bed Imogen snored and in between both their beds a draught blew cold. Leila's thoughts turned to Geraint. The other dark thing in her life...

Why had Geraint wanted to choke her? Had she just been in the way? Did he hate children? Especially other men's children? She had been the thing that tied her mother and father by more than just marriage. If she had died then that child-bond would have been untied. Lio would have been able to leave Tom without worrying about a custody battle or the effect the break up would have on her child. But Geraint would have been a fool not to understand what a mother feels for her child. That was what had stopped him; he had known he would lose Lio completely if he killed her child.

'But why does he still want to kill me?'

Maybe it was just an extension of how he felt then. He hadn't let go of Lio and he hadn't let go of his hatred for the child that had survived her. Maybe hate gave him a focus. Why else had he stayed all these years, in a place where he did not belong, in that dark bungalow no one else wanted?

Leila knew the answer already.

'He is here because I am here.'

At school, Leila was pre-occupied. In maths Mr Edwards threw his chalk at her because she was looking out of the window. It left a small explosion of white dust on her cheek and lower eyelashes, which she did not bother to wipe away. Imogen could see the return of the necrolatry in her and knew that she was best avoided at such times. Imogen still liked Geraint; if anything she liked him more now. She thought about him constantly and when she was with him in her dreams she whispered, 'Mr Noon.'

So was it Geraint? Leila, sitting on the school toilet mused over this question. If her parents' big row the day before the accident had finally prompted her mother to finish with Geraint, she might have been going to do just that on the day of her death. Of course it had *looked* as if she was running to him that day. How could Leila ever find out what was true? There seemed to be no way forward, unless someone somewhere knew Lio's thoughts towards the end.

'Did she confide in anyone?' she said aloud and her voice echoed off the grey-tiled toilet walls.

'Did she confide in anyone?' echoed Lisa much later, as she drove them home. 'Who do you confide in?'

'Me?' said Leila. 'No one really. But I was asking who you think Lio might have confided in.'

Lisa smiled, the imperious smile she used when she knew something. 'Leila, first you must tell me who *you* confide in. You must have someone you can talk to. If you tell me who you confide in, then you'll have the answer.'

Imogen was frowning fiercely.

'Okay, Imogen I suppose,' said Leila. 'And Gwyneth at school.'

She left Jude out, he no longer deserved a mention.

'There you are then. I'm the same,' said Lisa. 'We confide in our girlfriends. I'm sure it's always been the way.'

'Right,' said Leila. 'Now I see. But I don't even know if my mother had any girlfriends.'

'No,' said Lisa, 'I don't think she had many round here. I don't know about where she was before. But I do know of one friend she had in these parts.'

'Really?' exclaimed Leila. 'Who? Is she still here?'

'Yes, she is and I'm sure you must have met her. Almost definitely. You were friends with Jude Noon weren't you?'

'I was. What does he have to do with it? He's not a girl.'

'His mother was the best friend Lio had up here.'

'She was?' said Leila, shocked. 'He never mentioned it.'

Lisa rolled her eyes. 'Men don't think of important things like that, they miss the details. If Lio confided in anyone, it would have been Celyn.'

'But she is Geraint's sister-in-law isn't she?'

'Yes, but she was more Lio's friend. She doesn't have much to do with him. No one does.'

'So what are you going to do?' Imogen asked Leila.

'I don't know, but I've got a few things to say to Jude, if I ever see him again. Have you seen him?'

Imogen shook her head. 'No, not lately.'

Imogen almost went on to say that she *had* seen Geraint at lunchtime in Llan, but stopped herself. She would hug this to herself for now. Geraint had caught her eye and smiled as he parked his car on the high street. He had asked her how she was, and how Leila was. He had even asked if Leila was all right after seeing the life mask, as if he was really concerned for her welfare. Of course he was; Leila was, after all, the daughter of the woman Geraint had so hopelessly loved and was still faithful to, almost ten years later. He had looked a little better today. His fair hair was startling in the sunlight, blowing up soft and wispy (because it was quite long), making him look younger than he was. There was something in his eyes; a new recognition. Today he had seen her as a person in her own right, and he had appeared to find her interesting and attractive. They had talked for a short while about badgers and birds and she did not believe the Crow Woman anymore. Geraint had such delicate, soft hands, not the sort of hands that could do anything cruel. He was beautiful. He had even said that he might consider having another mould made of the mask, if it were possible, so that Leila could have her own copy. He had asked Imogen to leave it with him.

'Don't tell Leila yet,' he had said with a conspiratorial smile. 'We don't want to build up her hopes, do we? Leave it with me. I will speak to Arabella about it.'

Imogen held a piece of paper in her hand, which was hidden inside her coat pocket. The paper was warm and clammy from being held for so long. When she thought no one was looking, she would sneak a look at it to make sure the ink had not smudged. He had given her his phone number, but it was a secret.

As Imogen looked at Geraint's number, Leila picked up the phone, took three deep breaths and dialled. She would have taken some pleasure from this if only she wasn't so nervous. Now she could tell Jude, that no, she did not want to speak to him, she wanted to speak to his mother.

Jude answered. As she had hoped, and dreaded.

'Oh it's you,' she said. 'Hello…'

'Is that Leila?' he sounded surprised. 'It is! Do you know, I was just thinking about you. How are you?'

'I'm fine…' she said. 'Fine as can be.'

'What happened to you? Imogen told me you didn't want to speak to me. Was it because of Bethan?'

Leila found herself blushing and fought to keep her voice on a level. 'What exactly did Imogen say?' she asked.

'Can't really remember. I'm not seeing Bethan anymore now. I should have explained to you.'

'Oh, no, no,' Leila said, her voice rising. 'No, there is no need. I didn't really think you would… would…' she couldn't quite manage to say it, but Jude got the point.

'I've been wondering how you have been getting on with finding out about your mother,' he said.

She remembered then, and anger allowed her to regain her composure.

'Well,' she said, 'not a lot really. Nothing like that day in the library when I found out that I was there when she died. But of course you already knew.'

He would hear it in her voice.

'But Leila, you know it wasn't really my place to tell you,' he said. 'You are an awkward person to have as a friend.'

She felt affronted at being called an awkward person, almost self-pitying, but managed to recover the point of the phone call.

'You didn't even tell me what you *could* have told me,' she said resentfully.

'What's that?'

'That your mother and my mother were friends. How could you not tell me that?'

'I didn't think.'

'You must be thick Jude. Anyway, I didn't ring up to speak to *you*. I wanted to talk to your mother. Is she there?'

'Er… yes. Listen, I'm really sorry, how can I make it up to you?'

'Just get me your mother,' she said through gritted teeth, though she was on the verge of breaking down into tears. She so wanted Jude back. She missed him.

'OK,' he said. His voice seemed to waver. He covered the phone and called for his mother.

Leila's bottom lip trembled, her throat felt tight. She took another three deep breaths and tried to remember what she had wanted to say. All she could think of was how she wanted Jude back.

That weekend both Leila and Imogen went off on secret assignments. They did not confide in one another as they once would have. Nor did they confide in anyone else. Ann thought Imogen was going to meet Gwyneth in Llan, though she cycled off in the direction of Clocaenog. Leila set off cross country for Jude's house. His mother Celyn had invited her.

It was a hot day. Ants were scuttling about, holding the warm soil to ransom. The water, which had trickled down the side of the pale lane in rivulets throughout spring, had dried up. The stones, bleached in their dryness and sifted with white dust, made the pale lane paler. The warmth was unusual enough to be much appreciated by Leila who had set out early in order to enjoy a longer walk. She was going up to the ruin of Gwylfa Hiraethog first and she had a small lunch packed into her rucksack. Taking the meandering sheep path route, she took her time, stopping to watch pheasants flapping noisily up from the heather and checking the redundant shooting hides, as if she expected to find men in post World War I dress behind them, pointing their guns in the air.

Waiting, with dark eyes and neat moustaches. Of course there was no one crouching behind the small dry stone walls now; they were no more deadly than the damp mosses and lichen that mottled them. Everywhere the heather was coming into bloom, the air full of climbing skylarks and pirouetting swallows, the romantic ruin of the lodge looking dirty with the sun on it, like an old piece of leather with lots of eyes. Watching.

Leila looked back at Hafod, now distant, the whitewash shimmering in the sun. She hoped her father was not watching her route. He had recently informed her that Hiraethog was a special site with rare plants and important bird species. He did not think she should be tramping over it willy-nilly and the ruin was on private land where visitors were not welcome. Leila had argued that her feet alone would not do much damage. Imogen had argued it would be in a state if everyone said that. Imogen wanted to be a conservationist; she already knew she wanted to study ecology at university.

'It will be my job to make sure people like you use the proper footpaths.'

Leila had her own way of justifying her trespass, she knew her father's main motive was to try and keep her off the moor, away from Afon Ddu, away from Geraint, away from the ground tainted by Mr Parry's passage, but she told herself she was on an important mission.

It was a mile of tough uphill walking. As she climbed she was aware of how Gwylfa Hiraethog clutched her sight; it was impossible to take her eyes off it. She approached from the north side and here the climb was steep enough to conceal the ruin for much of the ascent. This added to the suspense. From the moment the ruin became concealed she climbed towards its invisible darkness and when it finally reappeared over the brink in its true immensity, it was always as astonishing as the first time.

First to appear over the skyline were the huge black chimneys and with each step upwards more of the lodge came in to view. As she marched, it marched to meet her, appearing slowly over the top of the hill, throwing its dark cloak of shadow over the purple heather and dominating all in its hideous, dead splendour. When she had made the last of the climb, on more gently sloping ground, she was brought to her knees by it (as she was every time). Struck down by a paradox of horror and rapture. She could see Lio there, walking with her sketchbook, sitting on the mossy stones, her bare feet resting on slates fallen from the roof and baked by the sun. She could see her stepping over the stones, as she herself was now, looking out at the view of everything. Of Hafod as a small shining light, the distant crumbs of other houses, the strips and plots of farmland, files of hedgerow, the woods of Llan, the cliffs over Afon Ddu, the moor road snaking over Hiraethog and to the south the closeness of Clocaenog's gloom. And behind her the blackened stone and sightless windows, silent, as if waiting for something.

But today she looked twice at the cliffs over Afon Ddu.

From Gwylfa Hiraethog the cliffs could be seen clearly enough. She could see there was no one on the cliffs. Yet if there had been someone there, she would have been able to watch without them ever knowing. A person standing on the cliffs could be seen, another person pushing them off could be seen, though it would perhaps be hard to identify exactly who it was. She held her breath for a moment as she realised. Gwylfa Hiraethog's empty eyes had been watching it all on that fateful day, had seen it just as her own immature eyes had, and yet neither could tell the story. She sat down in the short grass and moss without taking her eyes off the distant cliffs. They were deserted, no drama was being played out today and, after a while, Leila opened her sandwich box. There was still plenty of time before she had to be anywhere, and the weather was quite hospitable, the wind low. Next to her the lone tree that stood sadly next to the ruin unhunched its shoulders.

Her attention quickly wandered.

Which would last the longest, she wondered. Tree or house?

The house was only around eighty years old and already a stone skeleton. The staircase had fallen through, the inside was full of debris, the mossy stairs down to the cavernous cellars looked precarious, the cellars themselves terrifying. The lodge looked older than its years (part of its attraction), the roof was growing a patchwork of holes, but the chimneys still pointed to the sky in defiance. The tree nearby looked sad and stunted, perhaps the remnant of someone's attempt to plant a garden and the only tree which grew up there at 1,267 feet. Leila thought the tree would go first, despite the house's ruined state.

It was always a wrench to leave, but she would be late if she stayed any longer. Before she went she looked again at the view of Afon Ddu, and wondered if anyone had been visiting the ruin on that fateful day almost a decade before. Had the police thought to ask anyone? It was, of course, a long shot. How could they trace tourists who had been passing through the area ten years before? People who might themselves be dead now. She would save this for another day. Now she descended the south side towards Clocaenog.

Jude's mother had sounded slightly unnerved by Leila's request. She had not wanted to talk over the phone but she had admitted that Lio had confided in her shortly before her death. As Leila approached the house, she grew agitated, not only nervous about the interview, but about seeing Jude again. She was half relieved when, on the descent to the house, she saw his mother Celyn hanging washing out in the large garden. Celyn did not seem to sense her approach, even when Leila was standing right behind her and looking at the way her dark curly hair fell just short of the ends of her shoulder blades, which jutted out through her T-shirt. She was a small, slim woman, very different from Jude. Finally she turned and started with surprise at Leila's silent presence.

'Oh hello Leila,' she said, recovering quickly from the shock of finding her already there. 'I'll just finish hanging this out and then we can go in for a chat.'

'We can talk out here if you want,' said Leila, suddenly reluctant to see Jude again.

'Well, it is a nice day. I'll get us a drink and we can sit at the garden table.'

Leila waited outside, sitting on the edge of the shade of a large mountain ash. She could see Celyn pouring apple juice in the kitchen. Jude's bike was against the wall, but she could not see him anywhere. Celyn brought the drinks out. Leila watched her and thought she looked intimidated. She wanted to say: 'Don't worry, its all right,' but the words would not form, so she took the drink with a nod, which must have appeared curt, and waited.

'You mentioned the life mask on the telephone,' said Celyn, smiling and kindly. 'I never saw it, but I remember Lio talking to me about it. She wanted to know if I thought it was vain of her. I said that I supposed it could be interpreted as vain, it depended on who it was given to and the spirit in which it was given. She said it was for you, obviously for when you were older. It was an unusual gift and a very thoughtful one I think. I suppose that she knew that through being someone's mother she had become very precious to someone and she liked the idea that the dimensions of her face in its twenties would be preserved. I didn't like to pass judgement and I never saw it.'

It occurred to Leila that her mother might have suspected that something was going to happen to her. The coincidence of the timing of the unusual gift, which had immortalised her, and her death seemed too much. And Leila was more angry than happy to have discovered that the gift had been intended for her and yet she did not have it.

'I can't think how Geraint came to know about it,' mused Celyn, 'I didn't tell him, but it occurred to me that perhaps he'd found out thanks to his stalking, or else she must have mentioned it to him.'

'Stalking?' said Leila. 'You mean he used to follow her?'

'Yes, towards the end. She was unhappy with his clinging and the effect he was having on you, but when she told him to stop, he became worse. He became sneakier about it, and started watching her.'

'It sounds like half of the people who lived here were stalking my mother!' said Leila incredulously.

Celyn laughed.

'Well she was a striking woman.'

'Did my mother tell you that she was going to finish with Geraint and go back to my father?'

'Well,' said Celyn slowly, 'there was something Lio said shortly before her accident. She asked me not to tell anyone and I guess I didn't. I waited for them to come and ask me questions, but no one did, apart from the few questions initially asked by the police. They can't have thought me important because they didn't give me the chance to repeat it…' She paused. 'But, I am making excuses for myself. I could have gone to the police station or to your father and told them, but I didn't. Do you know I've probably only seen your father once or twice a year in all the years that have passed since, and rarely close enough to speak to him.'

'It's okay,' said Leila.

'I did truly mean to tell him, but it was difficult given that I am related to Geraint through marriage. My husband died long before any of this happened, as you probably know. You might not know that I tried to help Geraint through some of his worst times, so I suppose I was the last person Tom wanted to speak to. In the end I had to distance myself from Geraint for my own health's sake and of course for Jude.'

'Did you tell Geraint any of the things that my mother told you?' asked Leila warily.

'Oh no, and to be honest he never asked me, which I found a little odd.'

'So you've never told my Dad what you know.'

'No. Time passed all too quickly and then I saw your father with a new woman, I heard the gossip that it was serious and they were getting engaged, so I left it; it no longer seemed relevant.'

Celyn paused for a moment, seeming to swallow against her tension. She looked across her garden to where a blackbird was singing on the gatepost.

'Your mother had made a decision,' Celyn continued cautiously, attempting to gauge the likely effects of what she had to say. 'It was a hard decision. A decision about what to do with regards to her marriage and her relationship with Geraint. This was what she came to talk to me about. It must have been four days before she

202

died and the last time I ever saw her. She didn't want me telling anyone. She wasn't sure when she would be able to speak to both Geraint and Tom and she wanted to pick her moment. I was half tempted to tell her that sometimes there is never a right moment, but I decided to just be a friend instead of always giving advice. She told me that she was concerned about the way her life was going. Apart from Tom and Geraint, I was her only real friend in these parts. She realised she had got herself into a mess. She blamed her lust for adventure, and now all she wanted was to go back to having that quiet life of routine she had become so bored with. However, she didn't need me to tell her that she could never go back to that and, even if she could have done, it would only be a matter of time before it became inadequate all over again.'

Celyn paused to check that Leila was following everything she had said. It was a habit, to see that she was being understood; there was no point in continuing otherwise. Leila appeared distressed. She suddenly became animated and said: 'Oh no, I don't understand! You mean Lio had the mask done for me as a farewell present before she left us for Geraint?'

'No Leila, Lio was never going anywhere without you and certainly not to Geraint,' said Celyn. 'He made sure of that with his behaviour.'

'So what was my mother going to do?' asked Leila.

'Well, she couldn't go back to Tom either,' said Celyn. 'It may be hard to understand, but she had decided to leave *both* of them.'

Leila swallowed hard. She had not thought of this eventuality. She could only reply with a question. 'Forever?'

Celyn shrugged. 'I only know she had decided to cut off her relationship with Geraint completely, but if possible to maintain a friendship with Tom, since he was your father.'

'Was she taking me with her?' asked Leila. This was perhaps the most important part for her.

Celyn nodded. 'She was going to rent something just outside Llan. There was a nice cottage in the village, Tan-y-Fron, with woodland behind it; she just needed to check out the money situation. I said to her there was a chance Tom would give Hafod up for her, but she wanted to look into all the options. She wanted to concentrate on her work as an artist and her work as a mother. She felt she had lost her way with the affair and now it was time to take back control of her life. She thought she had been a bad mother, but I disagreed. She had made some bad moves but I had always admired the way she was with you and Jude.'

'So was this how she wanted it to be forever, just her and me?' asked Leila.

'Forever is a long time,' said Celyn. 'She couldn't see forever. There was a chance that she and Tom would have made up, eventually, if they were both prepared to live on slightly different terms. But she was quite determined, that day I saw her, to spend some time alone with you. She was happy too, if that's any consolation. She had been depressed for a few months. Geraint was troublesome and deceiving Tom was getting to her. When she made the decision to leave both of them, she was happier than she had been in a long time. It was a huge burden off her shoulders.'

'Is it possible she changed her mind inbetween the day she came to see you and the day she died?' asked Leila.

'I can't say for sure, but I doubt it. I know she had a row that day with Tom and the consensus is that she was headed out to Geraint's place. People round here seem to think she was going to leave Tom for Geraint, but I think she was actually going to finish it. People don't always behave logically when they are in the heat of a row, but I firmly believe, given what I knew of Lio, that she had made her decision and would stick with it.'

'So after finishing with Geraint she would have gone back to finish with my father?'

'Perhaps finish is the wrong word,' said Celyn. 'Your father was very important to her – she realised this after her affair with Geraint. She probably would have gone back to talk with him, to tell him she had finished with Geraint and to discuss an indefinite period of time apart for them both. Arranging for your father to visit you would have been a priority.'

'But none of this ever happened, because she died.'

'Yes,' said Celyn. 'It was a terrible accident.'

'But *was* it an accident?' asked Leila, watching for Celyn's response.

Celyn appeared vaguely surprised and looked at Leila a moment before saying, 'There was no evidence to suggest otherwise. You don't believe that it was anything else, do you?'

Leila shrugged. 'She was about to make a new start, and she was dealing with her problems, but I have often wondered if she was pushed.'

'But who would have pushed her and why?' asked Celyn.

At least she was not dismissing Leila's theory entirely.

'There seem to be only two people,' said Leila, somewhat encouraged. 'My father and Geraint; I believe they were both there on the cliffs that day.'

'But why would either of them want to kill Lio?'

Leila sighed, unable to articulate what was in her head, the dreams and visions of Lio, of her father, of the man with black sunglasses (Geraint) and of herself up on Afon Ddu that day.

'I don't know. Maybe they did not mean to push her, but they got into a fight and somehow she fell.'

'So, let me get this straight,' said Celyn. 'You are saying that you think they *both* pushed her?'

'No, not that,' Leila shook her head vigorously. 'Rather that they both could have. My father might have become angry about Mother taking me away from him; they may have fought over me. Somehow, my mother fell, or he in anger pushed her,' she paused, thinking how unconvinced she was of this now she had said it out loud to someone.

'And does your father know what you think?' asked Celyn.

'No. I suppose I don't truly believe that,' Leila sighed. 'But he *is* keeping something from me. I know he is.'

'Has he told you in detail what happened that day?'

'Yes,' Leila said, suddenly weary. 'The Crow Woman, I mean Arabella, backed up his story. I do believe him, but Jude said withholding truth is as bad as lying.' She blushed then, even as she said his name.

Celyn smiled, 'It can be,' she said. 'But what makes you think that your father is withholding anything from you?'

'I can't say… it's just a feeling I have.'

'Perhaps you need to tell him what you have told me today. It sounds like both of you need to talk. I know it is a painful subject for him, but he must also think of you. Do you think you can get him to talk to you about this?'

Leila sighed, 'I feel like I've tried and tried. But maybe, if I keep on pushing.'

'Right, now let's go back to Geraint. Why do you think he would have pushed your mother?'

'Because she was trying to save me. He wanted to kill me. Please don't be angry, I know he is your brother-in-law.'

'That's a serious accusation. Can you tell me why you think that?'

Leila took a deep breath, her voice began to tremble and her hand automatically went to her throat

'I remember something… it was him… he tried to choke me when I was four. I dream about it sometimes. I feel I am being throttled, a choking feeling in my throat, my father has taken me to doctors and hospitals and they have found no physical problem. So they came to the conclusion that I am having panic attacks in stressful situations, but that is wrong, because it can happen anytime.'

Celyn looked intrigued. 'And you believe the dream is linked to your throat problem?'

'Yes. It's a real memory of how the throat thing started.'

'And are you sure this really happened? I mean it could just be a dream that seems very real.'

'No, I know it happened,' said Leila. 'I'm not mad.'

'We may need to speak to your father about this,' said Celyn. 'If this happened we need to sort it out..'

'No!' said Leila, frightened. 'I don't want to see anyone. It's a secret, I don't want to tell anyone about it. I have a friend who I can talk to. A grown-up friend, but not my dad.'

'I'm glad you have someone to talk to. Is it Ann?'

'Oh no,' Leila winced as she spoke, 'no, it's Arabella.'

'Ok. Jude mentioned her. Why don't you talk to me too? It's my job to help people. You have come here to talk to me today. Perhaps you are looking for someone to help you.' She looked at her watch. 'I am expecting visitors but I can cancel. Would you like to stay a bit longer?'

'Perhaps,' said Leila dubiously. 'But I've told you everything I remember. It's just a dream, maybe I am imagining it.' She was fearful of the fuss that might result from her admission. 'I could have created this in my mind because of how he hurt me when he killed my mother.'

'Leila, why does there have to be a conspiracy behind your mother's death? Sometimes there are just freak accidents, tragic events with no reason, that no one can explain. People find that very hard to accept and it's normal to find it hard.'

'What are you saying?'

'That a mythology has been built up in this community about your mother's death. Why? Because she was young, beautiful, artistic and intelligent. No one could accept that she was stupid enough just to fall off a cliff.'

Leila sighed. 'There is no evidence to suggest that it was an accident, other than that no one saw anything.'

'And equally, no evidence to suggest that it was anything other than an accident. It's just that we always want explanations and sometimes we want them to be more exciting than they really are.'

'I've been told all of this before,' said Leila. 'But I don't think the gossip has affected me, I hardly hear any of it anyway. No, it's something else, something my father is keeping from me. That is why I think it wasn't an accident.' She was growing confused, her head filled with arguments she could not articulate.

Jude was coming out of the house, walking across the lawn. His hair catching the sun. Looking somehow like his uncle.

'I'm sorry, I have to go,' said Leila. 'Thank you for your time.'

She jumped up, almost upsetting the table in her haste and

ran before Jude could reach them. She ignored Celyn calling her back and Jude's cry: 'Leila!' Her throat was tight and she was choking.

Not far away, on the south side of Clocaenog, Imogen was saying goodbye to Geraint and getting onto her bike.

SIXTEEN

'He's going, leaving for good!' cried Imogen.

Leila was incredulous.

'Geraint is leaving?'

It did not seem to fit.

'Why is he suddenly leaving now?'

'He has had enough,' said Imogen, wiping away a tear. 'He wants to move on and leave the past behind.'

'He sounds almost sane,' said Leila. 'How did you get talking to him?'

'I was cycling to Gwyneth's when he stopped in his car. I was so shocked that I never went to Gwyneth's in the end. I came straight back to tell you, but you were ages.'

Leila frowned. 'Are you *sure* he's going?'

'Yes,' said Imogen impatiently. 'You didn't really think he would stay and rot here forever for your mother's sake did you?'

'No, but everyone else seems to think so. And they all think he is crazy.'

'Just like Mr Parry, and look what happened to him. They drove him to it. Look, there's no need to worry, he only wants to say goodbye and Arabella is coming too. She is going to make a mould of the mask for you. It's so you can have a copy. We owe it to Geraint to give him a chance.'

'I don't owe him anything,' said Leila. 'If it wasn't for him coming up here, my mother would never have died. And he shouldn't even have that mask in the first place. It was meant for me.'

Imogen sighed. 'Well, you will have to tell him that when you see him, but you'd better be careful or you'll end up with nothing. We have to go now. We need to hurry – before our parents notice.'

There was not enough time for Leila to think. Imogen was pushing her. She was troubled; it all seemed too easy.

'Are you sure Arabella will be there?' she asked. 'Have you heard from her?'

'Not directly, but he rang her while I was there…' Imogen stopped too late, and then she blushed.

'While you were *where*?' said Leila

'Where do you think?'

'At Geraint's?' said Leila in disbelief.

'Yes, that's right. I wasn't going to tell you – I knew you would make a fuss. I saw him in Llan a few times. We spoke; he talked about arranging this copy of the mask to be made for you. It was like he wanted to make it up to you; he feels guilty and he wants to do this for you before he goes. He won't ever come back.'

'And he asked you to go to his place?' asked Leila.

'Yes,' Imogen said impatiently, 'I'm not afraid of him, like you. He isn't that bad.' She touched her palm to her cheek self consciously, remembering the kiss he had put there earlier.

'I don't know about this,' Leila was tense, but she was putting her coat on nevertheless. 'Will Arabella be there when we get there?'

'Yes, he said five o'clock onwards. He's leaving this evening. Come on, this is for you, Leila!'

'I'm still not sure about it,' said Leila, 'but I'll come.'

As they left their bedroom, Leila slipped the sharp stone she had taken from a rock near Afon Ddu into her pocket. It was long and thin, and sufficient to cause injury if wielded in anger or need.

For the first part of the cycle over to Clocaenog, Leila nagged Imogen for details, though her words were snatched from her as they fell away from Hafod down the steep hill that led downwards between a leaning hedgerow of hawthorn and blackthorn. As they gathered speed she took a quick last glance over her shoulder and thought of turning back, but something made her continue, perhaps the same daredevil disposition Lio had possessed. Surely if Imogen was happy to go and Arabella was going to be there, nothing bad could happen. She hoped. She had wanted to tell her father about the mask and see what action he would take first, but it seemed there would not be time. This way, she might be able to bring the mask back as a surprise for him. But how would he take it? Would he want to see it after all this time?

As they reached a level section of the lane, Leila pulled alongside Imogen. She had never seen Imogen, careful, sensible, Imogen, cycle like this before. Her behaviour was somewhat alarming, but it was difficult for Leila to think straight at such speed.

'Imogen,' she cried, 'can I ask you something?'

Imogen did not take her eyes off the road ahead. 'What?' she shouted.

'Why didn't Arabella come and pick us up to go there?'

'No time,' came the reply, 'we didn't know what time you would turn up.'

This is not all for me. I just hope she can see past her infatuation, Leila thought as she found herself struggling to pedal fast enough to match Imogen's fevered cycling. She had always considered herself stronger than her stepsister, and it was disconcerting to find herself coming off the weaker of the two. Steeling herself she pushed onwards, pedalling harder, determined to match Imogen, even if she could not beat her. She hardly noticed their passage over the moor road. It was a smoothly surfaced road, favourable for cycling. But she did notice the drop into Clocaenog; it was impossible not to feel its cold shadow.

As they cycled hard into the gloom and Leila saw Imogen's breath rising beastly in the cool, damp air of Clocaenog she wondered if her stepsister had become possessed somehow. The shivering, quivering Imogen, who needed gloves and scarves to fiddle with in winter and sun lotion and shady hats in summer, was racing towards Geraint, leaping off her bike and propping it smartly against his beige bungalow.

'Come on,' she urged, glancing around only once as she marched to the door.

Leila hesitated, pulling her coat around her nervously and fiddling with the buttons, behaving more like Imogen than Imogen. The sun had gone behind the clouds since they had entered Clocaenog. Not that it needed to, the silent evergreens blocked it out anyway, but at least it was not as cold as previously. No drip, drip. No sound at all.

There was Geraint's beige car in the drive, the car that matched his bungalow, his sofa and his tacky carpets. Leila saw little sign of belongings packed into it, except for a duffel bag, stuffed full and sitting on the front passenger seat. As Imogen knocked eagerly at the door, Leila was suddenly filled with a sickening fear, which almost knocked her out. She backed away as the door opened. This was her last chance.

'Hello,' said Geraint in a friendly tone, as he stepped out eagerly to welcome them. 'I'm so glad you came Leila. I wanted to make everything right between us before I went. Has Imogen told you that I am leaving?'

Leila nodded, and coughed. Her throat was constricting, but she managed to ask: 'Is Arabella here yet?'

'Yes, come in,' he said. 'I've got coffee on. Would you like some?'

'Yes, please,' said Imogen enthusiastically, and Geraint smiled at her, almost as if there was some understanding between them.

'That's my girl,' he said. 'For you, Leila?'

'Not for me thanks.'

'Oh go on,' he said, speaking with a fiendish playfulness and a glint in his eye. As if they were friends. 'I can't stand having guests if they won't have a drink. I'll tell you what, I'll make you one and you can decide whether to drink it.'

As she walked into the dingy hallway, Leila shivered. The mucky walls were closing in to suffocate her. There was a stink of mould and decay.

'Take a seat,' he said, pointing to the beige sofa in the lounge, 'I'll just get the coffee.'

'Where is Arabella?' asked Leila, a note of urgency that she would rather have suppressed appearing in her voice.

'Oh yes, I'm sorry,' said Geraint, putting a hand through his flaxen hair and looking appealingly at her, as if he thought his looks could overcome his lies. 'She forgot something she needs to do the mould with and she's just popped back to her place.'

'And how long will she be?'

'Not long,' he said, withdrawing from the room. She watched him go, and then saw, once he was out of Imogen's view, the weirdness return. As he moved back into the shadow of the doorway, his eyes looked black again, intent on her. Psychotic.

She turned around in panic. 'Oh no;' she said quietly, but enough for Imogen to hear, 'please, let's go!'

Imogen tilted her head to one side, and regarded her. 'Really, it's all right Leila. Calm down will you. Come and sit here, you're not on your own. What *is* the matter with you?'

Leila stared at the beige sofa. Even older and dirtier now than it had been then, when she had lain face down as a toddler, her head stuck down its back. Why on earth was she here? Standing once again in the bungalow where he had once tried to kill her. Did she want to die? She turned to go, but found Geraint standing in the doorway, holding the drinks on an old metal tray, stolen from a pub like the ashtray on the table. There was nothing else left in the room, except for something lying underneath a red tea towel. The mask, perhaps... Leila thought she could make out the line of the forehead and the nose under the cloth. Perhaps it was true, perhaps he did want to make amends. She gripped the stone in her pocket and sat down tensely on the edge of the sofa, trying not to think of how she had lain on it helplessly as a toddler. She glanced at the new Imogen, whose hands were not in her pockets holding on to potential weapons but resting passively on the coffee cup in her lap; her eyes were on Geraint and shining with devotion.

Geraint sat down and smiled. His face creased and Leila saw his age in the lines at the corners of his mouth, yet in his thinness and the smoothness of his pale skin he had retained the look of a twenty-something, while his fine, shampoo advert hair could have belonged to a seven year old boy. It occurred to her that she had no idea of his age, possibly late thirties if he was the same as Lio would have been.

'Well,' said Geraint. 'What shall we do while we wait?'

Leila noticed he had no coffee. She put hers down on the windowsill, next to a dead plant, still standing in its pot like a wooden skeleton. Perhaps coffee had killed it. She leaned towards Imogen and whispered: 'Don't drink it.'

Imogen looked at her with disapproval. 'It's rude to do that,' she said.

Geraint smiled again and joined his hands.

Leila observed the small, smooth hands. They looked good for strangling and pushing. Perhaps now was the time to ask.

'Did you push my mother off the cliffs?' she heard herself say as if she was detached from her foolish mouth. Then she braced herself for the response, with a coldness entering between her shoulder blades.

The smile faded from his face and the muscle twitched on the left side of his jaw as it tightened. Then he put his eyes on her with an unnerving steadiness.

'I don't think you should be asking that question,' he said slowly. 'I don't think you want to hear the answer to that. I don't think you want to know who pushed your mother.'

Despite the fact that she was now gripped by fear, and leaning back stiffly away from him as much as she could, perched as she was on the edge of the sofa, not wanting to risk sinking into its depths, she said the next thing that came into her head.

'So, she was pushed, you admit it! And I bet it was you. She

214

was leaving you. I have it on good authority, she wanted rid of you.'

Imogen had nervously gulped down her coffee, and was saying: 'Don't be silly Leila, don't be ridiculous!'

Geraint smiled, again as if laughing it off. 'It's all right Leila. I'm sorry. We got off on the wrong foot. You have never liked me. I expect your father never had anything good to say about me and I suppose I can't blame him. Naturally he has told you that Lio was going back to him.'

Leila said nothing.

'Yet, the day before she died, she changed her mind, she was going to leave him for me.'

'Liar,' said Leila, choking.

'She was having trouble making her mind up,' he said, in a voice that sounded reasonable, 'she kept going this way and that, but let me tell you…she died on my side.'

'She was never coming to you,' snapped Leila.

Geraint shook his head. 'You were too young, you never really knew her. But I can see that you have suffered over her death and if you must believe that she was going back to Tom and you, then I will let you,' he spoke gently, but there was no compassion in his dark eyes, only a sarcastic glint.

With Imogen by her side, Leila indulged her growing anger, nothing could happen with two of them there.

'You killed her because you couldn't bear to lose her.'

He said nothing but stared at her with the same intentness in his empty eyes. It was as if he was waiting for something. He looked at Imogen and smiled. Imogen's breathing had become audible and regular, like when she was asleep. Geraint's smile widened. Leila turned and looked at Imogen. A minute earlier Imogen had leant back, now she was obviously unconscious. Her empty coffee cup had fallen over in her lap. In an instant Leila knew it: Arabella knew nothing of this little meeting. She wasn't coming back.

The rotten stench of cat fetor rose from the beige carpet like a bad genie. And from the other side of the room Geraint watched Leila steadily, his smile had evaporated.

'I think your sister must be a little tired,' he said quietly. 'Would you like me to call your father to come and collect you both?'

Leila thought with panic about her father's likely response and shook her head and then wondered whether she had chosen a much greater evil.

'What have you given her?' she asked in a voice that shook.

'Nice bit of herbal tea. She's probably tired after all that cycling.'

'Let's call Arabella' said Leila, her tone becoming increasingly strangled.

'No need,' said Geraint in a voice that was meant to reassure. 'Remember? She's probably driving here as we speak.'

'I'm worried about Imogen,' said Leila as she shook her sister vigorously, 'she's not waking up!'

'I've got something that might help,' said Geraint smoothly, 'you stay there and take care of her. I won't be a minute.'

'Imogen wake up now!' Leila whispered urgently, shaking her like a rag doll. 'I'm going to have to leave you. Sorry, but I will go and get help.'

Panic was making the room sway, but this was Leila's chance to escape. If she could get out of the bungalow she could cycle to the nearest house and raise the alarm. She had to go before the panic got too bad. As she reeled towards the door, a sudden rush of nausea made her swing slightly to one side and bash against the lintel. Now she was in the hall, but she was not moving quickly enough.

'Leila!' came Geraint's shout from the kitchen and then as she was at the door, trying to undo the lock, he was behind her.

'What are you doing?' he shouted.

'I... I thought I heard Arabella, I just wanted to go out and see if it was her.'

'Liar!' screamed Geraint in a rage that was so sudden that she turned fearfully to see the anger distorting his face.

He ran forwards, his small smooth hands extended towards her and she tried to kick out and throw him back, but his hands flew at her, one grabbing her by the hair, the other at her throat.

'Please don't!' she cried as the strangling feeling so tightened her throat that she gasped for breath.

'You can't leave without Imogen. You're a vicious, ungrateful girl. Get back on the sofa.'

Leila felt herself thrown towards the sofa, vaguely relieved that his hand was no longer on her throat.

But panic had taken over now. She could not think of anything except that she must escape.

'Stay there!' he shouted, 'I don't want to get angry, but you are making me *very* angry.'

For a second she paused, afraid of his volcanic rage, though even as she waited she could see it subsiding a little, as if he knew he had gone too far.

She rocked on her feet for a second, refusing to look at him and sobbing.

'Shut up!' he screamed, the rage fountaining upwards again.

He was standing near the door but she thought she could rush him. He was quite slightly built. She braced herself and then with a sudden explosion of adrenalin, she ran at him screaming as she did, 'Let me out!'

This time he pushed her back harder so that she unbalanced and toppled backwards onto the table with the tea towel on it. She slammed down painfully onto her back, hitting the table and knocking it sideways. Something had fallen with her and was underneath her. Broken into pieces.

He cried out as she recovered herself and pushed her aside in order to lift the tea cloth. The life mask was smashed.

'You,' he cried turning on her. 'You, you've done it again... You should have died, not her...'

He moved towards her as she froze, gasping in terror and trying to scream, but giving out little more than a strangled squeak.

'I should have done this years ago,' he said breathlessly crashing towards her, his right hand outstretched, 'before everything else...'

Leila might have used the last brief chance to try another escape, except that she had been crippled by the tightness in her throat and chest. Geraint's hands flew towards her like claws and now she knew beyond all doubt the reason for her throat trouble. She cried out and fell back onto the sofa, all her strength seemed to have evaporated. Even before his hand closed on her neck, her throat was constricting, stealing her breath, making it easier for him. She tried to find her right pocket with the sharp stone from Afon Ddu, but her hand seemed to fumble uselessly as if the strangling was stopping her limbs from moving too. She had dreamed of this, the flaxen hair falling forwards over a pale face contorted with hate and eyes with nothing behind them, no flicker of regret, just a cold anger accompanied by a depraved pleasure screeching at her from a blank, black void.

The world was shrinking all around her, her head exploding above her squashed neck, as if his grip was pushing everything into her head so that it bulged obscenely. She looked up at the corner of the ceiling, which was upside down, and sideways as she was pushed down on the sofa by his alternately one-handed and then two-handed grip. There was a large spider there, guarding a dusty web above the filthy lemon-coloured picture rail. She thought, 'I am dying; this is it and I don't know what is beyond this.' Even as she felt herself swimming towards a strange high point, a final panic shook her, giving enough reflex action for a final bid at escape, a sort of twitching which to Geraint must have looked like nothing more than the floundering of someone close to death. Geraint smiled, Leila's face felt blown up and red, taut, ugly. She had the stone, somehow and she stabbed it into his straining temples as hard as she could.

As she fell away from his hands, she felt everything fading into pixels and dots, brightness and darkness and a strange harmony, floating warm above the smashing and screaming and falling... Geraint falling on top of her and Geraint's blood on the sharp stone from Afon Ddu.

SEVENTEEN

'Why are hospitals white? So you think they are clean? Or is it so you think you are in heaven?'

Jude's voice came first, floating clear over the tang of antiseptic and the kerfuffle of voices at visiting time. It was the first thing Leila heard as she became conscious again. She opened her eyes and wondered why her neck was hurting so. There was Jude's face near her, not a dream, but real. His hair had grown longer and wispy at the ends, but his eyes were still bright green and he was complete with halo shining. He was back.

'I don't know,' said Imogen, not having noticed that Leila was awake, 'maybe they are white because white is cheaper.'

'She's awake,' said Jude softly, 'I'll run and tell Tom and your mother.'

Leila watched him go and the remembrance of what had happened took her back with the ferocity of the collapsing building that haunted her dreams. For a moment she writhed away from the terror, grasping the edge of the bed as if to jump out and make her escape. But Imogen grabbed her shoulders.

'Be careful Leila. You'll fall!'

Leila rolled back into what felt like a straight jacket of bright lights and crisp white sheets. It was too bright – all around – pallid walls, glossy floors and wan faces reflecting concern. And a headache spiralling within her skull. She turned slowly to Imogen.

'Is it true?' she asked. 'Did it really happen?'

Imogen nodded, but remained silent.

'I'm so, so sorry Leila,' she said after a moment, relieved that she could at last apologise, 'I've been so stupid. I'll never forgive myself.'

She burst into tears.

'It's ok,' said Leila hoarsely. 'Are *you* all right?'

'Yes, he gave me enough Valium to knock me out, though I deserved worse. You know you saved your own life, you got him with the stone...you did good.'

'How do you mean?' asked Leila, afraid, because she could not remember.

'You hit him with a stone... on his head... hard, I think.'

'Where is he now?' asked Leila, it hurt to talk and she could only manage a hoarse whisper and was having difficulty being heard over Imogen's loud sobs.

'Have the police got him? He killed my mother. I thought it was him. He practically confessed.'

Imogen had buried her head in the bed sheets and was shaking it from side to side.

'Have the police got him?' repeated Leila, but there was no reply.

Could Geraint be dead? she wondered.

'Where's my father and Ann?'

'They just went to get some food,' replied Imogen, wiping her eyes. 'They'll be back soon.'

'So have they taken him in?' asked Leila.

Now they can press charges over my mother's death, she thought, when no immediate reply was forthcoming.

Imogen shook her head again, 'Don't ask me, I don't know what's going on.'

Leila gave up and put her hand onto her throat. It felt stiff and badly bruised. She had come close.

Presently Jude reappeared.

'Your father is on his way,' he said, sitting down beside her and taking her hand. She was glad of the warmth of his hand and too tired to react with annoyance or embarrassment.

'Leila, I'm so sorry,' he said, 'I feel that it is partly my fault for encouraging you, for taking you that first time to see Uncle Geraint. I suppose I didn't know him as well as I thought. Please forgive me and please believe that I am nothing like him. Will you forgive me?'

Leila wanted to nod her head but thought better of it.

'It wasn't your fault,' she said, keeping her damaged neck still and trying to contain her words and the movement they required inside her mouth, away from her throat. She trusted Jude, she had no doubt in him now that she could see him there, sitting on her bed, smiling at her. Leila smiled back.

'Now we know what happened to my mother.'

Tom and Ann returned. Leila was relieved to see that her father was not angry; instead his eyes glistened with a fear she had not seen before.

'We're moving,' he said, as he stooped to give her a careful hug. 'I should have taken you away a long time ago. We are going as soon as you get out of hospital, we will go and stay with my brother.'

Leila murmured in agreement; for the first time she really wanted to go. It was as if the whole place had conspired in what had happened to her mother ten years before and what had happened to her now. All of it, including Hiraethog, Gwylfa, the Afon Ddu cliffs and even Hafod's bland white face looking out over the moor; all were defiled now. They always had been marked, she had known through the paradox of devotion and hatred she felt for them. She had almost died without seeing anything else.

Even Ann appeared sympathetic in a stepmotherly way.

'Don't you worry yourself,' she said to Leila. 'There is a policeman on the door.'

'Why?' asked Leila, her eyes widening. 'Is he still free?'

Tom flashed his annoyance at his wife and Leila saw that once again he had planned to protect her by covering up, by lying.

'I will be staying with you until you get out,' he said turning to her. 'The police will need to speak to you about what happened, when you are ready.'

'Where is Geraint?' asked Leila, she was getting impatient with them. Why could they not just tell her?

They all looked so afraid.

'I should think they have him by now,' said Tom, though his voice was shaky. 'He did get away, but he won't get far. You did so well in defending yourself. The injury will help them spot him.'

'What injury?'

'The one you inflicted on him, with a stone or something.'

She did not remember.

'What happened to the mask?' she asked after a moment.

'Imogen mentioned that,' her father replied. 'I'd never seen or heard of it until yesterday. I wish you'd told me about it Leila. If only you had listened to me about Geraint. If you'd asked me, I could have sorted things out for you.'

She looked at him doubtfully as he stroked her forehead. And in her head she said to him: *'I did ask you Dad. I asked you many times...'*

He was still talking, 'I know that Imogen was somewhat to blame here and she has learned her lesson. I'm just glad you're safe.'

'Did you get the life mask?' asked Leila, since he had still not answered her question.

'No, it seems he took what was left. There were just a few fragments. It was broken somehow.'

Leila could remember how. She remembered everything up until the mask was broken and Geraint had come towards her grabbing for her. After that she knew nothing, only that she had woken in hospital.

'You will stay won't you?' she pleaded, suddenly afraid.

'Of course,' he promised, 'I won't leave until you are ready to come with me.'

When Leila was well enough to leave the hospital and had gone through her story with the police, her father took her away to his older brother's home in Northumberland, far enough away to make Hiraethog seem like another world. It was then that she told him what she had discovered from Celyn. It seemed a long time since she had sat in that garden with the blackbird song and apple juice. She was sure that he did not know that Lio had intended to leave Geraint. She was sure that he had been haunted by the fact that Lio had been headed towards Clocaenog on the day she died. So long ago, so much pain in not really knowing. Instinct told her that her father had believed that Lio was going to Geraint. How much did it matter now that he had been wrong, was it too late?

She watched him as she told him. He showed little emotion and said less, but she could see the relief breaking out, behind his eyes, rolling back the lines at his mouth, bringing a tearful glitter, making him swallow hard. The power of helping someone like that made Leila feel strong. A sudden harmony in the midst of uncertainty and fear of the future. But she knew he had waited too long to hear it. Much of the damage was beyond repair.

For the first week, Imogen and her mother also stayed in Northumberland, but both went south to some of their own family after that. Leila was kept busy by outings almost every day, even when the weather was not conducive. She was kept so busy that she had to take time out, lying in her bed, in order to think things over. She felt safe there, sharing with her cousins who slept in bunk beds, with her father in a room to one side and her uncle and aunt in the room on the other side. But she could only sleep when she was sure the window was bolted tight, the curtains drawn and a night-light left on. She would not feel completely safe until Geraint was apprehended. And something else was unnerving her. There was a noticeable lack of interest in charging Geraint for her mother's murder. There was talk that he was also wanted for questioning about the circumstances surrounding Mr

Parry's demise, but the re-examination of her mother's fall was shrugged off citing 'lack of evidence.' And everyone said the important charge was the attempted murder on her, which was what he would go down for. They did not seem to understand that the ten-year-old murder of her mother was still the worse crime. It was all so frustrating; she was being treated as an invalid and no one would listen to her.

So Leila gave up. If she left it alone, solutions might come forth, conjured up by her unconscious. She thought about Jude instead. He was sending letters twice weekly, which she received like long-hoped for Christmas gifts. He furnished his scrappy notes (treasured by Leila as if inscribed on twenty pound notes) with reports on how he was getting on at school, amusing stories, jokes and harmless local gossip. Occasionally at Leila's request, he told her what people were really saying about the whole incident. She had become an overnight celebrity and everywhere the people who had treated her with suspicion now talked of how they wanted to help her if she should ever come back. They felt they now understood why she had appeared dark and morose. A child who felt under threat could be nothing else. Jude on the other hand was being treated with some of the derision and suspicion that was reserved especially for the relatives of villains. But Jude professed that he had broad shoulders and that he could understand these reactions, which only made him seem even more gallant to Leila.

'Do you think Geraint will contact you?' Leila asked him one night on the phone.

The line at the other end crackled and buzzed and for a moment Leila thought Jude had gone, but then he answered.

'No, we weren't that close,' said Jude.

'What would you do if he did contact you or your Mum?'

'We'd ask him to turn himself in and then we'd tell the police. Because that would be the right thing to do.'

'Really?'

'Yes really. You are more important to me now and he needs to be caught.'

And so the letters continued with Jude and Leila finding all of the attention very amusing. The idea of going back to Hiraethog slowly began to appeal to Leila, if only to luxuriate in being the biggest celebrity in town since her mother's corpse. And to see Jude, of course.

After four weeks in Northumberland, Tom had to return to work and Leila was left in the capable hands of her uncle and aunt. She began to attend her cousins' school, since she felt well enough to return to lessons. It was a small high school full of farmers' kids, not unlike the one in Llan. Her cousins Olivia and Joe had become good friends and protectors. They played out together in the long hay fields around the house, which was one of a small hamlet built into a west-facing wooded hillside, with a stony-bedded river like Afon Ddu, flowing at the bottom of the valley. There were lots of good things to do. They jumped out of trees into the long grass and stalked each other like wild animals. They built a den on private land, trespassed in a derelict bungalow in the wood and were chased off by the farmer's boys shouting, 'Get off our land!' Leila had never before had cause to wonder whose land she was wandering on; she had thought the immediate world was all hers. Unperturbed, they went back and built a bird table in the woods, waded across the river when it was low, balanced precariously on stepping-stones when it was high, watched in awe when it was swollen and uncrossable. Birds ate scraps on their low stone wall, snails nestled in the cracks in the bigger dry stone wall round the back and at night in bed they heard the badger rumbling about in the woods behind.

'I love it here,' thought Leila as she relaxed into sleep, 'Imogen would love it too.' But in her dreams Welsh words shone with phosphorescence like when, in the dark, they were caught by the beam of headlights and black letters jumped out from shimmering white signposts. Signposts which pointed the way back to places with underworld names: *Clocaenog, Hiraethog, Hafod, Afon Ddu.* And she could hear the wind howling through Gwylfa Hiraethog, just as it was, back there on the moor.

They visited at the weekends, Tom, the stepmother and Imogen.

Geraint had not been found but his car had been abandoned in Dover. Money totalling one thousand pounds had been taken from his account. It was all he had. There was much talk back in Llan and the town was divided into two camps. One believed that Geraint had committed suicide. The evidence was there, he had left his passport behind in Clocaenog and most of his belongings. The white cliffs of Dover were popular with suicides and a striking fair-haired man had been spotted at the café on the cliffs the day after he had fled from Clocaenog. It was the café where suicides often took their last lonely drink. The stepmother was in this camp. The other half of Llan disagreed. Geraint had spoken in the past of disappearing. The fact that he had left his passport meant nothing, he probably had a fake passport prepared in advance, after all he had been planning to leave. It was likely that the whole thing had been planned. He had crossed the sea and got away, and it was unlikely that they would ever see him again. So far a body had not been washed up, although no one had spotted him on the continent either.

Imogen was secretly of this last view. In spite of everything, when she thought of Geraint, it was still with an odd, distorted affection. She saw his hair shining in the sun and baleful eyes which could floor her with a look. He had brought a hint of darkness into her life, and she welcomed it.

'I don't think he's coming back,' said Tom, who was undecided between the two theories on Geraint's fate. 'We have decided to move back into Hafod until it is sold.'

Leila nodded. 'Am I coming back too?'

'Well, I was hoping you would finish school here for this year, but perhaps you could come back before we move. Then you can say your goodbyes.'

'Is Hafod sold?' she asked.

'Not yet, though we have a young couple very interested. But they do need to sell their own house.'

Leila hoped they would not be able to.

'Do you want to come back?' asked Tom when he saw how sad she looked. 'I thought you were happy here.'

'I am,' she said. It wasn't possible to have both lives, and her heart ached to go back to Hafod, but she could not say it because she knew everyone was against it and the tears that were welling up would not allow her to speak coherently. She ran away out to the woods to be alone.

'I think she should stay here,' Tom told the others. 'She will be safer here. It's not so much Geraint returning that worries me, because I think we've seen the last of him. It's her mind I'm worried about and the attention she'll get.'

Everyone agreed with Tom.

Out in the woods, Leila climbed a tree. She was still trying to master this skill, and could not climb as well as Olivia and Joe. There were few trees around Hiraethog, only slender, shimmering rowans and the commercial plantation pines that were unclimbable except when the wind felled them, when they were fun to balance on. But it was far more pleasant to climb these deciduous trees, with light flickering, whispering, dappling leaves and rounded crowns with thick branches to shimmy along. If she climbed high enough she could get a good aerial view of the whole valley. A different world to her own: a world of long, swaying meadows, black and white cows and wide rivers, green hills, green grass everywhere, and no heather. Wild flowers and garden birds: no gorse, no red grouse or soaring buzzards. No wind-haunted ruins, or raw moorland, just a derelict bungalow in the woods and wire fencing, stone walls, trimmed hedges, telegraph poles, smooth tarmac roads, the sound of the occasional car roaring up the hill and coasting down. With the pleasant valley breeze in her face, she turned to the south and thought of the moor. She had stopped crying now, and was quite pleased to have made it to the top of the tree through the watery blur of tears. Here she swayed precariously, but hardly noticed. She comforted herself with the fact that she would go back soon.

June brought better weather and the long dusks of summer. Leila often thought of Hafod in the light evenings when the sun immersed itself slowly, soaking the sky as it gradually set. Hafod always glowed warmly in these long, slow summer sunsets. Leila watched the gradual change of hues and pictured Imogen sitting on the bench on the patio, swinging her legs and watching the swallows dashing by. At such times Leila faced south and became submerged as if she was a goldfish in a bowl hallucinating, imagining the ocean. The letters from Jude sustained her and they talked through ink and paper as they had talked, before Bethan. She only hoped that Jude's obvious affection was not just a consequence of her recently acquired celebrity.

Her relationship with her own family was improved too; every night her father called her and once a week a letter from him, the stepmother and Imogen would slap through the letterbox. Sometimes this included letters from locals, obviously censored by her father, though a few slipped through the net. She was sure he would not have approved a letter sent by a nine year old who wanted to know what it felt like to be strangled. In spite of this she felt happier in many ways now than she had in a long time. Arabella sent frequent notes, reporting on the progress of the peregrines and the buzzards with accompanying sketches of the nests and views of Hiraethog that made Leila nostalgic. The family in Northumberland, her own immediate family, Jude and Arabella and all the love and attention she was getting made her feel protected and loved. Most of the time… In just a few weeks after her ordeal, her father had paid her more attention than he had in the whole of the preceding year. There were times when it made her uncomfortable, because it did not seem genuine, perhaps he was allaying his own guilt over what had happened to her. Then finally in the last week of June, he again asked her what she would like to do. Of course he knew what she would ask for.

It was subsequently agreed that she could spend a few days at Hafod. And with cruel irony it was on the day of her return that she saw Hafod sold and her father shake hands with the buyers, a young, smiling Welsh couple. There was only one person whose smile was broader than theirs and that was her father's. He could not hide his happiness at finally selling Hafod and he did not try. Infuriated, Leila slipped away and went up onto Hiraethog for the first time since the day she had almost died.

It was strange to be alone on the moor again after almost three months away. She realised how much she had missed it, the open expanse, the rolling heather, the hills and the boundless sky. It was not tainted after all, no more than it ever had been. Geraint's darkness could not add anything more to the moor's intrinsic shadow, it was far greater than one man. She looked around for a minute to check that she was alone, that she was not being followed, and then she was not afraid anymore. Not outdoors anyway.

She knew now that she really did not want to leave. Even in spite of what had happened to her, she could not abide the thought of giving up Hafod to anyone; it made her want to scream into the bloody sunset that was streaming hellishly over her head. When she thought of someone else waking up and looking out of her window at her view, while sitting on her window seat in her room, she could not bear it. She was overcome by nostalgia even before she had departed.

She ran up to the babbling stream and sat there in the heather and watched Hafod from a distance, observing the young couple emerge and linger in the yard talking to her father and Ann. Tom and Ann were eager to move into their new Victorian home in Llandudno. Leila had refused to go to the viewings and had failed to prevent Imogen going; she had put on a show of reluctance before returning full of enthusiasm. So there was no way out for Leila, she was too young to live by herself. Sometimes she dreamed of living with Jude. She was afraid that she might lose him, before she was old enough to really love him. And then there was her Lio. Why did she feel like she was about to betray her? She had failed because she had not brought her mother's murderer to justice. But at least she had driven him away. That was something.

Between the warm, running stream of her own thoughts, shining on her warm cheeks and the cool, careless babbling of the moor stream, the world was under water; the red ball of a diminishing sun and the angry sky couldn't change anything. Hiraethog was disappearing under lengthening shadow and drowning in watery obscurity. The tiny figures had vanished. Her father did not understand, could never understand, stuck as he was in his left-brain rationality (as Jude had once described it), he did not think that Lio was there anymore. To him death was final. He did not believe in the fishy swishy soul that Leila knew. He did not believe in fishy swishy souls at all.

'You've got to move on,' he had said. 'You can't keep clinging onto your childhood. You'll never lose it, it will always be there in your memory, but the time has come to start growing up.'

It was Ann who suggested a farewell party to say *hwyl fawr* to the place and the people. Even more surprisingly, she did not seek to dominate the proceedings but allowed suggestions from everyone, even Leila. Tom was easily encouraged. After Lio's death his counsellor had spoken of the importance of routine and rituals that could help them remember and at the same time, move on, hence the yearly ritual at the Afon Ddu cliffs. The party would be a final ritual to help Leila leave her childhood home and all of her childhood obsessions. She would have to learn how to give things up. Otherwise life would prove unbearably painful for her with its inevitable endings and uncertainty. Secretly Tom thought of it as *Leila's letting go party.*

It was Leila's idea to make it an all day party. They would begin with a walk up to the ruin, the highest point locally, which gave them a panoramic view of the moor all around and on a clear day as far as the distant blue of the sea. Tom was not keen on this mass trespass, but Leila was implacable and he gave in. There they would have a picnic, with those who wanted descending to the Sportsman's Arms for a drink, while anyone who wanted (like Leila) could linger on the moor before the late afternoon descent. Back at Hafod there would be a meal, outside watching the sunset if the weather allowed it, and they would sit out with the oncoming dusk, drinking wine and reminiscing about their years at Hafod. Before bedtime, Imogen proposed that they would have a final tour of the house, when the family, and anyone else who was staying over, would go from room to room, appreciating the details of everything they had lived with for so long. Telling their stories to each other and saying their last goodbyes together. Then the children would go up to bed, with their closest friends (Leila imagined Jude there), camping out on the floor with them, staying up for as long as they could. This was the way they would say goodbye.

Ann took on the planning of the event with enthusiasm. Without analysing her possible reasons for doing so, Leila instead thanked her at least for this. The date was set for a week before their final departure, which was scheduled for the 18th August. It had not escaped Leila's notice that their last full day at Hafod would be the 17th and the tenth anniversary of Lio's death, this was by design rather than by accident, and Tom had deliberately delayed moving . He knew it was important to Leila. On the last day they would take flowers and spend time on the cliffs alone; finally bringing down the curtain on their life on Hiraethog. While Tom eagerly awaited it, Leila blocked this solemn event out of her mind. She would not think of the end until after the party. The food was planned, the invitations sent out by letter and word of mouth and it became clear why the stepmother was renowned for her organisational skills at work. There was a rare buzz of excitement animating the whole household.

'Jude!' said Imogen one day as they argued over pudding. 'We haven't even invited him!'

Leila blushed, she was well aware of this and relieved that someone else had finally noticed.

'Do you want him there?' asked Imogen.

'I don't think he will want to come,' said Leila awkwardly. 'He has been very kind to me recently. But he says he is going abroad in August to do a summer work camp. So I don't think he will be here.' She gulped back the rising bubble in her throat, not wanting to admit that the party would be no good without Jude. Much to her dismay, Imogen nodded in assent and then seemed to forget all about it.

'Isn't it funny', Imogen said, 'this has really made us pull together as a family, like never before. You and my mother are almost friends for the first time ever. Why wasn't it always like this?'

'Because we never really tried,' said Leila, half-heartedly.

There was still no news of Geraint and people were becoming resigned to the fact that there might never be. Now that she was back at Hafod, Leila did not want to return to Northumberland and she was eventually allowed to stay on at Hafod, though Tom enforced a rule of her not being allowed out alone.

'I don't think Geraint would come back to watch the house or anything,' he said to Ann one night when the girls were in bed. 'But I can't even take the slightest risk with her now. I couldn't let it happen again.'

As the days passed Leila grew tired of having her freedom inhibited. When a weather report predicted that the warm weather would be temporarily broken by a storm, Leila came up with a plan to escape from her father's and Ann's over-bearing protection.

'There's going to be a storm today Arabella,' whispered Leila, the phone held between her ear and shoulder in the fashion of her father. 'Can I come to your house? Dad said I'm allowed if you come for me.'

'Yes, of course,' came the voice at the other end. 'I'll come over right away.'

The clouds were gathering darkly as Leila rode with Arabella in the rattling Land Rover.

'Can we go for a walk in the storm, Arabella?'

'I'm not so sure that's a good idea.'

'Oh please. I'm moving away soon. I won't see you any more and I want to feel free for one last time, because my father is keeping me in chains. He won't let me go anywhere without a grown-up.'

'Why do you want to go walking in a storm Leila? We've had so many lovely days lately.'

'Well, I suppose it's the sort of thing I can imagine my mother enjoying. She was an artist, like you. And now you are a bit like my second artist mother and I think my real mother would have said "yes".'

'Ok, Leila, you win.'

Arabella parked the Land Rover on her drive with the faint impression that she was being manipulated. Leila was already out of the vehicle before the engine had died.

'Come with me... Mother.'

Leila laughed as she said the word. It sounded faintly ridiculous. As soon as she was out, she began to run, without waiting for Arabella, without looking back. She had a feeling it was going to be the greatest storm she had ever known. She had to grasp it while she could. The wind had risen and the air was taking on a chill. Leila vaguely remembered a day when she, Imogen, Jude and Gwyneth had waited and watched for a storm with their bikes lined up against the wall of Hafod. They had decided they would chase the storm on their bikes, although they had not been sure of exactly how to do it.

As the wind rose and the air grew colder, it felt as if the elements were revving up around her. She continued to run, stopping only to look back briefly. Arabella was trotting heavily behind her, a long way back, her shawl was battering around her in the wind. She *was* the Crow Woman, not really Leila's mother.

The swish of the long marsh grasses serrating the thick air filled Leila's ears. She stopped to breathe and stood alone feeling the elements exploding about her, the world of nature screaming, running and hiding in fear, the rushing terror of the grovelling, writhing vegetation filling her senses. A sudden gust whipped up her hair and thrashed it across her face. At intervals the wind would lull and she imagined she could hear frightened cries at her feet, high pitched like field mice, and the swallows chipping to each other in fear (or was it excitement?) above. Then the sky grew darker in an almost theatrical manner and forked lightning struck. She was transfixed as white vein-like arms streaked down in grasping white flashes. The lightning was spectacular for its silence. The thunder came seconds later and Leila remembered, from that day of storm-chasing when Gwyneth had timed the storm's distance with her watch, that each second after lightning counted for about a mile. Presently the rush of terrorised vegetation was accompanied by the first heavy splats of rain spat from the dark, moving features of a sky screwed up with apoplectic rage. Leila found herself shrinking to her knees in the marsh grass, with her face into the wind, the long grass rushing in her ears, the earth beneath her vibrating and humming as if straining its bowels while the sky cracked and rolled like a head out of control.

At last the heavy air which had hung sluggishly all day was now circulating and refreshed, and a thousand horse's hooves seemed to thunder across the thin racing membrane of the swirling sky, breaking up the angry, black trouts of clouds that had suffocated their world all day. She remembered Jude and when she had first loved him. 'Come on let's chase it!' he had shouted. 'We are the storm chasers!'

Leila was standing still, ankle deep in something sludgy. She didn't want to leave the only home she had ever known.

The sky was wracked with thunder and seemed to groan and strain against complete collapse. The heavens had finally yielded and rain was falling down like an ocean unleashed.

'Leila!' cried Arabella as she floundered in the boggy ground. 'Leila, please come back. You'll get stuck!'

It was then that Leila realised she had walked into a bog.

'I don't want to move away,' she muttered and took another step into the mire.

'Come back, you're sinking!' shouted Arabella.

Leila did not speak, but moved further in, until there was no longer the hard ground beneath her feet. Until she was suspended in the mire, slowly sinking. She could see the dark sludge rising towards her knees.

'What am I doing?' she thought. *'I didn't mean to do this.'*

'Stop there Leila. I will help you,' screeched Arabella as she lumbered breathlessly towards Leila.

'It will be all right. You can come and visit whenever you want. Maybe, if you want to…you could come and live with me when you are old enough.'

Thunder sounded then with such a searing crashing that Leila thought her eardrums would burst with hearing it and a shiver went through her as she stood quite still, looking down, watching the mire rise over her knees.

'Leila, let me get you out…please! What about Jude! He loves you and I do and so do Tom and Imogen. Stop being melodramatic!'

Leila had begun to cry. She didn't know why she was standing in the middle of a cold, wet bog. Couldn't understand the swift and colossal darkness that had drawn her. Was the sadness always going to be with her?

She turned despairingly towards Arabella and held out her hands towards her.

'Help me.'

'Silly girl,' said Arabella, pulling Leila out and wrapping her shawl around her, 'let's go home and light the fire…'

The summer slipped by. The calendar in the kitchen counted down the days to the party. Imogen crossed them off with a red pen and Leila watched nervously, realising they were counting down the time left at Hafod too. Her encounter with the bog was a secret between herself and Arabella. Tom had been unimpressed by her requests to live with Arabella.

'Have you forgotten about Geraint? You *cannot* live here again.'

No, but I could run away from you, Leila thought.

The second half of July had been stormy, but for August the good weather returned. The swallows in the barn were bringing up their second clutch of chicks and Leila had put a blue ring around the 17th of August on the calendar for the ten-year anniversary of her mother's death. She thought of Geraint almost every day. Sometimes he was in the sea, as bloated as a leatherjacket, his eyes eaten by fish, his hair seaweed green and his arms and legs floating out like a spaceman. Other times he was on the continent, with his hair dyed black and cut short. He was learning French and had begun to wear small, round glasses. She did not like to think of the third option, that he was still here somewhere and that he was biding his time.

Jude was unable to come to the party and though she was devastated, Leila acted as if she did not care. He left a week before the day, but promised to try and return for the final farewell.

'It won't be the same without you round here,' he said. 'I'm really sorry you are going, but I can see it's the best thing for you.'

'Well, I can't,' said Leila, 'I want to stay here. I'm sort of enjoying being a celebrity. People ask me all sorts of things, like did I have flashbacks of my life when I was being throttled? And even, do I have a phobia about blonde-haired men now?'

'And do you?' asked Jude, a smile forming.

'Of all except for you, Jude.'

She looked away self-consciously.

He laughed. 'I'll try to get back to see you off.' Then he held her hand and kissed her cheek. 'Just for you, Leila…'

With Jude gone, Leila felt the darkness return and nothing, not being a celebrity, or looking forward to the party could fill it. The only chance was if her father would change his mind about moving, but that would never happen; contracts had been signed and officially Hafod was no longer theirs. Their new home in Llandudno had balconies and views of the sea. It was set on a steep hillside, had a patio and a small garden and neighbours everywhere, houses on all sides. Leila had by now been coaxed into seeing it; just the once. It was nice, she admitted that much. It was called 'Sea View' like thousands of other similar homes. She liked the balcony with the clematis curling around the balustrades and the fresh, slightly pungent sea air. She even liked the view of Llandudno attractively curving around its bay and the high, raucous cries of large yellow-billed gulls, a sound so evocative of seaside holidays. It would have been lovely for a holiday, but it was not Hafod and there was no Hiraethog.

EIGHTEEN

The night before the party Leila dreamed that a man was climbing through the still white fog waters; out of Llan with a bag slung over his shoulder. His hair held the dew in bright droplets… Tiny, shining crystals... Dark pitiless eyes. There had not been such thick fog for quite some time. He would be the surprise guest.

'Dad, is there a surprise guest coming?' asked Leila, twenty minutes later at her father's bedroom door, still groggy from sleep and alarmed by vivid dreams.

'A surprise guest? No, Leila. What makes you ask that?'

'Oh. Nothing.'

Leila went back to her bed and opened the curtains. She was troubled to see thick fog swirling around the window. White out. Normally it would have delighted her, but today it was distressing. Was Geraint coming back for her? Had Jude gone to an innocent summer camp in Germany or was he visiting his Uncle?

She distracted herself with a book and nervously waited for the day to begin.

*

By midday the farewell party had begun. The guests were arriving like ghosts in the spinning fog. They couldn't see beyond the cars parked along the pale lane and by the gates. Leila was hanging out of her bedroom window, looking down on them. She spied a few of Tom and Ann's work colleagues whom she did not know well, Ann's friend Bronwen and the Crow Woman with her fist around a big bunch of flowers from her garden and some of her own baking balanced between one hand and her belly. Jude's mother, alone. Leila's heart sank (she had held hopes...) and Mr and Mrs Roberts, the latter looking around nervously as if she was being hit by one of her flashbacks. It was a warm, muggy day. The damp fragrance of blooming heather was everywhere and out in the white the sad sea cries of invisible curlews could be heard. Like lost children. Hafod seemed to be on an island in the sky, for all around was the nothingness of fog swirling like dragon smoke.

All at sea... Leila felt like the captain of a ship, on the lookout for danger. It was a special day, she could feel the atmosphere of a big occasion, one of those particular days of which there can only ever be a few. She rubbed her skin because it was moist from the warm damp air. The impenetrable fog on which Hafod now floated would keep them hidden from unwanted visitors. Geraint would not find her here. But she would be looking out for him anyway. They were adrift, sailing away on the fog like Noah on the flood, climbing higher and higher, growing lighter and lighter. At least there was plenty of food for their voyage, she could smell the aromas of the feast as they rode transparently on the mist. She leaned on the window ledge and stared for as long as she could without blinking.

'It looks like it might be clearing,' said Mr Roberts from down below, breaking the spell.

Her father, standing next to him, nodded and pointed over to the fencing on the other side of the pale lane which was now coming into view.

Leila moved away from the window and went downstairs. The

connecting doors between the lounge and the dining room had been opened wide to make one larger room and everyone was gathered in here. Ann was pouring drinks and chatting to Bronwen, while in the kitchen Tom and Imogen were preparing a salad and the Crow Woman was unveiling her cake. She was nervous and laughing girlishly. Leila sat down with a sneaky glass of white wine and waited to be noticed, because since Geraint had tried to throttle her, people were being very nice to her.

'Thanks for coming everyone,' said Tom as he entered the room, 'I think the fog is lifting and it's going to be a good day... hopefully. So all those who are walking should set off within the next half an hour in order to make it there for noon. Leila will be leading the way up.'

Leila nodded and stood up and everyone turned to look at her.

As the walking party gathered outside the gates, Leila looked down the lane and realised the fog was indeed thinning since she could now see the house sign which was almost a hundred yards down the lane. The sign read: *Hafod – No through road.* It was falling sideways, its paint peeling off and the wood rotting. As she looked, a figure appeared there, pausing to look up as she looked down. Leila's heart lurched. She did not hear her father who was telling her to go and get her jacket in case of rain and then he too noticed the figure of a man approaching. He saw the fair hair and stopped breathing, rooted to the spot. The man had also stopped. Tom moved towards Leila and felt as if he was swimming, for his movement seemed too slow and a feeling of panic gripped him.

'Leila,' he said hoarsely. 'Come here!'

He reached out for her shoulder and held it.

Leila looked at her father and found a look of frozen horror. For a moment she too had been transported back to Clocaenog, reminded of that first occasion when she had seen Geraint in the mist stepping out from the pines like a vision. But this time was different. It was a trick of the fog. This was not Geraint.

'It's all right,' she cried grabbing her father's hand and pulling it away. 'It's Jude. Jude has come back!'

Emerging from the distance at which the fog had covered him, they saw it was the younger figure of Jude and that he had lifted his hand to greet them, completely unaware that he had been mistaken for another.

'Hello there, Jude,' cried Tom walking forwards his hand outstretched, his voice shaky with relief. 'It's a surprise seeing you!'

'Yeah,' said Jude smiling, 'It was like the tower of Babel and there was somewhere I thought I'd rather be. I was hoping to catch you before you set out.'

'If you want to join us, we're about to leave. Just waiting for Imogen to find her gloves, though goodness knows why she needs them.'

Jude turned to Leila, 'Hi,' he said. 'I was hoping to surprise you. I was going to jump out on you. Still I suppose you have had enough surprises for a lifetime.'

'Don't worry, this is surprise enough,' said Leila.

While the walkers ascended on foot, Bronwen, the baby, Mr and Mrs Roberts and Ann took their cars and the picnic hamper over the moor road to the Sportsman's Arms. The fog was lifting fast and before the walkers had begun the ascent in earnest they gained a view of the ruin, appearing intermittently from behind the last skeins of low cloud. Then it was lost behind the steepness of the climb. Leila found herself shaking, having not gained control of her delight at seeing Jude there. She walked alongside Imogen and Gwyneth, and Imogen's silence had not gone unnoticed. Leila suspected that Imogen had also briefly mistaken Jude for Geraint and she was right to. Imogen had felt strangely disappointed when the figure had not materialised into Geraint and, having been reminded, she was thinking of him even though she knew he would never think of her. She had decided he was still alive, albeit somewhere far away.

Two other girls, Lynda and Brangwirin brought up the rear with Tom, they were new friends of Leila's, made thanks to her new-found status. Tom who walked a little way behind the girls,

240

found himself occasionally glancing behind to check they were not being followed and then looking ahead to the figure of his daughter to check that she was still there. He told no one that he was carrying a knife.

Soon the climbers felt the sun warm on their backs and saw the view open up around them as the last of the fog disappeared. By the time the damp ruin came into view, coats were tied around waists and bottles of water were being lifted and swigged from. They walked around the ruin, admiring its unremitting gloom even in the full sun of mid-August. The picnic was laid out on the south-facing side and there were ample blankets and rugs for everyone to sit on. Jude and his mother shared a blanket with Leila. Celyn realised it would probably be her last opportunity to talk to Leila, for while at least, and she had waited for this chance.

'You are looking much better, Leila,' she said.

'I feel better,' said Leila, smiling and glancing over at Jude frequently.

'I'm glad,' said Celyn, putting her hand on Leila's arm. 'You've done so well. I'm astounded at the way you have recovered. You have a maturity beyond your years.'

'Do you think so?' Leila asked.

'Yes, I do,' replied Celyn, leaning closer. 'Lio would be so proud of you.'

'Did she talk much about me when she was with you?'

'Yes,' said Celyn, 'we were always talking about you and Jude and our plans for the future. I was still studying at the time. Lio wanted to move into illustrating. She was talking about doing children's books. She was doing well with the local market, selling paintings, particularly small landscapes, but also with her big red paintings, which had aroused some high-brow interest.'

Leila nodded, remembering the red ones.

'She wanted to become more self-sufficient, she was considering renting a shop.'

'So do you think she was leaving my Dad forever?'

'I don't know. All I do know is that she didn't want you to lose contact with your father, even if you weren't all living together;

she still wanted you to be a family as much as possible.'

'It's almost like a curse,' said Leila after a short silence. 'I can't help but fear that I will go the same way as my mother. I'm too much like her.'

'No, don't be silly,' said Celyn. 'You are like her in looks, nothing more, you needn't think your fate is already decided by your genes. I think it would be far healthier for you to expect to live to a ripe old age. Your life is your own, it isn't decided by what happened to your forebears. The danger of believing in a curse is that you could make it real.'

'What do you mean?' asked Leila.

'Well, if you believe bad things are going to happen to you, then they might just do that. You are not a clone of Lio. You have different gifts and talents and will take a different path in life.'

'Yes,' said Leila, 'I suppose I already am. I am going away from here, away from her life. If I keep away from cliff edges I should be okay.'

After they had eaten enough, the picnic debris was cleared away and most of the adults descended to the Sportsman's Arms, but Tom remained, unable to trust Leila to anyone. She tried to reassure him, but he would not go. He said he would retain a distance and that she should ignore him and enjoy her time with her friends, but not to worry, because he would be around. She walked around the ruin with Jude, watching Imogen skipping ahead and Gwyneth picking up slates, examining them and then dropping them noisily.

'I feel a bit sorry for Dad,' she told Jude, 'he is so afraid that something will happen to me if he doesn't watch me all the time. I suppose I should be annoyed, but I just feel sorry for him, he looks haunted by it.'

Jude nodded. 'More so than you. You seem to be coping very well.'

'I'm okay, still a bit afraid at night though. The dreams are the worst thing.'

'Do you mean you're having nightmares?'

'This morning I had a dream that you were coming back.'

Jude laughed, 'And that was a nightmare for you was it?'

'No. It's just that sometimes it looked like you in the dream and sometimes it was Geraint.'

'Well, he is... was my uncle. Unfortunately.'

'I know that you aren't like him Jude.'

'I think you will feel better away from here,' said Jude, walking with his head bent forwards, looking at the broken mossy slates which were scattered all over the ground. 'But you can't blame your father for worrying, because everyone is worried. All the parents are being strict with their kids, even though it is not likely that Geraint will come back, if he's still alive that is. He was crazy but not stupid.'

'Do you think Geraint is still alive somewhere?' asked Leila.

'Difficult question,' said Jude, 'and I'm not sure if I want to answer it.'

'Well I think he might be,' said Leila.

'Really,' said Jude looking at her sideways, 'and does that frighten you?'

'Only if I'm thinking about it in the dark or if I am on my own... I don't know if I shall ever be able to sleep on my own.'

'I don't think he's dead either,' Jude admitted. 'But I don't think he will live to a ripe old age. Without treatment his mental health probably won't improve and he always did have that fey look about him, like he wasn't exactly a creature of this world.'

'What, you mean like an alien?'

Jude laughed, 'Sort of... that and being fated to die young.'

Leila looked behind and saw her father some distance back, standing and watching awkwardly. He gave an apologetic wave and she smiled and waved back.

'I hope he will get better when we move,' she said, 'otherwise I will become deranged.'

Jude smiled sideways at her: 'No change there then.'

Leila went to slap him, but he ducked and circled around her laughing. It was beginning to feel like old times.

'I need to say some things to you,' said Jude when they had finished playing around. He appeared tense. The ruin of Gwylfa

Hiraethog was not one of his favourite places. 'This is going to sound funny coming from me, but I am going to say it anyway. No... keep walking,' he added as Leila came to a halt, 'I find it easier to say things like this while I am in motion.'

'Fine,' said Leila.

Jude smiled to himself, an awkward lopsided smile. He had rehearsed his words, but now he couldn't remember any of it.

'Leila, I want us to stay in touch... if you want to. I don't just mean occasional letters that dry up after a year. I want us to see one another too. I'll be learning to drive soon, so there is no excuse.'

Leila was taken aback by this, but could not resist smiling. She had wanted to say as much herself.

Jude hadn't noticed, he was too busy looking at the ground in front of him as he walked, 'I want us to stay in touch forever,' he said with a sudden passion, grabbing her arm. 'There's something I have with you that I have with no one else. It's like we are unconsciously linked. I can't bear the thought of losing you again. I don't even know if you feel it; sometimes I believe you do. There is a very real bond between us, at least for me.' He let go of her arm and took her hand more gently. 'We are the same in many ways,' he added.

Leila was looking at the ground and there was no immediate answer forthcoming so Jude, embarrassed now, filled the void with the next thing that came into his head.

'Did you feel like you'd seen me before – when we first met?' he said, but did not wait for an answer. His nerves made him talk quickly. 'I must admit that I did and then my mother told me of how we had met as infants. We were together all the time that our mothers were. You were a sleeping baby and I pulled your bootees off to try and wake you up. Then your mother died and I didn't see you for years.'

Leila couldn't speak at first. She concentrated her efforts on suppressing the smile that was trying to break out ecstatically. She felt hot-faced and shaky and the swishy fish was battering against her insides as if it was being reeled in. It was an effort just to walk in a straight line.

Finally, she said, 'Yes, I felt I knew you from before.'

He leant towards her and whispered, 'I think it must have been fated. My mother doesn't believe in superstitious fate, so don't tell her I said that.'

Leila said nothing, having become suddenly self-conscious and unsure as to what she should say next. She walked on hesitantly, looking straight ahead and down at the boulders and the slates that she had been carving dates on for every visit to Gwylfa Hiraethog, for as long as she could remember. The soul fish continued to fight, harder than usual, Leila thought.

'Leila,' said Jude when he could bear the silence no more, 'you haven't said if you feel anything back.'

Finally she looked at him, feeling her cheeks hot, the huge ruin passing her by, dark even in the sun and unreal like something on film.

'I think you know I do,' she said awkwardly at last, 'I always have.'

'Then we *will* stay friends?'

'Yes, we will.'

'I'll take good care of you,' he said.

'And I'll take good care of you,' she replied. 'Goodness knows you need it.'

Jude laughed. 'Not as much as you do, you loony. I know you too well.'

She nodded, but thought that perhaps he didn't know her as well as he thought. As he drew nearer to her, Leila recoiled involuntarily. It was probably just the fishy swishy soul she had long since given up trying to understand.

Jude saw the movement and thought it must be embarrassment. Maybe she was still too young to be kissed and with her father behind, even her cheek would be too much. Instead her put his arm round her and hugged her shoulders, removing it before it became anything more than brotherly. Leila looked up at his green eyes, and his smile and the blonde hair that was getting long and out of control. He was not like his uncle after all. He was Jude and she already knew there was no one else like him.

'Will you be staying tonight?' asked Leila.

'I hope so,' he said, 'but I'll need to ask your father and my mother.'

'I wish I didn't have to leave. It feels like the end of everything.'

'It needn't be the end of anything that you have now. You can come and stay with me. Hiraethog will always be here.'

'I hope so. But I wonder if we really will stay friends.'

Jude looked serious for a moment, and then brightened, 'Of course we will,' he said, 'and I'll come up to live near you when I'm old enough.' He laughed and lunged at her in jest, 'you won't get away that easy!'

No answer could have made Leila happier. To know that Jude would do all of that for her almost surpassed belief, but as she caught her father watching she changed the subject.

'I wonder what will become of the ruin,' she said.

'It'll probably get blown down,' said Jude. 'Then they might clear it all away.'

'You don't like it do you?' said Leila. 'I would be very sad to see that happen.'

Jude looked at her, his back to Gwylfa Hiraethog; he was avoiding looking at it. It was cold, hostile and dark to him. Yet he was also drawn to it. Drawn as if he enjoyed how cold it made him feel.

'How will it end?' asked Leila, not really expecting a reply.

'What do you mean?' said Jude and Leila saw him shiver.

'I don't know,' she said. 'It's just that I feel strange when I think of how life will carry on here when I'm gone. I've always felt a part of this place. I think I always will. I can't imagine having a life away from here.'

'You will come back to see me,' said Jude. 'You can still be a part of life here.'

Leila was quiet.

'Do you think it's haunted?' said Jude, making himself look at the ruin. Even though he did not like it, it had somehow heightened the experience of coming closer to Leila. He did not know what he wanted yet, only that he did not want to lose her.

'No, I don't think it's really haunted,' said Leila. 'It looks like a haunted house on a hill, but I don't think it is, not in a way that we could see or feel anyway.'

'So you think there might be undetectable ghosts lingering in this old lodge?' asked Jude, a teasing note in his voice.

'Perhaps just lost souls,' said Leila, smiling.

She looked around and saw that her father was talking to the Crow Woman and that Imogen and Gwyneth were running towards her.

'Come on,' said Imogen. 'Let's say goodbye to Gwylfa.'

They joined hands and walked together towards the ruin. Gwyneth stayed back with Jude.

'Goodbye Gwylfa Hiraethog,' said Leila, touching the dark stone of its southern wall. It was warm and dry now, baked by the sun.

'Hwyl Plas Pren,' said Imogen, using the derogatory local term for the ruin, as she bent to find a slate. 'We must date it.'

'Yes, and we have to leave the slate somewhere that we can find it if we ever come back,' said Leila.

'*When* you come back,' corrected Jude, appearing suddenly at their side, so that Leila was glad she was crouching near the ground, because her stomach moved as if she were on a swell at sea.

'Here, stand one on each side of me,' said Jude, putting his arms around them, 'Gwyneth wants to take a picture and I feel like James Bond.'

Leila felt the warmth and thickness of Jude's arm around her and remembered that moment because the air was balmy and sweet with heather bloom, it was summer and life was good, there were people she loved near her and they were high up, heads spinning at 1,267 feet. She pushed away the past and the future and moved closer to Jude, enjoying the present, the opportunity to feel his warmth. As she pressed closer and moulded into his side, she closed her eyes and saw Hiraethog collapsing and dissolving around her, awash with a red sunset, like one of Lio's paintings, and as she opened her eyes she felt the soul fish turning painfully against her ribs.

By the time they had made their way back and were warm and exhausted from the walk, Tom and Ann had begun serving the meal up. It was early evening and the sun was beginning to move into the west. Since the weather had turned out so well, the tables were set out on the patio. There were lamps out in case people wanted to linger after dark, a string of lights weaved hastily around the trellis by Tom and wine on the table. The delightful odour of the main dish of honeyed Welsh lamb – *oen Cymreig melog* – was billowing out of the lounge doors along with the chiffon curtains that had caught a breeze.

There was potted heather garnishing the centre of the table in-between the wrought iron lamps and the outdoor candles. Many varieties of the common heather of the moors, blooming with purple, pink and white double flowers, and coloured foliage in gold, silver, bronze and red. Tom liked cultivating heather. Lio had started it. He had taken over with great care since her death and now he was going to take them with him; they reminded him of Lio in better times. He could still see her, kneeling on the kitchen floor, pressing them delicately into pots, unaware that he was watching her. He had often watched her, and she had often been unaware. He had watched her from a distance even when she had thought he no longer cared for her and had lost interest in her. She had seemed unreachable at the time, cold and pale as marble. If only he had tried, he might not have lost her.

'Can everyone please take their seats,' said Ann, 'we are about to serve up.' She said it as much for Tom's benefit as anyone else's; he had that far away look again. She would be glad when they could put Hafod and Lio's ghost behind them.

When everyone had sat down and the wine was being poured, Imogen noticed there were thirteen people eating dinner.

'This is just like the last supper,' she said.

'Yes,' said Leila, 'and we've even got a Judas,' she looked at Jude who was sitting next to her, 'Jude-ass.'

'That's not nice,' said Jude in mock seriousness, 'I wouldn't betray you, would I?'

'I don't know yet,' replied Leila and something cold flipped over her heart.

It was half past eight. For dessert there was plum tart served with whipped cream. The wine had to be physically removed from Leila and Imogen who were drinking enthusiastically. As the sun set and everyone relaxed with florid complexions from warmth, wine and food and the youngsters cleared the plates away, Ann went inside and took up her seat at the piano. Leila, Imogen, Jude and Gwyneth tackled the washing up together. When they had finished, they found the grown-ups in various states of repose. The sky was fuchsia and the sun almost disappeared, Ann was still playing, Mr and Mrs Roberts had said their 'goodbyes' and left.

'Can we do our farewell tour now?' asked Leila, tugging at her father's arm. 'You look as if you will fall asleep, if you don't move soon.'

'All right,' he said, rousing himself. 'Who else wants to come? And where shall we begin?'

They began in the barn, looking up at the dusty eaves where several swallow's nests hung like papier-mâché sculptures and the scruffy nest of the barn owl was battened onto a corner beam. It had once been Lio's studio, though her paintings had long since been sold or packed away. Next to the barn was the hen house, to which the hens were returning after a day of strutting around their territory, marked by boundaries only they knew, but which stopped short of the open moor. Then there was the storehouse that was joined to the house. Before the affair with Geraint, Lio had gained permission to convert it into a large room. She had been talking of the possibility of another child. Tom could hardly bear to think of that now.

Inside the house they walked upstairs, Leila telling Jude to run his hand along the cold, stone wall that led upwards on each side of the narrow stairway. There were no handrails to hold on to, just the uneven, white wall. They noticed everything now, Leila pointed out the shadowy undulations on the walls, which had provided

249

something for her eyes to focus on and pick at through sleepless nights. Imogen drew attention to the ever-changing views of the moor from their bedroom window seat. Tom told of the spider he had half consciously watched in the corner of his room after Lio had died and how after it had gone, he had attempted to remove a yellow egg cocoon it had left, only to find hundreds of tiny spiders emerging as soon as he broke it.

'I inhale and exhale this house,' said Leila. 'It's a part of me.'

Coffee was taken on the patio in the cool evening air. There was the fragrance of Ann's container garden and the gentle rustling of the *Clematis* she had trailed around the patio doors in this sheltered spot (they would grow nowhere else). She had returned to the piano, Tom had stacked the tables away and everyone had gone home except for Gwyneth and Jude, who were sleeping over. The few clouds that had provided substance to the sunset had drifted away, and the heavens were ornamented with tremulous stars and the shivering half-light of a waning moon. Tired from his overnight journey, Jude reclined in his chair, facing out to the view of the moor. The moonlight faintly outlined him with a silvery, spritely luminosity creating a figure that was pale and phantasmal. Leila observed the unusual rapt stillness to his pallid complexion, and saw a vulnerability she had not seen before. It made her want to pick up a blanket and lay it over him, for he looked cold, like Lio. Like Lio lying at the bottom of the cliff, pale and dead. A quick sensation took her, powerful, and indescribable, rather like her hopeless feelings of attachment to the gleaming Hafod that stood over them and the dark Hiraethog spreading around them. A feeling of being closer to Jude than to her own soul and yet also further away than the edge of the galaxy. She could touch him briefly, just as she touched the heather, or the waters of the babbling spring, or the red feather of a grouse, but she could not hold onto him forever like she wanted to. She could not own him; he seemed as separate from her as the cold moon above.

Tom was lighting candles as Leila thought of endings. She was afraid that all the people around her would be gone too soon. She wanted time to stand still, now, on this night, and was suddenly painfully aware that it would not, and the times when she would feel so full of love for all that was around her, would be too few. Jude looked over and smiled at her, his face lost its pallor as he turned towards the warm gentle radiance of the lamps and candles. It was a relief to see that dead blueness fade, to see his skin warm and glowing and alive.

'I don't want to lose you,' she whispered, inaudibly, her lips barely moving.

He looked at her again, smiling faintly as if maybe he had half heard. Ann had finished playing her Rachmaninov and had joined them at the table. A peaceful quietness had stolen over them, which no one wanted to break because they did not yet want the evening to end, even though the air was growing cooler and a slightly stronger breeze was stirring the ivy that curled its way over the doors.

Eventually the hoot of an owl from the hawthorn that lined the pale lane roused Tom. Leila felt the burden of the end approaching, as time ran on all too quickly. Soon it would be exactly ten years from the day her mother had died and her last day in her home. Her only home. She felt it as a painful weight, pushing her down from inside.

The night advanced and Jude was allowed to sleep on the floor of the girls' room. After Tom had spoken to him in private, he was careful to place himself under the window next to Leila's bed, while Gwyneth slept with Imogen. Leila was unable to sleep seeing Jude curled up on the hard floor in a thin sleeping bag. She gave him her spare duvet to lie on, then returned to her bed and slept propped up on her pillows so that if she awoke in the night she would be able to see him, with the moonlight streaming under the curtains, making him a radiant ghost. It was the first time since she had almost been murdered that she fell asleep without a light on.

NINETEEN

The seventeenth of August came quietly. Tom was first to wake
that morning. He woke with the dawn and turned away from Ann.
He looked out of the window at the blue sky and the sunshine
and saw it was a day like that day ten years before. On that day
he had woken like this, with Lio lying beside him, sleeping. A
quarter of his lifetime ago. He had aged more in that quarter than
in any. And now Leila had grown from a chubby four-year-old
into a slender fourteen-year-old on the verge of womanhood. It
frightened him that a whole huddle of years had passed with him
lost in an ignorant haze. She was her mother without the lightness.
She did not seem artistic either, nor particularly academic, not like
Imogen, but older in another way. Wise for her years. He found
himself wondering who or what his daughter *was* and realized he
did not know. It was his fault, he had not paid enough attention to
her, the same mistake he had made with Lio. She had been a funny
and confident toddler, sometimes a little madam. But now he saw
an adolescent pre-occupied with death, a child full of dark looks,
silent unrest behind her green eyes and delicate white hands like
Lio's. Unnerving little hands, they were, reminding him of how

young she still was. Sometimes he wondered what it was like to be her and think like her. When he watched her now, the sad eyes and the thin throat floored him, paralysed him with dread. The red raw neck on which, in his dreams, he saw Geraint's hands holding her up like she was just a chicken, her legs dangling, her arms flapping. He had failed her, they had all failed her. He worried about what would become of her. Was it already too late?

Agitated, he moved onto his back and stared at the ceiling. Ten years was a long stretch. A whole decade. He could still remember that day, he had memorized it, made certain he was haunted by it.

Lio had woken shortly after him, they had talked and she had leant against his arm. He remembered the feel of her warm face resting there and how that gesture had felt like a reprieve. They had been getting on quite well, just talking as they lay there and he had felt that Lio was coming to a decision. There was a calmness in her eyes which always came when she had overcome something. He waited but she was not forthcoming and later he tried to force the issue, in the wrong way; he had never been much good at talking things through. A hard lump always seemed to form in his throat and then he felt he could not speak. Shouting was easier. He was in a way responsible for her death. Would she have gone up to the cliffs if they had not rowed?

Perhaps more than anything, the abrupt end to her life had haunted him. From her being alive and vital, lying next to him, talking quietly, her face a flower that had not yet passed its peak, to her lying broken and dead below the cliffs, her vitality oozing madly out of her; blood, cells and water. For what reason? Where did this sudden death come from? Why could he see no reason for it?

He got up and went downstairs. Ten years ago, he had been eating a breakfast of fried eggs and beans on toast and Lio was walking around barefoot with a glass of orange juice. He could see his younger self with her, as if he was watching a film. He found himself making fried eggs and beans again. Then he took them out onto the patio to eat. It was not like that day after all. There was no wind this time, but it was hot. The trees were not moving at all. He sat and looked from one to the other, the two rowan trees, the poplar tree in the paddock, the hawthorn tree and the whitebeam Lio had planted. Not a leaf stirred. He began to feel uneasy and continued to look from tree to tree, wanting something to rustle or flicker, but the trees stayed completely still.

Leila had also risen early. As soon as she woke the weight of what was to come had fallen on her from a great height. She felt dead inside. Jude had told her just to think of her new home, which she admitted was nice.

'Try to imagine all the things you will do there, the new life that awaits you, where Geraint can never touch you. Think of all the opportunities that await you, if only you open your eyes.'

'I can't think of it. I've got years ahead of me there, but only hours left here. I want to think of here,' she had replied.

She had seen Jude every day and would see him again for the departure the following day.

Like a zombie, Leila made her way down through the packed boxes and the stark emptiness of the house. She suddenly noticed all manner of blemishes in the cold morning light: damp patches, dents in the plaster, scuff marks, peeling paint, rust. Too heartbroken to speak she joined her father on the patio. His eyes looked slightly red and he sniffed heavily as he rose.

'I'll get you some breakfast,' he said.

'I don't want any.'

'There's some beans. You must have something if you want to stay on the cliffs for a good while.'

Leila consented. On the patio table she could see the two bouquets of flowers bought for the occasion. Larger and more extravagant than usual. There were heathers in hers too, taken from Lio's potted heathers, which grew in abundance since they had been transplanted into the garden borders. Little else would grow there in the wind.

'I'm being forcibly pulled up by my roots,' she thought.

They were away before Ann or Imogen arose. Neither Tom nor

Lelia wanted to see anyone else this morning.

'Which anniversary do you think is more important?' asked Leila as they walked out to the van.

'Ten years or twenty years?'

'I don't know,' said Tom. 'Perhaps for me it was one year.'

'Why one year?'

'I still wasn't over her death after one year, not that I ever really will be, but the pain was still quite acute then. I looked forward to the anniversary for a long time, the way you would look forward to a child's first birthday, not wanting it to come too quick, but wanting it to come all the same, so I could do something special on the day. In a way it was wrong of me, her deathday became more important than her birthday. I went to the cliff with flowers and sat talking to her for a while and just thinking and praying,' he sighed as he glanced at the blooms which Leila held upright and could hardly see over. 'A year is a funny length of time, it can seem like an age and equally it can seem like a moment. That was how I felt, like it was a lifetime since I had seen Lio alive, and yet also like it had only been yesterday since we were married, held you in our arms as a newborn, walked on the moors as a family… all the things we did before I got too busy. I suppose I still had a sense of unbelief. Even now I do.'

Leila nodded thoughtfully. 'I was only five then. Did you take me with you?'

It was a while before he answered. The question seemed to pain him.

'No, not that first year,' he said, 'I was afraid of more falls. You were headlong and crazy at five. You refused to speak for almost a year after Lio's death, but that didn't stop you from running here and there like a maniac and refusing to listen. You always did like your freedom, but still, you helped me through that first year. I don't know if I could have made it without you.'

'We must have helped each other,' said Leila.

Tom started the van up and put it into gear.

'I think this anniversary is the most important one for me,' said Leila after some thought, 'because I found out everything this year, I feel like I've grown up a lot, *and* I almost died.'

A ferocious butterfly would flutter in her father's stomach when she mentioned her brush with death so frankly and fearlessly. He pulled the seat belt and handed it to her by the way of a reminder. He was always careful about such things now.

'Is it adjusted properly?' he asked before he removed the handbrake.

'Yes, Dad.'

'I think ten is an important one,' he said. 'It's a long time after, a time when we can expect to be quite healed, but not too long not to remember. I think when it is more than twenty years it will begin to feel like another lifetime. But we will never forget, though it gets easier to live without thinking of it all the time, without waking up and feeling the burden weigh you down as you remember straight away and feel like it will never get any better. It is these painful experiences that are in the end the making of us. They help us to grow.'

On the cliffs, it was as hot as that day Tom remembered so clearly and Leila hardly remembered at all. They walked up together and Tom found himself edgy, unable to stop himself from looking around all the time, checking they were not being followed. He often saw Geraint in his dreams, the shadow man, vengeful, looking for people to blame. Tom was convinced that part of the reason for Geraint's attempt on Leila was to get back at him, but that was perhaps the smaller part. There was the other thing, the thing he would never tell Leila. He stole a look at his daughter, she was carrying her bouquet like a doll, holding it gently against her and climbing in earnest, looking straight ahead, unblinkingly as if in a trance. Once again he looked behind, but there was no one there.

Here they were again. Ten years later, two of them were back. Leila looked all around as she noticed her father had, but they were alone. There was no Geraint, no Crow Woman and no ghostly Lio. They went forwards towards the spot where the brambles that had caught Leila's sun hat still clung on to the edge. Tom held her back from going too close and they laid their bouquets against the small stone set in the ground, engraved with: *In Memory of Lio*. The stone was now adorned by small, intricate yellow lichens that gripped like barnacles and with a dusting of white weather spots. Together they planted a small Lio heather, Tom digging the hole with a trowel, Leila pressing it in with her small pale hands, frowning slightly, fully concentrating on the task being carried out. Like Lio but smaller and sadder.

They stood back looking at their miniature shrine, both feeling that Lio would always be more here than at her grave in Llan. Despite the obvious dangers, there was also an oft forgotten beauty. The exposure to the elements, the height (the highest spot, locally, except for Bryn Trillyn, where the ruin Gwylfa Hiraethog stood) and the view. Long before it had become the place that had killed her, it had been a place that Lio had loved. She had loved it for its peace, its sacred solitude, for the godliness of its spinning height and the vigour of its bracing winds. Afon Ddu was like a platform, a lonely piece of elevated land approached by a long, low ridge. It was as if it was all that remained, after the rest of the land had fallen away around it.

'I don't want to leave,' said Leila quietly, to her father. 'Can we look over the edge before we go?'

'Okay, hold my hand though.'

They walked forwards, Tom holding her hand tightly, though he too wanted to see over the edge today, perhaps it was because a decade had passed, perhaps it was because they were going. He remembered the spot near a boulder and looked right at it. There was nowhere else to look. As he looked something powerful wrenched at him and he felt himself sway with its power; he swayed so much that Leila looked up at him and he had to step back.

'Careful Dad. I don't want both my parents to die here,' said Leila.

Tom nodded and closed his blurring eyes. The horror, the futility and the sorrow were still there, fresh with a violent potency like a black bird attacking with its sharp, shiny beak. As if something out there knew that he would never come here again.

Seeing her father wobble near the edge and seeing his tears as he bowed his head, grimaced and fought to control himself in front of her, made Leila think they should not have come. She was sorry for him. Why stir feelings up by coming back all the time? Had he done this only for her, year after year? He had probably not wanted to come again after the first anniversary. She continued to hold his hand while he sniffed and gasped and tried to wipe his face with his free hand.

Leila's mind was full of confusion. No clear visions or answers came to her as she had hoped they would on this significant day. Had it been by pure coincidence that Geraint was up on the cliffs when Lio was there, perhaps taking a walk? Or had he been following her? Did he push her as soon as she finished with him? Or did he take his opportunity when Leila's hat blew off? Why had Geraint left the hated child behind? Did he not have the time because Tom was approaching the top, or, having not intended to kill Lio, did he run away in shock? Leila only wished she could remember more.

There was of course the possibility that it had not been Geraint, but an accident. It was also possible that she was not really a witness and that she had been facing the wrong way and missed the whole thing. She had that memory of Geraint in his sunglasses taking the photo, but that did not mean he was guilty. The mistrust and dislike she had felt was because of his attempt at strangling her. Leila's head was full of confusing voices, speaking against one another. She began to see now that she might never know the whole story and she felt strangely relieved. If it turned out that her mother's fall was just a freak accident, she would rather not know. Let it stay unsolved.

Tom wiped his eyes on his free arm and glanced at his watch. He breathed out the emotion and calmed himself again. The ten-year old wound had opened like a chasm and begun to ache, yet he realised now that it was not as compelling as it had been, it was a strange tender, bittersweet ache, not the excruciatingly painful, overwhelming agony of grief he had known. He could bear it now.

'Come on, Leila,' he said softly. 'Are you ready? We have to go.'

Leila nodded silently, looking all around as if to take in every detail as he led her away, still holding hands.

The end came swiftly.

'We won't see the swallows leave for Africa,' said Imogen, 'it's strange to think that this year they will still be here when we have gone. Yet, nothing will really change at all.'

When the last boxes had been loaded onto the removal lorry and it had set off, trundling down the narrow lane, Tom, Ann and the two girls walked around the empty echoing Hafod together. The house seemed lighter without all the furniture and possessions. The bare wooden floors resounded beneath their feet and their voices bounced and chorused off the thick, cold stone walls. When none of them were looking Leila clung desperately to the wall of her bedroom, the place where she had slept since she was a baby. She clung on to the cold, ungiving surface, clawed it hopelessly and pressed herself against it in an uncomfortable embrace, wishing the wall would absorb her, let her disappear inside it. With a need to consume everything and take it with her, she snatched one experience after another, the window seat, running her hands over its painted surface, drinking in the view it provided, the stairs climbing up and down, counting them, feeling the walls of every room which had to be seen once again and memorised forever.

Her father rescued her from the toilet, where she was looking at herself solemnly in an abandoned hand mirror. Then they stood together in the front yard and said goodbye to the wise, white face of Hafod. Jude and Arabella arrived as promised, to say their farewells.

Arabella's bosom heaved and ached as she hugged the girls tightly and did not try to stop her tears. 'Stay in touch.... you must

259

come and see me,' she cried, 'I'll miss you both so much.'

It was all that was needed to make Leila break down.

'You'll be back soon,' Jude said as he hugged her. 'You know I'll always think of you when I see this place. You'll get it back some day. It will be yours again. I'll buy it for you if I have to.'

Leila half laughed through her tears.

'Thanks Jude.'

'I'm not just saying it to make you feel better,' said Jude in earnest. 'I really mean it. I promise that you will have Hafod back some day.'

'What if they never sell it?'

'They will, I'm sure of it. I think it was only ever meant for you. But for now, enjoy your new life, until you come back. I will write soon. I love you.'

'I love you too,' she whispered.

It was Jude's words that helped Leila to leave quietly, though she felt as if the soul strings that attached her there were being forcefully ripped out. And the fishy soul too, pulled her back as she went, making her sick in the car as they drove further away. The hope that, with Jude, she would some day reclaim Hafod would sustain her through the difficult years of her adolescence and beyond, giving her something to live for and work for and at the same time setting her apart from her peers so that while Imogen blossomed and grew worldly, Leila became gradually more remote, withdrawing into herself.

TWENTY

TEN YEARS LATER

'I'm so proud of Imogen,' said Ann, watching her daughter being interviewed by reporters.

Tom nodded, frowning slightly. He was less enthusiastic, since the campaign Imogen was involved with was against a proposal for a huge wind farm for Hiraethog, of all places. It was a decade since they had left, but clearly they hadn't gone far enough or been away for quite long enough for all the ghosts to be excised.

Imogen was speaking to a reporter in the garden at their Llandudno home, trying to make it clear that she did not oppose wind turbines, only the proposed positioning of them. She wanted to see them offshore instead.

'So do you think there's a good chance of you stopping this wind farm development on Hiraethog?' asked the reporter.

'We have more voluntary organisations coming on board and there's been hundreds of letters of complaint sent to the council,' Imogen replied. 'Though, I suppose it depends on whether those balding, middle-aged men who make all the decisions are in touch with long term concerns rather than the usual short sightedness... No don't put that in.'

She paused and wiped her brow, it was hot and she had forgotten her hat and sunglasses. 'What I mean is, yes, I think we should win. Too many Sites of Special Scientific Interest (SSSIs) have been compromised and it's time we learnt our lesson. What's the point in designating land as special and then allowing damaging developments onto it?'

'But what about the argument that this is an environmentally benign way of getting energy for the future, after all it's clean, renewable energy, isn't it?' said the reporter.

'I'm not disputing that,' said Imogen. 'But there is a problem with the sites being chosen. Too often we are seeing areas of important but declining habitat being chosen by developers and as long as we allow them to trample over supposedly protected areas, we will continue to lose important habitat and see our landscapes degraded.'

Imogen could hear herself quoting her own dissertation, but her tone was passionate and beneath it her real reasons lay like moor bogs beneath spiky swamp grass... Pools of childhood attachment to a landscape and its people, to her own memories and to Leila, whose heart would be broken.

'This wind farm development, which will be the biggest in the UK, with the tallest turbines ever seen in the UK, will slice into that landscape, making it smaller...and then there's the noise...' she paused, to gather her thoughts.

'But if the wind farm doesn't go to Hiraethog then surely it will have to go somewhere else?' said the reporter.

'Well, what about developing the offshore potential? It's all too easy to bring these developments to a sparsely populated and poor upland area. Apathy is always an ally to this kind of thing. It's also scandalous that so little is invested in energy conservation. Why should places like Hiraethog pay the price of rampant consumerism? We're going the wrong way.'

Imogen was beginning to ramble, beads of sweat were appearing on her nose and she wished she could have prepared for this interview. She was ready for the pub – she had done enough for the day.

'So why do you care so much about Hiraethog?' asked the reporter. 'You haven't even mentioned the Mynydd Glyn Lws scheme.'

Imogen fished out a handkerchief and dabbed at her nose: 'The proposal for Hiraethog is huge. I have been involved with the other campaign but we've had more trouble convincing planners with this one. I have a personal interest too. I spent much of my childhood on Hiraethog and it's a place that means a lot to me and to many other people who have lived or who live there. The sad thing is, we would never have had this fight if Hiraethog had been included within the boundaries of the Snowdonia National Park. It wouldn't have even been an option then. It seems that planners care more about landscape protection than about protecting what is *in* a landscape. By that I mean the wildlife and plant species that sometimes seem to be the poor relations to the landscapes themselves, even though they make them what they are.'

'Perhaps you see something in this rather bleak landscape that others don't…' the reporter stopped her tape. 'Okay, I think that's all for now.'

'Do you want to come to the pub with us?' asked Imogen. 'We can continue this conversation there if you like. We're going in to town. I'll buy you a beer – heaven knows I need one.'

Leila woke from her afternoon nap with sweat on the bridge of her nose and warm cheeks. As she sat up she felt her hair sticking hotly to the back of her neck. She threw off the sheets and put her feet to the floor, but waited a full minute before hauling herself to a standing position. It was a hot day outside. She almost wished the hot days would come to an end. The sun-soaked outdoors could be seen through a gap in the curtains where a faint breeze lifted them aside and there was the drone of a bee in the window box drawn there by the open flowers of the French marigolds. Leila made her way to the window and looked out onto the terrace behind her flat. Everything was as she had left it, the sun lounger, her washing swaying on the line, a pot of sun lotion, an empty tea cup, her container garden of flowers and herbs and Lio's heathers.

She looked at the heathers, in full bloom now, just as they would be on Hiraethog. It would be cooler there with the altitude and the stronger breezes.

Where's Jude? she wondered.

It was five years since she had been to Hiraethog. Somehow she had not been back as much as she had intended. Gwylfa Hiraethog, the ruin, had fallen. The once glorious stone lodge had become a pile of rubble, except for part of the south wall and two chimneys, which leaned precariously and would not last. It was no longer the dark, fearsome house on the hill she had known throughout her childhood, but a mere remnant of that structure which had once dominated the landscape for miles around. And now Hiraethog itself was under threat from a wind farm development. She knew already what the wind farm would look like and how it would dominate the landscape, slicing through it, shrinking it, sucking it in. It would bring loud alien noises to a place that knew little more than bird cries and sheep talk.Whenever she thought of the future, she was filled with a sickening sense of impending doom. Yet still she wanted to go back, the desire had not abated in her ten years away. She desired Jude and Hiraethog just as much as she had then.

'Where *is* Jude?' she spoke aloud to herself, in annoyance now. She went to her dressing table and dabbed her face dry, then brushed the frizz on her hair down. It was time to go and find him. She could guess where he would be. Taking care to lock the flat behind her, she checked all around before crossing the terrace and walking down the narrow steps into the side street. She looked over her shoulder again before stepping into the bustle of the busy main street and turning her steps towards the pub on the other side of town. It was ingrained, this looking over her shoulder, it would be a habit for life. Even now her throat would constrict in stressful situations or when something brought it all back. Geraint had never been seen, nor heard of since the attack on her life. There had been a televised reconstruction to no avail. Very few sightings had been registered, most of them too vague to be definitely linked to him. No one had anything other than theories. It had occurred to Leila that he could even be in Wales. She might not know if she passed him in the street. Sometimes she looked for him, knowing that no matter what he changed, he could not change his fiendish eyes.

'Where is he?' Leila lifted and wrinkled her nose against the wall of smoke and the stench of beer inside the pub, having not found Jude in the beer garden outside. It took half a minute for her eyes to adjust to the dimness and to pick out the florid complexions of people who had seen too much sun and drink for one day. Then in the midst of the warm bodies and sweat, she found Jude and put her hands onto his arm.

She had startled him, but he turned round and smiled.

'I didn't think you would be so long, Jude.'

He looked at his watch, 'I know, I just realised a minute ago how late it is. I was just coming back. Imogen is over there with the others and there's a reporter there too...'

'Can we just go please,' said Leila, 'I'm in no condition to be standing about in here.'

'I know, I'm sorry,' said Jude, putting his arm around her. 'Let's get you out of here.'

Leila paused and laughed as they reached the exit and went out into the brightness.

'The baby kicked,' she said. 'Put your hand there Jude, it's turning somersaults.'

'I think our baby is going to come early,' said Jude.

'But most first ones are late.'

'Then we'll have to have a wager on it.'

They ate a Chinese takeaway that evening, sitting out on the terrace on their plastic patio furniture. Imogen was back from university to take a lead role in the wind farm campaign and Jude had a few days off from his vacation job. They were doing what they had wanted to do, Jude had just completed his psychology degree and Imogen a degree in ecology. Leila was proud of them, and occasionally envious. An intelligent and independent young woman had replaced the whingeing Imogen. She no longer followed Leila like a shadow, nor did she wail about cold hands and cold feet. She no longer had to cope with the bleak Hiraethog climate and, anyway, Imogen was by now famous locally for the beautiful woollen hat, scarf and glove sets she had begun knitting when she was fourteen, making her pocket money throughout college. Sometimes, it was too much for Leila when the two of them sat discussing courses and university life; she felt she had become one-dimensional, a person who had never wanted to do anything, a person who rarely considered the present, spending rather more time thinking of the past and plotting the future. There was only one thing she had ever really been *driven* to do, and that was to find out the truth behind her mother's death. Now it seemed her only ambition was to return to Hiraethog one day, to go back to Hafod as Jude had promised they would. Even after leaving Hiraethog, she still felt the fishy soul, flipping within, pulling at her, brushing coldly against the inside of her ribs. She believed she was meant to go back, she was only waiting now, waiting for the right time.

There was one major obstacle: her father could not bear her obsession with the moor and she could tell that he was secretly glad about the proposed wind farm development and the chance that the Hiraethog she loved might be destroyed. Since he had become ill and virtually bedridden, she had tried to hide her desire from him, had tried to be a good daughter, but she knew he could see it in her; in the occasional faraway look or lost moment.

Tom had found his own happiness advancing his career, until early retirement was enforced by cancer. Sometimes he felt he had been cursed by Lio, by Hiraethog and by Geraint, who he still saw in his dreams. And he saw that they were not satisfied with him, they wanted his only child too.

Ann had compromised her own successful career to nurse him, accompanying him as best as she could as the journey toward his inevitable demise took his mind into occasional darkness and delerium. And though he was haunted, Tom had never been back. Once he had turned his back on Hiraethog, Hafod and the ghost of his dead wife, he had done so forever. He had forbidden Leila's dream of returning and had become more adamant as he grew more sick.

'You must never go back to live there, you had to be rescued from that place, why do you want to go back? Can't you see it is dangerous for you?'

Leila argued that Geraint was gone forever. But Tom knew about her dreams, he had heard her waking and crying in the night for years. When she said she wanted to go back, even after all that she had been through, he feared she was mad. He blamed himself for making her mad, for not taking her away sooner. They had stayed far too long. His parenthood was a constant source of pain to him.

'I have to stop you, Leila,' he said. 'I won't let you use my money to go back there. My final wish, and this will go in my Will, is that you never return to that place as anything more than a day visitor. You must not go back there to live. I won't rest in my grave if you do. I firmly believe that no good will come of you if you go back. You must promise me you won't. I only want to see you settled, to see you with some direction in your life, some security, some happiness.'

She had promised, yet he saw the flicker of sedition in her eye and he did not fully trust her or understand her any more than he had understood her mother. And so he fought in his last days, fought against his daughter's obsession, which had brought him much suffering over the years.

But Tom was weak and he knew less about what was really going on than he suspected. He did not know about Leila's savings. While Jude had studied psychology and Imogen ecology, Leila had studied money.

A month passed and July brought a mixture of hot, dry days and cool rainy days. The time to give birth drew close and Leila grew impatient, because the heat was tiring her and she longed to be thin again, to see her own feet. She spent most mornings with her father, who was just as impatient for the birth. The cancer that had begun in his stomach, a kind of cancer not uncommon in upland areas and possibly linked to bracken spores (all the more reason for him to hate Hiraethog), had now spread to his bones. He suffered mostly in silence, grappling alone with the journey towards death. He was working his way towards acceptance, tying up his loose ends, trusting people to take over his responsibilities, letting go. But it pained him that his girl had still not done her letting go. He wanted to be there to see the baby, not just because he longed to hold his grandchild before he died, but also because he believed it could be the answer for Leila. If one thing could change her, it would be this child. And so they spent their mornings together, father and daughter, making small talk, discussing politics, looking at baby magazines, commenting on local affairs and, if he was well enough, admiring the view from the balcony on fine days and the summer borders that Leila had planted for him in the garden below. But there was always a prickly distance, an awkwardness, avoiding the subject of death and illness, of Lio and Hiraethog and the past.

'I think you will be the gardener when I'm gone,' said Tom on one of those lazy days as Leila sat by his side reading a parenting book. 'I might be ill, but I haven't failed to notice that you've planted a few varieties of your own. Tell me, what is that splash of red I see over by the pond? Is it a crocosmia?'

He pointed in the general direction, but lowered his hand abruptly when he saw how much it shook.

'Yes Dad,' said Leila smiling. 'I planted those in spring. It's a variety called 'Lucifer'.'

'And what made you choose it?'

'I like the colour red.'

She smiled again and he noticed for the first time that she was wearing red lipstick. It was not like Leila to wear much makeup and he had never seen her wear such a bright shade of lipstick before. Suddenly all the pleasantness of the morning evaporated and it was not summer anymore and it was not Leila sitting next to him. There was snow outside and it was Lio who sat by him, red-lipsticked and smelling of paint. The lipstick was smeared half across her face and her face was deathly pale, staring at him with a look of horror. She looked dead, sitting rigidly in an awkward position as if someone had taken her out of a freezer and forced her to sit there. Questioning him. Mocking him. He lifted his hand to his face and closed his eyes. It must be the drugs. When he opened them again, Leila was leaning over him and saying something to his blurred senses, but he could not tell what. He closed his eyes and slept.

On the twentieth anniversary of Lio's death, unbeknownst to her father, Leila went back to Hiraethog with Jude. Once they had left Hiraethog, Tom had not been interested in keeping up the ritual of the annual visit to Lio's grave and the cliffs, and for many years he had managed to prevent Leila from going, but this was the twentieth anniversary; it would be wrong not to go. Jude drove the car while Leila sat, uncomfortably large, in the back with the window down, noisily blowing, blocking out all chance of conversation. She watched Jude's fine blonde hair ruffling in the breeze, his strong, brown arms straight and stiff and his hands resting on the steering wheel. She could not see the concentration in his face. He was away, thinking, as the road climbed southwards towards the hills. All around them the big scenery began to unfold and the coast diminished into a flat, cluttered plain far below. She felt happy and content. Her morning with her father had gone well, she was enjoying those mornings spent sitting with him and the reading aloud, which soothed them both; she was enjoying too, the pregnancy in spite of its discomforts and the uneventful, relaxing summer, which was passing quickly and which she would forget all too soon. She still loved everything about Jude and they were going back to Hiraethog for the afternoon. Reason enough for enjoyment... The wind was blustering through the window, the weather growing duller and cooler as they climbed, and she wanted to laugh out loud and whoop for joy.

At Bylchau the baby kicked hard. They had come to the junction where the pale lane leading to Hafod went one way and the moor road stretched towards Hiraethog, Clocaenog and Afon Ddu in the other direction.

'Which way do you want to go?' asked Jude, slowing the car

down.

'Go towards Afon Ddu,' said Leila, 'and then Gwylfa. I want to see them both.'

'Are you really sure about walking up there in your condition?'

'I'll be fine if I take it slowly.'

He turned round and smiled. 'It is exciting to be back here together isn't it?'

'Yes,' said Leila, smiling back. 'Isn't it!'

They parked in a lay by and took the steep walk together, Jude holding the flowers and Leila's hand.

'I want to see Hafod as well today,' said Leila. 'Just from a distance will do, now it's not mine.'

Jude nodded. 'All right, then after we can go to my mother's for tea.'

'I want to go up to the ruin too, Jude.'

Jude's eyes went to the ground as they always did when she mentioned Gwylfa Hiraethog.

'Why do you want to go there?' he said after a moment. 'It looks like rain and it'll be so bleak up there. . It won't be what you remember.'

'I still want to go. It wouldn't be a proper visit if I didn't go up to Gwylfa. You can wait in the pub if you want.'

'No, I can't let you go alone. I'll come.'

They walked on in silence. The baby's kicks were becoming painful in their vigour, but Leila was happy again. On the cliff Lio's heathers were doing well and the memorial stone was still intact, if a little more weathered. Leila brushed golden lichen off it and traced over the words with her index finger. Then she held onto Jude and he held on to her and the baby.

It was a cool day on the moor, a light mist faded out the sun and it was beginning to drizzle so their hair stuck wetly to their foreheads and they were glad of each other's warmth.

'This is my chance,' whispered Leila.

'Your chance for what?' Jude whispered back after she did not elaborate.

'To set the balance straight, to bring life into the world. All I've seen is death, my mother, Mr Parry, Geraint maybe, my father next... But with this baby I can somehow make amends.'

'But those deaths weren't your fault,' said Jude.

'No, but I feel responsible somehow,' she replied, wiping her hair from her eyes. 'The baby is a gift. It's a new start for me, for us, away from the necrolatry Imogen used to accuse me of. Now I will nurture a new life, I will be a creative mother...I hope a good mother...and I hope I will be there for my child as he or she grows up. I want to last longer than my mother did. I can start living for life instead of death.'

Jude was not sure he understood her entirely, but he hugged her tighter and stood very still with her on the edge of Afon Ddu. He loved the open sky above and the feel of the cool, damp air on his face The swallows were flying through the drizzle, he could see their small, shining bodies following the contours of the moor below. At last, he and Leila had come home.

'Twenty years since she died,' said Leila as they descended. She had said this several times, as if getting used to the sound of twenty years.

'Such a long time... Twenty years since the day she took me as a four-year old up onto Afon Ddu. I'll never know why she went up there, whether it was to avoid Mr Parry, to meet Geraint or just because she felt like it. But I suppose I've come to accept that I will never know and I've come to enjoy the mystery and the myth. It's almost romantic, I suppose, like she has become a part of this misty, dewy old landscape.'

They walked on, Jude listened but said nothing.

'And I do want to stay in touch with her. I don't care if it is "necrolatry", I still want my ritual of visiting Afon Ddu and talking to her, because I think she's still out here.'

She turned to Jude and saw that he looked reflective. 'What are you thinking Jude?'

Jude looked at her. 'Oh just about how some religions believe in continuity of mind and spirit. It's as if a mind cannot be created at conception or destroyed at physical death. It changes and evolves through different rebirths and lives. So each different life is a bit like the heather that is growing on the moor now, compared to that which was growing when you were born. It is not exactly the same heather, but it comes from the same place.'

'Why were you thinking that?' asked Leila. 'Were you thinking that Lio might still be here?'

'I just wondered for a minute, what if she were reborn in our child? In a way you would have a chance to get to know her again, wouldn't you?' He looked at her quickly to gauge her reaction. 'Sorry, forget I said that, it was a bit of a stupid thing to say.'

Leila looked calm and thoughtful. 'I do believe in God, you know that. And I believe that my mother has passed on to a better place. Sometimes I wonder if she is watching me and whether she would be proud of what I have become. I suppose if I believed in the continuity of mind, then I could live with the comfort of knowing that my mother was not completely destroyed by her death.'

Jude nodded.

'What do you think Jude?'

Jude had picked a piece of heather and was spinning it around between his thumb and forefinger. He did not answer.

They found the ruin mostly rubble and Leila was saddened, though glad to see that part of the south wall and the two chimneys had endured through some heavy winds and harsh winters. She realised she had been wrong about the tree though, the old granddad tree still stood, stunted but firm and had once again come into leaf. Jude fidgeted around the ruin, looking at the heavy stone plinth that had once surrounded the doorway, while Leila enjoyed the view and the exhilarating height. She could just see Hafod, luminous in the mist, shining white, faraway now. She had half forgotten what it was like to live within those walls, all those memories she had tried to cram in before she left and make live forever were still there but had somehow become faint and dream-like. But it would be hers again, even as she looked at it, miniature with distance, she felt her eyes possessed it. Then she turned away and once again felt the rush associated with her hopes for the future, for renewal, the birth of a new life, a fresh start and through motherhood a greater connection to her own mother. Whether or not the old spirit of her mother would actually be in the body of her newborn child, she had already come to believe that it would be somewhere nearby. When she was refreshed enough, Jude led her back down and they went to see his mother, Celyn. And she told them that Hafod was on the market.

In spite of her father's wishes, Leila was certain her time had come. At first Jude was unsure, worried about Tom, worried that Tom was right in not wanting Leila to go back. Yet he wanted it, too. He and Leila shared an intense attachment to Hiraethog that no one else seemed afflicted by. Both wanted to go back, their love for each other only heightening this need to return. They were sure it was their paradise. So Jude's resistance was short-lived. As the baby quickened so did Leila, with a bloom in her cheeks they associated with an enriching pregnancy. One week before the baby was due Jude had the keys to Hafod in his hand, after what had been an alarmingly quick sale. It was September and Leila had vowed to tell her father of their secret after her child was born. Jude was afraid of the reaction, but accepted it had to be done.

'Hopefully, the joy of seeing his grandchild will somehow balance the pain of my going back there,' said Leila, unsure of herself in spite of her confident words. 'He will just have to accept it somehow. I'm twenty-four now, he can't control me for the rest of his life…'

She stopped short at those words realising, full well that it may not be long, then added more soberly, 'Unless, of course, I think he is too ill to take it…'

Tom did not question them as to where it was they went so often in Leila's car; with the morphine he was often slipping in and out of consciousness. They had moved some of their furniture down to Hafod and had spent some time decorating, mainly preserving the whitewash on the stone walls and painting the nursery in the yellow of the gorse bushes that bloomed on the edge of Hiraethog. With Imogen and the Crow Woman now in on the secret, the pressure to tell Tom was mounting and Leila had come to hate the secrecy and the deception. Was this how her father had felt keeping secrets from her all those years? She pitied him now for that pain and realised she had to tell him, somehow she would bring him round, show him how happy she was, and show him that she was safe.

Leila had to get away to think, so she went to Hafod with Jude for a weekend, their first weekend there alone as a couple. Jude was subdued, while Leila moved ecstatically from room to room. It was smaller than she remembered. The ceilings were lower than she was used to, the uneven stone walls crude. The low windows gave her neck cramp but the view was as spectacular as ever. She was vaguely disappointed to find she did not love it as much as she had thought she would, as much as she remembered. Something small pulled at her spirit, a small, cold slice of regret. She pushed it away and went downstairs to Jude.

Before she reached the bottom, there was an odd sensation of eruption in her abdomen and a warm rush of fluid, vital and alive, gushing down onto the stairs.

'Jude! Our baby is coming!'

Halfway through the next day their baby girl was born. She was long and glazed like a mermaid, but with tight, monkey hands and the bruised face of a fighter. Leila emerged from a twilight of pain, to hold the child, feeling nothing except huge waves of relief that it was over. The child had dark hair and that paradoxical wizened look typical of extreme youth. While Leila lay back in a haze of ambivalence during that first day, tired yet unable to sleep, she felt unburdened, yet also empty. As if she had lost something, as if the shiny thing that had flipped within her for as long as she could remember had left with the baby. As she lay incapacitated, Jude, anxious to do something, took the child and attempted to placate her. The baby was ferocious from the moment she was born, her arms waved jerkily, her legs propelled an invisible bicycle and she crowed relentlessly. Throughout the first night they looked at her with the wonder of new parents and when Leila finally slept, Jude took over, pacing the floors until the sun rose in a red sky.

The immediate bond Leila had hoped for was absent and she feared she would not make it as a mother. But by the end of the second day, she began to feel the beginnings of attachment to her daughter. The swelling on the baby's face had receded and she gained rare glimpses of dark, shining eyes blinking at her from another world. A warm, dark, underwater world. She sat for a long time watching the tiny form sleeping in its plastic trolley.

Ann brought her father to visit in his wheelchair. He had been determined to visit, though Ann was reluctant to let him leave the house. Out of his own environment, Leila saw how ill he looked, his skin grey and papery, his cheeks distended. But he was glad to be there and determined to hold the baby for as long as the visiting time lasted. It was a moving scene for Leila, to see him gauntly smiling through encroaching blindness, holding the child and looking long at her face, taking in every detail and memorising her features. The unfettered sleep of the child held the sick man transfixed, lulled and awed into a grateful, painless peace from which he appeared to gain a certain brief vitality.

'When are you coming home?' he asked Leila.

'The day after tomorrow,' she replied. 'They like to keep first time mothers in for four days here.'

She could not tell him that she had bought Hafod, not yet. She was still getting used to how fragile he had become.

She named the baby Lio Mair and was surprised when her father thought it was a good idea to name her after her grandmother. Perhaps he thought she would fill the gap left by her mother.

'I think we should stay around here for the time being,' said Jude.

Leila looked at Jude with his wispy, blonde hair and faraway green eyes, the strong arms and hands, the straight back and the proud posture with which he held himself. Then she looked at their daughter Lio, feeling a love that hurt for both of them. Watching the tiny child sleep she was overwhelmed by how much she had come to love her and the feeling of colossal responsibility which accompanied this love.

'What will become of us?' she said, a sudden panic filling her.

'We will be fine,' said Jude. 'Everything will be fine.'

Tom died in October as the leaves were turning yellow and the first frosts of autumn arrived. Leila was there with baby Lio. Despite being very weak, he had been holding the child, he had insisted on holding her. She was always peaceful in his arms, and Leila believed she was a healing influence on him; watching the child's dark eyes looking into the vitreous glaze in her father's eyes felt sacred. When he had given the baby up, he smiled and lay back, appearing strengthened and peaceful.

'I am happy for you Leila,' he said. 'She is a beautiful baby. She is like you were. What I see now makes me glad. You are a good mother and you have a wonderful, caring partner in Jude. I always liked that boy. I feel that you are safe, in spite of everything, in spite of the feeling that I failed you.'

Leila felt a lump rising in her throat. Now she would have to tell him about Hafod and she did not know how he would take it.

'Father, I have something to tell you.'

Her father was silent, smiling slightly, looking contented.

'As long as you never go back, I can rest in peace. Stay here, Leila. You have a new life here now,' he spoke quietly, almost as if to himself.

Leila shrank back. She would not, could not tell him. In her arms Lio stirred, lifting her small hands and spreading her long figures out like a magician. On the bed, Tom lay back and reached his hand out to touch Leila's arm. Then his eyes closed and his breathing stopped. Leila waited but it did not start again. He was gone. For a moment she thought she might scream, or run and call an ambulance, perhaps there was a chance to bring him back? Of forcing him to come back. But he was gone, quietly, after holding his beloved grandchild. Leila sat for what seemed like an age, but was probably only minutes. She sat and looked at every feature of the expiring man's face and let the motionless, relaxed hand rest on her arm for a while longer, while Lio the magician, as if struck by the same inertia, lay with her arms still raised, fingers stretched out like the points of stars.

The Crow Woman attended Tom's funeral. She was distraught and though her affair with him had ended over twenty years before, she exposed the endurance of her love for him by her intense grieving. She stayed with them for a while, though no one except Leila, Imogen and Jude would go near her.

'There is little left for me now,' she said. 'You don't know how much my life revolved around your family. You'll never know. In spite of myself, I have become a lonely old woman.'

'We will come and visit you soon,' said Leila, though inside she felt a vague revulsion towards her old friend.

Arabella returned home and burnt the painting she had made of the dead Lio long ago. She broke it clumsily on her knee and watched it licked by flames in her fireplace. From over her fireplace she removed a landscape of Hiraethog, replacing it with a portrait of Tom. He had not known of its existence. She had done it from a photograph. She had hidden it for years, worrying that he might see it and be angry. Her worries had been unfounded, he had never visited. The girls had visited her only twice after the move. She had found they no longer loved their old Crow Woman in the same way. They had not made themselves at home as in old times and there was an air of awkwardness about them, though out of politeness they tried to enjoy all the old luxuries like fresh produce from the garden, peregrines' nests and Welsh rarebit with real ale. When they left she felt empty with the realisation that no one loved her now. She had not seen them again until Tom's funeral.

But at least Leila was back on Hiraethog. There was a chance they could become close again. She remembered that day when Leila had called her "Mother". She had been so vulnerable then. Leila was still vulnerable even now. It was perhaps dangerous for her to be back on Hiraethog and she would need someone other than Jude to help look after her and the baby.

Alone at Hafod with a mug of coffee and November drizzle being blown against the window, Leila took out the old photograph albums and looked back at her childhood. Those long days of adventures seemed like another lifetime, that smaller version of herself, that figure in pictures, with the wisps of childish waves escaping from an anorak hood, the thin stalks of arms and the small hands holding onto sticks about to be thrown. The little smile in the thin, pale face; she could not believe it was her. She felt uncomfortably separated from the image, as if it were a ghost of her former self that was still running on Hiraethog somewhere.

She lay back in her chair and tried to remember. She thought they had been happy as children. For a few moments she heard the high, excited voices of herself and Imogen when they were small. They were running on the moors and their voices rang with a clear, cold quality, ringing against the hills like silver hammers on bright anvils. The exhilaration they had felt in nature then was never to be surpassed. Their small, unburdened bodies had been swept along by strong winds and they had heard the clear call of hurrying streams while they watched thunderous clouds crossing the sky. All of it she kept with her, glistening and mountainous like the white cumulus springing up fantasy islands over the brown moor. Flaming sunsets, lighting clouds and sky like lint paper and warming the earthy tones of heather-hugged moorland. The thrill of walking hot feet on short, cool mossy grass at summer's height and eating banana sandwiches and chocolate seated on mossy stream banks with toes dabbling tentatively in icy spring water. The magic of being small and yet able enough to complete the arduous climb to Gwylfa. Old enough, too, to know the feeling of being tiny against the enormity of the landscape unfolding on all sides, the feeling of being anchored by it, a willing part of its grand scheme. The spinning height was intoxicating for a young girl's senses. And she remembered the full moon nights when all was silver-lit and veiled. The madness of putting on woollens and running out into the cool air, especially after a long hot day, downhill with hell at their heels, howling like wolves.

Life had moved beyond the simplicity and ecstasy of living in the moment. Yet she felt she might regain something of it through her own child. Still sometimes she was taken back, when she let her hot, tired feet out of her grown-up shoes to feel their way through the cool grasses and mosses, and when she sat under the shade of a rowan tree and fell asleep to the soothing rustling and whispering of its quickbeam leaves. Or watching the shadows of leaves dancing and playing on the ground, her skin, or a wall at sunset, she found the effect narcotic, so that there seemed to be a rhythm developing, and the shadows were dancing to some predetermined beat which matched the beat of her own vital functions, and eventually through lulling the rhythm of her blood, sent her to sleep. Sometimes with Imogen and Jude she indulged nostalgia, though time had moved them on and it was just ritualistic homage to something they could not retain. They no longer had the seeing of children. No longer the keys to that kingdom.

In the next room Lio was sleeping with a peace that Leila loved to watch. Her hands were raised slightly, tiny fingers parted, as if she was floating. Her mouth was slightly open, her eyelids flickering delicately and small crescent moon smiles forming as she moved from light to heavy sleep. She was completely abandoned to her sleep, living her life somewhere else on another plane. Leila watched her daughter the way she watched the sunlight run over the moor, with an aching feeling of distance. She could never feel close enough, never hold her child with anything more than a momentary possession. And she was afraid of dying, afraid of being forced to leave her behind. She watched the child often, adoring the perfection of rounded nostrils and long eyelashes resting on flawless, glowing skin. As she watched, the baby suddenly twitched and shifted her position as if disturbed; the small voice sighed and the stars fell to rest on the quilt. A knock came quietly at the door. Reluctant to be troubled with company, Leila paused, hoping whoever it was would go away.   The knock came again, louder this time and insistent. She sighed and went to answer it. She was surprised to see the Arabella, but invited her in nonetheless.

'Is Imogen here?' asked Arabella.

'No, just Lio and me.'

'How is she?'

'Who? Imogen or the baby?'

'The baby.'

'She's fine. Asleep at the moment. She's three months old next week.'

'Already. If you ever need any help with her, don't forget my door is always open. I haven't seen much of you and I miss you so. Is Imogen still living with you?'

'No, she only came to stay. She's living with her mother, you know, Ann.'

The corner or Arabella's eye twitched.

'Do you suppose I could take a peek at Lio? I haven't seen her since I came to see you in the hospital.'

'I don't think that's such a good idea,' said Leila, a hard edge to her voice. 'She has just got over a cold and she's a little delicate. I don't want to expose her to any unnecessary germs. I'm sorry.'

'Of course,' said Arabella, her own face hardening in response as she closed her fists in her lap. So she was just a bunch of unnecessary germs nowadays. But she had a card to play...

'Leila,' she said after a moment's hesitation and an awkward silence, 'you look so tired, please let me help,' she ventured a hand on the girl's shoulder.

'I'm all right,' said Leila shrugging her off. 'Its only natural to be a little tired with a young baby. But of course, you wouldn't know.'

Arabella fell back into her seat like cut paper. Yet she would not give up.

Leila saw the hurt in her face and said, 'Sorry, that was underhand. I didn't mean it.'

But it was too late. Arabella had been alone and bitter for too long, harbouring knowledge that had eaten away at her from the inside and now, finally, she snapped. In a split second she committed herself to the thing she had thought she might do one day.

'Leila,' she said slowly, after another pause, 'I came here because something has been bothering me, bothering me for as long as I've known you.'

'What's that Arabella?'

'It's been gnawing at me for years and quite frankly, it is getting more and more difficult to just shut away.'

'What on earth do you mean?' Leila was beginning to feel agitated again; the Crow Woman of old seemed to have become a Crone Woman.

'It's about what really happened.'

'What *are* you going on about?'

'I'm talking about the death of your mother... how it happened.'

'I know,' snapped Leila, 'we all know, that it was just an accident,' she paused, she was afraid to let the Crow Woman go on and began to blabber. 'Okay, so there is a chance Geraint did push her as she tried to finish with him, but I have to live with the fact that I will never really know that because he has gone and perhaps we will never know where to. He might be dead. If he ever comes back, I'll get the truth out of him, but otherwise what's the point? There is nothing more I can do, it is over. History.'

'But Leila, you couldn't seriously think of speaking to him if he came back. He tried to kill you! I think sometimes that you trivialise danger.'

'I'm really tired,' said Leila irritably, 'so can you say what it is you wanted to say?'

'Ok. I'm here because I'm concerned,' said Arabella, 'and I believe it's time you were told the truth; you deserve to have someone with enough guts tell you the truth and, now your father is dead, there are only the two of us left.'

'What does my father have to do with it? And why are you saying all this *now*? What do you mean by only two of us left?'

'Leila, I cannot carry this burden any more,' said Arabella.

Now she had begun, she had to go on. 'I have to tell you that your mother *was* pushed, and your father and I saw who did it.'

Leila swallowed hard but said nothing as a feeling of dread crawled over her.

The Crow Woman carried on regardless: 'I had a short affair with your father when Lio was seeing Geraint. That was why I came to visit that day. I had to see him. I was in love with him, but I was worried because I felt he was tiring of me, I wanted to talk to him. I found him upset, Lio had just walked out on him after a row. I told him to calm down and not follow her, to let things rest and deal with it with a cool head later. At first he assented, but then he became agitated, he told me to leave, that it was a mistake. He was only with me to get back at Lio, but now he didn't want her to know. It had all gone wrong.'

Leila was intent on every word, yet frozen by the shock of what she was hearing.

The Crow Woman continued, 'He went out after Lio and you, and I followed. It may have been the end of our affair but I couldn't help being in love with him. You can't just switch love on and off. We had no chance of catching Lio before she reached the cliffs and I wanted to be there to witness what might be an ugly scene, although I realised my presence might provoke it. As we climbed Afon Ddu we could see Lio at the top with you, close to the edge. Then something white blew up into the air and towards the edge of the cliff. It looked to us as if it had gone over but it had actually caught in some brambles growing over the edge. It was your sun hat.'

'Who else was there?' asked Leila in an urgent whisper. 'It's like I remember, isn't it? There was a man there and he took a photo of Mum holding me, then he turned me away so I couldn't see while he pushed her over. It's true isn't it? Who was it?' Even as she spoke Leila knew she was confusing dates again. Shaking all over. Going mad.

She lurched towards Arabella and gripped both of the older woman's arms. Then she felt the return of the old, constricting feeling as if someone were gripping her throat. Arabella looked down and saw the clinging fingers, all white and bloodless like claws.

'Arabella,' growled Leila, the blood draining from her face. 'Who did it? Who killed my mother? Was it Geraint?'

'Leila, you remember it wrong,' said Arabella, with a deliberate slowness, delaying the moment. 'I don't know if you are remembering something that never happened, or an actual memory of another occasion on the cliff. Maybe a fabrication which helped you to cope with the pain and horror of what happened that day... Leila, we saw... Your father and I saw the person who pushed Lio.'

'Who?' said Leila, covering her face. 'Tell me who.'

Arabella took a deep breath.

'It was *you,* Leila. You. *You* pushed her.'

She paused to see the effect of her words. Leila had sunk to her knees, she was holding onto the older woman's coat and pulling down, a dead-weight. She uttered a small, strange crying noise, a strangled noise like a dying animal. Her face looked up hopelessly at Arabella. The older woman felt an oddly satisfying mixture of triumph and pain. Now she had Leila back, she wanted to weep for what she had done.

'You knew what you had done,' she said calmly. 'You pushed your mother off the cliff. She was retrieving your hat as you walked up behind her. We saw but hardly believed. There she was at the edge of the cliff, there you were walking unsteadily up behind your mother, screaming angrily. Your rage, even from that distance was alarming, more than a tantrum. Your arms were outstretched as you approached her as if you wanted her to lift you, maybe you did at first. Your mother turned her head at the last minute, she was saying something to you, but you carried on walking. Then you were pushing her, pushing her in the back of her legs. She managed to turn to face you, but you screamed and pushed her again. She cried out as she wobbled – for a moment we thought she would regain her balance, but she didn't. There was only despair in her cry. Despair at her own stupidity for allowing herself to ever get into that situation and despair at the thought of leaving you. It was all there in that cry. Then she went. She fell backwards.' The Crow Woman seemed to wobble backwards as if in empathy.

Leila was choking. It was as if a multitiude of hands had grabbed her throat and were squeezing altogether, not just Geraint, but everyone who had loved Lio. She grabbed the baby's nappy bucket and was sick. The Crow Woman stood over and watched. Tears were crowding into the corners of her eyes. What had she done?

'It was quick and merciful,' she continued more gently, 'and we ran to you as quickly as we could, screaming at you to get away from the edge. We thought for a moment that you would go after her, but you just stood looking over the edge, with a hand in your mouth and as we drew nearer we saw you were crying. You were crying so much, you didn't stop for ages.'

Leila had fallen against the wall. She banged the side of her head against it and broke one of Lio's handmade vases as she fell down. It was true. She knew that much.

'Who else knows?' she asked after a while, raising her hand against her strangled throat. 'Who is the other one?'

Arabella stared but did not speak immediately.

Leila had begun to sob again and then she seemed to come to her senses and she spoke, more quietly. 'Geraint,' she said. 'He saw too didn't he?'

Arabella nodded. 'I don't know what he was doing there, it appeared he arrived on the scene from the other direction some time before us. Perhaps you saw him and that was what made you angry at your mother. I know you didn't like him. He must have been on his way over to Hafod for Lio. He got into such a state...'

'That was why he wanted me dead,' said Leila, quietly realising. 'That was why he hated me so much.'

Leila was slowly moving away from the wall, aimless and without direction. Arabella managed to catch her in her arms, where she stroked her hair and patted her back. 'There,' she said. 'No one else will ever know. Don't tell Jude, Leila, you want to keep him.'

Leila looked up at the Crow Woman and in her misery decided that she couldn't possibly lie to Jude. That would only give Arabella more power over her. It was all too much to think of now.

'And I'll take good care of you Leila. No one will harm you if you let me take care of you. Then if...*he* ever comes back, I'll be here with you.' The old woman hugged Leila tighter and whispered, 'you were only a child. No one could blame such a young child.'

Leila remained passive in the Crow Woman's arms, though she wanted to beat her to a pulp.

She noticed a suitcase next to the couch and it occurred to her that she had to leave this place for a while, perhaps forever. Perhaps she would have to leave Jude behind too, at least until she had time to think it all over. She continued to hold on to the Crow Woman and turned to look out onto the moor at sunset. She no longer loved it.

'I need time alone now,' she said in a monotone, 'I'll be in touch as soon as my head is clearer. There might be things I'll need to ask you.'

'I'd like to stay with you,' said Arabella, 'at least until Jude comes home. I can't leave you alone like this. I hope I've done right in telling you. It's just that I've been thinking such terrible things. I've been thinking that it will happen again somehow, because you were back and you still didn't know.'

'I'll ring you if I need you. Just go, I need to be alone.'

The Crow Woman nodded and assented to being let out.

'I'm so, so sorry Leila, but I think its better that you know.'

As soon as she was gone Leila fell onto the couch. It was an hour before she resurfaced. Then she washed her face and sat for a while with an unfocused stare, wondering what to do next.

'I'll go for a walk on Hiraethog, that's what I'll do.'

It took time, dressing herself for the cold and strapping Lio into the baby carrier, so that by the time she was outside she was at a loss as to where she should go and what she should do. So she took the path she had been taking all her life, up the pale lane, through the gate and onto the moor. Lio fidgeted at first, but soon became quiet and sleepy with the warmth and the motion. It was not easy walking with the burden of her child, so Leila took an easy route to gain some height quickly. She followed the sheep path that began near the stream and rose up to some bare rock where she could stop and see from another perspective.

She was bigger and this landscape was smaller. This moor had been her home but how could she not look now at the ridge that rose to Afon Ddu and at that high place with dread? How could she not think every time she saw it, of what she had done? She had killed her own mother. How had her father coped so well? Had he secretly hated her? She would never know but she wished she could just say 'sorry' to him.

Dusk was falling on Hiraethog, the broken down ruin growing blacker with every second, as decrepit and defeated as her dreams of returning to a paradisical homeland. What a fool she had been! She was not that child anymore. That child would remain on Hiraethog forever, somehow resurrected whenever the wind blew through the ruin and when the cloud shadows and the descendants of her buzzards soared over the moor. Because that child was more a part of Hiraethog than a part of her. It was time to go. There would be another place somewhere that she could love.

'I'm a fool for bringing you here,' she whispered to the sleeping head of her baby. 'At least you've seen it now, but we will go far away from this cursed place and we will never see it again.'

What of Jude? What would he think of having a partner who had killed her own mother and then named their baby daughter after her? Surely Jude would understand how they must leave now that the truth was out. They could not stay and be haunted by it. Perhaps Jude was thinking the same. He had often been quiet and introspective since their return. Was he thinking how foolish nostalgia had led them astray?

Not for the first time, Leila wondered at the fickleness of desire. Now she wished with equal passion to escape the very thing she had yearned for for years.

Yet in the midst of horror, she felt a strange desire to fight and to survive. There was no misguided passion that would lead her up to the cliffs to throw herself off in penance, nor did she feel any wish to wade into a bog as she had on that stormy day long ago. Instead new landscapes seemed to bloom out of the dark cloud shapes, highlighted by the last of the light; a glowing band of yellowish sky beneath the indigo where stars trembled. She would question desire and passion at every turn. Wherever they went, she would not be reckless again.

Leila turned and with a deep breath headed back towards Hafod. From a distance she could see someone coming to meet her. From where she was, it looked like Jude.

Skin Deep
by Jacqueline Jacques

WHAT IF ...

...scientists had discovered how to transplant brains into new bodies?

...deep frozen brains from the time of the Nazis were discovered and transplanted?

...you fell in love with the transplantee without really knowing who he was?

In Jacqueline Jacque's playful and terrifying thriller, Max is the first successful transplantee, after the chilling discovery of six frozen brains in an abandoned cellar. Journalist, Clare, wants to tell the story, get her promotion – perhaps even a new relationship – but she can't see the nightmare she is being drawn into, until its much too late.

"From the psychopathic to the perplexed, all human life is here. Throw in a dark political plot and the result is a terrific thriller, combining violence, psychological suspense and romance. J Jacques is a highly intelligent writer who is in complete control of her medium"

Lorna Read, Women Writers' Network News

ISBN 1-870206673   £ 6.99